D1528252

PRAISE FOR TESS THOMPSON

The School Mistress of Emerson Pass:
"Sometimes we all need to step away from our lives and sink into a safe, happy place where family and love are the main ingredients for surviving. You'll find that and more in The School Mistress of Emerson Pass. I delighted in every turn of the story and when away from it found myself eager to return to Emerson Pass. I can't wait for the next book." - ***Kay Bratt, Bestselling author of Wish Me Home and True to Me.***
"I frequently found myself getting lost in the characters and forgetting that I was reading a book." - ***Camille Di Maio, Bestselling author of The Memory of Us.***
"Highly recommended." - ***Christine Nolfi, Award winning author of The Sweet Lake Series.***
"I loved this book!" - ***Karen McQuestion, Bestselling author of Hello Love and Good Man, Dalton.***

Traded: Brody and Kara:
"I loved the sweetness of Tess Thompson's writing - the camaraderie and long-lasting friendships make you want to move to Cliffside and become one of the gang! Rated Hallmark for romance!" - ***Stephanie Little BookPage***

"This story was well written. You felt what the characters were going through. It's one of those "I got to know what happens next" books. So intriguing you won't want to put it down." - ***Lena Loves Books***

"This story has so much going on, but it intertwines within itself. You get second chance, lost loves, and new love. I could not put this book down! I am excited to start this series and have love for this little Bayside town that I am now fond off!" - ***Crystal's Book World***

"This is a small town romance story at its best and I look forward to the next book in the series." - ***Gillek2, Vine Voice***

"This is one of those books that make you love to be a reader and fan of the author." -***Pamela Lunder, Vine Voice***

Blue Midnight:

"This is a beautiful book with an unexpected twist that takes the story from romance to mystery and back again. I've already started the 2nd book in the series!" **- *Mama O***

"This beautiful book captured my attention and never let it go. I did not want it to end and so very much look forward to reading the next book." **- *Pris Shartle***

"I enjoyed this new book cover to cover. I read it on my long flight home from Ireland and it helped the time fly by, I wish it had been longer so my whole flight could have been lost to this lovely novel about second chances and finding the truth. Written with wisdom and humor this novel shares the raw emotions a new divorce can leave behind." **- *J. Sorenson***

"Tess Thompson is definitely one of my auto-buy authors! I love her writing style. Her characters are so real to life that you just can't put the book down once you start! Blue Midnight makes you believe in second chances. It makes you believe that everyone deserves an HEA. I loved the twists and turns in this book, the mystery and suspense, the family dynamics and the restoration of trust and security." **- *Angela MacIntyre***

"Tess writes books with real characters in them, characters with flaws and baggage and gives them a second chance. (Real people, some remind me of myself and my girlfriends.) Then she cleverly and thoroughly develops those characters and makes you feel deeply for them. Characters are complex and multi-faceted, and the plot seems to unfold naturally, and never feels contrived." - ***K. Lescinsky***

Caramel and Magnolias:

"Nobody writes characters like Tess Thompson. It's like she looks into our lives and creates her characters based on our best friends, our lovers, and our neighbors. Caramel and Magnolias, and the authors debut novel Riversong, have some of the best characters I've ever had a chance to fall in love with. I don't like leaving spoilers in reviews so just trust me, Nicholas Sparks has nothing on Tess Thompson, her writing flows so smoothly you can't help but to want to read on!" - ***T. M. Frazier***

"I love Tess Thompson's books because I love good writing. Her prose is clean and tight, which are increasingly rare qualities, and manages to evoke a full range of emotions with both subtlety and power. Her fiction goes well beyond art imitating life. Thompson's characters are alive and fully-realized, the action is believable, and the story unfolds with the right balance of tension and exuberance. CARAMEL AND MAGNOLIAS is a pleasure to read." - ***Tsuruoka***

"The author has an incredible way of painting an image with her words. Her storytelling is beautiful, and leaves you wanting more! I love that the story is about friendship (2 best friends) and love. The characters are richly drawn and I found myself rooting for them from the very beginning. I think you will, too!" - ***Fogvision***

"I got swept off my feet, my heartstrings were pulled, I held my breath, and tightened my muscles in suspense. Tess paints stunning scenery with her words and draws you in to the lives of her characters."- ***T. Bean***

Duet For Three Hands:

"Tears trickled down the side of my face when I reached the end of this road. Not because the story left me feeling sad or disappointed, no. Rather, because I already missed them. My friends. Though it isn't goodbye, but see you later. And so I will sit impatiently waiting, with desperate eagerness to hear where life has taken you, what burdens have you downtrodden, and what triumphs warm your heart. And in the meantime, I will go out and live, keeping your lessons and friendship and love close, the light to guide me through any darkness. And to the author I say thank you. My heart, my soul -all of me - needed these words, these friends, this love. I am forever changed by the beauty of your talent." ***- Lisa M.Gott***

"I am a great fan of Tess Thompson's books and this new one definitely shows her branching out with an engaging enjoyable historical drama/love story. She is a true pro in the way she weaves her storyline, develops true to life characters that you love! The background and setting is so picturesque and visible just from her words. Each book shows her expanding, growing and excelling in her art. Yet another one not to miss. Buy it you won't be disappointed. The ONLY disappointment is when it ends!!!" ***- Sparky's Last***

"There are some definite villains in this book. Ohhhh, how I loved to hate them. But I have to give Thompson credit because they never came off as caricatures or one dimensional. They all felt authentic to me and (sadly) I could easily picture them. I loved to love some and loved to hate others." ***- The Baking Bookworm***

"I stayed up the entire night reading Duet For Three Hands and unbeknownst to myself, I fell asleep in the middle of reading the book. I literally woke up the next morning with Tyler the Kindle beside me (thankfully, still safe and intact) with no ounce of battery left. I shouldn't have worried about deadlines because, guess what? Duet For Three Hands was the epitome of unputdownable." - ***The Bookish Owl***

Miller's Secret

"From the very first page, I was captivated by this wonderful tale. The cast of characters amazing - very fleshed out and multi-dimensional. The descriptions were perfect - just enough to make you feel like you were transported back to the 20's and 40's.... This book was the perfect escape, filled with so many twists and turns I was on the edge of my seat for the entire read." - ***Hilary Grossman***

"The sad story of a freezing-cold orphan looking out the window at his rich benefactors on Christmas Eve started me off with Horatio-Alger expectations for this book. But I quickly got pulled into a completely different world--the complex five-character braid that the plot weaves. The three men and two women characters are so alive I felt I could walk up and start talking to any one of them, and I'd love to have lunch with Henry. Then the plot quickly turned sinister enough to keep me turning the pages.

Class is set against class, poor and rich struggle for happiness and security, yet it is love all but one of them are hungry for. ......Where does love come from? What do you do about it? The story kept me going, and gave me hope. For a little bonus, there are Thompson's delightful observations, like: "You'd never know we could make something this good out of the milk from an animal who eats hats." A really good read!" - ***Kay in Seattle***

"She paints vivid word pictures such that I could smell the ocean and hear the doves. Then there are the stories within a story that twist and turn until they all come together in the end. I really had a hard time putting it down. Five stars aren't enough!"

- M.R. Williams

ALSO BY TESS THOMPSON

CLIFFSIDE BAY

Traded: Brody and Kara

Deleted: Jackson and Maggie

Jaded: Zane and Honor

Marred: Kyle and Violet

Tainted: Lance and Mary

Cliffside Bay Christmas, The Season of Cats and Babies (Cliffside Bay Novella to be read after Tainted)

Missed: Rafael and Lisa

Cliffside Bay Christmas Wedding (Cliffside Bay Novella to be read after Missed)

Healed: Stone and Pepper

Chateau Wedding (Cliffside Bay Novella to be read after Healed)

Scarred: Trey and Autumn

Jilted: Nico and Sophie

Kissed (Cliffside Bay Novella to be read after Jilted)

Departed: David and Sara

Cliffside Bay Bundle , Books 1,2,3

BLUE MOUNTAIN SERIES

Blue Mountain Bundle, Books 1,2,3

Blue Midnight

Blue Moon

Blue Ink

Blue String

EMERSON PASS

The School Mistress of Emerson Pass

The Sugar Queen of Emerson Pass

RIVER VALLEY

Riversong

Riverbend

Riverstar

Riversnow

Riverstorm

Tommy's Wish

River Valley Bundle, Books 1-4

LEGLEY BAY

Caramel and Magnolias

Tea and Primroses

STANDALONES

The Santa Trial

Duet for Three Hands

Miller's Secret

HEALED: STONE AND PEPPER

CLIFFSIDE BAY SERIES, BOOK 7

TESS THOMPSON

A NOTE TO READERS

Dear Readers,

Welcome to the seventh installment in the Cliffside Bay Series. I'm so glad you found your way to the little beach town of my imagination. Although these books can be read as stand-alones, I think they're even better read in order. Regardless, I hope you enjoy the continued story of the Dogs and Wolves and the women they love. Happy reading. Xo

Tess

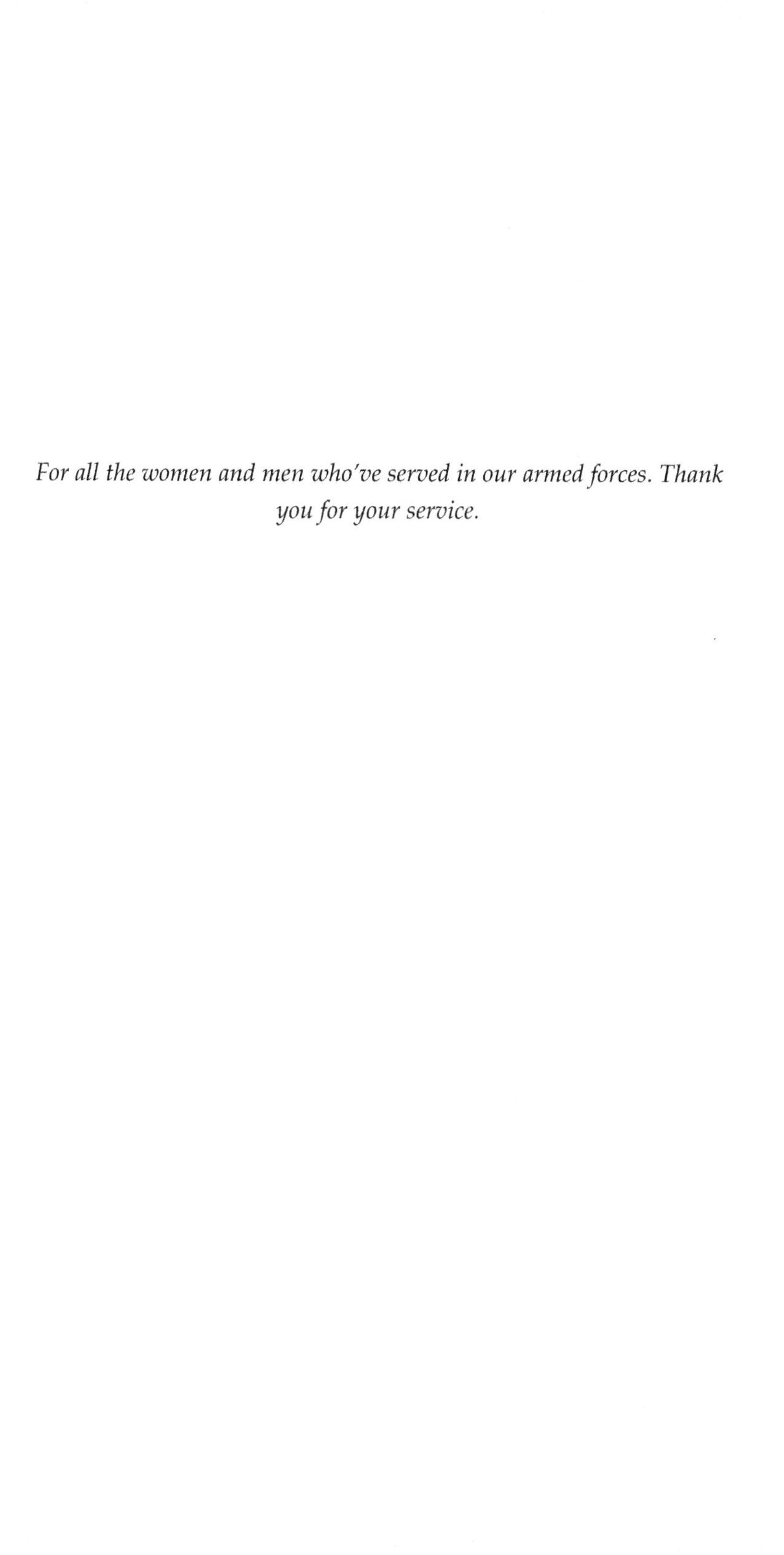

For all the women and men who've served in our armed forces. Thank you for your service.

1

Stone

Stone Hickman knew life was as fickle as a teenage girl. One moment everything was rainbows, unicorns, and chocolate drops falling from the sky. Without warning, unicorns turned into flying monkeys, and rainbows transformed into moody clouds that rained down those slimy canned peas he'd been forced to eat as a kid surviving on subsidized school lunch.

Today was all rainbows and unicorns. Given the number of canned-pea type days he'd had during his thirty years of life, he soaked up the unicorns and rainbows, grateful for each one.

He smiled with contentment as he stepped out of Cliffside Bay's only grocery store with a bag of breakfast items in his arms. Dozens of bins filled with flowers decorated the store's entrance. He breathed in the sweet scent of lilies and roses combined with the briny breeze of the sea. October sun rose over the eastern hills and drenched the town in orange and pink light.

The air snapped with crisp fall weather. Red and yellow leaves fluttered from sturdy branches of the oaks that lined the street.

In the quiet stillness of early morning, the sound of waves hitting the shore echoed faintly in the background.

Main Street was deserted. After Labor Day, the Northern California beach town emptied of tourists to resume its normal one-stoplight kind of existence. Residents of Cliffside Bay were not early risers on a Saturday morning. During summer months visitors flocked to town wearing beach attire, carrying umbrellas, picnic baskets, and sandy children. Their long stretch of beach had always attracted beachcombers from San Francisco, but since his brother, Kyle, had opened a luxury resort, visitors from all over the country swarmed their sleepy bedroom community. Between the resort and the newest tourist favorite, Dog's Brewery, the vacationer numbers in Cliffside Bay had exploded. The locals grumbled about traffic and people crowding the sidewalks and shops.

All the way to the bank.

Yes, life was good. Especially for a guy like him. After a dozen years in the marines, he'd returned to civilian life to fulfill his lifetime dream of becoming a licensed general contractor. He'd moved to Cliffside Bay to be near his siblings, Kyle and Autumn, and had lucked into a full-service construction partnership with four men who had quickly become his best friends. Among the five of them they had every step needed to construct or remodel residences and small businesses, from architecture to landscaping to interior design. Someday, he would build his own house on Kyle's property outside of town, but for now he was happily settled in an apartment with the interior design partner of the business, Trey Wattson.

He'd awakened yesterday to the news that Wolf Enterprises had won the bid to build a mansion for Autumn's heiress friend, Sara Ness. They'd survive another fiscal quarter. Hallelujah and amen. This was indeed a blessing, since he and the other Wolves,

Rafael, Trey, David, and Nico, had sunk every penny they had into the business.

So, yes, life was good. He had bacon in his grocery bag and blueberries to add to the pancake batter Trey was whipping up in their kitchen. It was Saturday, which meant he could get a good workout in and watch a little college football. He was reading this fantastic thriller recommended to him by Mary Mullen, the local bookstore owner. The woman was like a savant when it came to finding the perfect book for every customer. She was five for five with him. Later, he and the guys might go up for a beer at The Oar. Living right in town had its benefits, including their local haunt within walking distance.

Maybe Pepper would be there.

He sighed, thinking of her long legs and haughty chin and those flashing smoke-gray eyes that turned almost lavender when she looked at him. Usually accompanied by a salty insult thrown his way. She was the most beautiful woman he'd ever laid eyes on, and not that he was proud of it, but he was no stranger to beautiful women. He'd had a few in his days. None like Pepper Griffin, though. No woman in the history of the world could compete with her.

He yearned to have Pepper Griffin in the crook of his arm, but that was a goal for another day. Pepper was what his brother, Kyle, called a *stretch goal*. Mostly because she hated him. Getting her to fall madly in love with him, adopt a puppy, have his babies, and grow old together might seem unrealistic. For some men, anyway. But he was an optimist. Always had been. One needed that skill when life so often turned to canned peas. Someday, he would win her over. He just needed to crack through her perception of him. She hated military guys. Even former military guys like him. Not that he could blame her, considering four navy men attacked her when she was nineteen. He didn't know the details of the assault, only that it was brutal and had caused her to distrust and dislike military men.

If she'd soften toward him just a bit, he could show her his heart, and he might have a chance. Unrealistic? Maybe. However, he'd lived through three tours in Afghanistan. His marine buddies said he was like a cat with nine lives, considering the scrapes from which he'd escaped. Surely, given his propensity for landing on his cat feet, feisty, sexy, sassy Pepper Griffin could be his someday.

From the first moment he met her a little over a year ago and every time since, he'd had this tingle up the back of his spine, like a message from God. They were meant to be together. Like him, she was broken. Together they would heal. Not that he would tell anyone his theory, especially not the guys, but he couldn't shake the feeling. They were meant to be. So at night, on his knees, as he'd done all his life, he prayed. *Please, God, make me worthy. Show me the way to her heart.*

The answer was always the same. Not yet. Be patient. All in good time.

So instead of brooding over it, he lived his life and strove to be a better man with each passing minute. Once she finally loved him, he would be ready and worthy.

"Stone Hickman?"

He stopped mid-stride. Had he heard his name, or was it the rustling of the fall leaves in the oak above his head?

"Stone Hickman." The voice was that of a crackling, raspy longtime smoker.

He squinted into the bright sun to locate the origin of the voice. He had forgotten his sunglasses, and his blue eyes were sensitive to the light.

"Stone?" The voice again. He turned to the right. There, under the shade of a tall oak, a shadow moved. He drew closer. A shriveled gray woman stood with her hands clasped together. She wore faded jeans and a sweatshirt with a pumpkin on the front over her skinny frame.

She seemed vaguely familiar to him, like the first notes of a well-known song he couldn't quite place. "May I help you?"

"Stone Hickman?"

"Yes, I'm sorry, but do I know you?"

"No, no, you don't. Not anymore." Narrow dark eyes peered out from under a fringe of white bangs. Her weathered face reminded him of the skin of an elephant. She stepped toward him until they were only feet apart. "Your eyes are the same. I'd recognize them anywhere."

His chest hollowed and his legs went numb. Could it be? No. Ghosts didn't exist.

"I'm your mother." She smiled, and he knew her then. Her front right tooth had a triangle-shaped chip.

He recoiled and stepped backward. His mother. He'd been six years old when she left with the stranger in a black car. A man. Her *boyfriend,* his father had told them that night as he slumped on the floor with a bottle of whiskey between his legs.

"I assumed you were dead." That was the story he'd told himself. She'd died soon after she left them. Why else would a mother not return to her children?

"Not yet." She smiled again, and this time he saw his brother, Kyle.

He stared at her hard, trying to see the woman she once was. The pretty young mother of his memory was no longer evident. When he was a child, she'd had long, shiny chestnut hair. He had few memories of her. One was of her sitting in the chair by the window as she brushed the long strands, letting them dry in the warm pool of sunlight. He shook aside the vision.

"How did you find me?" he asked.

"Social media makes it so no one can hide." She raised a shaky hand to her hair and smoothed it as if she were a fifties beauty queen. "Even your brother with his changed name was easy to find once I found you and Autumn."

"We weren't hiding." Her tone made him defensive. She was the one who left, not them.

"It wouldn't have mattered if you were. A mother's instincts always find a way."

"After twenty-three years?" he asked, unable to keep the

bitter sarcasm out of his voice. Two minutes in and her presence had changed him. Chocolate drops out. Canned peas in.

"I know I have no right to see you," she said.

"It's been so long." He wasn't sure Autumn had any memory of her whatsoever. She'd been only four when their mother left. Kyle had been eight. He remembered a lot. Occasionally, if he'd had a few scotches, he'd tell them a story about her. Even now, after all these years, Kyle mourned her. That loss, that abandonment had shaped so much of who he was—a great father and husband. A great man. But in those unguarded moments when he talked about her, Stone saw the deep hurt that still swam through his veins. Was there anything she could say or do to repair the hole she'd left in their hearts?

"I just want to talk to you. Once is all I ask."

"Autumn doesn't even remember you." He wanted to hurt her. That surprised him. He hadn't thought he cared any longer. "Kyle had to become an adult and care for us when he was only eight years old. Did you think about that when you left us?"

"I left you with your father." She jutted her chin forward and fixed her gaze on him, her eyes like the dull plastic of a cheap button.

A bitter laugh erupted from his gut. "Dad? He was a drunk, and you knew it. You made the choice to leave three little kids alone with a man who couldn't even take care of himself."

"I know it was wrong. I had to go. I couldn't stay one more minute in that house with him."

Then kick him out. Or take us with you.

"I don't know what you thought you'd gain by coming here," he said. "It's been too long. The damage is long past repair."

Her shoulders slouched forward. Defeated so easily. A quitter. A leaver.

He hated her—wanted to lash out at her and hurt her as she'd hurt them. "You have a lot of nerve showing up here."

Her voice quivered. "I have something I need to tell you, and then I'll leave. I promise." She pulled a scrap of paper from her jeans and handed it to him. "Here's the number where I'm staying. I have a motel room up north. I'll be there for a while. If you change your mind, I'd like a chance to see you. All three of you. Will you ask them for me?"

"Why me? Why'd you approach me and not Kyle or Autumn?" That question was out of his mouth before he could evaluate why he wanted to know.

"Kyle was all brain, but you were all heart. You used to spend all day in the forest and come home with a special rock, or wildflowers or some other treasure, and present it to me. 'Don't be sad, Mama. I brought you a present.' I never understood how a little boy knew his mama was sad. I figured you'd be the most likely to agree to ask the others. Please, ask them to meet me for coffee. I won't bother you again."

"I'll ask them. No promises." He had no recollection of gifts from his forest adventures. Mostly, he remembered cutting down trees for firewood so they wouldn't freeze in the long winters.

"Thank you."

With that, she turned away and headed down the sidewalk. Her legs were like twigs. A long white ponytail swung back and forth behind her head, as if it didn't get the memo that it belonged to an old lady. He watched as she slid into the driver's seat of a beat-up Honda and pulled into the street. His gaze followed the car until it disappeared around the corner toward the highway. He realized he'd been clutching the bag of groceries to his chest so hard that he'd ripped a hole in the side where the carton of milk had dampened the paper.

Their mother. Here in Cliffside Bay.

She wanted money. It had to be money, or why would she have suddenly shown up in town? She'd probably read about Kyle's vast wealth, accumulated from years in the commercial real estate business. As the Mullen brothers liked to say, Kyle owned half of the strip malls in California. Women like Valerie Hickman didn't appear because they wanted to mend relationships with their children. She was desperate. No longer pretty, she could not attract a man to take care of her. Maybe she was sick. She looked ill—skinny and with that gray tinge to her skin.

All these thoughts floated through his mind in tandem with his heart softening with compassion for the woman who'd given birth to him.

Dazed, he ambled, bleary and unseeing, to the crosswalk in front of the grocery store. Directly across the street, Cliffside Bay Bookstore was dark, as was The Oar. No cars coming either direction. He stepped off the curb.

A great force yanked him backward just as a black SUV seemed to come from nowhere.

He toppled backward and fell hard onto the person draped around his waist and neck. The bag of groceries flew from his arms. The SUV raced off toward the highway, nothing but a flash of taillights. Slender legs in black leggings wrapped around his middle. She'd pulled him away from danger by jumping on his back, which meant she'd fallen with him. He shook his head and swallowed the taste of metal in his mouth.

A woman had yanked him away from danger. A *small* woman who smelled like spring flowers. He scrambled onto his knees and whipped around to meet the frightened, smoky gray eyes of Pepper Griffin. "Oh my God, are you all right? Did I hurt you?"

"What do you think? A giant man just knocked me on my butt. Onto a very hard sidewalk, I might add." Pepper sat with her long dancer legs spread out in front of her. All one hundred and ten furious pounds of her trembled as if she'd love to murder him despite having just saved his life. Black curls tumbled over her forehead, and red lipstick stained her pouty mouth. She winced and pressed both of her hands into the dent above her tailbone. "I'm going to have a bruise on my butt the size of your big head."

He knelt next to her and gently wrapped his hands around her upper arms, examining her from head to toe. "Did you hit your head? Did I break you?"

Her expression softened slightly. "No, you didn't break me." They locked gazes. The world around him faded. All thoughts of his mother and the truck disappeared as he let himself fall into the stormy pools of her eyes.

"You could have smacked your head." The thought of hurting this precious woman made *his* head ache. "Head injuries are very serious."

She laughed. "Calm down, Boy Scout. I'm not a delicate little princess. Dancers are tougher than most."

"Are you sure?" He resisted the urge to run his hands over her body to make sure nothing was broken. In the marines he'd been trained in first aid. However, he knew his touch would not be welcomed.

"I'm fine, other than I'll be stiff tomorrow. I basically leaped onto your shoulders to pull you backward. I've taken a million tumbling classes and hours of stage combat. My mom always said I was like a monkey. And you're a tree, so there you have it."

A beautiful, graceful monkey. She could climb up his tree anytime. *Shut up, gutter mind. Keep it classy.*

She slid her gaze to his hands still wrapped around her arms. "You can loosen your hold on me now. I'm just fine." Her eyes glittered as she raised her head to look at him. He wasn't sure if she was amused or about to launch into one of her attacks on his caveman ways. Last time it was because he called her a girl instead of a woman. Her sharp tongue had nearly slashed him into a million pieces. It had taken great control to hide how her anger hurt him.

He released her and apologized. Heat rose to his face. "I'm sorry." He grimaced. What a dolt. "Thank you for saving me. I feel like an idiot."

"Don't be silly. It wasn't your fault. I'm glad I was there." She moved to sit cross-legged on the sidewalk and flapped her hands, as if they'd fallen asleep. "That scared the crap out of me." Her eyes were almost too large for her delicate heart-shaped face and were a mixture of blue and gray that reminded him of the sky right before a thin layer of fog departed from the shore. "It came speeding out of the alley—like warp-speed fast. Thank God it's Saturday. Weekdays the high school dancers have class before school. They exit right around this time, all spilling into the alley while reading their cell phones and not paying a bit of attention to their surroundings. He could've plowed them all down." Even angry, she had the most delightful voice, like whiskey with a dab of honey. Actresses always had the best vocal tones. They were trained that way, he supposed. Not that he knew much about actresses, but he imagined they spent quite a lot of time practicing scales and such. "Didn't you hear the squeal of the tires? They about gave me a heart attack."

"No, I didn't hear a thing." Not a thing, other than the buzzing in his ears from the encounter with his long-lost mother. Stone tried to get up, but black dots danced before his eyes. He rubbed the back of his neck. "I was distracted—thinking about something else."

"It must have been a heck of a something to keep you from noticing a large black vehicle." She blinked, and her thick lashes swooped like the wings of a butterfly. Wings of a butterfly? *Did I hit my head? He* might have a concussion.

"I had a shock just before…this happened." He remained sitting as she leaped to her feet with the lithe and grace of a dancer. So much for stiffness. Pepper was a song-and-dance girl from New York. As was her best friend, Lisa, who was engaged to his best friend, Rafael. *Rafael and Lisa.* The happy couple. Meanwhile, he was sitting on the sidewalk with a carton of spilled milk leaking into the cement while staring into the eyes of the woman he loved. Who didn't love him.

Be patient. She just saved your life.

"How did you think so fast?" he asked.

"I'd just come out of the studio and was standing here looking for my phone. It always falls down into my bag." She gestured toward a duffel bag under the awning of the dance studio. "I saw it whip around that corner just as you approached the crosswalk. I guess my instincts just kicked in."

"Your ninja instincts?" he asked.

"I had no idea I was a ninja, but I'm glad she kicked in when I needed her." She offered him a slender hand to help him up, smiling down at him.

His big stupid heart turned over. Could there be a better smile in the entire universe? He looked away from her before he gave himself away. And now he was eye level with her tight bottom in those leggings. God, he was a pervert. He'd almost been killed and all he could think about were those legs wrapping around him. "I'm fine. I can get up by myself." As if she could lift him even if he wanted assistance. He probably weighed twice as much and was at least a foot taller. He scrambled, rather ungracefully, to his feet.

Pepper placed her hands on her hips. "You know, that car came out of nowhere. Like it was chasing someone." She pulled her sweater tighter over the leotard underneath and shivered.

"Really?" Was it chasing his mother? His mind whirled as the possibilities occurred to him. Fraud? Criminal? Grifter? Who was this woman? Was she even his mother at all?

He looked up to see Pepper regarding him with a suspicious glint in her eyes. "What did you just think of?" she asked.

"What? Nothing."

"Who were you talking to over there by the tree?" she asked.

He swallowed. "Um. Just a woman. Looking for directions." There was no way he could tell her before he'd even told his siblings. *That was my mother. She's probably a grifter and wants to extort money from my brother.*

"Maybe they were after her." She tossed her chin-length hair, then placed her fingers through her curls as if to tame them. They were as feisty and misbehaving as Pepper herself. "I mean, no sooner had she taken off than the car whips around the corner."

"Were you watching from the window?" he asked.

She blushed the shade of the red mums in front of the dance studio. "I happened to notice you. It's impossible not to. You're like the Jolly Green Giant."

He laughed. "That's mean." *She was watching me.*

"Well, the giant part anyway."

"I should get home. Trey's waiting for his ice cream." He surveyed the spilled contents of his grocery bag. A bottle of orange juice had miraculously gone unharmed and was now nestled against the curb between the street and sidewalk. A package of hamburger and a box of cereal were also intact. The carton of ice cream was facedown under a tree but seemed relatively unharmed.

Pepper helped him gather it all up, but the paper bag was useless now, ripped and soggy. She ran back to the entrance of the dance studio and rummaged around in her duffel, returning with a tote that had her initials embroidered on the side. *P.G.* "Here, use this." She thrust it at him. "I use this for groceries."

As he tucked the bottle of milk into the canvas bag, he noticed his hands were shaking. Whether from the adrenaline of his near-death experience or the resurrection of his mother, he couldn't say. "Were you headed to the store? Do you need this?" he asked, referring to the tote.

"I have another."

"Thanks for this. And for saving my life."

"You all right?" Pepper stepped nearer to him, concern knit between her brows. "You're pale and shaky-looking all of a sudden."

"I'm okay. I think."

She looked at her feet, clad in tennis shoes. "I'm headed to Lisa's. How about if we walk together?" Lisa and Rafael lived in the apartment next to Stone.

"Do I look that bad?" he asked with a smile. "I must, if you're offering to walk with me."

"You look like you're in shock, which makes me wonder if you'll walk into the street and almost get killed again."

He blinked, surprised by the kindness in her voice.

"I'd love to be escorted home." He gestured toward the crosswalk. "How about you take the lead?"

"Sure thing."

They crossed the street in silence and then walked a block east to the Victorian mansion set slightly off Main Street. Roughly a year before, Rafael Soto had bought the old house and hired Stone as his contractor to execute an entire renovation, including dividing it into six apartments. After working well together, along with local interior designer Trey Wattson, they'd decided to start their own firm, buying and renovating houses and apartment buildings. Through a happy turn of events, they were now joined by David Perry, architect and brother to Lisa, and Nico Bentley, landscape architect. Thus far, Wolf Enterprises had successfully renovated Autumn's cottage and built a house up north in the town of Stoweaway.

When they reached the wraparound porch of the building, he walked ahead to open the door for her. He let her take the lead as they traipsed up the stairs. Despite his agitation, he admired her nicely shaped bottom as she climbed the steps one by one.

At the third-floor landing in front of his apartment, he thanked her again.

"Don't make it a habit." She patted the tote that he held against his stomach. "I can't be expected to ninja you out of trouble every day."

"I'll try not to. I didn't survive three tours in Afghanistan to be taken out by a reckless driver on the quiet streets of Cliffside Bay."

Her mouth lifted into a sassy, almost flirtatious smile. "Saved by a woman in a leotard. What will you tell the guys?"

Was this his window? A signal that she might be open to a date? She'd softened a little. Maybe saving him made her feel powerful, thus rendering him less threatening. Thanking her for saving his life was the perfect excuse to take her to dinner. Wasn't it? What the hell, he would go for it. If he didn't ask, he'd never know. "I could take you to dinner. To thank you for saving my life."

Her eyes widened. "Dinner? With you?"

Instantly shot down. *Good job, dummy*. "Okay, I'll take that as a no." He made sure to keep his voice light, good-natured. No big deal. "Have a good weekend." He turned toward the door.

She tugged at the sleeve of his sweatshirt. "Wait. I didn't mean to hurt your feelings. I'd like to have dinner with you sometime. I mean, as friends. Just not now. It's not a good time. That's all."

"Sure, no problem." He smiled, but his mouth had gone so dry he wasn't sure his lips had actually moved. *Just as friends.* That might have hurt more than the rejection itself.

"It's nothing to do with you." Her fingers still grasped his sleeve. She seemed to notice and dropped her hand like he was a hot burner. "I have a few things to work out. I'm in therapy." The last sentence spilled out of her as though the pot on his burner had boiled over. She colored and let out an embarrassed snort. An adorable snort from her perky little nose. "Not sure why I just told you that."

"Hey, it's fine. And good for you. Therapy helped me a lot."

"*You* were in therapy?"

He almost laughed at the shock on her face. "Why's that surprising?"

"I don't know. You seem like the type who doesn't need any help being happy in their own skin."

"I am. Now. But I've had some stuff to work through." Cart-loads of stuff. He looked down at the tote in his arms. He might have to return to therapy now that his mother had reappeared.

"Does it work? Therapy?" she asked.

He raised his gaze to look into her eyes. The frankness and sincerity in her expression touched him in a deep, vulnerable spot of his own. "For me, yes. But it's not a magic pill that erases everything that ever hurt you."

"I wish it did." Her expression darkened.

"Me too." He studied her hands. She fingered the charms on the silver bracelet she wore around her left wrist. When he lifted his eyes, her gaze was fixed on him. Searching. Did she wonder what he'd like to erase? "Good luck with everything. I'm sure I'll see you around." He turned toward the door.

Once again, she stopped him by grabbing his sleeve. "Wait, one more thing." He circled back around to face her. She moved closer. The tote created a barrier between them, and he wished with a sudden fervor that it didn't. "Why would you want to take me to dinner when I've been such a brat to you?"

He raised an eyebrow, shocked. "I…I don't know. Just being friendly, I guess." *Because I love you.*

"I lied just now."

"About what?" he asked. This conversation was too much for his pea brain.

"If I were to go to dinner with you, it would not be as friends."

He held the tote tighter to his chest, a sliver of hope making its way up the back of his neck. "Are you saying you might say yes if I asked you another time?

"I might."

"Well, then, I'll be asking you again." He smiled, hoping it was as charming as hers. "If you gave me the chance to take you to dinner, I'd be the happiest guy in Cliffside Bay."

A line formed between her eyebrows. "What if our date was a total disaster? Then you'd be unhappy."

"True. But it won't be a disaster." He lowered his voice, hoping to seduce her a little with a cocky promise and a husky tone. "It'll be the best night you've ever had."

She tilted her head to the right and swallowed. He'd gotten to her with that one.

"What makes you so sure about that, Stone Soup?"

He shrugged and pursed his lips as if thinking it through. "Well, Pepper Shaker, no one's ever complained in the past."

"Yes, but have they raved?" She elongated the last word.

"If there were an app that ranked men on their dating skills, I'd be ranked all fives, baby."

She laughed and rolled her eyes. "It almost makes me want to go out with you simply to knock you down a peg."

"I have an unflinching self-confidence. It's impossible to squelch."

She adjusted the strap of the duffel bag on her shoulder and peered up at him through narrowed eyes, as if seeing him for the first time. "I believe that, actually."

"Yeah, so about this date we may or may not have in the future—how long should I wait before asking again? Is there a specific waiting period?"

"I'll let you know." She brushed up against the bag as she leaned closer, transfixing him with her eyes. Then she raised up on her dancer toes and pressed her velvety lips to his cheek. A wave of her perfume washed over him. She smelled of the forests of his youth, woodsy and floral, perhaps honeysuckle mixed with cedar. He was intoxicated, made bold, by her nearness. If he hadn't held the tote, he might have gathered her into his arms and kissed her properly. Fortunately, the environmentally conscious grocery carrier saved the earth and lovestruck giants. "All teasing aside, I'm glad you're okay." With a dramatic twirl, she disappeared into Lisa and Rafael's apartment.

Dumbfounded, he stood in front of his door with one hand pressed against the spot where her mouth had landed for too brief a second. Was it possible that a friendly peck could be felt in every nerve ending?

Be patient. Your time will come.

2

Pepper

For Pepper Griffin, therapy sessions were like high school all over again. She was trapped like a bug in a jar. The world went on outside the glass, but she could not participate, tortured as the last of the season's sunny afternoons faded. The bracing snap in the air invigorated her, made her feel more alive. Fall breezes, with their hints of woodsmoke and dried hay—and here in Cliffside Bay, the briny sea—sharpened her mind. The layers of protection over her heart thinned under the piercing blue sky. Oh, how these crisp autumn days made her greedy, wanting more. Without them she might become as brittle and cold and gray as the winter to come. She longed to be in Maggie's backyard dancing with baby Lily as the fall light doused the landscape in gold. They could laugh and breathe under the bright yellow leaves of the aspens.

Instead, she fidgeted in the counseling office of pudgy Cora Sandberg, PhD. Good old Cora with her basset-hound face, always serious, contemplative. Cora knitted during the sessions, her needles clicking with unremitting cheerfulness in direct juxtaposition to her sad eyes.

The office smelled of lavender. For hours after she left, the cloying scent clung to Pepper's clothes.

Knitting and lavender. All the rage these days. Everyone and their mother trekking to remote parts of the Pacific Northwest to gather around lavender fields and remark on their beauty and scent before returning to a bed-and-breakfast to drink tea and knit endless numbers of scarves.

"Why don't you know how to drive?" Cora asked a lot of questions.

Pepper's role was to answer them and somehow be cured of her tragic past. Yes, that was slightly dramatic, but for heaven's sake, how long had she been here today? Surely the clock on the table next to the bowl of lavender sachets was wrong. Fifteen minutes. She'd only been here for fifteen minutes!

Did therapy make everyone feel somewhat suicidal?

Cora halted her knitting. The brown scarf went limp in her lap, like a tired beaver. She reached for the plastic water bottle next to her chair, then sucked from the straw while observing Pepper. "Is that a hard question for you to answer?"

"What was the question again?" Pepper's mind had drifted off as she fixated on the layers of lipstick on the straw of the water bottle. How often was it washed? How many days or months did the red stain represent?

"I asked why you can't drive."

Pepper's cheeks warmed. "I grew up in New York City. You don't need a car there. In fact, it's much better not to have a car. Plus, I like walking. Did you know most questions can be solved while walking? It's also great for learning lines. Something about the physical movement makes your memory keener."

"Are those the only reasons?" Cora resumed her knitting.

Pepper shrugged. "Not exactly." She told people it was because she grew up in New York City. That was a lie. Technically, she grew up in the Hamptons and went to college in New York City. Everyone in the Hamptons drove cars, usually fancy, shiny, fast cars. The truth was seedier and more complex. She had a phobia about driving. Undiagnosed thus far, although Cora might do the honors before the session was over today.

Her stepfather, Dack, had tried to teach her. After coming inches from a lamppost during her first lesson, he'd been a less enthusiastic teacher. That night he'd suggested driving school.

The second time out, with a grumpy driving teacher who looked as though he'd recently stepped out of a biker club, she managed to hit a person. In her defense, she barely tapped him as she pulled out of a parking space at the driving school. Her victim had been clearly intoxicated in the middle of the afternoon—which likely was the reason for his homelessness—and had stumbled in front of the car with a sudden swiftness. She was driving five miles an hour. Not fast, thankfully. Still, in her shock, she slammed on the brakes. Hard. The teacher's forehead smacked the dashboard. The homeless guy was fine. Drunks tend to bounce. Her teacher, unfortunately, had a sizable bump on his forehead. Pepper Griffin was kicked out of driving school. They wouldn't even give her parents their money back. The story had spread like a wildfire in the dead of summer. By the next morning, all the kids at her small private school knew about her near-homicide. Everyone had a great laugh at her expense, which further sealed her determination never to attend a high school reunion.

After giving her teacher a concussion and almost taking out a harmless albeit drunk homeless guy, Pepper had decided her driving career was a lost cause. Having access to the great freedom machine, as Dack called it, wasn't worth the pressure of being responsible for killing someone. Cars were completely irresponsible in the wrong hands. And hers were all kinds of wrong. Furthermore, talk about an exercise in trust. At any moment, a car could veer into your lane and, boom, it was all over. The best you could hope for was that you were wearing clean underwear.

"Why is it that I always think there's more to the story than what you tell me?" Cora asked, not unkindly or with a hint of accusation. Her voice was always flat and even, like the smell of antiseptic in a medical clinic. All very clean and tidy but without an ounce of warmth.

That said, the woman was good at her job. She cut right through Pepper's bullshit and zeroed in on the truth.

"I have a phobia. Is that what you want to hear?" Pepper asked.

"Of driving."

"I almost killed a man when I was in driving school. So now I don't drive."

"Was that so hard to say?" Cora asked.

Pepper wanted to let out the world's longest sigh and roll her eyes like a thirteen-year-old girl shopping for clothes with her mother. She refrained. "It was a little hard."

"Why?"

"It's embarrassing."

"And therefore, makes you feel vulnerable," Cora said.

"Yes." *Vulnerable.* The most overused word in America.

Knitting, lavender, and vulnerability. Even better when done together.

Cora set aside her knitting. "I've been doing a little research about the craft of acting since you became my client. My niece is studying the dramatic arts in college and is a great source of information. I've learned that much of the initial training is focused on becoming vulnerable so that you might adequately express human emotion. Yet you seem to have difficulties doing so. Even with a therapist."

"Playing a part is different from being me." Being Pepper might look easy from the outside, but the inside was as complicated as one of those thousand-piece puzzles Dack loved.

"Could we try something new in the spirit of making progress as quickly as possible?" Cora asked. "When I ask you a question, don't censor yourself. Just say the first thing that comes to mind. I promise not to judge you."

Cora was as relentless as her knitting needles.

"I'll do my best," Pepper said.

"Are you having any luck finding a place to live?"

Ah, yes. Now they'd come to her second problem and cause of embarrassment. Ironically—given her earlier brush with the almost-homicide of a homeless man—she was homeless. Thirty-one years old and a perpetual guest. A mooch. Not because she was a day drinker like the poor guy she hit with the front bumper of a Chevy. Thank goodness. She had enough problems without adding drinking to the list.

"My options are somewhat limited." With her funds from the latest acting gig already drying up like her skin in hot weather, there was no way she could afford a place in Los Angeles or Cliffside Bay. Thus, she had made mooching a professional sport. "It's hard to find a rental in Cliffside Bay, and I don't have much money."

"Yes. We agreed that it would be a challenge. At the same time, you expressed a deep desire to have your own place and rely less upon your friends. You're sure to *remain* stuck if you never take actions to change your situation. Did you take any steps we agreed to last week?" Cora crossed her legs at the ankles. Her shoes were black with a buckle. *Raggedy Ann shoes.*

"I did not," Pepper said.

"Why is that?"

Cora was not the kind of shrink she'd anticipated. Pepper had assumed she'd be the type who asked a leading question at the beginning of the session and then wrote psychoanalysis type stuff in a notebook while the client rambled on about their feelings. Not Cora. Although she looked like someone's grandma with her knit dresses and comfortable shoes, she was a real ball-breaker—always pushing for progress on Pepper's to-do list and bugging her about being more proactive about her life and work. Cora had no clue what the acting life was like. One didn't just will a job your way. There were thousands of girls hoping for an audition for some crappy television show. When she'd mentioned this to Cora in a previous session, the irritating woman suggested goal setting and vision boards and being clear about your intentions.

"I had a place until my best friend fell in love in like two seconds." Pepper hadn't meant to say that out loud or with such a biting, bitter tone.

Pepper and Lisa had planned on renting an apartment on the second floor of the Victorian, but an unforeseen set of circumstances had prevented their plans. First, Lisa fell in love with Rafael and decided to move in with him. Second, Lisa had asked Pepper to give up the apartment so that her twin, David, and his two young children could move in. She'd agreed without hesitation. The poor guy's wife had been dealing and distributing drugs from her minivan while their children slept in the back seat. She was murdered when the bad men she worked for learned the FBI was about to arrest her. They killed her before she could make a deal in exchange for information. At least, that was the theory.

When she wasn't in LA for an audition, Pepper stayed with Maggie and Jackson and their adorable baby, Lily, in their idyllic house down a country road five miles out of town. Yet another couple blissfully in love and having perfect little babies. They were all around her. It was enough to make a lonely girl even lonelier.

Pepper, Lisa, and Maggie had attended four years at NYU together and then spent another eight in pursuit of Broadway careers. Oddly, Maggie was now a folk-rock star, and Lisa was the "it" girl of Hollywood.

And that left Pepper.

An *almost* movie star. Who was she kidding? She wasn't an almost anything. Other than her recent part in a slasher movie and a long list of Broadway chorus girl credits from her time in New York, she was more moocher than actress. Her character in the worst horror film ever made had been killed in the first twenty minutes. Filming had wrapped in August, so the movie hadn't yet released. Technically, she didn't know that the film was bad, but she had a distinct suspicion. The script had been terrible. The other actors had been young and untrained with no tricks to elevate terrible dialogue or rescue the implausible plot. Unless the editing team was a bunch of magicians, there was no hope for the thing.

Alone. Out of work. Bitter. Worst of all, jealous of her two best friends. Which only made Pepper's suspicions about herself abundantly clear. She was a bad person. Just like her biological father. Selfish, self-centered, self-absorbed. All the words that began with *self*.

Her response seemed to energize Cora. She leaned forward and fired off the next question. "This is the second time you've mentioned Lisa's rapid engagement. Do you disapprove?"

"No. I don't disapprove. I'm happy for her. Rafael's a great guy. She finally met the right man." Even if he was former military. "I can be glad for her and sad for myself." Pepper had recently learned something about friendship she hadn't known before. One could be happy for a friend's good fortune in parallel with feelings of jealousy and abandonment.

"What makes you sad about her engagement?" Cora asked.

She kind of hated Cora. "I'm being left behind."

"Everyone's moving forward but you?" Cora asked.

Right. Lisa and Maggie had thriving careers and supportive partners who adored them. She was broke and alone.

"And I feel like a mooch," Pepper said. "A pathetic loser."

Her stepfather always said visitors and fish go bad after three days.

Even Jackson, Cliffside Bay's young and saintly doctor, might tire of her frequent presence in his home. The same worry didn't apply to Maggie. They were like family. Sisters by choice. For years, she and Lisa and Maggie had shared apartments in New York City. In the early days after college, they'd lived in a one-room studio together. They were sardines in a can back then. She'd loved those times.

"I'm fine to stay at Maggie's. As long as Jackson doesn't get sick of me."

"Why would he get sick of you?"

"I don't know. It's just that..." She looked down at her lap. "I'm often too much for people."

Cora smoothed a plump hand over the arm of her chair as if petting a cat. "What does that mean?"

"Unless they want to have sex with me, most men dislike me." Men wanted her to shrink down to their size. "I say what I think and don't pretend to be dumb just because men love to feel superior."

"Can you give me an example?" Cora asked.

"Not off the top of my head, no."

"All men are not the same. There are men who like women who challenge them."

Pepper shrugged. "Maybe."

"May I ask you something?" Without waiting for an answer, Cora asked anyway. "Why did you start therapy with me?"

"Lisa and Maggie thought I should." Pepper squirmed, remembering the conversation. Maggie had been insistent that she talk about the trauma she'd experienced at nineteen. Four sessions later, she hadn't yet told Cora about the awful night on the subway.

"Do you know why they wanted you to see someone? Did something happen among the three of you that prompted the request?"

Pepper picked at the fabric of her jeans, buying time. "I had an argument with Lisa and Maggie."

They'd been in Lisa's kitchen washing up the dishes from one of the Sunday-night dinners with the residents of the Victorian when Lisa brought up the subject of Stone.

She winced as she remembered the conversation.

"I'd appreciate if you'd drop this ridiculous and unfounded

animosity toward Stone." Lisa handed her a cup to put in the dishwasher. "You were so rude to him tonight that I was actually embarrassed for you and for him."

"I wasn't rude, just distant." Anger widened the space between her breastbones. She came out fighting. "I don't like him. What's it to you?"

"He's my friend and Rafael's *best* friend. I don't like the way you talk to him. It makes you seem petty and spoiled."

"I don't have to like him just because you want me to."

"For heaven's sake, Pepper, you don't even know the guy. How can you hate him?" Lisa slammed a rinsed plate onto the counter instead of handing it to her.

"You spent like two minutes with Rafael before you decided you loved him. What's the difference?"

Lisa gaped at her, like a stunned fish. A fish with the face of an angel.

Pepper scuttled away from the sink. The minute she'd said it, she knew it was so far out of line as to be a zigzag. She placed her hands on the edge of the cooktop and took in a deep breath, waiting for the explosion from her friend.

It didn't come. When Pepper had the nerve to look, Lisa was simply standing there with her hands tented under her chin. Her light blue eyes shimmered. From unshed tears or anger? Pepper couldn't be certain.

"You're the one who told me hate is *not* the opposite of love. Indifference is. Right?" Lisa asked.

"That's right." Her father's behavior had taught her that lesson far better than any definition in a textbook.

"You're not indifferent to Stone Hickman. Which is what this is all about, and you know it."

"You're wrong." Pepper glared back at her friend.

"You haven't allowed yourself to get to know him because you're wildly attracted to him."

"What're you talking about? He repulses me."

"You can lie to yourself all you want, but I know this isn't about him, other than the fact that he used to be a marine. Maggie's right. Your weird revulsion toward the sweetest guy around is about what happened to you, and you've never dealt with it. If you spent time with him instead of doing everything in your power to alienate him, you'd see what a wonderful person he is. He would never hurt a woman."

"I've dealt with it fine. I'm strong. Not everyone has to spend thousands of dollars at the shrink to work through stuff," Pepper said.

Lisa's eyes filled with tears as she took two steps back and slammed into a corner of the counter. "How can you say that to me?" Her voice trembled. "Take it back."

Pepper's stomach lurched as she realized what she'd said. Lisa had spent time in a mental facility when she was younger. Recently, she'd started intensive therapy after being at a concert where dozens of people were gunned down by a monster with an automatic rifle. "I didn't mean you. I'm sorry. I just meant that I don't need therapy. I'm fine."

Lisa drew near enough that Pepper could see the shimmer in her friend's eye shadow. Lisa tapped her lightly on the chest. "Listen to me. You're going to call the therapist's number that Jackson gave you, and you're going to make an appointment."

"I'm a grown-up. You cannot make me."

"Do you value our friendship?"

"Of course I do. You know that. You and Maggie are my family," Pepper said, hoping not to choke on the tears that gathered at the back of her throat.

"Then you're going to do two things. You're going to get into therapy and deal with the trauma from that night. And in the meantime, you're going to do whatever it takes to get along with Stone. No more smart remarks or mean glances his way. No more antagonizing him. You're going to treat him with the kindness and respect he deserves."

Before Pepper could answer either way, Lisa turned on her heel and fled the room, leaving only the scent of her perfume.

Now Pepper looked up at Cora. Rip the bandage off. There was no other way. "I was raped when I was nineteen."

Cora flinched as though someone had slapped her. "I'm so sorry." A slight pause as Cora adjusted her skirt. "Are you ready to talk about it?"

"My friends think I should. They believe it's messing up my relationships with men."

For once, Cora didn't ask a follow-up question. The silence was like a bowl of heavy cream between them. They both wanted to dip their fingers in but weren't sure how.

"I don't want to talk about it," Pepper said, finally. "I mean, it was a long time ago. Shouldn't I have moved past it by now?"

"Time does not heal all wounds," Cora said. "Despite what people say."

Pepper unlocked her knees and rose from the chair to walk over to the window. Cora's office was in the front room of her house. Her home sat at the base of the southern hill and looked out to the sea. The lawn butted up against a section of the boardwalk that ran above the long stretch of sandy beach. Several potted planters with mums decorated Cora's front steps. A woman with two small children in a double stroller had stopped at the edge of Cora's lawn to adjust the baby's blanket.

"Do you think talking about it will help?" Pepper asked.

"I wouldn't be in this chair if I didn't."

Pepper ran her finger along the edge of the windowsill. The smooth white trim paired well with a soothing blue.

Blue was supposed to calm a person. She'd read that somewhere.

"Tell me what happened," Cora said. "Just the facts."

She remained at the window. A gust of wind tickled the chimes that hung from a rafter of Cora's covered porch. They made such a lonely sound, like a high-pitched, staccato cry for help. "I was on the subway late at night. The car was empty other than me and four navy guys. They were drunk—staggering and belligerent—and cornered me. 'Let's take turns.'

That's what they said right before they grabbed me. Three held me down while one raped me. Before the next one could take his turn, the police came. I learned later that a man in the next car had seen them cornering me and had called 911."

An image of the navy men dressed in whites floated before her. It was forever ago, but she could see their mean faces in detail. One fair with freckles. Another had a crooked nose, as though it had been broken in a fight. The third man who held her had a thick, bulging vein in the middle of his forehead. The rapist had eyes like Hitler.

"Eleven minutes. That's how long it took before the cops showed up," Pepper said. "But it seemed like a lifetime."

She forced her eyes to focus on the woman with the stroller to keep the images of that night from crowding her mind. The young mother kissed the baby on the head as she tucked the blanket tightly around her.

"Were they charged?" Cora asked.

"Yes. I made sure of that." The police had taken her to the hospital. "Rape test and the whole thing. They went to prison."

The woman outside the window got behind the stroller and set off down the sidewalk. Pepper watched her blond ponytail sway back and forth, as if it were happy. Free as could be. What would it be like to be live without the weight of the past? She turned back to look at Cora. "I wish I were normal. Because of them, I'll never be."

"What would normal be for you?"

Pepper walked to the chair but didn't sit. What would it be? "Light. Free. With a man who loves me. Not one of the guys I usually choose. Someone good. Someone who would be good to me. But I can't seem to pick the right one." An image of Stone Hickman flashed before her eyes. "There's this guy. The type I'm talking about. One of the good guys, like Maggie and Lisa have."

"Tell me about him."

Pepper shoved her hands in her boyfriend jeans to keep them from flailing about. As she talked, she circled the room. "His name's Stone Hickman. He's Rafael's best friend. A former marine. For so long now I haven't been able to look at a man in a military uniform without thinking about that night."

"Understandable."

"Stone likes me. Even though I'm mean to him, he's always nice to me." No matter how cold she was to him, the man was unrelenting in his optimism and sunny disposition. Frankly, it was baffling. He thought she couldn't stand him, yet he never ceased to be polite and often flirtatious.

"And you like him?" Cora asked.

"Before I knew he was a marine, I was instantly attracted to him. We met at a party and there was this huge spark between us. I felt drawn to him."

"But now?"

Pepper rested her elbows on the back of the chair. "Now I just feel confused and conflicted when I see him." He often looked as if he was on the verge of laughing. For some reason, this annoyed her. Often, she wondered if he was laughing at her. She suspected he found her silly. Not that she could blame him. She acted silly when she was around him. He made her edgy, nervous. She fidgeted and snarled like a trapped animal whenever he was near.

"His military background triggers you."

"Exactly. I know intellectually that one has nothing to do with the other. It's like this switch turns on, and I feel this rage. This misplaced rage. But something weird happened today." She told the story of the SUV almost hitting Stone. "I pulled him out of danger, or he would have been killed. I saved him. Don't you think that's strange?"

"I'm not sure I follow."

She flushed, embarrassed. "Surely it isn't a coincidence that it was me who happened to be there? Like God has a plan or something. Maybe I'm supposed to give him a chance?"

Cora's gazed flickered to the small clock on the table. "I'm afraid our time is up."

3

Stone

STONE SPENT the rest of Saturday contemplating what he was going to do about his mother's sudden appearance. After a run on the beach and a serious workout at the gym, he'd texted both his siblings to see if they wanted to meet for dinner. Kyle texted back that he was out of town for just one night. He'd taken Violet for an overnight in the city and left their four kids with the nanny. Autumn said she had plans for that evening as well. They agreed to meet Monday at Kyle's house. Although he was anxious to speak with his brother and sister, he was relieved to let it ride for a few more days. He needed time to decide how in the hell to tell his siblings their mother had reappeared. In addition, he wanted more time to think about what he wanted to do about it.

Instead of stewing about it, he decided to instigate a night out at The Oar with the other Wolves. Winning Sara Ness's project was reason for celebration. They'd all agreed with much enthusiasm.

After a shower, he wandered into the kitchen to wait for the rest of the Wolves to arrive. He'd just popped the cap off a beer when Trey entered the kitchen dressed in nice jeans and a checkered button-down shirt that hugged his trim physique.

Stone looked down at his faded jeans. Maybe if he dressed better, he'd have more of a chance with Pepper. Nice clothes cost cash—money he didn't have to spend on frivolity. He needed to keep his attention where it belonged. The business and saving for his own home.

"Hey, where've you been all day?" Stone asked as he got up to fetch another beer for his roommate and friend.

"I took Autumn into the city. She wanted to look for a little patio set for her deck. Everything's on sale right now."

"That's cool."

After working together to decorate her cottage, Trey and Autumn started spending time together perusing antiques and furniture shops in the city or cooking meals together. They acted like best girlfriends, dashing Stone's hope that they would fall madly in love. Maybe it was just as well. Trey was bitter after his contentious divorce and claimed he would never get married again and had no interest in having children. His sister was the opposite. Although she didn't talk about it much, he knew her greatest desire was to get married and have a family.

Any guy would be lucky to have his gentle, smart, and pretty sister. She needed to put herself out there, but her physical scars made her shy and insecure. One of her legs was disfigured from the car accident. She never went anywhere without makeup to hide the scar on her right cheek and dressed in pants or skirts with long boots. Her former boyfriend hadn't helped her self-confidence. She wouldn't tell Stone exactly what went down, other than he hurt her. Stone wanted to punch the guy just thinking about him.

Again, he wished she and Trey would become more than just

friends. Trey was nice. Like the nicest guy ever. But if there was no attraction between them it wasn't as if it would develop just because Stone wanted it to. The heart loved who it loved. Take him, for example.

Pepper. What was she doing tonight? Maybe he'd run into her at The Oar. Damn, his thoughts were like a stupid circle that always came back to her.

Trey took the opened beer from him and jumped on top of the counter. "You look funny. Something happen?"

Stone sat at their table. "Very perceptive of you. I had a weird day." Over the course of a few minutes, Stone told him about the woman and then his subsequent saving by Pepper Griffin. "She jumped on my back and pulled me out of the way. I landed on top of her."

"That must have been fun for you."

"It would have been had I not been so totally freaked out." Stone shared his fears about the fast vehicle being connected to the woman claiming to be his mother.

"Whoa. You think?"

"I have no idea, really."

"Do you think it's really her?"

"I haven't seen her since I was six, so I can't be certain. She looks like an old lady. It's not a stretch to think she's probably had a tough time of it. She sounds like a smoker."

"Did your mom smoke?"

"Not that I remember." He searched the recesses of his brain, but no memory of either of his parents smoking came to mind. "Just when things were starting to gel for Autumn and me here, now this. And Kyle seems like he's got it all together, but there's deep pain under all that bravado. He took her leaving the hardest of all of us."

"Autumn told me how he basically raised you guys," Trey said.

"She shared that with you, huh?" Interesting.

"Sure. We talk about everything. You wouldn't think so, but

we have a lot in common."

"How so?" Trey had grown up wealthy in San Diego. The Hickman kids had grown up in a trailer on the edge of someone else's pig farm in Nowhere, Oregon.

"We both almost died when we were in high school." Trey said it casually, as if this were common knowledge.

"I didn't know that."

"Yeah, I got this weird blood infection. They couldn't figure out what was wrong with me. I was months in the hospital. They told my parents to get ready to say goodbye." He grinned. "But I guess I was too ornery."

Trey didn't look ornery. He was a "boy band" type of pretty. Everywhere they went, women swooned over his light blue eyes and perfectly symmetrical face and wished he would father their children. And that nose. It was like a nose in a catalog at a Hollywood plastic surgeon's office.

"Like your sister, I had a long recovery," Trey said.

"I'd never have guessed." Trey was in great physical condition now, lean and fit.

"It's been twenty years and my mom still calls every day to check up on me. I'm thirty-four, and she still asks if I'm taking my vitamins."

He wished he had a mother like that.

They were interrupted by a knock on their front door and then David Perry's voice. "Anyone home?"

"In here. Come on in," Stone said as Trey jumped from the counter.

Stone followed Trey out to the living room.

Architect first and man second, David carried a long tube containing a set of house plans, even though this was supposed to be a fun night.

Stone slapped him on the shoulder. "What's up with the work stuff?"

David flushed. "I know this is supposed to be a night of debauchery, but I just came from meeting with Sara to go over the plans." David seemed to prefer working to playing, but the Wolves were slowly breaking him of his golden boy habits.

"Well, what did she think?" Trey asked.

David grinned and sighed at the same time, obviously relieved. "She loved them."

"You must be psyched," Trey said. "I'm always ecstatic when a client likes my proposal."

"For sure." David placed the tube on the sofa table as if it were a precious newborn baby and shrugged out of his black peacoat. "Especially Sara. She's got that posh rich-girl vibe that scares me."

Stone chuckled as he took David's coat. "She's super sweet, though. I've known her since she was a pimply-faced college freshman."

Sara Ness was Autumn's best friend from college. Newly widowed with a small baby, she'd hired the Wolves to build her a house on a piece of property outside of town. A huge house. Because she was richer than God—an heiress to a major fortune. Her massive wealth was their good luck. Without the personal connection to Autumn, they wouldn't have had a chance in Hades of securing the deal. As Kyle always said—success was at least partly due to who you knew.

David swept away a few wheat-colored waves from his forehead as he looked at his watch. "I told Lisa I'd check in on the kids before we go out, but she gave me strict orders not to. They do better if I just stay out rather than come home and leave again. Abandonment issues." He said the last part as if it were a joke, but Stone knew he didn't really find it amusing. His wife's death had been hard on his young children.

After losing his wife he'd moved to Cliffside Bay from Iowa to be near his twin, Lisa. When his sister was in town, she always offered to babysit so David could go out with the guys.

Rafael showed up a few minutes after David. Rafael and Lisa were home for another week before leaving for a month in LA. With her filming schedule, she was gone for weeks at a time.

Depending on their work commitments, Rafael went with her. As the head of finance and business operations of Wolf Enterprises, Rafael could work remotely from the apartment he shared with Lisa in LA. Stone gave Rafael a lot of credit. Being engaged to the "it" girl of Hollywood was not exotic vacations and champagne with every meal. Instead of being able to enjoy each other, Rafael was on the constant lookout for paparazzi or crazed fans. His former position as head of Brody and Kara Mullen's security had trained him well for his new role.

His phone buzzed with a text from Nico that he was already at The Oar and to get their butts down there ASAP.

"I wonder how long he's been there already," Rafael said with a smirk. "Flirting with his favorite bar owner."

"I thought Nico was staying away from Sophie?" Trey asked.

"Supposedly they're just friends," Rafael said. "But I think Sophie has other ideas."

"Not with her brother watching her every move," Stone said. Zane Shaw and his sister, Sophie Woods, owned The Oar as well as being partners in Dog's Brewery. Zane had made it abundantly clear that he didn't like Nico anywhere near his sister. Which was a shame, because she liked Nico, and they had a lot in common despite their age difference. Sophie was only twenty-two. Nico was in his early thirties like the rest of the Wolves.

The situation was further complicated because Zane and Kyle were best friends. The Wolves were grateful and reliant upon Kyle's financial investment into their company. The tangled web of small-town life was like that. Not that Stone would have it any other way. He was a small-town boy and always would be. A man could breathe here in this little town by the sea.

They walked together down to The Oar. The sky boasted a brilliant twilight blue that hinted of a wondrous starry night ahead. October, he'd learned since moving to Cliffside Bay, brought moderate sunny days and crisp, clear nights. Stone breathed in the brisk evening air scented with the sea and eucalyptus trees. According to the locals, a wet winter was coming. He'd heard on the news that the entire country was expected to have an early and harsh winter. Something about weather patterns and climate change, all above his comprehension. California residents up and down the state would welcome the rain, even if it meant fewer opportunities for construction. The chance for fires lessened with each day of rain.

That said, he felt a sense of urgency to break ground on Sara's house as soon as possible. Beating the rainy season would provide the opportunity to finish the house by spring. If they could exceed Sara Ness's expectations, she would recommend them to her wealthy friends, and suddenly they would have a legitimate business.

A blast of warmth hit Stone's face as the door closed behind them. He took off his jacket, feeling hot. Too bad there were no outside tables this time of year. Even though it was chilly, he much preferred the fresh air to the manufactured heat. He tugged at his collar and breathed in the scent of grilled food and beer.

Sophie waved to them from behind the bar. Blond, tanned, and legs for miles, she looked like the beach itself. No matter what time of year, Sophie Woods was summertime in a person.

Nico Bentley was waiting for them at a table in the corner with his nose in a book about the planting regions of the California coast. He looked up to greet them with his typical joyful smile. The guy was never in a bad mood, always congenial and even-tempered. During their last project if anything bothered or worried him, he came right out and expressed it, making him an ideal business partner. If Stone knew what someone wanted, it made it a heck of a lot easier to give it to them.

The Oar was quiet for a Saturday night, with about a half-dozen tables in the restaurant occupied. The bar section was full of happy weekend night drinkers. The locals liked the months between the Labor Day weekend and Memorial Day weekend.

No crowds, and the drinks were half price during happy hour. The Wolves were particularly fond of the cheap drinks.

They joined Nico at a table for six. His chair faced the bar, probably so he could keep an eye on Sophie. David plopped next to him. Stone and Trey took the seats opposite. Rafael had just lowered his muscular frame into the chair on the end of the table when a waitress who looked about twelve years old brought the menus over and passed them around. She gave them an apologetic smile. "I'm too young to serve alcohol, but Sophie will bring you whatever you want."

"You tell her one of us will come to her," Nico said with a glance toward the bar. "She's too busy."

"I'll get the first few pitchers." Rafael stood. "Couple of IPAs?"

"Ask Sophie to pour us the seasonal one," Trey said. "She told me it's stellar."

"Please ask her to pour a glass of whatever red blend she has open for me," Nico said.

After the waitress left, Stone tossed a sugar packet at Nico. "She has a special bottle open for just you?"

"If you must know, I'm here many nights for a glass or two." Nico tossed the sugar packet across the table at Stone. "It's merely good business to have a bottle open for one of her regulars."

"Yeah, but wine?" David asked. "Dude, you're killing our reputation."

Nico laughed. "I don't know what reputations we have, other than being complete losers with women." He tipped his head toward Rafael. "Except for him. Lucky bastard."

"Wine." David shook his head again, as if disgusted.

"Do I lecture you about how much sugar you put in your coffee?" Nico asked David.

"Yes, you do." David picked up the wayward sugar packet and wriggled it in front of Nico's face. "And I'll continue to have my coffee with two sugars, thank you very much."

"All I'm asking is that you try green tea for a week. You'll start feeling one hundred percent better," Nico said.

"I feel fine." David rubbed under his eyes. "If I could just get Laine to sleep in her own bed, I might not be so tired. She kicks all night long like she's in a race or something."

"No luck, huh?" Stone asked.

David gave a weary shake of his head. "She starts in her own bed, but the next thing I know I wake up to a hot little body next to me. By that time, I'm too tired to carry her back to her room."

"What about when you want to bring home a lady?" Trey asked.

David guffawed and slapped the table. "Like that's ever going to happen. I wouldn't be able to stay awake long enough to make anything happen even if I could charm someone into the house of sippy cups and spilled cereal."

"You need a single mom. Someone who gets it," Nico said.

"I think my situation is a little more complicated than most women would want to be involved in. Like, what am I supposed to say when a date asks me about my late wife? She had brown hair and dealt drugs out of our minivan until she was murdered by her thug bosses."

The table grew silent for a few minutes.

"Did you try the grief support group down at the church?" Trey pushed his black-framed glasses up his nose.

"Not yet," David said. "I tried to go the other night, but I just stood outside the door for about fifteen minutes and then turned around and went home."

"Baby steps," Stone said. "Give it some time." When he'd returned to civilian life, he'd been flummoxed by the smallest complications. Autumn had helped him start fresh. He'd moved in with her while he was studying for his contractor license. That's when they'd decided to look for Kyle. Coming here had changed so much for him, given him a fresh start. David needed more time to heal. It hadn't even been six months since his wife's murder.

David studied the sugar packet, turning it over and over on the table. "I'm okay, guys. I'd rather not talk about it. Let's talk about you guys, not me."

"We're here for you if you ever do," Nico said.

David mumbled, "It's good to be out. That's enough."

"How's Mrs. Coventry?" Stone asked Nico, hoping to change the subject.

Nico brightened. "She's doing pretty well. Dr. Waller paid her a house call earlier today, and he said her blood pressure's down." He smiled and leaned back in his chair. "Dr. Waller said he thinks it's my home-cooked meals. She was getting way too much salt from those frozen dinners."

Nico lived up on the very top peak of the hill above town in a bungalow he rented from an elderly widow, Judi Coventry. Rentals were hard to find in Cliffside Bay. Finding a bungalow had been a stroke of luck. Mrs. Coventry owned one of the oldest houses in town on a large lot that included an amazing view of the ocean. A bungalow sat adjacent to the house, which she rented to Nico at a low rate in exchange for help in the garden and with errands, such as grocery shopping and tending to the flowers.

"I'll probably stay over at your place tonight," Nico said. "But I'll scoot out early. I've started making Mrs. Coventry breakfast and coffee. She doesn't eat anything until late afternoon unless I make her oatmeal with just a touch of maple syrup."

"Maple syrup? I thought you were against corn syrup," Stone said.

"You may not realize that real maple syrup comes out of a tree and is sweet enough just as God made it," Nico said.

The table erupted in good-natured jeers.

"You Californians are just plain weird," David said. "In the Midwest if it doesn't have corn syrup in it, then it's not food.

"Seriously, though. It sounds like you're taking on a lot with this lady. You don't even know her," David said.

"She doesn't have anyone," Nico said. "It's the least I can do. And she's such a sweet old lady."

Trey patted Nico's shoulder. "You have the biggest heart around. Just be careful. You don't realize when people are taking advantage of you."

Rafael appeared with two pitchers in his hands. "Sophie's bringing the wine. She insisted." He said this with a pointed look in Nico's direction. "And what's this I hear about a dog?"

"If you're referring to my recent adoption, then I'm guilty." Nico put a hand over his heart and made a face. "I couldn't help it. When Jen looked at me with those big eyes, I was a goner. We kind of picked each other."

"What were you doing at the shelter in the first place?" Stone asked, even though he knew the answer. Sophie had asked him to go with her to help pick out a dog.

Nico threw up his hands. "You know I can't say no to that girl."

"You're going to get yourself into trouble with her," David said. "Trust me. I'm an expert on trouble."

"I'd love to be in trouble with her," Nico said quietly. "But I've made it clear I'm not interested."

"You mean, you're pretending not to be interested," Stone said.

"Right." Nico glanced up at the bar. "It's hard as hell. She's awesome."

"How is it that you came away with a dog and not her?" Rafael asked.

"She wants a bar dog, and she said she'll know it when she finds him or her," Nico said. "Talk about something else. She's coming this way."

Rafael immediately launched into the subject of football, so by the time Sophie arrived with Nico's wine they were in a heated debate about what San Francisco should do about their quarterback problem. Since Brody Mullen retired, the team had been a disaster.

Sophie set the glass in front of Nico and whispered something in his ear that made him chuckle. When she straightened, she greeted the rest of them and then sauntered off on her long, tanned legs.

Nico's gaze followed her until Stone punched him on the arm. "That girl's going to make me lose my mind. Do you know what she whispered in my ear?"

"Do tell," Trey said.

"She said, 'There's a bottle with your name on it on my bedside table.'"

"Goodness," Rafael said. "She's not exactly playing it cool."

Nico groaned. "I'm telling you guys, she's my kryptonite. Do you know how badly I want to take her up on her offer?"

"Dude, you've got to pull yourself together," Stone said.

"Getting with her would be a disaster on so many levels," Rafael said.

"I know. I know. But there's something about her I cannot resist," Nico said.

"Well, you need to. For all our sakes," Stone said. "Getting on the wrong side of Zane Shaw is not a good idea."

As if God was punishing him for his lack of sympathy toward his friend's plight, Pepper Griffin walked in the door wearing tight jeans and black stiletto pumps. She had a sassy orange scarf in her black curls that looked retro and posh. His stomach fluttered. Actually fluttered, as if there were birds or butterflies flying around inside him.

He didn't know which of them had it worse. Him or Nico. All he knew was they were both headed for trouble if they didn't keep it together tonight.

"Hey," he whispered to Nico. "Keep it cool."

"Cool?"

"With Sophie. Like, don't get drunk and follow her upstairs."

"Should I say the same to you in regard to the black-haired doll who just walked in here?" he whispered back.

"Yeah. You should. You most definitely should."

4

Pepper

FROM THE SIDEWALK in front of The Oar, Pepper spotted Stone's chiseled face. She was embarrassed by their intimate conversation after he'd nearly been killed by a speeding car, and the last person she wanted to see was Stone. She'd run over the conversation a hundred times since, chastising herself for telling him about therapy. Seriously, who just let that pop out of their mouth to a guy they had an enormous but confusing attraction to? Her instinct now was to make haste in the other direction, back to Lisa's to spend the night watching television. She almost told her friends to go in without her. However, what excuse wouldn't make her sound like a crazy person?

Autumn and Sara were new friends—relationships she wanted to cultivate. For one thing, they were also single. Since everyone else in this town seemed to be happily married or headed there, a bitter single girl needed a few plus-ones to hang with. In addition, she liked them both tremendously. Sara was guarded and maybe a little shy, but intelligent and interesting. Pepper had met her at a party at Kyle and Violet's a few weeks back, and they'd spent hours talking about a variety of subjects. They shared a love of theater, art, and fashion. And Autumn? Other than being Stone's sister, there was nothing to dislike about her. She was kind, generous, and down-to-earth. Just like her brother.

She followed behind Autumn as they entered the bar. Unless you watched carefully, you would never spot the slight hitch in her left leg.

"Hey, I may lean on you by the end of the night," Autumn said once they were inside the bar. She sometimes used a cane, but tonight she was without it. "After a few drinks I can get a little topsy-turvy. But I hate to bring my cane to a night out. I feel like an old lady."

"I'm on it," Pepper said. "And you're nothing close to an old lady. You look great tonight. I love your hair."

She gave a shy smile and ducked her head. "Thanks. I'm not used to going out, but I'm trying to be bolder." Autumn was a beautiful woman, with gorgeous fair skin and a mass of thick auburn hair that fell past her shoulder blades. This evening, she was dressed in black jeans and a light green sweater that matched her eyes.

Pepper had chosen a flowy blouse with blue dots, ankle skinny jeans, and black pumps. Her hair would not behave, so she'd arranged a scarf in that mess, hoping it looked trendy and not silly. Everyone was so much more casual out here. Back home in New York, she, Maggie, and Lisa always wore cocktail dresses out for a night on the town.

Sara shrugged out of her black leather jacket and reached up to touch the messy knot of reddish hair on top of her head, as if to check it was still there. On some it would look unkempt. Not Sara. She was fierce and tall, with a muscular, athletic body, like a warrior queen. The type who set trends, not followed them. Pepper had to admire her short green wool skirt and knee-high black boots, as well as her sleeveless sweater in winter white. Not everyone would notice this, but Pepper knew just by looking at her that every item of clothing on her body was from a high-end designer. Years working retail made her and Lisa experts. They could spot couture a mile away. That outfit probably cost three thousand dollars. Must be nice to be an heiress.

As they huddled in the entrance, Pepper couldn't stop her traitorous eyes from looking Stone's way. He was sitting in the back of the restaurant with his buddies looking like heaven in faded blue jeans and a tight black sweater that clung to his muscular shoulders and chest.

She spoke sternly to herself. Pay attention to your new friends, not Stone Hickman.

When Autumn had called to see if she wanted to go out with them for dinner and drinks, she'd jumped at the chance. Especially since she'd faced a night alone with Maggie and Jackson, who she felt quite certain wanted to put the baby to bed and have wine and sex in front of their fancy fireplace. Lisa was busy babysitting David's kids and had asked if she wanted to come over and run lines with her. Selfishly, that was the last thing Pepper wanted. The thought of running lines when she wanted so desperately to have work herself made her completely depressed and filled with awful jealousy. She'd been contemplating going out alone when Autumn called and offered to swing by to get her.

"Where should we sit?" Autumn asked. "Oh, great, there's my brother. He'll be giving me the stink eye all night."

"Why's that?" Pepper asked.

Sara laughed. "He doesn't like it when the two of us drink. It's a big-brother, overly protective thing. My brother has it, too."

"That sounds nice," Pepper said. She'd always wanted a brother. Sadly, her mom and Dack hadn't been able to have other children.

Sara pointed to a table by the window. "There? Away from Stone?"

Autumn nodded. "Pretend like you don't see them."

"Good luck with that," Sara said as Stone lifted a hand in greeting.

The three of them traipsed across the restaurant in a row and settled into the hard chairs. A server came over right away with menus and took their drink order for a bottle of white wine. Stone showed up soon thereafter.

"Ladies, care to join us?" he asked.

"No. Definitely no." Autumn crossed her arms over her chest. "We're having girl time."

"Fine. I can take a hint." He grinned. "But may I say before I go that you all look beautiful this evening."

Pepper felt the heat rise to her cheeks and made a great study of her menu. Was it her imagination or did his gaze seem to linger longer on her?

"Thank you," Autumn said. "Now go away."

"Come over and say hello at least. After you eat," he said.

"Will do," Sara said. "By the way, David's plans blew me away. A few tweaks and we can get started."

Stone beamed. "We won't let you down."

"I've never been less worried." Sara placed a hand on Stone's arm. "I'm proud of you and delighted to be one of your first clients."

A shock of jealousy shook her. Stone and Sara had a past, obviously. Was it sexual? She really hoped not, because she liked Sara and would hate to spend the rest of the night imagining stabbing her with a fork.

"Nice scarf," Stone said to her. "You look like a movie star. Oh, that's right. You are a movie star."

Before she could say anything, he hustled away.

She watched his tight rear in those jeans walk to the other end of the restaurant until she realized the other women might notice. If they had, they didn't let on. Both had their noses in the menu.

"I'm starving," Sara said. "I met with David about the house plans this afternoon and haven't had anything since breakfast."

They talked for a bit about what they were going to eat. Pepper didn't feel particularly hungry. After her session with the therapist, she'd felt the urge for a cocktail, not food. The waitress brought the bottle of wine. They all decided on the Brody salad. Once that was settled, they toasted to a night out, then started talking about Sara's house plans.

Pepper only halfway listened. She tried but she couldn't seem to stop obsessing about the nature of the relationship between Autumn's best friend from college and her brother. Finally, after the salads arrived and the other two were quiet for a moment, she had to ask.

"You guys go way back?" Pepper asked. "Like Maggie, Lisa, and me?"

"That's right," Autumn said. "We were college roommates freshman year. I'll never forget the first night. We're lying there in our little twin beds talking about where we're from and everything and next thing I know Sara's told me she's Sara Ness and that her dad started the famous hamburger chain Burgerland, and did we have those in Oregon?" Autumn laughed. "She pronounced Oregon weird, like Oar Ah Gone."

"I did not," Sara said.

"You did. And I was so freaked out by how rich you were I was stunned into silence," Autumn said.

"That didn't last long," Sara said. "A few minutes later we started talking and haven't stopped since."

Pepper smiled at the two women across from her. "You two almost look like sisters, you know that?" They both had light brown hair with red highlights and were similar heights. Although Autumn was fair with a scattering of freckles and had eyes the color of a mountain green lake. Sara had a darker complexion, wide cheekbones, and light blue eyes.

"People tell us that all the time," Sara said.

"Especially since you copied my hair," Autumn said.

"She's such a liar. I'm the real redhead here." Sara made a face. "Don't believe a thing out of her mouth."

"Fine, I did get some red highlights recently, but only so that I didn't feel like drab Dora around you," Autumn said.

"So you've known Stone a long time then, too?" Pepper asked, using her best blasé face.

Sara looked up from her salad and glanced at Autumn. "When did he come home for leave that first time? Were we sophomores?"

"Yes, because we were in the apartment across from campus by then," Autumn said. "I remember because I found some girl draped over Stone on that ugly plaid couch we had."

Sara laughed. "That was after the party over at Zoe's. If I recall correctly, Stone was very popular."

"It was disgusting," Autumn said.

"So, you and Stone...were you guys ever a thing?" Pepper asked Sara.

Sara made a gagging noise. "That's gross. He's like my brother."

Brother. Okay, now we're getting somewhere. I won't have to stab her with a fork.

Autumn set aside her fork and watched Pepper with a suspicious glint in her eyes. "Why do you want to know exactly?"

"No reason. Just making conversation." Pepper popped a section of avocado into her mouth.

Both the ladies across from her laughed.

"That's a good one," Sara said.

"He's available, you know." Autumn picked up both her knife and fork and cut into a piece of grilled chicken without looking at Pepper. "But I got the distinct impression you didn't like him."

"He's impossible not to like, and he's very attractive," Pepper said. "I'm sure there's a million girls who think so."

Autumn sipped her wine. Pepper watched as the women exchanged sideways glances. "Okay, I'm going to come clean.

The reason we asked you out tonight was to get to the bottom of this thing with you and Stone."

"Thing? We don't have a thing," Pepper said as her face heated to the degree of the perfect latte.

"He's smitten with you," Sara said. "As a matter of fact, I don't think I've ever seen him look at someone like he just looked at you."

"Agreed," Autumn said. "So what I need to know is this—are you sassy to him because you like him and don't know what to do about it?"

Pepper cleared her throat. She should've ordered a scotch. "I'm not sure."

"Which means we hit it right on the head," Sara said, looking delighted. "I knew it. I could see the way your eyes followed him at that party a few weeks ago."

"She's the one who suspected your feelings," Autumn said. "Sara notices everything." She said the word *everything* as if it was in capital letters.

"Did he tell you I saved his life?" Pepper asked.

"He did, in fact," Autumn said.

"Isn't it strange that I happened to be there?" Pepper stuck the tines of her fork into a cherry tomato. "Right at the moment?" She held her fork up, using the tomato like a highlighter. "Do you think it means something?"

Both the ladies nodded. "What else could it mean but that you're meant to be?" Autumn asked.

5

Stone

Monday evening around six, Stone parked his truck in front of Kyle and Violet's four-car garage. He grabbed a bottle of wine from the passenger seat and hopped from his truck. Before heading inside, he took a moment to admire the house. Kyle had wanted a traditional-style home, with pillars, dormer windows, and bright white paint. Given their childhood, it didn't take a genius to know why.

Building this house had been Stone's first project as a licensed contractor. Kyle had insisted he take the job, even though he'd only recently been licensed. Heading up the project on this house had changed so much for Stone, both personally and professionally. He'd had a concrete example of his work to use during bids, which led to the Victorian remodel for Rafael and their subsequent partnership. However, the personal effect this house had on his life meant even more. The addition of every nail and board had drawn him closer to his brother. For twelve years they'd been estranged, but it took only a handful of months to forgive, to reconnect, to become brothers again. Now it was as if those twelve years of separation had never happened. Kyle was his big brother. They were a family as they'd always wanted to be now that Autumn had moved to Cliffside Bay. This town, this house, represented their second chance. With the bonus of Violet and the four children, Stone felt grounded. For the first time, he felt that they were all where they were supposed to be.

He hoped like hell the reappearance of their mother didn't cause a rift among the three of them. After all the healing that had transpired between them, it would break his heart if they lost one another again.

As a child he'd loved to work with wood. His hands and mind, so restless in the classroom, had calmed while sanding a piece of wood or repairing a leak in the roof of their trailer. The smell of sawdust or plaster was the scent of contentment. On the bus ride home from school, he'd stared out the window at the homes of the other children. Kyle, too, had studied them, but with an envy that fueled his ambition. He vowed to one day have a home of his own. Whereas Stone observed them with curiosity. How had it been constructed? What material and labor went into building that shingled roof or wraparound porch? Could he someday be the person who made something so beautiful?

The path to that dream proved circuitous, including multiple tours in Afghanistan and ten years in the marines. Autumn had been the one to convince him it was time to leave the military and pursue a career as a contractor. He hadn't regretted it for a moment. Although he didn't do all the work himself, he spent many days working side by side with the construction staff. He fell asleep at night physically fatigued and his mind content, knowing he'd spent his day doing honest work with the talents God had granted him.

The work he and his partners were doing filled him with

pride. Wolf Enterprises made spaces in which families would make memories. A house was not just the materials it was constructed from, but a space where love lived. The walls of their homes would witness babies' first steps. Kitchen islands would host countless nights of homework. Pasta sauce made in one of their kitchens would soothe the sting of a teenager's first breakup. Footsteps running up a stairway would tell a father his son had returned home safely from a school dance.

He'd noticed during his thirty years on earth that most unhappiness came from yearning for what one didn't have instead of gratitude for what one had. Stone understood his gifts were simple, but they were his. How he chose to use them defined his life, gave it purpose and meaning. He understood many men, including his brother, would not consider his work interesting or fulfilling. Men like Kyle were inspired by the thrill of the deal—the esteem that came from being a man in the power seat. They were men who wore red ties. Not Stone. He was a faded jeans and calloused hands kind of man. And that suited him just fine.

He walked across the manicured yard to the front door, admiring the two redbud trees Nico had planted at the base of the front steps. The wooden swing Stone had hung from the branch of an old oak swayed in the breeze. Fall mums in pots bloomed in cheery red on the front porch.

He didn't bother ringing the bell. Violet was expecting him, so he let himself in, shutting the door behind him. Tonight, the house smelled of baby powder, pumpkin spice, bacon, and Violet's perfume. The scent of love.

He called out. "Hello there. Anyone home?"

Dakota came running down the stairs. "Uncle Stone. You have to see my new train track." His nephew hugged him around the legs with every ounce of his five-year-old body. "It goes all the way around the playroom now."

Stone's knees cracked as he knelt to Dakota's level. "Cool."

He held up the bottle of wine. "Let me give this to your mama and then you can show me."

Dakota nodded, his round blue eyes innocent and earnest. "Sure thing. Mama's in the kitchen." He lowered his voice. "Don't say anything about the bad smell. She was making a pie and then the babies started crying and it burned all up."

"I don't smell anything bad."

"Wait until you get in the kitchen," Dakota said. "Just pretend like it smells completely normal."

"I won't say a word." He made a zipping motion over his mouth.

Dakota slipped his hand into Stone's. "Between you and me, those babies are a lot of trouble."

"The twins or all three of them?" Stone asked as they walked down the hallway to the kitchen.

Dakota shook his blond head in obvious disgust. "All three of them. I'm the only one who isn't crying my head off every other minute."

He stifled a laugh as they entered the large, modern kitchen. The air did smell faintly of burned pie. As promised, he kept that to himself.

"Mama, Uncle Stone's here," Dakota said.

"Hello, Uncle Stone." Violet gave him a quick smile and wave before returning to the pot she was stirring on the cooktop. "Hang on a minute. I don't want my sauce to burn. I already burned the pie." His sister-in-law wore an apron over a mint-green tunic and yoga pants. Her glossy brown hair was pulled back in a ropy braid.

Dakota smacked his forehead with the palm of his hand, as though he couldn't believe his mother would confess after he'd gone to the trouble to warn their guest.

Three high chairs with three babies were lined up in a row on one wall of the kitchen. Mollie Blue was a little over two, with chubby pink cheeks, blond curls, and sea-blue eyes. Although they were not biological siblings, Mollie and Dakota looked like they could be, other than their personalities. Unlike his precocious nephew, Mollie was shy, docile, and attached to her mother. To Stone's dismay, she wanted nothing to do with him. In fact, she hid her face in Violet's legs whenever he approached.

The fifteen-month-old twins, Hope and Chance, were both dark-haired like Kyle but with the brown eyes of their mother. Now their faces were covered in avocado. As he approached, Hope screamed a word that sounded almost like his name from her high chair and held out her arms. She was the outgoing twin, always quick to giggle or ask to be chased. She loved her Uncle Stone, which rendered him a big, mushy slave to her every bidding.

A ball waited at the foot of Chance's high chair. Chance loved anything to do with balls—throwing, kicking, chasing. Wherever Chance was, a ball was sure to be close by.

"Mama, can I show Uncle Stone my new train track?" Dakota asked.

"Have your dinner first, and then yes." Violet pointed at a plate set on the kitchen table.

Never one to argue, Dakota climbed onto a chair and went to work on his turkey-and-vegetable dinner.

Stone kissed Hope's head. "Did you get a haircut?"

Hope nodded and put a sticky hand on top of her stick-straight brown hair. She now had a bank of bangs. "She looks like a flapper," he said to Violet. "And way too grown-up."

"Her hair was hanging in her eyes," Violet said as she turned from the stove. "I was afraid she was going to trip. And she refuses to keep a hair clip in place."

He chuckled. "Hair clips do stifle a person, don't they, Hope?"

In response, Hope smashed more avocado between her fingers and grinned at him. That smile went straight to his heart. She grunted, then sucked the avocado from her fingers and kicked her fat legs.

"She's not so into her baby fork, either," he said.

"Not nearly as efficient as fingers," Violet said.

He kissed Chance next. He'd also had a haircut. All the unruly baby wisps had been trimmed and tidied. "What are you doing to these babies? They look way too grown-up."

"I know." Violet turned from the stove. "They're starting to look like kids, not babies."

"You have to have more," Stone said.

Violet grimaced. "Please, don't even get Kyle started on that tonight. He truly wants another one."

"He's a madman."

"Exactly what I told him." Violet sighed. "Even with the help of the weekday nanny, I'm exhausted."

"You don't look it. You're glowing." His sister-in-law was a stunner with those chocolate-colored eyes and skin like toffee. She had a figure like a teenager, despite having given birth to three of her four children.

She wiped her brow with one forearm while continuing to stir her sauce. "I'm back to teaching yoga down at the dance studio. It's been good to get out of the house."

"Good for you."

"I feel a little guilty about leaving the kids with Millie in the mornings, but it's really helping my sanity."

"Don't feel guilty. You deserve a little time to yourself. Plus, you have to take care of you in order to take care of them."

She waved her spoon at him. "Have you been reading Autumn's magazines?"

He laughed. "My sister's taught me a lot about women." Stone leaned over to kiss Mollie's fair head. She tucked her chin into her neck and refused to look at him. "Hi, Mollie Blue. I missed you."

"Say hello to Uncle Stone," Violet said.

"Hi, Uncle Stone." Only Mollie's mouth moved. She stared into her tray and went perfectly still, like a bunny under the gaze of a ferocious cat.

"I brought wine." Stone set the bottle on the island.

"You didn't need to bring anything." Violet fiddled with the red knob on her gas cooktop, adjusting the temperature.

"I don't smell anything but babies' heads and enchilada sauce."

"Very diplomatic of you." Violet tilted her head, regarding him. "You look weird. Is something wrong?"

"No, nothing." He would wait until Kyle and his sister were here to share his shocking news.

"Good." Using the wooden spoon as a pointer, she gestured toward the wine. "Open that, please, and pour me a large glass."

He went to the drawer where she kept the wine opener and used it to nudge the cork free. By the time he finished, Violet had set four wineglasses out on the table. She was like a vampire the way she could move around without making a sound. He poured each of them a glass and inquired about the whereabouts of his brother and sister.

"Autumn will be here any minute. She had to work today. Kyle's finishing something up in his office. Some deal he's trying to close by the end of next week." Violet accepted the glass from his outstretched arm. "Cheers. Now sit with Dakota so you're not in my way."

Stone sat on the opposite side of the table from his nephew. While Violet worked at the island scooping tablespoons of enchilada meat into tortillas, she filled him in on the latest happenings with the children. The twins were into everything, including Violet's best lipstick, which now decorated a solid square foot of the playroom's walls. Yesterday, Mollie had managed to get her head stuck between the posts on the stairway railing. Kyle had to remove one in order to get her out. "Which took a few minutes."

"She screamed bloody murder the entire time," Dakota said with a disgusted shake of his head.

"She did." Violet wiped her hands on the front of her apron. "If we had neighbors, they would've had us arrested."

"What else is happening?" Stone reached across the table with his long arm and ruffled Dakota's hair. "How's school?"

"Fantastic. I excel at school. But Mom says not to talk about that too much in front of other people because it sounds like I'm bragging."

"We just attended his kindergarten parent-teacher conference." Violet continued to fill and roll tortillas, placing them side by side in a glass casserole dish.

"How did that go?" Stone asked. "I always hated conference time." Mostly because his dad never showed up to one.

"It went awesome. Mrs. Blakely said I'm a nice young man," Dakota said gleefully. Although Kyle wasn't his biological father, they shared the same wolfish grin. "And that I'm the smartest in the whole class. Maybe the smartest kid she's ever taught."

"Dakota, what did I tell you about bragging?"

"Sorry, Mama. But she did say that. I heard my dad tell Uncle Lance."

"Your dad was always the smartest one in his class, too," Stone said.

"Were you?" Dakota asked.

"No. I was the strongest but dumb as a brick."

Dakota giggled and slapped the table. "Uncle Stone, a person can't be a brick."

"Your uncle is *not* dumb as a brick," Violet said. "He's just being modest."

Stone winked at Dakota and whispered under his breath, "Not really."

"They want to move Dakota up a grade." Violet poured the enchilada sauce over the rolled tortillas. "But I'm against it."

"She thinks I'm too short," Dakota said.

"I do not think you're too short." Violet shot Dakota a rather scary mom glare. "He misunderstood something I said to Kyle while he was *eavesdropping*."

"Which I got sent to the naughty stairs for," Dakota said with a world-weary sigh. "They never want me to hear any of the good stuff."

"What I said to your father in a *private* conversation is that you're small for your age and it would be even worse if they skipped you up a grade. You don't want to be the smallest kid in class."

"What do I care? I have a big fat brain, why do I need to have a big body, too?" Dakota asked.

Stone stole a glance at Violet, who had her hand over her mouth, clearly trying not to laugh.

"There's sports to consider." Stone took a serious tone with Dakota even though he wanted to howl with laughter. "Sports might matter to you later."

"Right." Violet put the enchilada casserole into the oven and set the timer. "Plus, he has so many nice friends in his class."

"Dad says Mama's obsessed with having friends," Dakota said. "Even though I have no trouble making them. I'm like a magnet to other kids."

"Dakota Hickman." Violet clutched the collar of her blouse. "What have I done to make you so full of yourself?"

"I have good self-esteem, Mama. Just ask Mrs. Blakely."

Stone laughed. This kid killed him. "I've always been a magnet to the ladies."

"You have?" Dakota's eyes widened.

Stone shrugged. "Totally. It's a family trait. You'll be the same way."

"A magnet to the ladies is not an appropriate lifetime goal, Dakota Hicks." Violet tossed the last of the chopped carrots into the salad bowl, then turned toward the babies. "It looks like everyone's done with dinner and ready for baths."

Kyle entered the kitchen. "Did I hear something about baths?"

Mollie held out her arms. "Dada."

"Hello, baby girl," Kyle said to his daughter.

"They're ready for baths," Violet said to Kyle, then mouthed the words, "Thank God."

"Roger that," Kyle said to his wife. He slapped Stone on the shoulder in greeting. "Welcome to the chaos."

A few inches shorter than Stone's six-foot-three frame and not nearly as wide, Kyle's was a sinewy strength compared with Stone's bulk. His older brother's facial features were chiseled with a rougher tool than Stone's, but they had the same stubborn square chin, thick brown hair, and intense blue eyes.

"How does this work exactly?" Stone asked. "Aren't you guys outnumbered?"

"I take a shower," Dakota said. "All by myself. Which helps them tremendously." He said the last word slowly, but with amazing diction considering his age. No wonder Mrs. Blakely thought he was a genius.

"It does help that Dakota's growing so independent," Violet said.

Dakota grinned at his dad, who grinned right back and then high-fived him.

"One of us does the girls and the other handles Chance." Violet lifted Hope from her high chair and kissed her cheek. Hope giggled and kicked her legs. "Chance thinks bathing is a combat sport."

"I get to stay up later than the babies," Dakota said. "Thirty minutes more." This last bit of information was followed by a satisfied smack of his lips.

"Which means you have time to show Uncle Stone your train tracks before you head to the shower," Violet said.

Dakota jumped up from the table but halted when Violet frowned at him. "Right. Sorry, Mama." He picked up his plate and took it to the sink.

Kyle strode across the kitchen and yanked a few paper towels from the holder. Stone watched in amazement as Kyle and Violet worked in tandem to get their children ready for the next phase of the evening. Faces and hands wiped. Trays washed. Sounds of the disposal chewing the leftover bits from dinner mingled with the babbling from the babies as they waited to be unbuckled from their chairs. Finally, they returned, unclicked their belts, and hauled them up into their arms. With one twin on each hip, Kyle led the way with Violet and Mollie following closely behind.

"Wow," Stone said.

"I know, right?" Dakota asked. "Can you believe how much trouble they are?"

Minutes later, Stone plopped on the floor of the playroom. It was tidy and organized, and wooden boxes tucked into shelves held copious toys. Children's books lined several shelves. Labeled plastic bins contained craft supplies. Several beanbag chairs retaining the imprint of tiny bodies filled one corner of the room. Dakota's train track ran the circumference of the play area.

His nieces and nephews were lucky children. The cycle of poverty had been averted by his brother. From what he knew of Violet's cold upbringing, it seemed that cycle had also been broken.

He listened to Dakota describe the tracks in detail and how he'd created a whole new section for his train to go around. "See there? It's a new loop." Dakota pointed. "I'm going to make a new part of town with my Legos."

"Like your dad buying up commercial real estate."

"No, like you. Building things."

This kid gave him the lump-in-the-back-of-the-throat thing on a regular basis.

After a few minutes, Violet called for Dakota to take his shower and get ready for bed. Stone was instructed to go downstairs and wait for Autumn.

His sister arrived just as he descended the stairs. Dressed in a sage-colored peacoat and black boots, she looked sophisticated and fashionable.

"You look beautiful in that coat." He took it from her and hung it in the closet.

"Thank you. It's new. Trey spotted it in the window of a boutique and insisted I buy it. He said it matches my eyes." Was it his imagination or had the sea air made his sister even prettier? Her fair skin looked dewy. She'd gotten golden highlights in her auburn hair that were very flattering. "What? Do I have something in my teeth?"

"No, you dork. You look great. I think Cliffside Bay agrees with you."

Autumn punched him on the arm. "You're biased." She glanced toward the stairs. "Did I miss the kids?"

"Yes, Kyle and Violet are putting them to bed."

"Oh well. It couldn't be helped. Work was really busy. I guess cold and flu season is already here."

They went into the kitchen, and he poured her a glass of wine. The kitchen filled with the spicy scent of the enchiladas cooking in the oven. While they waited for Kyle and Violet, Autumn told him a few funny stories from her day, as well as that of a young mother who'd cried when she saw the bill for her child's medicine. "I wanted to cry, too," Autumn said. "Deductibles bite."

"That poor lady," Stone said.

"I know." She tapped a finger against her wineglass. "How did your night at The Oar end up?"

Startled at the abrupt change in direction, he shrugged. "Good. Why?"

"I had an interesting night."

"Yeah?" It hadn't seemed interesting. Much to his disappointment, the three ladies had eaten their dinners and left right afterward. The live music had started at nine, and he'd talked himself into asking Pepper to dance. Next thing he knew, they were gone. "You left kind of abruptly."

"Sara's sitter called. The baby had a fever."

"Is she all right?"

"Fine, yes. Just a virus." Autumn tucked her hair behind one ear. "However, I did a little intel on our friend Pepper."

"What do you mean a little intel?" What had his sister done?

"Sara and I both think she likes you."

A bolt of hope shot through him. "Yeah?"

Before she could tell him more, Violet and Kyle returned to the kitchen just as the alarm for the enchiladas chimed. His stomach churned, knowing it was time. He had to put Pepper aside and tell his sister and brother the news of their mother's reappearance.

When they were all seated around the kitchen table, Kyle gave thanks before they dug into the enchiladas. Stone ate some of his dinner before clearing his throat. It was time. He had to tell them. Get it over with. "Something weird happened yesterday."

"You mean almost getting run down by a SUV?" Autumn asked.

"In addition to that, yes." Stone pushed his plate away, suddenly nauseous.

Autumn and Violet immediately looked over at him with concern in their eyes. He never turned down Violet's enchiladas.

"What is it?" Violet asked.

Stone wrapped his fingers around the stem of his glass and fiddled with the wine charm. "I don't know how to say it, so I'll just come right out with it. A woman approached me outside the grocery store. She claims to be our mother."

Kyle dropped his fork. It made an awful clattering noise as it fell onto the china. Violet gasped as her hands flew to her throat. Autumn simply stared at him.

He told them what he could remember of their conversation. Since the unexpected encounter, whenever he thought about the woman and what she'd said to him, it was as if a thousand bees hummed between his ears. The entire incident seemed like a dream. He'd been able to put it aside for hours at a time. However, saying it out loud made it all too real.

"Do you think it's really her?" Autumn asked.

"She didn't look anything like I remembered," Stone said. "But we were so young when she left that I barely remember what she looked like."

"And Dad burned all her pictures," Autumn said. "I have almost no memory of her."

"I do." Kyle's eyes had darkened to the shade of a twilight sky. His voice sounded eerily calm. "I was eight when she left. I'd be able to tell if it's her."

"She wants to see us," Stone said.

No one spoke as the gravity of that statement filled the room.

Kyle's face had reddened. He pushed away his plate and clenched his hands together on the tabletop. Autumn moved food around without looking at anyone. Violet watched Kyle.

"Her desire to see you doesn't mean you have to." Violet spoke gently, in the same voice she used to soothe one of her children. "I've learned that not all family deserves to be in our lives."

"Do you want to see her?" Autumn asked Stone. "I mean, again?"

"I don't know," Stone said. "I was so taken aback I couldn't think straight. And then right afterward, the SUV almost took me out. I can't help but think they were related. Maybe the truck was chasing her."

"Like she's in some kind of trouble?" Autumn asked.

"Maybe," Stone said.

"It would be an odd coincidence if not," Violet said.

Kyle stared at his plate. "The day she left has replayed in my mind a thousand times. She was like a brick wall. Nothing penetrated her resolve to leave us." He took in a ragged breath before continuing. "I begged her to stay. I grabbed on to her leg and she dragged me across the muddy yard, then shook me off like I was a pesky dog." He looked up at Stone. "Why, after all this time, would she want to see us?"

"Maybe she wants to make amends?" Autumn wiped the corner of her eyes with a napkin. "Did she seem well-intentioned?"

"I'm not sure. She said she just wants to see us once and then she'll leave us alone," Stone said.

"Women like her only come back to their families for one reason. She wants money," Kyle said.

"She didn't look like she was doing well financially," Stone said.

"What did she drive?" Kyle asked.

"An old Honda." Stone suppressed a manic laugh. Leave it to Kyle to ask about her car.

Kyle's eyes glazed over as he stared into space, his expression stoic. "That's funny, because I always imagine her in a black car like the one she left in."

Stone sobered. His brother had taken the brunt of her abandonment. Kyle had been old enough to feel the rejection and the burden of responsibility. Stone and Autumn had been allowed to remain children. Kyle had not.

"Kyle, it's totally up to you whether we see her or not," Stone said.

"I appreciate that, but it's not fair," Kyle said. "You two should decide for yourselves. I can tell you this. The only reason I will see her is to let her know exactly the mess she left and the toll her absence took on all three of us."

"I might like to see her," Autumn said in a small voice. "Just to get my questions answered."

"Like how she could leave her own children?" Kyle asked.

"Yes. For one." Autumn reached for her glass of wine and took a generous sip.

Kyle ran a hand over his thick brown hair. "I used to lie awake at night and make a list of all the things I'd like to say to her. You know the saddest part of all? Even after she left, I still loved her. If she'd come back, I would have forgiven her everything."

"We love our parents, even when they're monsters," Violet said.

"Can you forgive her now?" Autumn asked. "If her intention is to be in our lives?"

Kyle stilled and gazed at his sister for a long moment, as if deciding his answer. "My immediate response is no. Anyone who leaves their three young children isn't someone I want to know. But then I remember how I left you two. My reasons for doing so were complex and made from brokenness. The three of us pieced this family back together through understanding and forgiveness. Maybe if we understood why she left, we could forgive her."

Again, the silence returned to the room. They were never quiet in one another's presence. Typically, when they were together, they laughed and talked over one another. He and Kyle gave each other grief. Autumn bugged him about whether he was interested in anyone. There was an occasional moment when one of them needed advice. He didn't want this woman to ruin what they had. The foggy buzz in Stone's brain cleared. His thoughts careered around his head like one of those bouncy balls they sold at the dollar store. Should they see her for closure? To tell her how much she hurt them? Did she want to be in their lives, or did she want money? Forgiveness? Absolution?

"We have to see her," Autumn said.

"Violet, what say you?" Kyle asked.

"Obviously, it's up to the three of you to decide. I'll support you either way. We've all come a long way together in a short time. You three and the little ones upstairs are my whole heart—the family I always wished for. I don't want you guys hurt. Be prepared that it might not go well. Like with my dad, you might have to walk away for your own health."

"I agree," Kyle said. "We shouldn't go in with expectations of a happy ending."

"Just information," Autumn said.

"So, we see her and go from there?" Stone asked.

"Agreed," Kyle said.

"Agreed," Autumn said.

Violet put her hand on her husband's forearm and looked at each of them in turn. "Whatever happens, we're a family. Nothing changes that."

Stone raised his glass. "To family."

"To family," they chorused.

6

Pepper

Pepper pressed her nose against the glass of Lisa and Rafael's third-floor apartment and peered down into the parking lot of the Victorian. Stone was washing his oversize truck. Without a shirt.

His back muscles rippled in the sunlight as he scrubbed the hood. Locks of brown hair flopped over his forehead. His hair was longer than when she first met him. Last summer, he had it cut military short. *Former military.*

Light blue surfer shorts rode low on his hips. A slight tug and they'd slip off. To distract herself from wicked thoughts, she pinched the skin on her wrist and looked up at the sky. A jet made a white streak against the blue.

It wasn't her fault that she couldn't stop looking at him. Most women would find his bronzed skin and unruly dark hair sexy. His angular facial features were interesting and rugged. The man was beautiful.

There's this guy.

She'd admitted it to Cora. Had said the words out loud. Stone Hickman. *I have a thing for Stone Hickman.*

The truth made her dizzy.

She shivered, despite the warmth of the sun coming through the window. Her gaze returned to him. The muscles of his shoulders flexed as he moved the brush in systematic, thorough circles. She pressed her thighs together. Did he touch everything that way?

He dropped the sponge in the bucket near his feet. Suds splashed onto his calves. He picked up the hose and fiddled with the nozzle until spray leaped from the hose and onto the truck. After the soap was washed away, he changed the spray to a mist and turned it on himself. Water gleamed off his bronzed skin. What did he think this was? A gun show?

There should be a crime for being that ridiculously gorgeous. Extra time behind bars for being shirtless in October. It was California. No one wore clothes out here.

Stone turned the mist to a mild stream and brought the hose to his mouth. The muscles that ran down his thick neck pulsed as he drank.

Just then, he looked up and saw her watching. Before she could back away, he waved.

Her entire body lit on fire. Oh God, what do I do? Wave back? Pretend I wasn't watching him?

He waved again, this time with the hand holding the hose. The stream of water bounced and circled. If she didn't know better, she would have sworn it was in the shape of a heart.

She waved back. It would be immature not to.

He tapped his watch and said something to her. She couldn't hear him. Fine, she would open the window. Again, she didn't want to be rude.

She unlocked the fastener and lifted the window. "What did you say?" she yelled down to him through the screen.

"I said, has enough time passed? Can I ask you out yet?"

"It's only been two days." Her entire body went hot. Please, God, don't let anyone else in the Victorian have their windows open.

"Okay, just checking." He grinned. "Are you joining us for Group Dinner?"

Group Dinner was a new tradition in the Victorian. All residents of the building and whomever they wanted to invite all dined together on the wraparound porch. Rafael had purchased outside heaters for the winter months. Whenever he and Lisa were in town, they usually put one together for Sunday or Monday evenings. The two bottom apartments were occupied by Rafael's mother, Mama Soto, and her best friend, Ria. Lavonne, also a bachelor, lived next to David on the second floor. Rafael and Stone usually grilled, and the rest of the building contributed a side dish. Sometimes Maggie and Jackson joined them. Occasionally, Stone's brother, Kyle, and his wife, Violet, and their four children came as well. Like one big, happy family.

Pepper was the bitter aunt they felt obligated to invite.

"Yes, I'll be there."

"I'll save you a seat next to me," Stone said.

"We'll see about that. I have to go now. Some of us have things to do other than prancing around in our underwear."

He threw back his head in laughter.

Smiling, she shut the window.

Twisting one of her black curls around her index finger, she looked at the clock for the twentieth time. Her agent was supposed to call about a role in a television show she'd auditioned for last week when she was in LA. They'd had her come back three times. Her chemistry with the lead actor had been good. Still, it was an action show about a group of FBI agents. Who would believe her playing a cop? She was skinny and ashen, more suited for a chain-smoking anorexic than a muscular agent.

Lisa and Rafael came through the front door with bags of groceries in their arms. Pepper rushed forward to take one.

"You're staying for dinner, right?" Lisa asked. "Rafael's going to do his famous chicken."

"Sweetheart, it's not exactly famous," Rafael said as he held the kitchen door open for the ladies to pass through. "I've only made it two times."

"Yes, but it's so good." Lisa flashed him her dazzling smile. Rafael's features melted into warm caramel every time she smiled at him. The man would die for her. That was obvious every time he looked at her the way he was doing now.

Would anyone look at her that way? Was she too damaged, too messed up? Was it her destiny to grow old alone? *Crazy Aunt Pepper.*

She and Lisa unloaded the groceries while Rafael put them away. He had a precise order to the cupboards. Pepper had learned that the hard way when she'd put the cereal box in the wrong cabinet. Rafael was too polite to say anything, but a muscle near his right eye had started twitching and hadn't stopped until the cereal box was in the right place.

Pepper would agitate Rafael within a matter of minutes. One waylaid towel on the floor or crumb in the butter and he'd kick her to the curb. Lisa didn't seem to mind Rafael's fastidious ways. Perhaps she was accustomed to someone obsessively tidy because of her mother. Pepper's stepdad claimed there was someone for everyone. Rafael and Lisa seemed to prove this theory.

Lisa sat at the kitchen table. "We wanted to talk to you about the wedding. We've decided to have it in December."

December. "So soon?" They'd just gotten engaged in August. "What's the rush? Are you pregnant?"

"Very funny." Lisa and Rafael exchanged glances. "It's more about my mother than anything else. I want to plan it quick and dirty before she can stick her nose into things."

Lisa's mother was notorious for her passive-aggressive behavior. Planning a wedding was Mrs. Perry's perfect wheelhouse. If Lisa allowed her into the process, it would soon become Mrs. Perry's wedding and not Lisa and Rafael's.

"That makes sense," Pepper said. "But isn't she punishing you with silence right now?" Mrs. Perry and Lisa had barely spoken since David decided to move to California. David was Mrs. Perry's golden boy. His decision to start over out west had not been a popular one with her. Because he was her golden boy, she had to blame Lisa.

"Yes. I've hardly heard from her," Lisa said. "But once we set a date, she won't be able to stop herself from coming out here to 'help' me." Lisa made quotes with her fingers as she said the word *help*. "And with my filming schedule for *Indigo Road*, this gives us a chance to be married and take a honeymoon before I have to be back on set at the end of January."

If Lisa wanted to have it in December, then Pepper would make sure it happened. "We can totally do this. It'll be tight, but if we start planning right away, it'll be fine."

"Will you help me?" Lisa asked.

"Try and stop me," Pepper said. "Where do you want to have it? Do you remember the place you found in Colorado?" Years ago, Lisa had read an article about a small tourist town in Colorado with a little white church and a neighboring lodge perfect for a reception. She'd ripped the pages of the magazine out and put them on the refrigerator. Every day Lisa would tap the photo. "Someday, Pepper. Someday."

"Yes, but that was just silly talk." A flush had crept up Lisa's neck. She glanced at Rafael, then back to Pepper. Lisa seemed nervous, maybe even embarrassed. "We only care about getting married. The wedding is secondary."

"Mama wants it to be a church," Rafael said.

"The Catholic church?" Pepper asked. Lisa was about as Protestant as a girl could get.

"Mama's approved the nondenominational church in town," Rafael said. "She's a sucker for that steeple."

Lisa smiled and hugged herself around the middle. "I adore

that steeple, and the church is so old-fashioned and perfect. It's exactly the type of church I dreamed about getting married in when I was a little girl."

"No, you didn't. It doesn't look anything like the little white church you picked out," Pepper said. Why was her friend acquiescing? Was it to please Rafael? Because if that was the case, then she needed to give Lisa a good talking-to. Everyone knew the wedding was for the bride. The groom's or his mother's wishes were not even allowed into the discussion.

"It's close enough." Lisa spoke quickly, as though the wedding was of no real significance. "Jackson and Maggie are members at the steeple church, so they already talked to the pastor and he's agreed to marry us. We have to become members too, which isn't a problem. We need a church."

"He has us down for December twenty-second." Rafael's brown eyes sparkled, as if this was the best idea for a wedding in the history of man. "And Zane's reserved one of the private rooms at the brewery for the reception."

"The brewery?" Pepper's stomach tensed. What the heck? The industrial-style building with the exposed beams and tall ceilings was fine for a brewery, but for her friend's wedding reception? No. This wasn't right. Plus, the room was too small. They'd only get about twenty people in there. Mostly, though, this was not what her friend had wanted. Not before Rafael and his mama.

Lisa knew her too well. "I know what you're thinking. Too small. Not fancy enough."

Pepper blew a stray curl from her forehead. "For starters."

"We want this to be a small affair. Just family and close friends," Lisa said. "The brewery's perfect. We'll have a nice sit-down meal. A few toasts and then we're off to our honeymoon."

"But what about dancing?" Pepper asked.

"I don't dance." Rafael plunged his hands into the pockets of his cargo shorts.

"Well, Lisa dances. She loves to dance," Pepper blurted out before she could stop herself.

"I've danced enough in my lifetime," Lisa said with an evasive shrug of her shoulders.

"Wait a damn minute. None of this is what you wanted," Pepper said. "You wanted a wedding in the mountains. With snow."

"You did?" Rafael stared at his fiancée as if he'd never seen her before. "You've never mentioned that."

"She most certainly did. I wanted a castle in France and she wanted a mountain wedding." Pepper wasn't about to let this go. Her friend would have the wedding of her dreams if it was the last thing Pepper ever did.

Lisa's gaze was on Rafael. "It was just a whim after a few glasses of wine one night. We saw this magazine article about a little town in Colorado. It was a fanciful notion, that's all."

"She had the article stuck on the refrigerator for years," Pepper said.

"Tell me more," Rafael said to Lisa. "Please."

Lisa's cheeks now matched her pink neck. "It was a little white church with a red door."

"She loved that red door," Pepper said.

"It was nothing, really," Lisa said.

"Tell him about the lodge and sleigh rides." Pepper paced between Lisa and Rafael, her low sandals clicking on the hardwood floor.

"There was a lodge there, like something out of the 1940s, with high beams and quaint little rooms." Lisa's expression softened. "Couples rented the entire thing out and had whole wedding weekends. There were sleigh rides and bonfires in a fire pit. I imagined the sleigh taking me from the church to the lodge. It was stupid."

"And she'd have a white faux-fur coat over her dress," Pepper said. "And when she arrived at the entrance to the lodge, her groom would pick her up and carry her inside, so she didn't wreck her shoes in the snow."

Lisa shook her head. "Seriously, it was just an immature notion. The wedding will be much better in Cliffside Bay than some place we've never been to. Photo shoots can make a place look way better than it really is. And this was at least five years ago. The lodge could've gone out of business for all we know."

"Doubtful," Pepper said. "And the town was built around tourism. You can bet everything's quaint and pretty."

"Think of how pretty Cliffside Bay is at Christmas," Lisa said. "With all the lights in the trees."

"I'm pretty sure there won't be sleigh rides in Cliffside Bay," Pepper said.

"I'm not a gambling man, but I would bet on that," Rafael said gently as he crossed the room to sit next to Lisa. He tilted her chin upward until she met his eyes. "Tell me the truth. Is this what you want?"

Lisa managed to shrug even with Rafael's hands on her shoulders. "We already agreed. It's not about us. This wedding is for your mom."

"Bullshit. The wedding is about you two." Pepper moved the fruit bowl from one end of the counter to the other before realizing Rafael wouldn't like that, and returned it to the original spot. "For heaven's sake, Lisa, for once in your life do something for yourself."

Rafael hadn't taken his eyes off Lisa. "Sweetheart, she's right. I'm sorry if I made you think my mother's feelings were more important than yours. I thought you wanted something quick and dirty."

"I want to marry you. The wedding is *not* the main thing. The next fifty years is what I care about," Lisa said.

Rafael took Lisa's hands. "Although I appreciate that sentiment, that isn't really the point. I want you to have the wedding you imagined. I'll do anything to make you happy. You know that. If you want a wedding in the church with the little red door, I'll move heaven and earth to make it happen."

Lisa shook her head. "Even if I still wanted this, it's not realistic. I'm on set for *Indigo Road* for the next month. I don't have time to plan a remote wedding."

"Then I'll do it," Pepper said. "Every bit." It wasn't as if she had anything else going on that mattered. "I'll go there and arrange the whole thing."

"Everything for the holiday will be booked," Lisa said. "It's October already."

"I know you hate this kind of thing," Pepper said. "But you're one of the biggest movie stars in the country right now. I'm pretty sure they can make it happen for you."

Lisa waved her hands in front of her chest. "No way. Not if it means someone else's wedding gets pushed aside."

"Let me look into it. That's all I ask," Pepper said. "I need an excuse to get away. I'm going crazy waiting to hear from my agent about work I'm not going to get."

"The mountain air will be good for you, Pepper," Rafael said. "A change of perspective is always good."

She looked at him, surprised he intuited what she'd been thinking. "I agree." She glanced back at Lisa. "I've been feeling really sorry for myself for months. It'll be good for me to focus on something else." Truthfully, she was quite sick of herself.

For the next few minutes, they talked about numbers. They wanted to keep it small, so the guest list was around thirty. Which meant they'd need accommodations of at least fifteen rooms and a facility that could handle a small reception with a sit-down meal.

"There's one other thing," Lisa said.

"What is it? I'll make it happen," Pepper said. She hadn't felt this energized since filming the horror flick.

Lisa tucked her hair behind her shell-like ears. "It's just that..." Her voice tightened in a very nontheatrical way.

Rafael cleared his throat. "I'm going to ask Stone to be my best man."

Pepper arranged her face into her best fake smile. "That's great. It'll be fun to hang out with him during all the festivities." If the groomsmen outfits included shirts, she should be fine.

Rafael's face washed with relief. "Good. I wasn't sure how you felt about him."

Pepper inwardly winced with guilt. They'd been worried to tell her about Stone, which was unacceptable. "Stone's a great guy."

"He is?" Lisa asked. "I mean, I know he is, but I thought you...well, never mind."

"Maybe I'll ask him to help me throw an engagement party," Pepper said.

The joy on Lisa's face heightened the guilt. What kind of friend was she to make Lisa worry over this?

"I've been unfair to Stone," Pepper said. "It's just my baggage." *My triggers.* "Don't worry, I'll be on my best behavior."

Lisa jumped up from the table and gave Pepper a tight hug. "Thank you."

"I'm sorry about everything," Pepper whispered before letting go and moving over to stand against the sink.

Rafael glanced at his watch. "I need to pop next door for a moment." He kissed Lisa on the cheek. "I'll be back soon to get the chicken ready."

For a man who said he didn't dance, Rafael rushed out of the kitchen with a move just shy of an échappé.

Lisa opened the refrigerator and pulled out a jug of water. "Is therapy helping?" she asked.

Pepper leaned against the sink. "Cora's really in my face. Which is what I need. I finally told her about what happened to me."

"That's good."

"I told her something else, too. You were right about Stone. I have a thing for him, which has made me act like a child."

Lisa's mouth dropped open, then shut just as quickly. "I knew it."

"Fine. You were right. About him and therapy."

"What're you going to do about Stone?" Lisa asked.

"I don't know. Maybe say yes the next time he asks me out."

"The next time? Spill it."

"Well, it started when I saved his life." She told Lisa about pulling him out of the way of the car and their conversation afterward. "I totally blurted out that I was in therapy, which made me feel like a complete fool. But then he said he used to go and it really helped him."

"The man is full of surprises," Lisa said.

"He really is. Anyway, I am truly sorry. About our fight and how I've been to Stone."

Lisa cocked her head to the side and smiled her sweet, kind smile that made a person feel like the most important person in the world. "We're all a work in progress. No matter what, I'll always be here for you."

"Even when I'm a pain in the butt?"

"Even then."

7

Stone

STONE'S HAIR was still damp from his recent shower when he heard a knock on the door. He yelled out to Trey, who was in the kitchen making their contribution to Group Dinner. "I'll get it."

"Good. I'm elbow-deep in biscuit dough and mint leaves."

Biscuits? When had he learned how to make biscuits? And how did they go with mint?

Stone crossed the room and yanked open the door. It was Rafael.

"Hey, man, come on in," Stone said. "You want a beer?"

"Sure. That'd be great."

"Wait here. I'll grab us a couple. Trey's in the kitchen making biscuits."

Rafael blinked, then laughed. "Trey knows how to make biscuits?"

"He's been keeping things from us."

Trey looked up when he came into the kitchen. He wore an

apron over his nicely draped jeans and ruby-red shirt. Trey—always dressed like he was going to the country club.

"Hey, man, Rafael's here for a beer. You want one?"

Trey looked up from his task of painstakingly plucking mint leaves from their stems. "Sure. I'm almost done here."

Stone peeked at the oven. Sure enough, a pan of biscuits. In *their* oven. Weird.

Stone fetched three beers from the refrigerator and twisted the tops off before setting one on the counter next to Trey's bowl of watermelon chunks sprinkled with feta cheese. "Interesting salad," Stone said. Watermelon and cheese together?

"Your sister gave me the recipe."

"Really? She never made that for me," Stone said.

"She found it on that food channel show we watch together."

Oh, brother.

He took the beers out to the living room. Rafael had turned on the football game between Cleveland and Minneapolis. "You come over to watch the game?" Stone asked as he handed Rafael a beer. He was always happy to watch football on Monday nights with Rafael. Trey wasn't that interested. He was more a soccer fan, which Stone found boring. How many times could they run down the field and not score a goal?

"Nah, I came to ask you a question. Lisa and I set a date for the wedding. December twenty-second."

"Congratulations. That's great, man."

"Thanks. And I was wondering if you'd be my best man."

Stone did a double take. "Me? Really?"

"I can't think of anyone else I'd rather have."

"Dude, I'm touched." He was. Although they hadn't known each other long, they'd formed a deep bond. "I'd be honored."

"You've been a good friend to me," Rafael said. "And Lisa's grown really fond of you and Trey since we all moved in here."

"She's the best."

"Yes, she is." Rafael was squirming like a kid in church.

"Something worrying you?"

"What? No. Well, kind of. I just found out Lisa wants a whole different wedding than I thought. Pepper told me Lisa always wanted a mountain wedding with snow and sleigh rides and a church with a red door."

He didn't exactly follow, but he nodded as if he did. "That doesn't sound much like a wedding in Cliffside Bay."

"Not much, no."

"What're we going to do about it?" Stone asked.

"Pepper offered to go scout out this little town they read about years ago. There's a white church with a red door and a lodge. If we can get it booked, I think we should do it there."

"Yeah, man. A girl should have the exact wedding she wants."

"I agree. Which has me worried. Lisa was just going along with whatever Mama suggested. I'm not sure you've noticed, but Mama's personality is big enough to fill a stadium, and Lisa adores her."

"Lisa's a people pleaser," Stone said. "I get it." He would have done the same thing in her shoes. Mama Soto was interested in the lives of the residents of the Victorian. They all wanted to please her because she was so good to them. All it took was a bowl of cereal for dinner and Mama Soto was all up in their face about proper nutrition and eating like a man, not a boy. She was the mother they all wished they had, including Lisa. "Lisa cares more about making you and Mama Soto happy than any church with a red door," Stone said.

"What makes me happy is for her to have what she wants."

"Well, then, I guess we're glad we have Pepper Shaker around to shake things up." If only she wanted to shake things up with him.

8

Pepper

As predicted, Pepper ended up next to Stone at Group Dinner. They were on one end of the long table, inches from each other on the bench. She was so close to him that she could feel the heat from his body. With his left hand, he lifted a beer to his mouth. She'd noticed he was left-handed before. His right arm, browned from the sun, rested in his lap.

He took up more than his share of the bench. His two thighs equaled three of hers put together. Any time she happened to glance downward, she found herself staring at his tanned and muscular thighs displayed in yet another pair of board shorts. At least he had his shirt on.

He smelled of sunshine and soap with a hint of shaving cream. A small amount of the cream remained just below his left ear. She wanted to wipe it away for him. No, that would not be a good way to break the tension between them. Or would it? Should she lean over and tell him?

He turned to look at her, moving his entire large torso in her direction. "Are you staring at me because I'm beautiful or is there something on my face?"

She flushed with heat. "Yes. There." She pointed to the spot next to his ear. "It's shaving cream, maybe?"

He swiped at his face with a napkin. "Thank you. I often miss that spot."

"No problem." Pepper made herself busy rearranging her silverware.

"I told you we'd sit together tonight," Stone said.

"Don't get a big head over it."

He grinned. "No scarf tonight?"

She touched the top of her head. "No. My hair decided to behave today."

"I liked it. For the record."

While everyone wandered over to take a seat, she smoothed her hand over the slick tabletop, admiring the wood. Lisa had told her Stone made it from boards he'd rescued from an old barn. He'd put it together using only tongue and groove instead of nails or glue. Even her unpracticed eye could see the care he'd taken in choosing the refurbished wood and how it went together. He'd made benches instead of chairs. Which was why she was now seated inches from him.

"Did you know I made this table?" Stone asked, leaning close.

"I heard something about it." God, could she sound any more like a thirteen-year-old girl? "I always meant to tell you how much I like it." There she went again, fawning like a silly girl with a crush. She *was* a silly girl with a crush.

"It was fun to make. I'll make you one if you want."

She smiled. "I need a home first."

"Any luck with that?"

"Not really. There are so few rentals. And I'm not exactly gainfully employed. At this rate I'll be living with Maggie and Jackson until I'm fifty."

"It was nice what you did for David."

"Oh, well, it was the least I could do to help."

"Look at that sunset," he said.

From where she sat, Pepper had a perfect view of the sun setting, spilling orange and pink across the horizon.

"I love this time of year," she said.

"Me too. I want to spend every moment outside before winter comes."

She glanced at him, amazed he felt the same way she did about fall.

"Pink and orange must be your colors," he whispered in her ear. "You look beautiful in this light."

"Stop flirting with me." She smiled, more pleased than she should be.

"Never."

Mama Soto clapped her hands. "Time for a prayer, and then we will eat." An immigrant from Mexico, Rafael's mother had a smidge of an accent. She often slipped between English and Spanish in the same paragraph.

As Mama Soto gave a prayer of thanks, the sun took its final descent, leaving vivid pink stripes across the sky.

Everyone uttered amen and then they started passing a platter of grilled chicken and various salads around the table.

"Chicken?" Stone held the platter of chicken in front of her. "Rafael and I grilled it to perfection."

"I'll be the judge of that." She met his gaze briefly before choosing a piece.

He chuckled and handed her the platter. "You'll see."

"You're nothing if not self-confident." She gave the platter to Ria, who sat next to her.

"Come on, now. How could I not be when I'm clearly awesome?" Stone heaped potato salad onto his plate before passing the bowl to her.

She passed it along to Ria, who was cutting up a piece of chicken into small pieces for David's toddler, Laine.

"Not a fan of potato salad?" Stone asked.

"Mayonnaise is a foul combination of oil and egg yolks and should not be eaten by humans."

"I see." Stone lifted one eyebrow, clearly amused.

There's this guy.

As she ate, Pepper scanned the table. It was the usual suspects. Lisa, Mama Soto, and Ria made up the female contingent. Four-year-old Oliver, David's son, sat on a booster between the two older ladies. His daughter, Laine, sat in a portable high chair strapped to the bench.

The conversations had splintered into three separate discussions. At the far end of the table, Rafael and Lisa were chatting with Mama Soto and Ria about their upcoming trip to LA. Rafael would work remotely while Lisa filmed several episodes of *Indigo Road*. Several months back, Rafael had given his notice to the Mullens. With Lisa's fat paychecks, they didn't need the money. She wanted Rafael to have the flexibility to join her for filming. They'd promised never to be away from each other for more than a week at a time.

A pinch of envy tightened the muscles of her stomach. It had been the three of them for so long, and now she had to share Lisa and Maggie. From the moment they'd met in college, the three girls had been inseparable. They'd shared everything for twelve years. Heartbreaks and a hundred different awful jobs. Terrible apartments and looking for money in the couch cushions so they could buy a bag of beans to make soup. Auditions and dance classes and nights on their ratty couch drinking wine from a box and talking until two in the morning about everything and nothing.

And then one day, Maggie got the call that her father was dying. She decided to go home to Cliffside Bay and get the truth from him before it was too late. Maggie and Lisa had taken it as a sign that it was time to give up on their dreams. Lisa went back to Iowa. Maggie went home to California and learned the truth about her father—how he'd manipulated the truth to keep her from her childhood sweetheart, Jackson. It didn't take long for Maggie and Jackson to fall back in love and get married. Now Lisa was engaged to Rafael. Pepper was the one discarded and left behind because her two best friends had replaced her with men.

She missed the old days in a visceral way that made her skin hurt and her bones ache. For the first time in her life, she felt alone.

Pepper took a sip of wine and listened in on the conversation happening opposite her. Trey and Nico were discussing an art exhibit they'd attended in San Francisco. David and Lavonne were dissecting the merits of a parenting course they'd attended at church last week. A stranger might find it odd to hear men discussing parenting, but around this table it was a normal occurrence. Lavonne was Honor and Zane's nanny. He took care of seven-year-old Jubie and her ten-month-old brother, Sebastian, while their parents were at work. David was raising his two young children by himself.

Given the conversation, apparently Oliver was struggling with nightmares and sleepwalking. The little one, Laine, was sleeping in his bed every night. Having lost their mother suddenly must be so hard.

Pepper had no memory of living with her biological father. She'd been only two when her mom moved to the Hamptons. From then on, she saw her dad once a year. Like clockwork, he showed up the day after her birthday to take her to lunch and give her a card with a twenty-dollar bill tucked inside.

She nibbled on her chicken and the watermelon salad and chastised herself for thinking about her father. Great way to wreck a good mood. Her gaze moved to Stone's muscular thighs. What would it feel like to sit on his lap? She was small, and he was deliciously big.

"Can I get you anything?" Stone asked, startling her from her brazen thoughts. "More wine?"

"What? Sure, yes." She hadn't realized her glass was empty.

Stone filled it again. She took another sip, then another. The alcohol loosened the tension in her shoulders. Her mind quieted slightly.

"Sounds like you're on wedding duty." He smiled down at her as he wiped at his square jaw with his napkin.

He *did* have the prettiest eyes. Dark blue with thick black lashes.

"Yes, did Rafael tell you about Colorado?" She lowered her voice and spoke close to his ear, hoping he would do the same.

He leaned closer, matching her volume. "He did. Is there anything I can do to help?"

She matched his quiet tone. "Maybe. But first, I have to say something. I'm sorry I've been a brat to you. You've been nothing but nice to me."

He blinked, and his eyes widened a smidge. "Think nothing of it. Plus, you saved my life, so we're even."

"Well, that's true. It does kind of trump the other stuff."

"Totally. And I'm serious. If you need anything, just let me know."

She had a sudden idea. "What are you doing later in the week?"

His eyebrows twitched. "Not much. We're waiting for the permit paperwork to go through on the new house. Why?"

"How would you feel about joining me on a reconnaissance trip to Colorado?" Pepper looked away, flustered suddenly. It was a strange thing to ask. She knew it the moment the words were out of her mouth.

His dark blue eyes had narrowed, as if he expected her to pull a mean-girl prank on him. "Why would you want me to go?"

She fought the prick of embarrassment that wandered up the back of her spine. There were practical reasons she could use his help, which were convenient excuses to get him alone for a few days. "I don't know how to drive."

"You need a driver. I am available for such duties." The

corners of his eyes crinkled with amusement. He ate another bite of his potato salad.

She studied him. Stone was one of those people who could seemingly eat without moving their jaw. He was like a hundred-year-old tree, this man, all steady and uncompromised with a strength that seemed rooted into the ground. Nothing could make him falter or blow away. A still person. There were faint lines near his eyes—proof of a man who laughed frequently.

"It's not just the driving. I'd like you to go with me," she said.

"You would?"

"Yes. I might even let you take me to dinner while we're there."

His eyes danced, tormenting her. He was way too good-looking for his own good. Or hers. "Fine. I'll go. But if this is just a ruse to get me into bed…I accept."

Her eyes stretched open until her lids hurt. "I can't believe you just said that."

"I'm just a humble country boy with no way to fend off a wicked city girl."

The low, sexy tone of his voice made her entire body tingle. She leaned even closer, inches from his ear. "If there's a wicked one between us, it's certainly not me." She caught a whiff of his neck. A craving for the taste of him made it hard to breathe.

He brought his hand to his chest as if she'd wounded him. His eyes still pranced and danced, as though he was laughing his head off without making a sound. "I'd love to take that to a test."

"I'm not sure you know this, but sometimes you're annoying. Not everything's funny." Her mouth twitched. Stone was funny. And sexy. However, it would take a crowbar to wrench that truth from her.

"Most things are funny, including you," he said.

"That statement is a perfect example of the expertise you bring to the art of annoying others."

He laughed, deep and throaty. She liked the low rumble of it, how it sounded like the engine of the vintage cars in the Fourth of July parades of her childhood. "I'll try very hard not to annoy you from now on." Using a spoon, he chased an elusive piece of watermelon around his plate.

"Good luck with that." She reached over to his plate and stabbed the wayward watermelon with her fork. "It's always better to stab than chase." She waved the fork in front of his nose before popping the watermelon into her mouth.

"I'll keep that in mind." His gaze appeared to be fixed on her mouth as she swallowed the watermelon. The air seemed to still and warm, as if a tropical storm were about to unleash.

"I'm sorry if my good attitude about life bothers you." He scratched under his chin with the end of his spoon. "I developed it because much of my life has rained canned peas."

"Canned peas? Those awful ones they served in school lunches?"

He cocked his head, watching her. "You know the ones?"

"I'm familiar with their heinousness, yes."

"I figured rich girls didn't have to eat those."

"Canned peas infiltrate all levels of income." She shuddered dramatically.

He grinned at her. "I find them a useful metaphor for the stuff life's thrown at me."

Raining canned peas. It was an apt metaphor. Stone Hickman was smart. Damn him. Nothing attracted her more than wit.

Aware suddenly of eyes upon her, she looked over to see Lisa staring at her—communicating with her eyes exactly what she thought.

You have it bad for him. I so called this.

She sent a silent message back. It's not nice to say, "I told you so."

Pepper turned back to Stone. "I'm in awe of the cleverness of your metaphor and humbly ask that I might borrow it from time to time."

"It'll cost you," he said. "A game of truth or dare during our trip. That's my price."

"You're kidding, right?"

"I'm dead serious." His midnight-blue eyes burned into her. "Have you ever met someone you desperately wanted to know, but they can't stand you?"

"No. Everyone likes me." She meant to sound flippant. Instead, she sounded breathless.

He brushed her hand with his thumb. "I like you."

His touch sent a lightning-bolt shock of energy through her entire body.

"I want to get to know you, Pepper Griffin. Like every detail. I want to have the chance to show you who I am."

"I'd like that too." For a moment they stared into each other's eyes. She knew just what he meant about life raining canned peas. She'd had a truckload of them during her thirty-odd years of life. As the light faded around them and the others were having conversations of their own, the world became smaller. "Good. When is the earliest you could accompany me?"

"The day after tomorrow," he said.

"I'll look for tickets. We'll have to fly into Denver and then drive the rest of the way up to the mountains."

"Should I bring my driving gloves?" he asked.

"You don't really have driving gloves?"

His shoulders lifted in a slight shrug as he smirked at her. "I might."

"You can bring your gloves, but leave those shorts behind." She boldly tugged at the hem of his right leg under the table.

"What's wrong with them?"

"Nothing, if you're on the beach. Otherwise, they make you look like an overgrown man-child."

"Isn't a *man-child* always overgrown?"

She shook her head, pretending to be irritated but secretly impressed at his clever wit. "Again, annoying."

"I don't even know when I do it."

"Just stop talking."

"Yes, ma'am."

"And don't call me ma'am."

"So many rules," he said. "Should we put a contract together?"

"Great idea. You can get that started after dinner. Right now, I have another mission. Watch and learn the subtle art of doing something bad and begging forgiveness later." She tapped her glass with the end of her knife to get everyone's attention. "I have an announcement. Lisa wants a snowy wedding in the mountains."

Mama Soto's mouth dropped open. Lisa sent a death stare from the other end of the table.

"She does?" Mama Soto asked before turning to Lisa. "Is that right, love?"

"It was just an idea I had after seeing an article about this little mountain town," Lisa mumbled, and ducked her head, clearly mortified.

"Stone and I are going on a reconnaissance mission," Pepper said. "As best man and maid of honor, we will scout out the situation and report our findings. We'll be leaving the day after tomorrow and won't come back until we have planned the perfect wedding."

Lisa continued to stare at her, but with less of a death glare. Rafael leaned back in his chair with a satisfied smile. "Excellent idea. We'll leave it in your capable hands. We all want to give Lisa what she wants, right, Mama?"

Mama Soto reached across the table to pat Lisa's hand. "Anything and everything."

"There's this church with a red door," Lisa said. "*And* a steeple."

"I love red doors," Ria said. "It sounds lovely."

"Like a postcard," Mama Soto said. "Why didn't you say what you wanted?"

Lisa's expression had gone from shocked to a pretty pink rosé wine. "All I truly care about is marrying your son."

Mama Soto's black eyes shimmered. "You're a sweet angel, but all little girls dream of their wedding day, and you should have the one you want."

"Thanks, Mama," Rafael said.

"I'm a bossy old lady," Mama said. "I'll not say another word." A short pause. "As long as it's a church, that is."

"Yes, ma'am," Rafael said as Lisa beamed down at Pepper.

A conversation ensued about the location of the church with the red door and the lodge where they hoped to have the reception. During all of it, Pepper remained acutely aware of Stone. She could feel him next to her even without touching, as if the bulk of him were already familiar to her.

After dinner, everyone pitched in to clean up before parting for the evening. Mama Soto, Ria, Lisa, and Rafael broke out the cards and moved to play at the low table on the other end of the porch. Lavonne begged off, saying he had an early morning. David took the little ones up to his apartment to put them down for the night. Given the dark smudges under his eyes, Pepper guessed he wouldn't be far behind them. Stone disappeared upstairs without saying why.

She really wished she hadn't noticed and that she didn't care.

"I'm going upstairs to read," she told the group.

"I made up the guest room," Lisa said. "Clean towels are in the cabinet under the sink."

Pepper thanked her and trudged up the stairs to the third floor. As she arrived on the third-floor landing, Stone was coming out of his apartment, a bottle of scotch tucked against his side.

She halted. The landing outside the apartments was dim. They were alone. She waited for the familiar sense of panic that came when she was alone with a man in a dark space. It didn't come.

In fact, she wished he would ask her inside for a drink.

"You going to bed already?" he asked.

"Not bed. I'd rather read than play cards."

He nodded and ducked his chin to his neck, as if contemplating what to do next.

"I wouldn't mind a drink, though. If you wanted to invite me in." She flashed her best flirtatious smile, known to make men swoon. Would it work on Stone?

He stumbled backward as though she'd pushed him. "Really? Sure. Yeah, come on in." He opened his door and stepped aside to allow her to pass through.

She'd been in the apartment once or twice before, but never after dark. Trey had decorated it in masculine grays and blues, with a comfortable leather couch and several floppy easy chairs. Eclectic pottery collected during Trey's travels were displayed on shelves and on the fireplace mantel. Tonight, with the lights turned low, it felt cozy and seductive. She slipped off her ballerina flats and left them by the door.

Stone fixed them both a scotch and handed one to her before turning on the fireplace. Then he folded himself into the oversize blue chair, which shrank compared with his large frame. Pepper wandered the room on bare feet, sipping her scotch and looking at the abstract paintings on the wall. She stopped to admire a wooden bowl of blown-glass ornaments in shades of the sea.

Stone said he'd brought the glass home from one of his trips to Spain. "Most everything else is Trey's."

"They're so delicate and pretty." She picked one the color of a hazy blue sky and held it up to the lamp. The light changed the hue to a smoky blue. "This is my favorite."

"Mine too. It's the same shade as your eyes." He paused for a moment, as if considering what to say next. "The color changes depending on the light. Like your eyes."

She placed the glass bulb carefully back in the bowl and turned to look at him. "You noticed the color of my eyes?"

"Maybe." His gaze flickered over to the fire. In the glow of the flames, the sharp angles of his cheekbones softened.

She crossed to the fire and stood with her back to the gas flames.

"Do you ever sit still?" he asked with an amused arch of his brow.

"Stillness is for sleeping, nothing else."

He chuckled as he stretched his legs out over the ottoman and snuggled deeper into the cushions of the chair. "Good point."

"You have a physical job. There must be a reason you chose it." Her legs were warm, so she left the spot in front of the fire and sat on the end of the couch closest to Stone.

"True. I like working with my hands or body and coming home tired but satisfied."

She watched him lift his drink to his hard mouth. What would it feel like to be kissed by him?

"Did you work today?" she asked, hoping to distract herself from thinking about his lips.

"No, not today. I surfed this morning. *Tried* to surf. Jackson's teaching me, but I'm terrible."

"These Californians are weird. Obsessed with the beach and running around half-naked. Have you noticed that no one wears clothes here?"

"I have, and I've embraced the culture thoroughly."

I've noticed.

For the next few minutes, they talked about places they'd lived and their differences. She learned that Stone had grown up in a small town in Oregon where it rained a lot. He'd been stationed in South Carolina and Georgia as well as several bases in Afghanistan during his service. She was surprised at the ease with which he shared the details of his past, including how poor they were growing up and how joining the military had saved his life. "Not that I didn't see a lot of bad stuff in the service. I did. But the marines gave my life a direction instead of staying in my small town after high school. It gave me a way out. I didn't want to end up like my dad."

"Does he still live there?" she asked.

"No, he had the decency to wait to die until my sister was eighteen. By then Autumn was in college and I was already enlisted. It was like he waited until we were gone."

"I'm sorry."

"Yeah, me too. He had a sad life, which makes me sad," he said.

"What about your mom?"

"She left when I was six and never came back."

He said it so casually she didn't know how to react.

"Don't look so stricken," he said. "Things happen. People move onward."

"It's not as simple as that."

His mouth curved into one of his laconic smiles. He lifted one shoulder in a half shrug. "I know. But I discovered a long time ago that feeling bitter or resentful only hurts me, not the other person."

"I wish I could be like that. My real dad's one of the biggest theater producers in New York. He told me in no uncertain terms that he would not help me. I haven't spoken to him in ten years. Before that, I saw him once a year on my birthday. I'm bitter and resentful." She smiled to let him know she was joking. Kind of.

"It's his loss." His voice, low and tender, was like a soothing balm on a cut.

"Maybe. I don't know. Anyway, my stepfather is my dad. He raised me from the time I was seven. He's great." Alarmed at the tightness at the back of her throat, she didn't elaborate further. Crying in front of Stone Hickman was not on her bucket list.

They were quiet for a moment. Pepper resisted the urge to pace around the room.

"This day sure didn't turn out like I thought it would," he said. "I never thought I'd be having drinks with the prettiest girl in the world."

The prettiest girl. Right. "You're so full of it."

His dark blue eyes glittered as he brazenly returned her stare. "I'm not."

"You do not think I'm the prettiest girl in the world."

"How would you know?" He tapped the side of his head. "You have no idea what's in my mind."

She avoided his gaze by taking a sip of her drink.

"Am I not supposed to compliment you?" he asked. "Because if that's a rule, it's going to be nearly impossible. You're beautiful, funny, and sweet."

She grinned and swept her hand back and forth over the arm of the couch. "I might be the first two, but sweet is a stretch. I'm obviously difficult."

He shrugged and grinned at her. "I don't find you difficult."

"Liar."

He looked straight into her eyes. "I never lie."

"Come on. Everyone lies. Little white ones, at least."

"This would be the perfect time to employ a white lie," he said. "I could avoid answering this question with a good deflective white lie. But that's not how I operate. I've never hidden the fact that I have a huge crush on you."

"But..." She trailed off. Her brain couldn't keep up with this man and his honesty.

"But nothing. I happen to like feisty women. They keep things interesting. Add a little *spice* to life." He smiled at his own joke. "I'll tell you what I think about you, if you want."

She didn't say anything. Apparently, he took that as a sign to go ahead.

"I think you're the most beautiful woman I've ever seen. I also find you clever, interesting, and damn entertaining."

"Entertaining?"

"Yeah, in a scary horror-film kind of way—like will she bite off my head and feed it to the wolves or jump out from a closet and stab me to death?"

She burst out laughing. "I thought I was supposed to be the dramatic one here."

"If I asked you why you took an immediate dislike to me, would you tell me the truth?"

She opened her mouth to answer but closed it just as quickly. What could she say that didn't make her sound like a lunatic? "I thought we covered this earlier. I'm sorry and all that."

He smiled, kindly. "Your friends tell me it's because I'm a former marine."

Her friends told him that? Her *traitorous* friends who had no business sharing anything of the sort? Especially not with Stone Hickman.

What would Cora tell her to say? She would probably advise an honest answer in the spirit of vulnerability. Well, screw vulnerability.

"What did they tell you?" She couldn't keep the angry tone from her voice. How dare they talk about her?

"They didn't tell me details, only that you were assaulted by a group of navy men when you were in college." He leaned over the arm of the chair and looked at her intently. "There's no reason to be upset with them. They were quite clear that it wasn't their place to talk about it."

"Then why did it come up at all?"

"Do you remember the night we met?" Stone asked. "At my brother's place?"

"Sure." How could she forget? The first time she'd spotted him standing on the lawn at Violet and Kyle's lawn, she'd felt her mouth drop open with admiration. With his broad shoulders and Adonis-like face, she'd found him wildly attractive. In the time it took for him to cross from the pool to the patio, she'd already started regretting her decision to give up men for the next year. They'd launched into an immediate round of flirtatious sparring. That is, until it came out that he was a former marine.

That was like a bucket of ice water on her libido.

"Your friends spoke up to explain your odd behavior. One

minute you were at the table flirting with me and the next you were headed into the darkness."

Still, not their place to share.

"I'm sorry that happened to you," he said.

She didn't answer other than to shrug one shoulder. What could she say? *Yeah, me too.*

"For the record, I would never hurt a woman," he said. "Not all military guys are bad. Most of us aren't."

He didn't have to say anything further for her to hear the subtext. *We do the work no one wants to do.*

She returned to her careful examination of her drink. "I'm not *unaware* that it's an irrational response."

"That's not really the point. We don't get to pick and choose how we react to something or someone. Everything is influenced by our pasts."

She looked up from her drink to find him watching her. "Do you ever wish you could forget certain parts of your past?"

"Many, many times. But that's not the way it is." He raised his glass. "And tonight's not one of them."

"I'll drink to that." She clinked her glass to his. For a moment, she was lost in his eyes. "I'm glad you invited me in tonight."

"I'm glad you asked to come in."

"I promise I'll be nice during our trip," she said.

"I promise to tease you less. Although that'll be hard."

"Because I'm so entertaining?" She made a stabbing motion in reference to his previous description.

He laughed. "They won't let you bring a knife on the plane."

"I guess you're safe then."

"Trust me, Pepper Griffin. Nothing about you makes me feel safe." He said it low and sexy with his eyes all droopy and seductive.

She tingled. With desire. No. No, no, no. This was not in the plans.

It was the booze playing games with her brain. That's all.

Damn scotch did it to her every time. Why didn't she stop at just one? Because that's not the kind of girl she was. Never had been. Everything was all the way in, even when it was to her detriment.

Stone Hickman was proving to be more of an issue than she thought possible. Not in the way she'd expected. He was not irritating or infuriating or impossible or idiotic. No, he was not any of the *i* words. Why did he have to be so nice? He hadn't been sarcastic or impatient and hadn't lost his cool even once. Which was a miracle given how she'd tried to push his buttons over the last few months. Not Stone. He was calm, rational, caring, and so smart.

She liked him. What had she done? She'd let her guard down and now she flipping liked him and they were about to travel together to a romantic location all alone.

As usual, Pepper Griffin, you've made a messy situation even messier.

9

Stone

THE NEXT MORNING, Stone held the door for his sister as they entered the Cliffside Bay Bookstore. Autumn had her cane with her, dangling from her wrist, in case she needed it. She hadn't said anything, but Stone guessed she brought it in case the day proved emotionally draining. He couldn't imagine it wouldn't. This was the day. They were meeting with Valerie Hickman. God help them all.

Mary Mullen was at the register. She smiled shyly at them. With her husband, Lance, they'd renovated the old bookstore to add a soda fountain and coffee shop. With an open concept, patrons were able to buy a coffee or a soda before perusing the bookshelves for a new read. Despite the challenges of owning an independent bookstore, Lance's vision of a community gathering spot for people of all ages had come to fruition. Tourists flocked to both the bookstore and the café during the summer months. During the off-season, book-loving coffee drinkers and high school students who hung out and did homework at the soda fountain kept the business afloat.

"Did you enjoy *Seahook*?" Mary asked in her quiet librarian voice. Stone assumed she'd honed that particular tone from her years as an actual librarian.

"I love it," Stone said. "I'm not finished yet. Six hundred pages is no joke. I'm a slow reader."

Mary nodded, smiling as her dog, Freckles, wandered over for a few pets from Autumn.

"What're you two up to? Do you need a gift for someone?" Mary asked.

"No, we're meeting a woman who claims to be our long-lost mother," Autumn said, lightly.

Mary's eyebrows shot up. "Really?"

"You could say that." Autumn explained how long it had been since they'd last seen her.

"Kyle's talked about it a few times. You must be in shock." Mary placed a hand on her stomach. She wore a knit dress that clung to her narrow frame. For the first time, Stone noticed her middle looked a little round. "I can't imagine leaving my children." A shadow passed over her pretty features. Mary had lost a child years ago, during her first marriage.

"We can't either," Autumn said.

Mary must have caught him staring at her midsection, because she laughed. "Yes, that's a baby bump you see there. I'm five months pregnant."

"I'm sorry." His cheeks burned. "I didn't mean to stare."

"Don't be sorry. I'm thrilled to be having another. Lance too. We saw my doctor in the city last week and she reassured us the baby is perfectly healthy. We'd been waiting to tell people until we were sure."

"How old is Faith?" Autumn asked.

"Only thirteen months. Like her, this one was a surprise. We weren't planning on adding to our family so quickly, but God blessed us again." Her eyes filled. "Life has a way of surprising us, doesn't it? One never knows when love will change your life."

"I'm so happy for you," Autumn said.

"Let us know if you need a babysitter," Stone said. "Autumn and I love babies, don't we, sis?"

Autumn's eyes twinkled. "My giant brother here has a definite thing for babies."

"You'll make someone very happy one of these days," Mary said.

The bell above the door sounded. Stone turned to see Kyle walking in with his cell phone pressed to his ear. He waved and then finished up his call.

Kyle seemed surprisingly calm. The anger from the other day had disappeared and he was back to his usual fun and playful persona. "Hello, all. No sign of Mommy Dearest yet?"

"Kyle," Autumn said in her best sister voice.

"Don't fret. I'm just kidding." He squeezed Autumn's shoulder and punched Stone in the arm before greeting Mary. "How're you feeling, Mrs. Mullen?"

She patted her midsection and gave him a rueful smile. "I suppose Lance told all the Dogs our news?"

"You know we all blab like teenage girls." Kyle grinned. "Lance was practically bursting with happiness. Not going to lie—I felt a little jealous. I went home and told Violet we should make another one."

Autumn smacked him on the arm. "Bite your tongue."

"I'm with Autumn," Mary said with a laugh. "Four is plenty."

"You ladies are no fun," Kyle said.

"We should get some coffees." Autumn gestured toward the café, where a barista was currently making a drink for a customer.

"I was thinking about shots," Kyle said.

"It's ten o'clock," Autumn said, obviously scandalized.

"Just kidding." Kyle offered his arm to Autumn. "Come on. I'm buying."

A few minutes later, they took their coffees upstairs to the reading loft that overlooked the entire store. Stone and Autumn settled on the comfortable couch with their identical double lattes. Kyle sat across from them in a chair and shook open the *Wall Street Journal*. The morning was foggy and chilly, making the cove in the bookstore even more pleasant. The air smelled of freshly brewed coffee. Below them, Mary shuffled between the stacks putting new books on shelves. Freckles was curled into his doggy bed for a midmorning nap.

His stomach churned with nerves when he heard the chime that indicated a new customer. He looked down and saw Valerie Hickman. Her hands were shoved in the pockets of her jacket as she scanned the store. Mary greeted her and seconds later pointed up to the loft.

"That's her," Stone whispered.

Kyle stood and watched as the woman claiming to be Valerie Hickman climbed the stairs. By the time she reached them, she was out of breath. Stone could smell the cigarette smoke on her clothes.

She and Kyle stared at each other like a bull and a matador.

"Well, I'll be damned. It *is* you," Kyle said.

"Hi, Kyle." Valerie stood on the last step and gripped the railing as she caught her breath.

Autumn used her cane to get to her feet.

He watched his sister carefully. She hadn't taken her eyes off their mother. Her complexion had leached of color. The tie at the neck of her silky blouse quivered. She was shaking, he realized. He put his arm around her shoulders.

Valerie watched them with a hungry look in her eyes. "Hello, Autumn."

"Do you recognize me?" Autumn reflexively covered the scar on her cheekbone.

"Your eyes are the same," Valerie said. "You turned out real pretty. Like my mother."

Autumn touched the handle of her cane. "I was in an accident when I was fourteen."

"I know." Valerie stared at the cane. "I read about it in the papers."

"It was only in the local papers." Autumn's shoulders tensed under his arm. "Were you living near us?"

"I lived in Eugene."

"You were a half hour away and you never came to see us?" Kyle asked.

"It was complicated." Valerie wavered slightly, as if she might collapse.

"Would you like to sit?" Stone asked, gesturing toward the empty chair.

Valerie stepped forward, then sat gingerly in the lounge chair.

The men waited until their sister had resumed her position on the couch before sitting. An awkward silence fell among them. The scent of fresh scones wafted up from the café. Below them, a delivery man asked Mary where to put the boxes.

Kyle sat with his hands folded in his lap, glaring at Valerie with absolute hostility. Finally, he spoke. "Let's plow through this and get on with our days. We all have jobs to get to. What do you want?"

"I wanted to see you. Just once." Under Kyle's angry scrutiny, Valerie had seemed to shrink.

Some of the color had returned to Autumn's cheeks. "What do you want from us?" She faltered and looked over at Kyle for help.

He remained eerily quiet with his hands now splayed out on the arms of his chair.

"I have something I need to tell you." Valerie's eyes were brown and dull like tarnished metal.

Stone felt an odd desire to smooth things over, which was

ridiculous. Valerie didn't deserve his loyalty. Still, she seemed so old and small and fragile. It must have taken great courage to come to them.

"But it sounds like you had some questions for me first," Valerie said.

"We want to know, quite simply, why you left," Stone said.

"Not why. How. *How* could you leave us?" Kyle asked.

"We were so little," Autumn said. "We needed you."

Valerie stared in front of her with glazed eyes. She reached in her bag and pulled out a packet of cigarettes. "Have you ever felt like you were living someone else's life? Like you'd been stuck into a world you didn't belong? Living with your father was... hard. Every time we'd get a little ahead, he'd blow his paycheck on booze. I worked ten-hour days cleaning other people's houses, then came home and took care of you guys. I was dead inside—just going through the motions. And then I met a man who offered me a new life." She shook a cigarette from the packet and held it between her fingers as if she expected one of them to offer a light.

"Did you ever miss us?" Autumn's voice trembled.

Valerie fingered the cigarette and glanced up at the ceiling. "Every single day."

"Why didn't you come back for us?" Autumn asked.

"I'm sure I seem weak. You've all done so well for yourselves with so little. I wasn't strong. I couldn't rise above my circumstances. I lived in that dead-end town all my life. My own dad was a drunk who died in a bar fight when I was four years old. My mother was cruel and abusive. I got pregnant with Kyle at seventeen and had to marry your dad. Repeat, repeat, repeat. Red came along, and I had a chance to be something besides tired and poor and married to a drunk like my mama."

"You could've taken us with you," Autumn said.

"Red didn't take to children," Valerie said.

Kyle was shaking his head as though he couldn't believe

what he was seeing and hearing. "So you just tossed us aside and got in his black car and drove off."

"Cadillac. It was a Cadillac," Valerie said under her breath.

"You deserted three children for a man you hardly knew." Kyle's voice had grown in volume. His eyes glittered with hatred.

"I knew him," Valerie said. "I'd known him for a while."

"You left us. It doesn't matter if you'd been sleeping with him for a month or a year, Mother." Kyle spat out the word *mother* as if it were a vile disease. "You left your children."

"I didn't murder you like some of those women do. The desperate ones."

All three of them stared at her in shock.

"What I mean is, I did what I had to do. It was best for everyone. I was useless. A shell. I couldn't seem to get out of the fog. I was depressed. I realize that now, but at the time I thought there was something wrong with me that I couldn't love you. Your father was a drunk, but he loved you."

That was true. As useless as he'd been to look after them or even provide basic needs such as food and shelter, he'd never raised a voice or hand to them. He loved them as best he could. Maybe that was true of Valerie, too.

Valerie's hands shook. "I'd lost the ability to care for you. I was nothing but a ghost. Don't you remember how I could barely get out of bed? I went to work cleaning the houses and then I'd come home and sleep until it was time to go to work. I understand now that I needed help. But back then all I could see was how wrong it was for me to stay. You were better off without me. I knew that without a doubt."

"We weren't better off," Kyle said. "I had to become a parent at eight years old."

Valerie remained silent for a moment. A myriad of emotions crossed her haggard features. Regret, defensiveness, anger, and finally a great sadness. "My own mother beat me on a regular basis. She told me I was worthless, and she wished I'd never been born. I never had the chance to learn how to be a good mother. And then my thoughts started turning ugly. I began to plan how I would do it. Suicide, I mean. One of you always needed something. Things I couldn't give—that I didn't know how to give. I couldn't cope. It was better for me to leave. I thought if I left, your father would step up."

"He didn't," Kyle said. "When you left with that man, it broke him. He started drinking more."

"He lost his ability to work," Stone said. "We had to take care of him."

"He was useless," Kyle said. "In every way. He sucked down any paycheck he ever made. After you left, he didn't last much longer at work. I had to get a job to support us."

Having taken the brunt of the responsibilities, it wasn't surprising that his brother had no mercy for their father. Stone, however, remembered a few tender moments. The guy had tried, but life was just too much for him. He was a weak man overwhelmed with the pain of life. However, maybe if he hadn't been weak, they wouldn't have grown so strong?

"Kyle raised us," Autumn said.

Valerie examined her hands. "I'm sorry. Truly. I'm sorry we were your parents. You deserved better."

For a moment that seemed like a week, no one said anything.

"When did your father pass?" Valerie asked.

"He died right after Autumn went to college," Stone said. "Peacefully in his sleep."

"That's something, I guess," Valerie said.

"I always thought so." Stone met his mother's eyes. A moment of sympathy passed between them. An understanding that life was often cruel, and any small mercy was a blessing. The best his father could hope for was to die in his sleep. How far he and his siblings had come from their father's legacy.

"He was asleep for most of his life," Kyle said. "Why should his death be any different?"

Valerie met Kyle's hostile gaze with a soft murmur in the

back of her throat. "I can understand why you're angry. At both of us. We didn't do our jobs. I'm sorry, Kyle. I wish I'd been capable of being the mother you deserved." She cleared her throat. "As far as your dad goes—he never really had a chance. His family was poor. There weren't diagnoses for learning disabilities…for people like us. I feel certain he was dyslexic. He could barely read. I don't know if you knew that. His entire childhood was about shame. And shame leads to only bad places."

Kyle leaned forward and fixed his gaze on their mother with eyes that seemed capable of boring a hole through her head. "Do you know what the other kids called me?"

Valerie shook her head.

"Pig Boy," Kyle said. "They called me Pig Boy. Do you know why? Because I smelled bad. And do you know why that was?"

Valerie didn't say anything, just looked at him with tired, red-rimmed eyes.

"Because you and Dad didn't do what you were supposed to do. You left us with a man-child. So we went to school with dirty clothes and no baths because God knows it was much better to blow an entire month's paycheck or welfare check on booze instead of getting the hot water turned on."

"Kyle," Autumn said softly.

Kyle ignored her and kept his eyes on their mother. "What is it that you want?"

Valerie looked at each of them in turn. "I wanted to say I'm sorry. I'm sorry I was a terrible mother. I'm sorry I left you to raise yourselves. Leaving was the only way I could survive. Red provided that chance."

"Was Red good to you?" Stone asked. "Did you have the life you wanted?"

"We didn't stay together but a few years. He left me for someone else—he couldn't live with someone who was sad all the time. Years later, I was diagnosed with depression, and the doctors gave me medicine that helped a lot. I married again.

Jason was a good man who took care of me until he got sick. He died of cancer two years ago. There was a lot of debt from his medical bills. I lost our house because of it. I have a job down at the dollar store as a clerk and live alone in a small apartment. I get by. Paycheck to paycheck, but it's enough. I have my shows on television. I have a library card so I can read whatever I want. Sometimes my friend from work comes over to watch a movie. It's a fine life." Tears ran down her weathered face. "But there isn't a day I don't regret leaving you kids."

"Why didn't you come back, then?" Autumn looked like the little girl she'd once been, all eyes in her wan face.

"By the time I got myself on the depression medication, too much time had passed. I knew I wouldn't be welcome. I'd caused you all enough turmoil without showing up again."

"Why now?" Kyle asked softly. Stone couldn't be sure, but he thought his brother might be softening a smidge.

Valerie stuck the cigarette in her mouth, then perhaps remembered where she was and plucked it out again. "I wouldn't have bothered you, but I'm in a little trouble."

Here it was. The ask.

Stone exchanged a glance with Kyle. He raised one eyebrow as if to say, *I told you so.*

"One day, I saw an article in the Eugene paper about the car accident." Valerie's face crumpled. She sucked in a labored breath. "After I got better, I kept tabs on you three. I had a few friends still in town, and I'd call and ask for updates. You all seemed to be doing well. I learned about Kyle's scholarship to USC, and I was so happy for you. I knew his education could be the ticket out for all three of you. Then, like I said, I saw the article about the accident. I knew those Miller people. The two who caused your accident were the sons of the Miller I went to high school with. He was a mean boy. An even meaner adult." A darkness crossed her face. "When we were in high school, I had some trouble with him."

"Trouble?" Autumn asked.

"The worst kind of trouble. When I was fourteen—at a party. Well, anyway, you can fill in the blanks."

Autumn made a sound like a wounded animal.

"I hated that whole family before, but after I heard what they'd done to you, it was like I went temporarily insane. Autumn, you were the same age as I was when…the thing happened. Maybe that was part of it, but I couldn't stop thinking about revenge."

Stone held his breath. Where was she going with this? Why would she bring up the car accident?

"We don't talk about that night," Stone said.

Autumn's pretty features had turned stony. When she spoke, her voice was level and firm. "When we all found one another again, we talked it all through. We came to terms with what happened and agreed that we would no longer let it define the direction of our lives or our family. We have nothing else to say about it. We've moved on. Together."

He'd do almost anything to avoid talking about the incident that had torn them apart. As Autumn said, when she and Stone had found Kyle, they'd hashed it all out and come to an understanding. Kyle had felt the accident was his fault. The guilt ate at him—made him believe they were better off without him. Except for sending money regularly, he dropped out of their lives for twelve years. He even changed his last name from Hickman to Hicks.

Now, though, the memory of that night wedged into his rapid thoughts. Stone had been home trying to patch a hole in the roof of their trailer in the rain. The downpour had gone on for weeks and ravaged the house. While he worked, Kyle and Autumn had gone into town for groceries. Coming out of the grocery store, they'd run into the Miller brothers.

The Miller boys had been violent bullies since grade school. For years, Kyle was their target. When Stone was fourteen, he beat the bullies within an inch of their life. The bullying of Kyle had stopped. However, from then on, they had a vendetta against the Hickman siblings. Stone had known it was only a matter of time before they tried something. That night, they did.

They'd approached Kyle and Autumn in the parking lot of the grocery store. Drunk. One of them had tried to grab Autumn —threatened to have their way with her. Kyle had managed to shove them to the ground and get her into the car. He'd torn out of the lot and down the highway. The Miller brothers had chased them. The roads were slick. Speeds were high. A collision happened. Autumn was badly hurt.

The Miller brothers had caused the accident that scarred them all for life.

"Those young men were terrible people," Valerie said.

"We know." Kyle's mouth twisted bitterly.

"They died in a house fire," Valerie said, as if that might be news to them.

"We know that too," Kyle said.

"I set that fire." Valerie lifted her gaze to peer at each of them in turn and continued, so softly he had to lean closer to hear her. "I knew we'd never get justice for what they did to my little girl. So I took care of it."

They all stared at her.

A hot iron rod pierced Stone's chest.

Their mother had set the fire. She'd covered the house in gasoline and tossed a match onto the porch and let the entire thing burn to the ground. The Miller brothers had been asleep in the front room. Cops surmised they'd been passed out from a bender, given the booze bottles in the same room where they died.

Stone couldn't breathe. His stomach clenched. He thought he might be sick.

"You set the fire?" Autumn whispered. "They knew it was arson. The cops investigated Dad, but he had an alibi. He was at the bar with the other regulars. Stone was at school. His teachers vouched for him. I was at physical therapy. Kyle was already away at college. They told us it would probably remain unsolved. Which it did."

"Not that we cared," Stone said, finding his voice, but keeping it low, aware that Mary was downstairs. "Autumn and I were just relieved it wasn't Dad." He'd experienced several days of terror, worried the old man had set fire to the house in a drunken rage. Who would have ever guessed it was their absent mother? Not him.

Valerie straightened, and for a split second Stone saw Kyle in the angry tilt of her chin. "I made sure you all had alibis. I'd do it again. Those pigs didn't deserve to live."

"Keep your voice down," Stone said, gently. He didn't think anyone could hear them and the bookstore was mostly empty, but the clandestine nature of their discussion worried him.

Kyle had not moved or taken his eyes off their mother. "You set the fire. You killed the Miller brothers."

"For vengeance," Autumn said.

"I figured by now no one would ever know it was me. Turns out someone did. Someone does." Valerie set aside her cigarette. "Or at least that's what they want me to believe." She dug into the inner pocket of her jean jacket and pulled out an envelope. "I got this in the mail." She handed it to Stone. It was addressed to Valerie Hickman from Cathy Kemper.

The letter inside had been crumpled and then smoothed. He uncurled it from its trifold. It was a typed letter on ordinary computer paper.

Dear Valerie,

I'm not sure you'll recognize my name, so I'll explain who I am. My mother was your friend Trish Kemper. She passed away last month. Before she died, she wrote down a confession about her part in the fire you set. She felt a lot of guilt about the murder of two young men. I'm prepared to go to my own grave with the knowledge, but it's going to cost you. Around here, it's real well known that your son Kyle is rich. If you want me to stay quiet, he needs to send a cashier's check for five hundred thousand dollars. Real simple. Either he sends me the money, or I go to the police with what I know.

Please email me at cathyk@dmail.com to let me know you've received this letter and when I can expect my check.

Sincerely,

Cathy

The letter fluttered from his hands and landed on his lap. With shaking hands, he gave it to Autumn, who read it, then passed it to Kyle.

"This is extortion," Kyle said. "We'll go to the police."

"If it's the police, they'll know what happened and arrest her," Autumn said.

"What did this Trish Kemper do to help you?" Stone asked Valerie.

"Nothing really, other than she told me where you would all be. I waited until Kyle was away at college. And she told me your routines. Where you would be certain times of the day…" She trailed off, looking defeated. "I never actually told her what I was going to do, but she must have come to her own conclusions after the news broke."

"What should we do?" Autumn asked Kyle.

Kyle crossed his arms over his chest. "I'm not giving this woman a dime. If I do, she'll come back for more. That's how these things work. We have to figure out a different way to get rid of her."

Valerie was shaking her head vigorously. "No, you've misunderstood. I don't want you to pay the money. I came here to tell you what happened—to explain myself—before I turn myself in."

"What? No," Autumn said. "Those people have already taken enough from us. You're not spending the rest of your life in jail."

Valerie started to cry, silently. Stone handed her a napkin from under his coffee cup. His chest ached. Despite the past, this woman was their mother. She was so skinny and fragile. He hated to see her cry. She'd obviously had crippling depression, which explained why she left them. He couldn't help but see the parallels between Kyle and their mother. They'd both thought Autumn and Stone were better off without them. As far as whether she loved them or not—murdering the Miller brothers was certainly a crime of passion.

He tried to conjure remorse for the Miller brothers, but nothing came. All he could see were their mean, beady eyes and bloodied noses. They'd trapped Kyle under the bleachers by the football field. When Stone found them, he'd pummeled them without mercy, fueled by a rage born from years of his brother's slouched shoulders and fearful eyes. One of them had looked up at him from the ground where they lay sprawled. "You can't protect that virgin sister of yours every moment." He'd raised his foot to bash in their teeth. Right then, the truant officer had come out the back doors of the high school. Stone and Kyle had run.

For the next two years he had kept a close watch on Autumn. Either he or Kyle was with her when she wanted to go into town. They made sure she went straight home after school. Kyle would bring her into the diner while he worked as a busboy if Stone had to be somewhere in the afternoons.

Of all of them, Stone understood the rage that had made their mother light a house on fire. He'd been ready to bash their heads in.

Autumn fiddled with the bracelet, turning it around and around her wrist. "We'd have to get that signed confession from her. And even then, we wouldn't know if she'd made a copy."

"There's no way out of this," Valerie said. "I've been through every scenario in my mind. Kyle's right. People like her won't go away. Turning myself in is the only solution."

"Wait a minute. Let me think this through." Kyle rested his head on the back of the chair, staring at the ceiling. Autumn looked over at Stone and raised her eyebrows. Kyle always seemed to find a way out of any tricky situation when it came to people. Making deals was his business. But what happened when the person he needed to make a deal with was essentially a criminal?

Kyle sat up and looked over at their mother. "Are you serious about turning yourself in?"

Valerie mumbled a yes as she dabbed at the corners of her eyes. "The last thing I want is to drag you all into this."

"When did you start taking medication for your depression?" Kyle asked. "Was it before or after you set the fire?"

"After. Why?" Valerie lifted her head to look at him. Mascara had smudged under her eyes.

"What if I were to hire a high-powered attorney? One who could build an insanity case?" Kyle asked.

"It would cost a lot of money," Valerie said. "Too much."

"I'd rather spend it on that than give it to a woman trying to blackmail us," Kyle said.

"But would she have to go to jail?" Autumn asked. "Even if she pleaded guilty due to insanity?"

"Depends," Kyle said. "With a history of depression that goes back years, we might have a chance."

"Why would you do that for me?" Valerie asked.

"No matter what went on in our past, you're still our mother," Kyle said. "We're not going down without a fight."

STONE'S STOMACH GROWLED. He looked over at Pepper, who was gazing out the window. They'd been in the car for about an hour, steadily climbing after leaving Denver. The higher they climbed, the prettier the scenery. The countryside was a splash of green and gold, lush forests of firs and pines interspersed with bright yellow aspens.

"You hungry?" he asked.

They'd talked on the airplane nonstop about everything from current events to movies to hilarious stories from Pepper's various jobs. The time had passed quickly, and before he knew it, they were landing in Denver. Now they'd fallen into an easy compatibility, all talked out for the time being.

"Starving." She fidgeted in the seat, tugging on the seat belt as though it was choking her. "And I need to stretch my legs."

"Something quick, like a sandwich." They hadn't eaten since the airplane, and that was hours ago already.

He took an exit promising a sandwich shop on its road sign. They found the place easily, nestled in a brick building. He parked, and they went inside together. The place was warm and smelled of freshly baked bread.

"Yum," Pepper said.

His mouth watered looking at the menu written in bright-colored chalk that hung above the counter. Stone ordered the brie-and-ham sandwich. Pepper ordered a grilled veggie wrap with no cheese. "I'm dairy intolerant," she said.

"I feel you." The pierced young man behind the counter wore a beanie and a silver tongue ring that clicked against the roof of his mouth when he talked. "Dairy's the devil." The skinny punk stared at Pepper as though he wanted to eat *her* for lunch. This was what happened when you had a beautiful woman by your side. Men drooling and vying for her attention. *Not today, Beanie Boy.*

She appeared not to notice Beanie Boy's admiring glances as she picked up a plastic-wrapped cookie and read the ingredients. "I'd love this, but there's milk and butter in it."

Beanie Boy pointed at another stack. "Those are like totally vegan."

Didn't the category vegan imply they were *totally* vegan? From what he understood, there was no *kind of* vegan. *In or out, Beanie Boy.*

Pepper smiled politely at Beanie Boy but declined the vegan cookie. "Maybe another time."

"Do you live here?" Beanie Boy asked Pepper with a hopeful lilt at the end of the sentence.

"No, we're on our way to Emerson Pass," Pepper said.

"And we're kind of in a hurry," Stone said with a pointed glance in Beanie Boy's direction.

"No worries, man. I got you covered," Beanie Boy said.

Stone sipped from his coffee while they waited. The cozy shop was empty other than Beanie Boy, who was now slapping together their sandwiches while simultaneously shooting moony glances Pepper's way.

Pepper, oblivious, stared out the window with a worried furrow in her brow. "Do you think it's going to snow?"

"Looks that way," Stone said. "I hope so."

"You do?"

"I love snow."

"It's pretty but messy."

"Nah. You're with a country boy. I know how to drive in the snow."

"Did you have a lot of snow in Oregon?"

"Not a lot, but occasionally. Depended on the winter." He gave an involuntary shudder, remembering the cold from their winters in that trailer. That thought led to the next. His mother. Why did she have to come now, when things were going so well for all three of them? The haunted look in Kyle's eyes had scared him, reminded him of what his brother had been like in the months following the accident. Yet he couldn't help but be sucked into the idea of helping her. She was a destitute old lady who desperately needed their support.

She was a murderer. Their mother was a murderer. How could he reconcile that?

He looked up to see Pepper watching him.

"You all right?" she asked.

"What? Sure, fine. Just remembering a few cold winters from when I was a kid."

She frowned and looked as if she was about to ask a follow-up question but was thwarted by Beanie Boy's announcement that their sandwiches were ready.

Stone leaped to his feet and grabbed the sandwiches from the counter. Pepper suggested they eat on the road to save time. "We have a lot to do today."

"Agreed."

Beanie Boy called out to them as they walked out the door. "Come back anytime."

When they were outside, Pepper giggled. "How old do you think that kid is?"

"Twelve?" A quick glance at the window told him Beanie Boy watched them from the window. "He's in love."

They strode across the lot in tandem. "Perhaps I should move to Colorado. So far, men seem to like me here."

"I'd reckon men like you in every state, Pepper Shaker." *It's impossible not to fall in love with you.*

"Stone Soup, you say the sweetest things." Her eyes snapped like fireworks on the Fourth of July. He could almost hear the crackle.

When they reached the car, Pepper groaned and looked at her feet. "Could I have picked worse shoes?"

She was right. Ballerina flats with no socks were possibly the worst, other than open-toed sandals. The rest of her outfit consisted of a thin sweater and skinny jeans. He refrained from commenting on the inappropriateness of her attire. Autumn had taught him well. He knew some things were best left unsaid.

He opened the passenger-side door for her. "Get in there." His fingers had already stiffened from the cold. "Do you have anything else you could wear? And what about a jacket?"

"I brought boots and a down jacket, but they're in my suitcase in the back." She shivered again.

"I'll get them for you."

She hesitated, as if she didn't want him in her suitcase. But a sudden gust of cold wind must have convinced her otherwise. "Thanks."

He handed her his sandwich bag. "Hang on."

He scooted around the car and opened the trunk with a push

of the button. Her suitcase was black and had a designer label etched into the side. He unzipped the case and opened the lid. "What the heck, Pepper Shaker? Did you just shove everything in at once?" Her clothes were a jumbled, tangled mass of various colors and textures, as if she'd yanked them off hangers in a great hurry and tossed them into the bag. Toiletries were stuffed into the side pockets. One boot was on top of a cashmere sweater. The other was buried under several pairs of lacy underwear. Fortunately, the boots looked as though they'd never been worn so there was no mud to ruin the soft yarn of the sweater.

"Don't forget socks," Pepper said from the front.

"Right. Socks." He grabbed the boots, then stared down at the mess. How would he ever find a pair of socks? He moved the sweater aside, and two pairs of jeans. To her credit, they were folded. Under the jeans were several more sweaters and a down jacket. He pulled out the jacket and set it aside. Finally, he found a pile of socks under a makeup bag. Right next to a lacy red bra. He swallowed hard as he grabbed the thickest pair of socks.

"Did you find them?" Her voice sounded tinny and shaky.

"Yes, I've got them." He quickly shoved everything back inside the bag and zipped it closed.

She was shaking by the time he returned to her.

"Put this on first." He wrapped the jacket around her shoulders. She slid her arms inside the sleeves. He squatted and zipped it all the way up to her pointy chin. The jacket was white and fluffy. She looked like a marshmallow with legs. He chuckled.

"Is it the jacket?" she asked. "Do I look ridiculous?"

"A bit like a marshmallow with legs."

"This is exactly why it was in the bag."

"An adorable marshmallow," he said.

She rolled her eyes.

Still kneeling, he slipped her ballerina flats from her feet. Her toes were icy cold. He warmed them between his hands with a vigorous rub. "Why didn't you tell me your feet were so cold?"

How could feet be this narrow and hold a girl upright? Her toenails were painted red—perfect little squares against her white skin.

"I didn't want to seem high maintenance." She moaned softly as he continued to rub her feet.

The sound shot right through him. *Think of baseball.*

"That feels so good." She paused for a moment before blurting out, "I packed quickly. I'm not usually this messy."

Stone chuckled as he unwrapped the socks. "What did you say about snow? It's pretty but messy. Kind of like you."

She gave his shoulder a playful punch. "I'm not that pretty."

He looked up at her. "You're very pretty. And you're messy."

She pressed her bare toes against his chest. "I can put my own socks on."

"I've got it." With quick movements, he had her feet encased in socks and into the boots in less than thirty seconds.

When he rose to his feet, she was staring at him as though they'd run into each other at the airport and she couldn't quite place where she knew him from.

"What?" he asked.

"You know your way around feet," she said.

"That's not all I know my way around." He grinned, which made her blush and look away. "Now, get in there. We've got a wedding to plan." He waited for her to slide her legs inside before shutting the door.

As he slipped into the driver's seat and started the engine, he reminded her to turn on the seat warmer. "It'll take the chill off."

"Yeah, good idea." She poked it with her long, slim finger with the bright red nail polish. He loved red nails. They reminded him of an older era. This blue and black polish some of the girls wore now always made him think of corpses. He inwardly cringed. One of many comments he'd said to a lady that had gotten him into trouble. Women didn't like their fingers compared to corpses. In hindsight, it seemed obvious. Why this occurred to him after the fact was almost as mysterious as women. One thing he'd learned over the years. A man like him should keep his trap shut unless he had a fail-proof compliment ready.

Was now a good time for a compliment? He had one on the tip of his tongue, and it was one hundred percent truthful, which he'd also learned was best. Smart women could always tell when a compliment was disingenuous. "I like your nails. They look refined, all short and round like that. And red does it for me." *Does it for me*. Wrong. Too sexual.

She stiffened, then slowly shifted in the seat to look at him. Way too slowly. He cringed, waiting for the onslaught of all that pepper spice.

Instead, she smiled up at him. "In a million years, I would never have pegged you as a man who noticed my fingernails."

"I notice a lot of things."

"Do you now?"

"When it comes to you, yes ma'am, I do."

Pepper's cheeks flushed pink. "You're full of surprises today." She turned away, busying herself by plugging in her phone. A man with an English accent gave him the instruction to turn left at the end of town.

Stone unwrapped his sandwich and took a big bite before getting back on the road. "I've never heard a dude as the voice before."

"An English accent is so hot." Holding her wrap in both hands, she nibbled from the corner, then set it back in her lap. The way she hunched over her food reminded him of a chipmunk or squirrel. The cutest chipmunk ever.

"Would you like me if I had an accent?" He winked at her.

"You've got to stop this winking thing. It's awful. Secondly, an accent would have no effect on your hotness."

"So, you're saying I'm hot?" he asked in his best English accent.

She burst out laughing. "That's the worst accent I've ever heard."

"Say it isn't so." He made a face at her as if he were crushed. "How will I ever make it as an actor?"

Pepper's eyes went from dancing to dull. "Only one of us in this car is pursuing an impossible goal. I'm envious of you and your achievable dreams."

He took another bite of his sandwich before answering. "You don't really think it's impossible for you?"

She shrugged and looked out the front window. "I don't know. Lately, I've been wondering if I should give up. Maybe I'm not good enough."

"Seems to me it's a matter of luck."

"Perhaps." She nibbled from her sandwich.

"I'm the king of pep talks. If you ever need one."

"Is that right? How'd you develop that particular skill?" She gathered her wrap into her hands and took another chipmunk bite.

"My sister and I are close. She's needed a lot of them over the years."

She didn't say anything, only nodded. A woman understood why Autumn needed encouragement, even though she shouldn't. "Autumn's really pretty. And sweet."

"That she is."

"How come she doesn't have a boyfriend? She was too busy grilling me to tell me much about her own love life."

"Wait, what did you say? Grilling you? About what?"

Pepper's eyes twinkled up at him as she chewed, then swallowed. "She was trying to get it out of me whether I have the hots for you."

"And?"

"I think we both know the answer to that."

"Do we?" he asked.

"We do."

A zing of pleasure coursed through him. Maybe she liked him a little. Did she? For now, he'd go with yes. He had the rest of the week to make it true.

He bit off another portion of his sandwich. "This is so good."

She looked at it with a dreamy expression. "Tell me about the cheese."

"The cheese?"

"Describe it to me."

He took another bite. How did one describe cheese? "It's creamy and has kind of a nutty flavor. The sandwich is warm, so it's all melty."

"Oh, God, that sounds so good."

The throaty way she said it in combination with throwing her head back gave him a lot of ideas, none of which had anything to do with food.

The hot British guy broke his daydream. "Continue to follow this road for ten miles."

He finished his sandwich and crumpled up the wrapper before stuffing it in the empty bag. "That hit the spot."

"I was surprised you didn't order two."

"Why's that?" He glanced in her direction. She dabbed at her mouth with a napkin. How were her lips that naturally red? It was like they were stained with juice from a pomegranate.

"You always have two huge helpings of food at Group Dinner." She stuffed her half-eaten wrap into the bag and tossed the entire thing in the back seat.

"Busted." She'd noticed that?

His ears plugged as they continued to climb elevation.

"You want music?" she asked.

"You have any country?"

She seemed to think about that for a moment. "Hang on. I think Dack made me a playlist one time." She flipped through her phone. "Yes, here it is. Dack titled it 'Classic Country.'"

The voice of Don Williams filled the car.

"This music makes me want to take a nap," Pepper said.

"Bite your tongue. He's iconic. There's no question in life that a country song can't answer."

"You sound like Dack." She rested her cheek against the seat and looked at him with eyes that reflected the gray sky. "If you had any question about whether I like you or not, this should answer it."

"Why's that?"

"I would only listen to this playlist for one other man, and that's my stepdad."

Well, okay then. This was a unicorn-and-rainbow kind of day.

10

Pepper

DESPITE THE COZY CAR, a surprisingly enjoyable playlist, and the company of Stone Hickman, Pepper was happy to see the city limit sign for Emerson Pass, Colorado, appear. As they drove into town, a lone snowflake fell from the sky and landed on their front window.

"Maybe we'll get snowed in together." He slowed the car as they entered the main street of town.

"Snowed in?" Not that she would mind being with Stone in a cozy hotel room, but the thought of being stuck in the mountains scared her a little. She was a New Yorker, accustomed to speed-dial takeout, a coffee shop on every block, and the ability to walk to whatever else one might need.

He chuckled. "There could be worse ways to spend a few days."

"As long as there's heat, food, and booze, I'd be fine." And no blackouts. She hated the dark.

He grinned as they pulled up to a red light. "I'd keep you warm, Pepper Shaker."

"Is that a promise?"

"Yes. And I never break my promises."

She looked out the window, distracted from the gorgeous man beside her by the quaint brick buildings and charming shop fronts, including several restaurants, a candy shop, and at least three ski stores. "This place is beyond cute."

"It looks like a movie," Stone said. "Starring us?"

"That depends on if we can get a wedding planned before we leave. Otherwise, our scenes will be deleted and left on the cutting room floor."

She craned her neck to look up at the sky. Emerson Pass, nestled in the Rocky Mountains, had once been a mining town but was now built around ski slopes. The town itself seemed dropped squarely in the valley. In every direction, dramatic mountains reached toward the sky, majestic green punctuated by shades of gold, copper, and brown. Above town, the ski slopes were like thick brown snakes waiting for the first snowfall. Lifts hung motionless in midair, lonesome and a little bereft.

She had the fanciful sensation of being in a snow globe before it was shaken. With that thought, another snowflake dropped on their window.

All along the street, aspens with bright gold leaves rustled in the breeze like a percussion instrument. They passed another ski shop and a store that sold high-end kitchen gadgets.

"Look at the aspens," she said. "Their leaves seem to dance, don't they?"

"I always think they're waving to me."

She turned to observe him, to commit his profile to memory. The angles of his face seemed carved and smoothed from the finest instrument, like a classic sculpture. She wondered if he had any idea of his beauty. Did he ever think of it when he looked at himself in the mirror like her actor friends in New York? Her profession was a constant examination of one's own appearance. How would your face translate to the big screen, the small screen, the stage? Her female peers were obsessed with what they ate or didn't eat and how it changed or preserved their bodies. An actor's or actress's appearance was discussed and evaluated to a nauseating degree by agents and directors and peers. She suspected Stone was free of these thoughts. What an envious way to live, concerned with things outside of yourself. He was like the aspens' leaves, free to flutter gently in the breeze.

He glanced at her and smiled. "You all right, Pepper Shaker?"

"Yes, I'm fine. Admiring your profile."

He touched his fingers to his jaw. "I made sure to shave this morning. Just in case I get to steal a kiss later. I wouldn't want to scratch your perfect skin."

An eruption of excited anticipation danced in her stomach. There might be a kiss later. Was this what it was like to be with Stone? Would there always be another moment to look forward to? Would he always make her feel hopeful and excited and happy to be alive?

"What's the name of the lodge again?" he asked nonchalantly, as if he hadn't just promised to kiss her and thrown her into fantasyland.

Pepper lifted her phone from the bag at her feet to look up the address. "Willows Lodge. According to the map, it's one mile from here." She instructed him to turn left when they reached Blue Spruce Street. After a few minutes, they saw a sign for the lodge and turned down a paved driveway that ran between a meadow of straw-colored grasses and more of the golden aspen trees in the company of green firs. Soon the lodge appeared, nestled at the foot of the ski mountain. With wide beams and natural wood, it looked, to Pepper anyway, exactly as a ski lodge should.

"Is it like the picture?" Stone asked.

"Other than the snow, yes." The photograph from the magazine had captured the landscape blanketed in white. Today it blended into the brown ski slopes and smoky gray sky. Several wide snowflakes landed on the window.

As they drew nearer, Stone said he'd drop her at the front. "I'll find parking and bring our bags."

"No need. We'll just valet."

"Valet, huh? So, that's how it's done in Pepper's world?" He raised a teasing eyebrow.

"I'm afraid so." She flashed him a sassy grin. "Is that a problem?"

"I'm usually the guy parking the cars, but I'll go with it for now."

Her hand sprang out to touch his arm. "I love that you offered. But I want this to be nice for you. You don't have to take care of everything for me. It's bad enough you have to drive me all over the place."

"Driving you is my honor. And being with you is all the nice I need."

Swoon.

When they pulled up to the entrance, several attendants dressed in khakis and white shirts rushed out to greet them. Bags were collected from the trunk and set onto a rolling cart. Pepper made sure to grab her extra pair of shoes from the car, slipping them into her purse. Soon, they were inside the lobby. Out of the corner of her eye, she noticed Stone slipping the valet a five-dollar bill. Having worked in the service industry for most of her adult life, she appreciated people who tipped well.

She imagined what Lisa would say. *Of course he's a good tipper. He grew up poor.* She had a theory that people who were raised with little were always the most generous when they could be.

The lodge was not as big as the photographs had indicated. The lobby had an old-school vibe, with dark distressed woods and river rock. She detected the faint hint of smoke from the fire that roared in the enormous stone fireplace. The clatter of silverware came from the restaurant adjacent to the lobby. Picture windows displayed a meadow and the ski mountain. Several couples were reading, curled up in armchairs or love seats. A family with young children played cards at a coffee table near the window.

Lisa would love this place.

"I'll check us in," Stone said.

"Sure. The rooms are paid for. One of Lisa's stipulations."

"Even better."

Lisa had insisted that she and Rafael pay for all expenses, along with strict instructions to enjoy herself. And be nice to Stone. So far, those instructions had been quite easy to follow.

Pepper waited near a table with jugs of infused water and several canisters of brewed coffee as Stone approached the front desk. Despite his size, he moved with grace and an ease that indicated a man comfortable in his own skin. He was remarkably unflappable, as though nothing much bothered him. She could imagine what a good soldier he must have been.

In addition, he had impeccable manners. She'd noticed it on the plane with the flight attendants. *Please, thank you, do you mind, hate to bother you*—that kind of thing. He'd been gracious with Pepper as well, offering to order her a coffee when their flight was slightly delayed and insisting that he fetch it while she stayed with the bags. He was a man who dedicated himself to others. His service to his country, for example. The way he cared for his sister. His smile when he held his baby niece.

Being with him made her want to be a better person. And God knew there was a lot of room for improvement.

A young staff member named Sheila with a fringe of black bangs welcomed him and began the process of checking them in. Sheila made eyes at Stone while she explained where their rooms were. This had happened with every woman they encountered that day. Young, old, or middle-aged—it didn't seem to matter. They were all charmed by Stone Hickman. Not that she could blame them.

When they were checked in, Pepper sidled up next to Stone

and asked Sheila if they could speak to the event planner. Sheila turned suddenly dismissive. "Do you have an appointment?"

"No, but I left her a message," Pepper said. "We're here to plan a wedding."

Sheila's face fell but she did the best to hide her disappointment with a somewhat disturbing fake smile. "You're getting married?"

"Not us," Pepper said drily. "Our friends."

"We're more like the wedding coordinators," Stone said.

"Okay, well, that's nice." Sheila ignored Pepper and smiled at Stone. "Mindy's office is down the hallway and to the right."

They followed the direction of Shelia's outstretched arm. The door to the office was open, and a woman was on the phone, talking softly. She looked up and smiled, then mouthed, "One minute," and waved them toward the chairs across from the desk. A nameplate on her desk read Mindy Madden.

Stone waited until Pepper sat before dwarfing the simple office chair. His legs were almost as cramped as they'd been on the plane.

Mindy hung up the phone and turned to them with a smile. Pepper guessed her to be upward of fifty, but maybe younger. People probably aged faster under all this sun and dry air.

"What can I help you with?" Mindy asked with a resort-sized smile, after introducing herself.

"We're here to inquire about a wedding reception and renting most of the lodge out for guests," Pepper said.

"Excellent." She reached for a paper calendar. Paper? Wild West, indeed. Mindy flipped several pages before looking up at them. "What season were you interested in for next year?"

"Next year?" Pepper asked. "No, we were actually hoping for this December."

Mindy twitched and cocked her head to the right, like a puppy trying to understand a command. "This December? I'm afraid that's impossible. Every weekend is booked into September of *next* year."

"It's a small guest list," Pepper said. "And my friend, the actress Lisa Perry, has her heart set on this place as well as the church with the red door." Shameless name-dropping, but these were desperate times.

"*The* Lisa Perry?" Mindy asked.

"That's right." Pepper almost cringed. She was not accustomed to this yet. Her friend was famous. "Money is not an issue. However, she wants to have her reception on December twenty-second. Of *this* year."

Mindy placed her hands on the calendar and went completely still, as if the pages were a Ouija board. Would it spell out the right answer? "How many guests are we talking about?"

Pepper exchanged a worried glance with Stone. "No more than thirty. But they all need accommodations."

"I see. Well, as much as I'd love to help, unless there's a last-minute cancellation for the Ward and Fordham wedding, there's nothing I can do. They've rented the entire lodge for that weekend. I can't bump anyone off the list, even for Lisa Perry. Big fan, by the way."

"How solid are the Ward and Fordham couple?" Stone asked. "Any chance they might break up?"

Mindy brought a hand to her mouth, as if she were trying to keep a burst of laughter from escaping. "I'm afraid they seem quite happy."

"What about the week after Christmas?" Pepper asked.

"The winter here is a very popular time for weddings," Mindy said. "I can't imagine there's an inn or hotel in town that could accommodate you."

"Do you know anything about the church with the red door?" Pepper asked as she pulled the pages of the old article out of her bag. She unfolded the crumpled page and set it on the desk. "See there. Do you know if that church is still around?"

"Oh my, yes. It's been around for a hundred years," Mindy said. "It's not a quarter mile from here. We often partner with them for weddings. My friend's husband is the pastor there. I can probably cash in a few favors and get you in there for the ceremony, especially if Miss Perry is open to a morning slot."

"She might be," Pepper said. "I mean, I'm sure she is. But her dream included a sleigh ride from there to here."

"That's unfortunate. There's just no room at the inn," Mindy said, with a pleased snort over her own joke.

"Oh, okay." Pepper deflated. This was not going as she'd hoped. Plus, comparing a wedding to the birth of Jesus seemed rather blasphemous.

"What about other places in town?" Stone asked. "Is there any place you can think of?"

"There are several others as well as smaller inns," Mindy said. "But, again, I highly doubt you could get any rooms. It's Christmas, and many, many families come for ski vacations."

Pepper looked up at the ceiling and steadied her breath. Lisa would be disappointed, and it was all Pepper's fault. Why had she brought all of this up? She should learn to keep her big fat mouth shut.

"However, I do have an idea for you," Mindy said.

Pepper sprang to attention. "You do?"

"There's a large cabin about ten miles up the southern slope of the mountain. During busy tourist months, the owner rents it out for family reunions and small weddings. I just talked to Mr. Lake this morning. He's elderly and had put it on the market last spring, hoping to sell. After his wife died, he doesn't have the heart to keep it. However, the offer he received on the place fell through at the last minute. He called just this morning to tell me he'd like to rent it out this winter and put it back on the market in the spring. In the past, I've often directed people to him and a few other rental houses if I didn't have rooms here. The Lake House only has eight bedrooms, so she might have to limit the guest list or have people share the loft space."

"Is it nice?" Pepper asked.

"It's a lovely home. His wife had wonderful taste. Big fireplace and high ceilings. The rooms all have nice beds and furnishings. If it tells you anything, I live here in town, and I had my family reunion there two summers ago. We had a magical time."

"Magical? That sounds good," Stone said with a hopeful lilt in his voice.

"Especially for a wedding weekend." Without thinking, Pepper tapped Stone's knee with her knuckles. "Do you know if there are any places here that would cater a dinner for the reception?"

Mindy smiled and made a purring sound at the back of her throat like a contented cat. "I have a daughter who's just out of culinary school. She's back living with me until she can get her catering business going. I'd consider it a Christmas miracle if you'd consider her for the job."

Pepper's mind had turned to high speed by then. She wanted to get up and pace around the room to think better, but she crossed her ankles under the chair and jiggled one foot instead. "Maybe we could hire her for the whole weekend. She could cook out at the house, right?"

"She'd be delighted." Mindy picked up the receiver to the landline phone. "Shall I call Mr. Lake and let him know you'd like to meet him up there to take a look at the place?"

"He's there now?" Pepper asked.

"Yes, he came to town thinking he'd be signing papers, but the deal fell through. He sounded quite discouraged when I talked to him. He'll be happy to have at least one weekend filled." She picked up a blue sticky note from the desk and squinted at it before dialing the numbers.

As she spoke to Mr. Lake about the nice couple needing a wedding venue for their friends, Pepper stole a look at Stone. He sat with one ankle crossed over the opposite knee, the corners of his mouth lifted in a slight smile. Unlike her, he didn't waste a movement. He was like a massive old tree in a man's body. Nothing could shake him.

He must have felt her looking at him, because he turned his face toward her. "It's going to be okay," he whispered. "Don't lose faith."

Mindy hung up the phone and beamed at them. "He would love to show you the place in the morning." She scribbled a few notes on to a blank sticky note. "Here's the address and directions. You can't miss it. Climb straight up Aspen Mountain Drive about ten miles. His driveway is marked with a rather large sign that says The Lake House."

"Is there a lake?" Pepper asked, imagining ice-skating.

"There's a pond," Mindy said. "Lake is for their last name."

She flushed, feeling stupid. "Right. Duh."

"It's a great name for a guy who owns a cabin in the woods," Stone said.

"Does the pond freeze over in the winter?" Pepper asked.

"It does. The house has various-sized skates, too," Mindy said before she picked up the phone again. "Let's call about the church."

They waited while Mindy talked to her friend and then the friend's husband. She explained the situation and then quieted, obviously listening to the answer from the other end. "That's wonderful," she said into the phone. "I'm sure you're right. I'll call right away. Thanks so much." Once again, she beamed as she placed the receiver back in its holder. "Apparently, the Reed and Morris couple were not as unwavering in their love as my Ward and Fordham couple. They called their wedding off just this morning. He has a spot for a two o'clock ceremony." She scribbled on yet another sticky note, then handed it across to Pepper. "Address is there—it's a quarter mile up the road. He'll meet you there in fifteen minutes."

"Wait a minute. If they called off their wedding, would there be rooms booked in one of the other inns?" Pepper asked.

"Maybe they'd have enough rooms to make up for whatever the house doesn't have?" Stone asked.

"I'm way ahead of you," Mindy said. "He said they had a

block of ten rooms at the Aspen Inn. I'll call Rob right now." She was already dialing the phone. For the next few minutes, they listened as she shared the particulars with Rob. "Great. They'll be so pleased." With a jaunty flick of her wrist, she placed the receiver back onto the phone. "All set."

"I could hug you," Pepper said.

Mindy smiled and rose from her chair. "I could hug you for providing my daughter with her first big job. Granted you like her food, that is. How long are you in town?"

"Just a few days," Pepper said. "But if you give us her number, we'll call and see if she'll meet with us before we go."

"Excellent." Mindy walked them to the door and shook hands with each of them in turn. "I'm sorry I wasn't able to help, but when you two are ready, give me a call and we'll get your wedding scheduled."

An awkward giggle burbled up from her stomach. "We're not engaged."

"Not yet," Stone said, completely deadpan. "I have the next two days to get her to fall in love with me."

Pepper let her eyes twinkle up at him. "I don't think Mindy's interested in your fantasy life."

Mindy smiled up at Stone. "More than one couple's fallen in love at the Lakes' cabin. At my family reunion, two babies were made, and my niece fell in love with my son's best friend."

"Did he fall in love with her too?" Pepper asked.

Mindy tilted her head to the right with a puzzled furrow to her brow. "Pardon me?"

"I think it's assumed he did." Stone lifted his eyebrows, teasing her. "Unrequited love isn't usually described as magical."

"I'd better stay in town then." Pepper nudged Stone's rib cage with her elbow. "Just to be safe."

11

Stone

Stone's stomach fluttered as Pepper held out her arms and twirled in a graceful circle in the middle of the church aisle. "Isn't this place amazing?" She pointed to the windows. "Look at the stained glass."

He agreed. The church was as promised—white with a red door and the most magnificent steeple. Mama Soto would approve of its quaintness and tradition. There were wooden pews the color of strong tea and blue-and-red stained-glass windows.

"I can see why it's a popular place to get married," he said.

Pepper pointed to the wooden cross that hung over the pulpit. "Especially if you want to get married in a church." She let out a sigh. "I haven't been in ages."

Stone wasn't the most habitual church attendee, especially lately. His relationship with God was personal. He felt his presence when in nature or when he worked with his hands. "I haven't been much either. Sometimes Violet drags me along."

"I loved church when I was a kid." She picked up a stray Bible from one of the pews and held it against her chest. "What about you? Were you a choirboy?"

He stuck his hands into the pockets of his jacket and made a face. "No one wanted me in the choir, trust me."

She laughed. "That's where I got the entertainment bug—singing in the church."

He smiled, imagining a smaller version of Pepper standing up in front of the congregation. What had she looked like? All eyes in a small face? Gangly arms and legs?

"My stepdad used to brag about me to all his friends about my solos. I pretended to be embarrassed, but I loved it."

"*My* dad said religion was for idiots who needed something to get them through the day. Ironic, given his worship of cheap whiskey. When she was around fourteen, Autumn wanted to go, so I started taking her." Kyle had left for college by then and it was just the two of them and Dad, who'd faded into a nonperson by then. The car accident had transformed his sister from pretty cheerleader into a mangled mess of fragility. Her recovery took months. In the middle of the night, her cries from a bad dream or the throbbing pain in her legs would wake him. He'd bring her a pain reliever he'd stolen from the first aid kit at work and sit with her until she drifted back to sleep. On one of those nights she'd asked him if he would take her to church. Never able to say no to her, he'd agreed. At first, he'd attended with Autumn so she wouldn't have to go alone, but after a time, the sermon messages seemed to be directed right at him. By the time he left for the marines, both he and Autumn had been baptized.

Pepper watched him, her body still for once. "Was it after her car accident?"

"You know about that?"

She set aside the Bible as her cheeks flooded pink. "I asked

Violet about what caused her limp. Kind of nosy of me. I'm sorry."

"No, she doesn't mind if people know." He paused for a moment, thinking about his sister and how her lame leg shamed her, made her feel unlovable. "She'd rather have people ask than just stare at her with the obvious question planted on their face." Both Autumn's legs were marked with angry red scars from the accident and subsequent surgeries. Her left one, crushed in the accident, was misshapen, despite multiple surgeries. She never allowed anyone to see them, dressing in long skirts, boots or pants.

Pepper's expression darkened. "I get it." She tilted her head downward. Curls fell over her cheek, hiding her expression from his view.

"We were both lost and needed comfort. The church provided it." He looked up at the cross. "It was good to have him with me over there…in Afghanistan."

"It was bad, wasn't it?" With a soft expression in her eyes, she tapped the back of the pew, almost as if it were his shoulder.

"It was. Yes."

"You don't like to talk about it."

"That's right."

She lifted her chin and looked him in the eyes. "I understand."

"I know." An urge to take away all her pain almost made him stagger right there in the aisle of the church. His arms were heavy with the weight of their desire to reach out and pull her into him, comfort her, caress her hair and kiss her mouth until the sadness in her eyes departed. If God would grant his wish, he'd spend his life trying to ease her pain.

"You really think we can pull a wedding off by December?" he asked. *Stay in the lane of safer topics.*

Her face brightened. "I have no doubts whatsoever." She moved from the aisle to stand in one of the rows. Her hands wrapped around the back of the pew. "Were you surprised they got engaged so quickly?"

He grimaced, feeling disloyal to Rafael to admit his reservations. Especially since he was halfway to heedlessly in love with Pepper. He might just beat Rafael's record. Would it happen in two days? Before the day was done? "I was. A little. I *do* believe when you know, you know. But I didn't think he stood a chance in hell of winning her heart."

"Really? Why would you think that?" She asked the question as if genuinely curious rather than accusatory.

"You two are beyond classy. Rafael and I are working-class guys."

"That's very nice of you to say." She gave a vehement shake to her head, making her glossy black curls bounce. "Lisa couldn't care less about that. She fell for him the minute she met him. However, I didn't think it would happen this fast."

"You didn't think people can fall in love in three weeks?"

"Three weeks? They were together three days and she called to tell me she was in love with him. I *was* a little worried, but I'm not now. Lisa knows her own mind. He obviously adores her. That said, if he hurts her, I swear to God, I *will* kill him."

"What if she hurts him?"

She sucked in her bottom lip and stared at him for a moment. "Are you serious? Have you met Lisa? She feels bad when she slaps a mosquito. She's not going to hurt him."

"Rafael would die before letting anything happen to her."

She suddenly looked so sad he wanted to scoop her into his arms and tell her he would be that man for her. *Too soon. Take it slow.*

He resisted the urge to touch her by shoving his hands in his pockets. "Trust me, Pepper Shaker. Someday you'll have a man in your life who feels that way about you."

Her eyes widened a fraction. "How'd you know that's what I was thinking?"

"It's the same look my sister gets sometimes. I get it. Whenever I'm around Lisa and Rafael, my life seems pathetic."

She moved to his side and tilted her gaze upward. The glimmer of the glass windows stained her skin blue. "You're hardly pathetic."

He did a quick tug of one of her curls before he could stop himself. "*You're* magnificent."

She twisted her neck to look up at him. "Stone Hickman, did you just pull my hair?"

"I'd like to do more than that."

Her chest rose and fell as she took in a deep breath. She turned to face him. Her eyes were the color of a silver star. "Like what?"

It was his turn to have his breath hitch. "I'd like to give you everything you've ever wanted."

The corners of her eyes crinkled. She shook her head, teasing him. "As sweet as that is, I don't think you could get me the role of Hedda Gabler on Broadway."

"Hedda who?"

"It's a famous play. My father's company is doing a revival of it for spring season. Hedda's my dream part. I'm perfect for the role, but there will be a hundred others auditioning. They'll give it to someone well known." She shrugged. "As if my father would grant me an audition spot anyway."

"Why not?"

"Long story. I'll tell you about it some other time."

"What's something I *could* give to you?" he asked. "Like right now."

She placed her palm against his chest, but kept her eyes fixed on his neck. Could she see how fast his pulse throbbed? "You could take me to a nice dinner and open the door and pull out my chair and charm me with your bad jokes and sweet smile."

This woman made it hard to breathe. He'd never known what the phrase *take my breath away* meant until now.

"Pepper Griffin, will you give me the honor of taking you to dinner tonight?"

"Nothing would please me more." She tilted her chin upward. Her lips parted slightly.

The time was now. He would kiss her. Leaning closer, he took one last look into her eyes to make sure he was reading her signals right. He breathed in her scent and leaned closer.

The doors of the church burst apart with a clamor and crash, like the parting of the great sea. They jumped apart like guilty teenagers.

"Hello there." A skinny man with an abundance of slicked-back black hair greeted them. Wearing a vintage-style suit with narrow, tapered ankles, he looked strangely like Buddy Holly. Stone expected him to belt out a tune rather than speak. "Pastor Jordan at your service. Sorry I'm late. The wife needed a little loving before I left."

Next to him, Pepper made a sound between a chortle and a gasp, then murmured, "Oh my."

"We're trying to make a baby. One must answer to God's time, not our own, but when the ovulation window's open, it's open. You know what I mean?"

"Sure. You bet." Stone bit the inside of his lip to keep from laughing.

"God created an ovulation window for a reason." Pepper's tone was one of insouciance, as if it were a typical conversation to have in a church with a pastor they'd just met.

He was crazy about this girl.

"She has this app on her phone," Pastor Jordan said, "that lights up like the word of God himself. And boom, it's time."

Pastor Jordan might not pass the Mama Soto test. He made a mental note to tell Pepper they'd best keep this conversation under wraps.

"Now, tell me about your friends," Pastor Jordan said.

Pepper launched into the biographies, covering Rafael's

heroic service to his country and Lisa's dream to have her wedding in this little church.

"That article was my idea." Pastor Jordan smiled wide, revealing large, overly white teeth. "It's not enough to preach the word of God. A good pastor these days needs a marketing mind."

"It certainly caught our eye," Pepper said. "She had it on the refrigerator for years."

"Well, isn't that sweet?" Pastor Jordan said.

Pepper went on to explain about Lisa's profession. "I don't suppose you've heard of her?"

"Yes indeed. My wife loves *Indigo Road*." Pastor Jordan's eyes gleamed. "Now tell me about their beliefs. Are these people of God?"

"Sure. I mean, they're not like deacons or anything," Pepper said, for the first time sounding nervous.

"We do have a small fee for weddings," Pastor Jordan said. "And we're always appreciative of donations on top of that fee. We have a lot of needy families here in Emerson Pass that could sure use a boost up, especially around Christmastime."

"Of course. Lisa's known for her generous heart. I can't imagine she wouldn't be more than willing to contribute to a good cause."

"Excellent. Let's talk over the details in my office." Pastor Jordan pointed to a door near the pulpit. "And secure the spot with a credit card."

"I think I'll get some air," he said to Pepper.

She nodded and gave him an understanding smile. "I'll just be a moment."

After they left, he wandered outside. Snow was now falling in large, fat flakes. At least a good inch had stuck since they'd been inside the church.

He strolled across the lawn, enjoying the soft flakes on his face. The churchyard wasn't much more than a patch of grass and a gravel parking lot. He found a wooden bench under an aspen around the corner from the main entrance. A silver plaque said, "In memory of Rebecca Sizemore: wife, mother, friend, child of God."

Wife. Mother.

All day he'd been able to put aside the thoughts of Valerie and her spectacularly epic announcement. Frankly, the trip with Pepper couldn't have come at a better time. Being near her made everything else in his life fade from consciousness. Unfortunately, out here in the fresh air, the events of yesterday came crashing in, pushing aside the fun of the last few hours.

Kyle had texted that morning to enjoy the trip—he was taking care of the *other thing*. He actually referred to it as the *other thing* instead of *our mother's possible murder charge*.

His thoughts were interrupted when Pepper bounded down the stairs of the church. "We booked it." Beaming, she dashed across the parking lot and threw herself into his arms. "Pastor Jordan has us on the calendar." His arms wrapped around her waist. She wriggled like an exuberant puppy.

Her ivory skin glowed pink from the cold. Flakes of snow caught in her black hair in an uneven pattern, reminding him of fine lace. He moved his gaze to her red mouth. If only Pastor Jordan hadn't interrupted, he'd know what those lips felt like against his.

Her chest rose and fell against him. A curl dropped over one eye. Keeping one arm wrapped around her waist, he brought his hand to her face and swept the wayward lock away with a dart of his index finger. She flicked the tip of her tongue against her upper lip.

"Rose Red," he mumbled under his breath. That's who she looked like. Rose Red from the fairy tale.

"What did you say?"

"You look like the character Rose Red from the children's story."

The corners of her mouth lifted in a slow smile. "Isn't that the one with the giant bear?"

"I think so." He couldn't remember exactly. "All I know is I was in love with the picture of Rose Red in the storybook."

"I could fall in love with a giant bear," she said. "As long as he was a gentle bear, like you."

"I'm not nearly as furry as a bear."

"I meant the gentle part, not the furry part."

His knees nearly buckled. His arms tightened around her waist. He would get his kiss now, under the falling snow. As before, she tilted her face toward him.

"You're so beautiful," he said as he dipped his mouth to hers.

With perfect timing, the doors of the church opened and out came Pastor Jordan. This time, instead of jumping apart, Pepper started to laugh and rested her forehead against his chest.

They disentangled as Pastor Jordan crossed over to them on his skinny legs and squinted into the dim light. "Still snowing. Weird for this time of year."

"Will we be able to drive in it?" Pepper asked.

"Sure, won't be more than a few inches," Pastor Jordan said. "Heavy snowfall's weeks away. Nothing to worry about."

"Great, we're headed up to the Lake residence tomorrow," Stone said.

"Lake?" Pastor Jordan asked. "As in Ralph Lake?"

"That's right," Pepper said. "We're going to see about renting his house for the reception."

"It'd be a super choice," Pastor Jordan said. "He spared no expense. Perfect location for a family party. As long as you don't mind the ghosts."

"What?" Pepper flinched and moved closer to Stone. "Did you say ghosts?"

Pastor Jordan laughed. "I'm teasing. It was just a rumor spread by the locals to scare the tourists. Not a bit of truth to it."

Pepper's shoulders relaxed. She slipped her gloved hand into his, and he thought he might die of happiness.

"Pastor, any recommendations for dinner?" Stone asked. "Something romantic?"

"Can't go wrong with Simon's Bistro," Pastor Jordan said. "Tell them I sent you. The owners are some of my best parishioners."

They said their goodbyes and hopped back into the rental.

"You don't really believe in ghosts?" Stone asked as they drove away from the church.

"Kind of."

He laughed and poked her in the shoulder. "Not you, Pepper Shaker. You're not afraid of anything."

"That's where you're wrong. I'm scared of ghosts, the dark… and clowns."

"Everyone's afraid of clowns," Stone said. "Even bears like me."

Her curls splayed over her pink cheek when she turned sideways to look at him. "If I had a bear with me, I might not be afraid of a silly clown."

"Bear at your service."

And when she beamed at him with the light of a million stars, he couldn't imagine ever being without her.

12

Pepper

THAT EVENING, at a table by the window, they drank Chianti from tumblers and dipped crusty warm bread into olive oil. Outside, snow danced under the light of the streetlamp. Inside, a candle flickered happily between them. Opera music played in the background. White tablecloths, dark paneling, and sections of exposed brick made her feel as if she were in Italy, not a mountain pass in Colorado.

Pepper drifted to another place—a sanctuary far from her troubles and where everything but Stone Hickman faded from consciousness.

He wore a pair of black jeans and a button-down shirt, rolled up at the sleeves. When he'd come by her room at the lodge to fetch her, his hair had still been damp and combed into obedient lines. By the time the antipasti arrived, those silky strands had dried and now fell over his forehead in rebellious waves. Occasionally he brushed the wayward locks aside with a quick flick of his wrist. However, other than to take a bite of food or to sip from his glass, his gaze never left her. Emboldened by this unfiltered adoration and attention, she chattered on, answering his questions and telling stories of her life.

She told him of the summer she'd spent in Europe with her parents, recalling the apartment they'd rented in Paris and of high-speed trains to Italy, Spain, and Germany. She shared how the trip had changed her perspective and exposed her to art and history and awakened a deep love of historical fiction.

Over the second glass of wine and the pasta course brought by the formal white-haired server with posture like a dancer, she told him the story of her short and unfortunate driving career. He doubled over with laughter as she described the terror on the instructor's face when she hit the poor man. "I decided right then and there that driving was not for me."

"I could teach you. I taught my sister."

"I'd prefer to be driven, thank you very much."

That made him laugh again. "I'll drive you anywhere you want to go."

Their server poured more wine into their glasses as they twisted the pasta around their forks and murmured with pleasure at the explosion of tomato and garlic on their tongues.

"Tell me about New York," he said. "I want to know everything."

She told him about the auditions, waitress gigs, her parts in the chorus of big productions, and of lean days of rice and beans with Lisa and Maggie.

All the while, he listened and listened. She could almost hear him listening.

And she loved it. She loved the feeling of being with this big, easy man. She basked in his attention and felt herself bursting open as if she were a flower too long in the dark. Her petals opened toward him, as though he was the sun.

When the tiramisu arrived, she took one last sip of wine and watched him dig in with enthusiasm. The man could eat. He'd managed to eat his portion and half of hers. It made sense, given his size and the number of calories it must take to fuel those muscles.

"What does a theater major study exactly?" he asked.

She described the program to him in broad strokes: classes in vocal technique, dance, acting, audition preparations, and the more academic study of classic plays and history.

Through it all, he nodded and asked intelligent questions. How did someone become an actress? Was it just talent or could a person learn? She told him about the Stanislavski method she'd studied at school. "The program strips away the layers of protection we develop over the years, breaks you wide open so that you tap into what it felt like when you were a child, before you learned to hide your weakness and pain. Once you tap into your own truths, you use them to convey the emotional life of the fictional characters you play."

"It sounds awful." His brow furrowed as he dipped into a creamy layer of tiramisu. He held his spoon midair. A droplet of cream spilled onto the table. "In a strange way, it's like the marines. During training, you're stripped of everything, tested physically and mentally to the brink of exhaustion. By the time you're through, you're fully indoctrinated into the fold. They made sure we were ready for combat and that we knew how to have one another's backs."

"What was your job?"

"I was an amphibious assault vehicle—AAV—operator. Give me any terrain in the world and I could drive over it."

The pride in his voice hit her right in the gut. She blinked away the sudden tears that gathered in her eyes. To hide her emotion, she took another sip of her wine. "What made you want to enlist?" she asked when she'd gained control.

His face darkened in expression, like a shade snapped shut against the sun. He swiped the spilled cream from the table with his napkin. "It's complicated. Growing up, we were poor. You may not have families like ours where you grew up, but we were those kids with the clothes that didn't fit. We were scrawny because there was never enough to eat. A lot of times we didn't have power because my dad drank up his paycheck. We went to school dirty and in clothes that hadn't been washed for weeks. This will probably be hard to believe, considering how he is now, but Kyle was skinny and weak. Kids bullied him. They called him Pig because of the way he smelled. I'm sure they would've done the same to me, but I was always scrappy and tough. No one came near me. The minute I got big enough, I started kicking the ass of anyone who picked on Kyle. That evolved over time. I started protecting all the kids at school who got picked on, not just Kyle. The bullies backed down, and I loved it. I loved the powerful feeling it gave me, like nothing could break me. I could do something that mattered to other people, that made life easier for the innocent. I've always had this urge to fight. I don't know if it was because of my childhood, or if I was just born this way. Then the marines came to my high school and told me this craving I had to fight could actually be useful. I could serve my country and tame this beast that lived inside me at the same time. Marines are the first ones in, and we go in fighting. We root out evil and take it down." He splayed his hands on the table and hung his head.

"Do you still have the urge to fight?" she asked.

The congenial expression returned to his face. "Nah. Ten years in active service cured me of that. I fought enough. I'm more interested in love now." He grinned. She smiled back at him. His grin was infectious. Her mouth seemed destined to mirror his whenever she let the thing loose.

"Were you ever scared?"

"Sometimes, sure. But our training made us move without hesitation. A lot of times it wasn't until later that I realized how close we were to death." He crossed his arms over his massive chest and grinned. "There were some close calls. My buddies always said I had nine lives, like a cat. Trust me, some events I'd love to forget."

"Wouldn't it be great if we could pick and choose our memories? Think of how free we'd be."

"One of the things they taught us in training was to always keep moving forward, no matter the obstacle."

"That's a good philosophy," she said. "But not always easy to do."

"For other people, maybe. But you're tough, Pepper Shaker, with the heart of a marine. I'm not worried. Whatever you want, you'll get."

They shared another smile, and she felt as though she was in a club of two. Pepper and Stone against the world.

She watched him eat the rest of the dessert, enjoying the way he relished each bite. "Did you ever think about going to college? Like after the military?"

"Nope. Never occurred to me." He shrugged and simultaneously raised one eyebrow. "It seems to me that unhappy people are often struggling to belong in a life not meant for them. The classroom is not for me."

"I can relate. I was a terrible student when I was young. Until I was diagnosed with ADHD and dyslexia, I could barely read."

"No way."

"Yes way."

"But you're an actress. Aren't you all good at English class and deciphering poetry and stuff?"

"I am now, but before they diagnosed me, everyone but my mother thought I was stupid." She flinched, remembering her father's reaction to her report cards.

Stone pointed at her with his fork. "I would've pegged you for the smarty in the front of the class."

She snorted. "Even after I was successfully medicated, I wasn't the smarty in front of the class. The only thing I've ever been good at is being a theater and dance geek. So you're not the only one who hated school. I agree, sitting in a cubicle all day, stuck in a chair, would also be my personal hell."

"We have more in common than you thought." His eyes seemed to dance in his rugged face.

"Don't look so smug. It's very unappealing," she said, laughing. "Anyway, it turned out that my problems led us to the best thing that ever happened. We went to see a respected pediatrician in the area. Dr. Mack. He diagnosed my learning problems and managed to get my mom to fall in love with him in one fell swoop."

"That sounds like a movie," Stone said.

"It kind of was. I fell for him big time, too. He started out as Dr. Mack and I kind of merged the D and the Ack into Dack. He's the most romantic person in the world, like even worse than Lisa. He says he fell in love with my mother the first time he ever met her."

"If your mother's anything like you, I'm not surprised."

"Flattery will get you everywhere, Stone Hickman."

"Good to know."

She continued her story, despite the happy hum in her chest. "Unlike my real dad, Dack's always been in the front row of everything with his recorder in his hand. The last time I saw my biological father, I asked him to come to my sophomore showcase at college. I trekked to his office and asked him right to his face, thinking there was no way he could refuse. He did."

"What was his excuse?"

"He said he'd been to see me in the showcase the year before. I was shocked. I'd had no idea he'd even been there. He said, 'I saw more than enough to know from last year's horrendous performance that you're as untalented as your mother.'"

Stone gasped. "No."

She laughed at the shocked look on his face. "Yes. Dear old Dad's quite the charmer."

"That's awful. I'm sorry."

"I'm not. If he thought that would discourage me, he was dead wrong. It made me want to fight harder for my dreams. Not just to prove him wrong, but for my mother. When she had me, she had to give up on her acting career. My dad doesn't marry the young actresses he seduces. His talents consist of making spectacular musical theater events and seducing young and naive actresses. My mom was just one of many. They met when she had a part in the chorus of one of his musical productions. She was the conquest of 1987, which subsequently resulted in me."

"The year of the Pepper. A great year." He lifted his glass and tapped against hers.

"When he found out she was pregnant, he turned the entire affair into a business deal." Pepper patted her hands together in a gesture of efficiency. "Just like that he had us all packaged up into a monthly column on his expense ledger and sent off to live in the Hamptons. In exchange for discretion about the identity of her baby's father, he gave her a nice allowance." She took a sip of wine, thinking. "My mom doesn't talk about that time much, but he broke her heart and killed her dreams. She'd come to New York from Minnesota at eighteen. At twenty years old, she was offered a role in what she assumed would be the catalyst for her career, and it ended up being the end of it. That said, she never once said she regretted having me. In fact, it was the opposite. She said my birth made everything that had come before trivial and meaningless. She always says I'm the best thing she ever did, which is kind of sad when you think about what a mess I make of things."

"That's somewhat subjective," he said, sounding both gruff and tender at the same time.

"Maybe so, but I have high standards."

"It might help to cut yourself a little slack."

"By the time she was my age, my mom had a ten-year-old. I think about that sometimes and wonder if she's ever resentful."

"Doesn't sound like it."

"Things changed for us when Dack came along." Her voice thickened with emotion.

She picked up her wineglass and reclined in her chair, watching him set aside his dessert plate.

"This has been a damn good first date, don't you think?" he asked.

"It's been a wonderful first date."

"I can't wait to get home and write about it in my journal."

"You don't really have a journal?"

Deadpan, he picked up his glass without taking his eyes from her face. "I totally do. Hello Kitty on the cover."

She burst out laughing. "Hello Kitty?"

He continued with his poker-faced delivery. "I'm wounded. Just because I'm a guy doesn't mean I can't love that little white cat."

"I happen to love Hello Kitty. If you're nice, I'll show you my purse."

Finally, he broke character and laughed. "I've been looking for one of those."

"Had I known, I would've brought it on our trip." She wiped her mouth and set her napkin aside as the server arrived with their check. For the first time, she noticed the place had emptied. They were the only table still occupied. "Have we kept you?" she asked the server.

"Not at all," he said with a gracious tilt of his head. "This is my place. We stay open until the last customers are satisfied."

"You're Simon?" she asked.

"That was my father. I'm Simon the second. It was my pleasure to serve you. It's not every day I get to watch two people fall in love over my wife's cooking."

Fall in love? She flushed and examined her nails.

She reached for her purse, but Stone was way ahead of her. He slipped the waiter a card. "My treat. I asked you, remember?"

Simon retreated with Stone's card.

"Thank you for dinner," she said.

He held her gaze. "There will be a thousand more if I have my way."

Her breath caught. *A thousand more*. Was it possible they might have that?

After Simon returned with their receipt and a plea to please come again while they were in town, Stone helped her into her jacket, zipping it up to her chin as he'd done earlier that day. While she pulled on her gloves, he put on his quilted navy-blue coat. Then they stood in the doorway of the restaurant, smiling at each other like two fools.

"I almost forgot." He reached into his pocket and came out with a white knit hat. "I noticed you didn't have one, so I picked this up for you at the gift shop."

She touched the silky yarn with her fingertips. "Put it on me?"

"Sure." He slipped it on her head and tugged it over her ears. His fingers lingered by the side of her face. "Beautiful. The hat's nice, too."

"Thank you," she whispered.

He broke away and opened the door for her and they exited to the sidewalk. Frigid air immediately froze the end of her nose. The fat flakes from earlier had thinned into flecks of ice. Under her feet, the sidewalks were slick. About six inches had accumulated since they'd first driven into town, but it appeared to have stopped.

They set out toward the car. She walked with care, worried about slipping on the icy sidewalks. Other than her face, she was toasty in her down jacket, thick jeans, and tall boots.

"It's slick. Hold on to me." Stone offered his arm and she took it, snuggling close to his side. Earlier, the street had been lined with cars, forcing them to park four blocks north of the restaurant. Now they took their time, stopping to gaze into dimly lit shop windows. The blanket of snow made the world quiet. Under the awning of a bookstore, Stone halted. He disengaged his arm from hers and turned to face her. For a long moment, he looked into her eyes until she looked away, shy under his scrutiny. He made her feel like a schoolgirl. A giggling hot mess of a girl.

"I've had it bad for you since the moment I first set eyes on you," he said. "Am I crazy to think I have a chance with you?"

Her heart raced. She was grateful for the thickness of her jacket. No need for him to see how hard her little heart was working. She lifted her chin to look up at him. The lights from the display window gave her enough visibility to see the earnestness in his eyes. "Not crazy. Not at all."

He brushed her bottom lip with a gloved thumb. "Now that Pastor Jordan is home with his ovulating wife and cannot interrupt us a third time, should we kiss and see if I'm right?"

"Right about what?"

"That we could light all of New York City with the electricity between us."

She was certain he was right, but she wasn't about to suggest his theory go untested. "A science experiment, of sorts?"

His mouth lifted in a slow, sexy smile. "I was never much for school, but this is the kind of science project I can get behind."

She laughed and buried her face in his chest, unexpectedly overcome with nerves. The slick material of his jacket was both yielding and cold.

"This isn't something I take lightly." His voice had turned serious. "I'd walk the earth three times just to hold your hand, let alone kiss you."

Had anyone but Stone said it, she would have laughed. But he wasn't like other men she knew or had known. He was utterly guileless and transparent—the opposite of the players she'd had the misfortune to fall for in her past.

He wrapped his arms around her waist and spoke huskily into her ear. "It's been a while since I've kissed a woman, but I'm pretty sure it's impossible with your face buried in my jacket."

She tilted her face upward so that he might kiss her.

Kiss her he did, his mouth soft and warm and tasting of

tiramisu and wine. She'd expected a tender kiss, but this was hard and demanding and awakened every nerve ending in her body. She put her hands in his glorious silky hair and kissed him back. Her breath caught when his arms tightened around her, and the kiss deepened, grew more urgent.

When their mouths finally broke apart, he stroked the side of her face, then trailed his fingers over her mouth. "I guess I was wrong. That kiss would light both New York and Paris."

For the first time that night, she couldn't think of a thing to say.

"You scare the hell out of me, Pepper Griffin."

"I didn't think you were afraid of anything."

"I'm afraid of you," he said softly. "Very much so. I'm afraid you're going to break my heart."

"If any heart gets broken, it'll be mine."

He tugged her hat over her ears and kissed her nose. "No one will ever break your heart again if I have anything do with it."

LATER, when she was in her bed, she closed her eyes and replayed their first kiss. And the one after that, stolen by Stone Hickman in the doorway of her room before he gave her a gentlemanly smile and loped off down the hall.

What a day this had turned out to be. She curled into fetal position with her arms wrapped around a pillow. He hadn't asked to come in, and she was glad. As much as she would have liked to have more kisses, she wasn't ready to sleep with him.

Since the assault, her relationship with sex had been complicated. Her last boyfriend had grown weary of her erratic behavior when it came to their physical life. One day, she was fine; the next, memories of that night pushed aside any pleasure. After that boyfriend, she'd had a brief affair with her costar in a play who turned out to be married. She'd had no idea until his wife showed up to opening night. She'd rewarded him with a candlestick prop over the top of his head. The next day, the director had fired her. Men like that always stuck together.

After that last disaster, she'd sworn off men for a year. The year had stretched several months past her promise. Frankly, she'd been happier without the hassles of trying to figure out what the man of the month wanted. They were a lot of work. Curling up at Maggie's with a good book proved to be a lot more satisfying than chasing some idiot simply because she needed validation that she was lovable.

But Stone Hickman was a different man all together. He wasn't like anyone she'd ever dated. She knew even without discussing it that he would wait until she was ready to take it to the next level. Thanks to her friends' big mouths, he knew about the assault. She suspected that made him even more gentle and careful of her feelings.

When she'd told Dack and her mom about what happened, they'd been heartbroken. She almost wished she'd kept it from them. For years afterward, they'd called her every night before they went to bed. Home at holidays, she'd catch them watching her, looking for signs of distress. She'd developed a mask for them as well as Lisa and Maggie so they would believe she was fine. She hated that they worried about her, grieved for her. The men had hurt more than just Pepper. They'd also caused pain to the people who loved her.

Her phone buzzed on the side table. Would it be Stone? Maybe Dack? Sometimes he texted her from the East Coast when he couldn't sleep, knowing it was three hours earlier for her. The man was a texting maniac.

It was Stone. She smiled at the screen.

Hey. You still awake?

She texted back.

Yes.

Just wanted to say good night. And say thanks for the best day I've had in a long time. Maybe ever.

Ever? That seems like a stretch.

Only if you've never had a Pepper Shaker in your life.

She giggled as she typed a response.

You probably say that to all the girls.

Never. Only you.

She sent back a smiley-faced emoji. How did a girl reply to a man so outrageous?

Another text came in from him a second later.

Would you like to meet at nine for breakfast before heading up to the house?

Sure.

Great! Good night, beautiful. XO

Night. XO

She curled back around the pillow and closed her eyes. Minutes later, still smiling, she fell into a sound sleep.

13

Stone

The next morning, after a breakfast at the lodge coffee shop, Stone ushered Pepper into the car. No sooner had they pulled out of the driveway than it began to snow. They drove through town and turned up the mountain road as the sky dumped snow, thick and fast. The flakes were enormous, like an inch in diameter.

Pepper pressed her hands against the dash. "Should we drive in this?"

He'd asked the locals at the coffee shop about the snow warning. They'd brushed his concerns aside. Snowplows were as regular as clockwork, they'd assured him. A guy behind the newspaper had told them that the forecast said that it would snow for about an hour this morning. All clear after that.

So they'd set out, figuring locals knew what they were talking about. He wasn't so sure now.

Pepper wrinkled her nose, her head moving to the rhythm of

the windshield wipers. "These flakes are huge. Like blizzard huge."

"I was just thinking the same thing."

She pulled out her phone. "I'm checking the weather app. Maybe that guy didn't know what he was talking about." A few pecks with her thumbs later, she looked over at him. "It says it will stop by eleven and turn to rain."

"Great. We'll be fine."

They drove another mile through the white curtain of snow, unable to see more than a foot in front of them. He gripped the steering wheel. Despite all the missions where he'd driven an AAV across all kinds of dangerous terrains, he was nervous. Pepper was precious cargo. He swallowed to unplug his ears. How high up did this guy live, anyway? Would they be able to get down the mountain? In the twenty minutes since town, at least three inches had accumulated. This might be a bad idea. *Too late now, dummy. You're halfway up this monster of a mountain.*

Pepper made a little sputtering sound with her mouth. "We lost service. No bars."

He reached into his jacket pocket and handed her his phone without taking his eyes from the road. "What about me?"

"Nothing." She placed his phone in the cup holder between them. "We're almost there, right?"

At this point he was driving about fifteen miles an hour. They hadn't seen another car since town. Did the locals know to stay off the roads? A spasm of fear crawled up the back of his neck.

With his teeth gritted, he continued up the hill. Just when he'd almost given up of ever getting there, Pepper let out a little squeak and pointed out the window. "There's the sign."

"Thank God." He slowed and turned into the driveway. The car zigzagged. He steered out of the slide and spoke reassuringly. "Don't worry. I'm good in the snow."

Pepper stayed completely silent and still with her hand gripping the handle above her door.

Do not let her know you're nervous. He unclenched his jaw.

Driving about five miles an hour, they inched down the driveway. It had obviously been snowing for longer up here than in the lower elevation. There was a good foot of snow on the ground.

Finally, the house emerged. It was massive with thick beams and a long porch, and the roof was completely covered in snow, other than the two stone chimneys. He parked the car in the driveway and looked over at Pepper for the first time since they left. Her skin had leached of color, and she'd bitten off all her lipstick. "You all right?"

"Yes. You did very well. I wasn't at all worried." She gave him a tremulous smile.

He reached over and gave her hand a quick squeeze. "I'm sorry I scared you."

She brushed his cheek with the fingers of one of the gloves. "You didn't scare me. The mountain and snow are a different matter."

"We're here safely. I just don't know how we're getting back down this mountain."

Her eyes widened but she didn't say anything, simply reached down to her lap and tugged her hat over her head.

"Wait there. I'll open your door." When he stepped onto the ground, his boots sank into the soft, dry snow. The thick forest around them was quiet and perfectly still. He caught a whiff of woodsmoke.

After he opened Pepper's door, he offered his arm. "Hold on tight. I don't want you falling on my watch."

She pressed his arm tighter against her side. "I'm a little freaked out."

"Don't worry, we'll be fine," he said as they traipsed across the driveway, sloshing through snow.

"Do you think we can get back to town?" Her voice sounded thin and high.

"I'm not sure." He squinted up at the sky. Several flakes landed in his lashes.

"I hope Mr. Lake's nice," she said. "And doesn't mind a few houseguests."

When they reached the snowy steps to the porch, he dropped her arm and took her hand instead. "These could be slippery."

Once he had her safely on the porch, they took a moment to look back at the yard. At least an inch of new snow already covered the top of his car. He turned away and banged the heavy knocker on the front door. They waited. He knocked again. Another minute passed. No one came to the door.

"Oh, there's a doorbell too." Pepper stepped forward and pushed the button. A loud and rather long chorus of notes played behind the door.

They waited. Still, no one came.

"This is weird." She wrinkled her nose and rubbed her gloved hands together.

"It's also strange that he didn't call back to warn us about the snow." It had obviously been snowing longer and harder here than in town.

"Do you think he's okay?" Pepper asked. "Try the door. See if it's unlocked."

It was. He opened it wide enough to stick his head through. "Hello. Anyone home?"

No answer. He stepped aside so Pepper could precede him. He followed closely behind. She gasped when she saw the magnificent front room. Picture windows looked out to a frozen pond. Soft rugs and comfortable couches and chairs arranged around a stone fireplace invited lazy afternoons and family time doing puzzles.

"There's a fire," Stone said. "He's here. Somewhere." No one left a fireplace unattended unless they were planning on returning.

A tray of cheese and crackers was laid out on the coffee table, as though someone expected visitors. He strode over to the windows and looked out to the yard. A red hat lay in the snow. A thin layer of ice covered the pond. Stone drew in a deep breath. His chest tightened. Had Mr. Lake fallen through the ice?

"There's a hat," he said.

She joined him at the window. "We have to look for him."

Without further discussion, they jogged across the room and outside, where their pace slowed considerably. They trudged through the snow and around the side of the house. Finally, they arrived at the hat. He examined the ice over the pond. There didn't appear to be a crack. He sighed with relief. Stone turned in a circle, scanning the rest of the land. There was a woodshed to the right of the house.

His breath made a cloud in the cold air. "Let's check the shed."

He moved through the snow as quickly as he could, wishing he had snowshoes. When he reached the shed, he called out, "Hello. Anyone here?"

No answer. Pepper arrived, slightly out of breath. "Try the door."

He did so. Locked.

That was when they heard a faint moan. It was the sound of someone in pain. "Hello?" Pepper called out, her voice remarkably loud and resonant.

"Where's the sound coming from?" Stone did another full circle, but the heavy falling snow made visibility dim.

"There," Pepper said. "Do you see?"

He followed her gaze. About a hundred yards from the house, a lump, almost covered with snow, lay prone on the ground. The house had blocked it from their view when they arrived. "It's got to be him. He must have fallen."

Stone set out with wide strides impeded by the snow. He tripped and fell. Scrambling upright, he trudged forward until he reached the fallen man. Faded blue eyes looked up at him.

"Mr. Lake?" Stone asked.

"Yes." He moaned, as if speaking had made the pain worse. "I fell. I think I broke my leg. Hurts too much to get up. I've been out here for hours." Mr. Lake closed his eyes. "I've been praying you guys got here soon." He wore heavy boots and a jacket, but he was shaking, either from shock or cold.

Stone knelt over him. "Don't worry, sir. I'm a former marine. I'll get you inside the house. Which one is it?" He assumed it was his right leg, given the awkward angle of the lower leg.

"Right one," Mr. Lake said. "Shinbone, I think."

"I'm going to do this as gently as possible." He scooped his arms under Mr. Lake and lifted him easily out of the snow. Mr. Lake was a small, slender man. Not more than a buck fifty if Stone had his guess.

Stone took a few steps until Mr. Lake cried out.

"I'm sorry, Mr. Lake. Just hang in there. We'll get you inside and comfortable."

Pepper stood a few feet from him with her gloved hands over her mouth, her eyes wide and frightened. "What should I do?" she asked.

"Go ahead of us and open the front door."

She turned and trudged through the yard on her long legs.

Mr. Lake shuddered in his arms but made no more moans of pain as Stone followed Pepper. It seemed like a mile but was probably only a hundred yards. He took the steps as carefully as he could but managed to jostle Mr. Lake nonetheless. Pepper was there, holding the door open. Stone went through sideways. The last thing Mr. Lake needed was his leg slammed against the doorframe.

"Where's your bed?" Stone asked when they were inside the warm house.

"Down the hall. First door on the left," Mr. Lake said, faintly.

Stone, happy to walk without the cumbersome snow, moved quickly across the broad living room to the hallway. Again, he did the sideways maneuver to get his patient inside.

A king-size bed, a chair, and a large dresser were the only furniture. Pepper had run ahead and pulled back the top covers. Stone placed the broken man on top of the sheets.

"Can you ease out of that wet jacket?" Stone asked.

A flash of pain played across Mr. Lake's face as he pulled one arm, then the other, out of the jacket. Stone reached behind him to slip it off his bony torso.

Pepper leaped forward to untie his boots and gently tugged them off Mr. Lake's feet.

Stone peeled his gloves from his hands and shrugged out of his own jacket. Outside the window, snow continued.

"Should we call 911?" Pepper sneaked another pillow under Mr. Lake's head, then tucked the down comforter around his shoulders.

Mr. Lake grimaced. "There's no way anyone's getting up the road. I didn't figure you two would make it. If I'd been inside, I would've called to tell you not to try. This storm came out of nowhere."

He and Pepper exchanged a look.

"Mr. Lake, on a scale from one to ten, how's the pain?" Stone asked.

"I'd say a seven," he said through chattering teeth.

"Do you have any pain meds anywhere in the house?" Stone asked.

"There's some Advil in the medicine cabinet. And maybe a few pills from my shoulder operation last year." Mr. Lake indicated the door across the room with a point of his chin.

"I'll get them." Pepper sprinted across the room while shedding her coat.

"You have any booze?" Stone asked. "That'll warm you up and take the edge off."

"Sure. Bar in the living room has whiskey and vodka."

Stone left him to search for a whiskey and a glass. He wouldn't mind one for himself, but he needed a clear head. It was up to him to set the man's leg.

The liquor cabinet had glasses and several bottles of whiskey. He poured a generous amount into a tumbler before returning to Mr. Lake.

Pepper had him propped up on some pillows and was just taking a glass of water from Mr. Lake's trembling hand when Stone returned. "I gave him a few of the prescription ones," she said. "They're just really strong ibuprofen with a splash of codeine. My dad's a doctor," she said to Mr. Lake.

"Drink this." Stone set the tumbler in Mr. Lake's hand.

"Don't tell my daughter-in-law." Mr. Lake managed a smile, then downed at least half the whiskey. "She's always lecturing me about drinking and painkillers, like I'm some pill-popping maniac."

"This is a unique circumstance," Pepper said. "But she's not wrong."

The muscles in Mr. Lake's face had started to relax. He drank the rest of the whiskey. By then, he'd stopped shivering.

"I need to take a look at your leg," Stone said. "You all right if I cut your jeans?"

"It's either that or have you yank them off me, and I can't say that sounds super right now," Mr. Lake said. "Not in front of this beautiful young lady."

"Where do you keep your scissors?" Pepper asked.

"There's a pair in the kitchen in the knife rack," Mr. Lake said. "Nice and sharp."

Stone poured Mr. Lake another finger of whiskey and encouraged him to drink it. His patient didn't argue.

"Good call on the booze, son."

Pepper reappeared with a pair of scissors. "Will these do?"

"Sure." Stone took them from her, then crossed over to the window and pulled back the curtain. "How long after a blizzard before they clear the roads?"

"Depends on the blizzard," Mr. Lake said. "But this is Colorado. They're equipped for this kind of thing. Might be a day or two, but it'll happen. Only danger is if it freezes."

He turned back to look at Mr. Lake and Pepper. She'd moved to the chair, still for once, other than clasping and unclasping her hands.

"Do we just wait it out?" Pepper asked.

"No other choice," Mr. Lake said. "We'll be comfortable here. I'm stocked up on food and booze. You two can make yourselves at home while we wait for the snow to stop and then the plows to make it up here."

Stone drew back the covers and set to work cutting the jeans off at the knee. He muffled a curse at the sight of the broken fibular bone pushing against the skin of Mr. Lake's skinny shins.

"How bad is it?" Mr. Lake asked.

"I've seen worse," Stone said. "I'll put a splint on it until we can get you to a doctor."

"Do you know how to do that?" Pepper asked.

"Sure. I had a lot of training in the military for this kind of thing." He flashed her a smile and flexed his hands together like an athlete preparing for a weight-lifting competition. "I have many talents you don't yet know about."

"I'm sure," Pepper said.

Mr. Lake guffawed, albeit faintly. "You two mind curtailing the flirting until after you've got my leg in a splint?"

Pepper laughed as she went around the other side of the bed. "How about I flirt with you instead?"

"That's a splendid idea," Mr. Lake said with an impish smile.

Pepper perched on the side of the bed and returned Mr. Lake's smile. Stone chuckled to himself. The old man would forget everything else if she kept looking at him like that. "Would you like to hear about my role in a movie?"

"You're a movie star?" Mr. Lake asked.

"Not a star, but I've been in a movie. Do you want me to tell you what it's like?"

"I do. How many takes before you get the finished product? I've always wondered about that."

"Well, that depends. Some of my costars in this thing were awful…like excruciatingly bad." Pepper launched into a full story about her time on set. Between her melodic voice, the painkillers, and the booze, Mr. Lake seemed to be in a lot less pain. In fact, he seemed to be enjoying himself. Who wouldn't? Pepper was the greatest painkiller a man could have.

She was the greatest.

"Do you have kindling for the fire anywhere?" Stone asked.

"In the basket by the fireplace," Mr. Lake said. "My maintenance guy always leaves a big stack."

After assuring Mr. Lake that everything would soon be fine, Stone left the room to fetch a piece of wood. The fire was almost completely dead, so he stuck a few logs on top of the last of the burning embers. When he returned to the room, Pepper was sitting on the other side of the bed next to Mr. Lake pressing a cloth against his forehead.

"Everything all right?" Stone asked.

"I thought it might feel good to him to have a warm cloth on his forehead."

Mr. Lake nodded. "This darling girl is just what the doctor ordered."

"She doesn't like it when you call her a girl." Stone winked at Pepper.

She flashed him a sassy smile. "I don't mind if Mr. Lake calls me that."

Mr. Lake patted her hand. "We have an understanding, Pepper and me."

"I leave my girl with you for a minute and you're already making your move," Stone teased Mr. Lake.

"Apparently, she likes a man with a little more experience under his belt." A dreamy expression had smoothed Mr. Lake's features.

Pepper sparkled up at Stone. "What can I say? I love Mr. Lake's house."

Mr. Lake closed his eyes and mumbled, "It's considerably prettier with you in it."

The drugs were doing their job. Mr. Lake would soon be asleep.

"You lose power around here?" Stone asked Mr. Lake.

"The power could go out?" Pepper asked with a slight elevation in vocal pitch. She removed the cloth from Mr. Lake's forehead.

"Happens sometimes," Mr. Lake said. "I'm surprised a city boy like you knows that."

"I'm not a city boy, Mr. Lake. The town I grew up in was smaller than this house."

"I knew there was something I liked about you." Mr. Lake trailed off, then began to breathe evenly.

"This is good. Won't feel a thing now," he said to Pepper.

"You sure you don't need me?" Pepper hesitated at the end of the bed.

"I'd rather you not see this," Stone said.

"You're my hero." She leaned down and gave him a kiss on the cheek. With that, she left the room and Stone got to work.

14

Pepper

Pepper hurled one log, then another on the fire. Once they caught, she paced around the living room, wiping imaginary dust from vases, running her fingers along the books on the tall shelf, and turning the television on and off using the remote she found on the square coffee table. The television worked, at least. When they'd been outside, she'd spotted a satellite dish. If the power stayed on, at least they'd have some connection to the outside world. This venture up the mountain had thus far been nothing short of terrifying.

Although he hadn't said so, she could tell the condition of the roads and the lack of visibility had spooked Stone. He drove in that blizzard like a rock star, but his white knuckles gave him away. Pepper was accustomed to snow, having grown up in the Northeast, but was not at all familiar with narrow mountain roads in the middle of a snowstorm with no cellular coverage.

She shuddered to think what would have happened if Stone hadn't proven to be such a capable driver.

Another tremor passed through her at the thought of elderly Mr. Lake outside in the snow with a broken leg. How much longer would he have survived out there had they not come along? She had no interest in being in a real-life *stuck in the wilderness* adventure. Those were better in the movies.

She'd been relieved to leave Stone to do the splint alone. There weren't many things that rattled her. No one auditions for theater directors once a day for a decade and remains frightened of much. However, being stuck on a mountain in the middle of a blizzard scared her. She also couldn't stand the sight of anyone in pain. Mr. Lake was putting on a brave front, but he wasn't a good enough actor to hide the flashes of pain that tweaked his face. The last thing she wanted was to witness Stone fixing the splint.

She picked up her cell phone, hoping for a signal. No bars. Was this always the case or was it the blizzard? If it was always this way, Mr. Lake must keep a landline up here or he wouldn't have been able to call them earlier. She scanned the room once more. No phone. She moved to the kitchen and found one on a corner desk. Thank God.

She picked it up, praying for a signal, and sighed with relief at the buzzing sound. How long had it been since she'd heard that sound? Even her mother had gotten rid of the house phones and gone exclusively to cellular.

Pepper dialed Lisa's number first. She'd had the same number for twelve years, so she had it memorized. It rang a few times before Lisa picked up, sounding wary. "Hello?"

"It's me," Pepper said.

"I thought it might be when I saw the area code. Why aren't you calling me on your cell phone?"

"Do you have a minute? Because it's a long story."

"Yes, I'm in my trailer waiting to be called to set. Rafael went to get us lunch."

She conveyed the adventure of the last twenty-four hours. "Stone's in the bedroom putting a splint on Mr. Lake's leg. There's no way we're getting out of here anytime soon."

"I knew this was a bad idea." A sigh and then high-pitched groan—both sounds of Lisa fretting—were clear despite the miles between them. Pepper could almost see her pacing around her trailer with the phone pressed to her ear.

"It's a great idea. The blizzard's only a minor setback. Wait until you see this house. It's perfect for your wedding weekend." As she said all this, Pepper walked back into the living room to check on the fire. The logs had caught and were burning nicely, casting a cheery glow into the dim room. "Plus, we're totally safe here. There's even a fireplace in case the power goes out."

"The power? But you're afraid of the dark."

A fissure of fear broke through her resolve to remain brave. "Yeah, I know. Let's hope it doesn't come to that."

"Is Stone taking good care of you?"

"Totally. He's like lumberjack marine guy." She told Lisa about how he'd kept them from sliding off the road and how he'd lifted Mr. Lake from the snow and carried him inside the house. "Now he's in there putting a splint on his leg like it's something he does every day."

"Wait a minute. What's going on? Your voice is different. Oh my God. You're falling for him."

"Don't be ridiculous."

"You are. You're falling for him. I know that voice, all husky and giggly at the same time."

"Maybe a little. It's kind of impossible not to." Pepper glanced toward the hallway. How was he doing in there?

"I knew it. I knew it." Lisa sounded way too smug for Pepper's taste.

"You knew what?" Pepper asked.

"That if you could get past the whole military thing you would see how special he is. How kind. And smart."

"And funny. Not to mention solid and strong and just everything anyone could want."

"Right?" Lisa sniffed.

"Are you crying?" Pepper asked.

"Maybe a little. I can't help it. I'm just so happy."

"Don't get ahead of yourself. We've only been on one date. Plus, I'm no good with men. You know I'm not."

"It doesn't matter. The games we had to play with other guys aren't relevant when it's the right man. And Stone's like Rafael. Real. No games. They're not like the guys we knew in New York."

"For one thing, they're not actors," Pepper said.

"Right. Shoot, they're calling me to set. You guys stay safe and warm…and cozy."

"Very funny. Could you drop a text to my mom and let her know my phone isn't working? I don't want her to worry."

Lisa agreed before they said goodbye.

After she hung up, Pepper returned to the kitchen and set the phone back in its cradle. She rested her elbows on the countertops and looked around the rustic but high-end kitchen. Her mom would love the light granite countertops paired with dark walnut cabinets. An island in the middle of the kitchen had room for eight to sit comfortably. She traced her finger along a streak of gold in the granite, imagining Lisa and Maggie here with their families. All the kids would be running around playing while Lisa and Maggie made dinner together. Rafael and Jackson would be in the other room talking about sports or politics or whatever it was men spoke of to avoid intimacy. After dinner, the families might play board games around the fireplace.

Could she see herself in that scenario? Try as she might, she couldn't think of being there without cringing in embarrassment. The mooch. The crazy aunt who wasn't really anyone's aunt, just Mommy's weird friend who always showed up at holidays like a stray cat. She did not fit in the pretty picture with her friends and their families. In under two years, everything had changed. They were no longer the glossy, gorgeous trio out for a night in New York. Her friends had moved on and grown up, and here she was yearning for a time that no one wanted to return to but her.

The day had flown. Outside, the light faded with every passing moment. Soon it would be dark. Should she get dinner started now? She wasn't exactly the domestic type. The last time she'd made anyone a meal was...well, never. Lisa cooked for them back when they were in New York, or they ordered takeout or picked up something from the frozen section.

She opened the refrigerator, pleased to see it well stocked with fresh meat and vegetables. Even with her limited skills in the kitchen, they wouldn't starve.

Under the island, the glow of a wine refrigerator caught her eye. She opened one side and pulled out a bottle of white. Surely Mr. Lake wouldn't mind if she opened it? He didn't seem the type to begrudge a guest an adult beverage, especially since they'd rescued him from the snow. She found an opener in the drawer above the cooler and had just popped the cork when Stone appeared.

"Hey now, there's an idea," Stone said. "Now that I've got the patient splinted and he's fast asleep, I'd kill for a beer."

"There are some in the main fridge," she said. "Bottom shelf."

He opened the doors of the refrigerator and made a low, appreciative growl before coming up with a beer in his hand.

She handed him the bottle opener. He thanked her and popped the top with a practiced flick of his wrist. Instead of drinking from it, he left the bottle on the island and crossed the room to ease a wineglass from where it hung over the counter.

"Classy place." Stone poured a nice-sized portion of wine into her glass. "Mr. Lake is all fixed up and sleeping soundly."

"Do you think he'll be all right?"

"Sure thing. We'll take him to the hospital the minute we can get out of here. They'll put a real cast on him. He'll be fine."

"I hope it stops snowing soon." She looked away from him to

the windows. Outside lights had come on, illuminating the falling snow.

"Don't worry. I'll keep you safe." He reached for her hand and pulled her to him. "You were spectacular today."

"No, I was a full-on hot mess from head to toe," she said.

"From my view, you were cool, levelheaded, with extra credit for distracting the patient with your charm and beauty."

She placed her hands palm-down on his chest. "You were nothing short of phenomenal yourself."

He kissed her until she was dizzy and almost staggered out of his arms. Being here with him was dangerous. She hadn't thought of it until just now. One thing could lead to another here. A fire, wine, good food, and not even a phone to distract them. Anything could happen. She disentangled from his arms. "This is weird, right? Snowed in together after only one date?"

"I'll be a perfect gentleman. I swear."

"Good. I think."

He laughed and pulled her toward him. But instead of kissing her, he wrapped his arms about her waist and lifted her onto the island. "You say the word, Pepper Shaker. I'll go at your pace."

"Even if it's slow? Like hare slow?"

His expression sobered. He tugged playfully on one of her curls. "You lead. I'll follow."

She wrapped her legs around his waist. "Are you hungry?"

"I'm starving."

"You want to play house with me and make dinner?"

He lifted his eyebrows and gave her a sultry, searching look that set her on fire. "Playing house with you sounds like the best offer I've ever had." He lifted her from the counter and set her on her feet. "What do I do?"

She scooted across the kitchen to the refrigerator and pulled out a package of ground beef and a few potatoes. "How about hamburgers?"

"Nothing sounds better."

She set the package of meat on the counter. "I've seen you slap patties together for Sunday-night dinners."

"On it." He rolled up the sleeves of his flannel shirt, then washed his hands at the sink.

She handed him the dish towel hanging from the oven door.

He thanked her with a peck on the lips. "Playing house is fun so far," he said.

She found a skillet in one of the drawers and placed it on a burner on the large cooktop. "This looks like a good pan. Right?"

He laughed as he ripped open the package of ground beef. "Do you not cook?"

"I know nothing."

"Let's try not to burn down the house. We have enough trouble." He divided the meat into four sections and started pounding together a patty between his large hands.

She tore her gaze from the bulging muscles of his forearms. God did a particularly good job on Stone Hickman. Everything about him was bigger and brighter, more vibrant than other people. What would it be like to have him in her bed, to learn every inch of him?

"Hey, Pepper Shaker, you all right?"

She jumped. "What? Yes, I'm fine."

"Good. You looked a little flushed for a minute there."

Just picturing you naked. Nothing to worry about.

"I was wondering how to make the potatoes," she said.

"Cut them up into little pieces and put some oil on them? Lisa made them that way once." Stone sprayed a layer of oil into the frying pan. "I have a limited repertoire, and hamburgers happen to be on the list." He twisted the red knob of the cooktop, and a flame leaped to life. He set the frying pan over the heat. He waved the spatula at her. "Get to work, young lady."

For the next few minutes, Pepper bustled around the kitchen while Stone fried the burgers. She turned the oven on and cut up potatoes, then tossed them in oil before spreading them on a cookie sheet. She poked around the refrigerator and found a head of lettuce, a tomato and a jar of pickles.

Soon the kitchen filled with the aroma of frying meat.

"That smells amazing. I'm starving," she said.

"I guess traipsing around the yard in the snow burns a lot of calories."

She settled onto one of the counter stools with her wineglass.

"Did your family have dinner together when you were growing up?" Stone asked.

She jerked her head up, surprised by the question. "Most nights, I guess." Evenings had just been the three of them. Often, they ate together in front of the television watching old movies. Dack had taken her education of film very seriously. "We liked to eat and watch movies together. My mom isn't much of a cook, but she can pick up takeout like a boss."

"That sounds nice. The watching movies together part." He made a sound somewhere between a snort and a laugh. "We were lucky to have food, let alone a movie."

"Oh, Stone."

"Ah now, don't give me that sad face." He patted his chest. "I'm all big and strong and well fed now."

For the next ten minutes, as she cut up the lettuce and tomatoes and Stone cooked the burgers, she asked him questions. By the time the burgers were done, she'd learned that he'd played football in high school, worked as a bag boy at their local grocery store, and had his first kiss in Ellen Moore's hayloft with Patti Newman. He'd also shared how the three Hickman siblings had worked as a team to take care of one another after their mother left. Stone was the woodcutter and roof fixer, while Kyle worked after school and managed the bills. Autumn cooked and cleaned. When she asked him about his mother, he changed the subject.

With the spatula in one hand, he crossed his arms and regarded her from across the island. "This playing house thing is super fun."

"Other than poor Mr. Lake and his broken leg, I'm enjoying myself immensely."

"I'll check on him after dinner," Stone said. "But I suspect he's out for the count."

She moved to the window. Thick snow continued to fall. She watched an individual flake as it traveled to its destiny, then another, then another.

The alarm for the potatoes beeped. She opened the double doors of the upper oven. A waft of hot air pushed against her face. The heat could melt the mascara off her eyelashes. However, the potatoes looked crispy, just like Lisa's. She looked around for an oven mitt and found one by the cooktop.

She reached in and began to pull the pan out, but the doors weren't open wide enough, and she touched her wrist to the side. Instant pain. She yelped and thrust the baking pan onto the granite countertop.

Stone rushed to her side. "Are you all right?"

"I burned myself." She rushed to the sink and turned on the cold water. Holding her wrist under the stream, she cursed under her breath.

Behind her, he sprinted to the freezer and yanked open the door. "Here's an ice pack." He moved over to where she still had her arm under the cold water. "Sweetheart, let me see."

Sweetheart. It was such a nice word, especially out of his mouth and directed at her. She allowed him to take her arm and put the ice pack on the singed skin. Basking in his attention, she barely felt the burn.

"Hold it on there for me." He turned back to the oven and shut the guilty doors.

"It's not bad," she said. "It was stupid. I should've opened the doors wider."

He took her by the uninjured arm and steered her toward the table. "You sit. I'll bring your food."

She followed his directions. The man was good in a crisis.

He picked up the empty plates and hustled over to the cooktop, where he'd assembled the burgers and buns. "I decided to let you put the ketchup on yourself. I'm assuming the amount is a very personal decision.

"I should've warned you about those doors." He set her plate down in front of her.

"Warned me? How would you know I'd do that?"

"I didn't, but still, I'm supposed to be taking care of you."

"Despite your obvious desire to save the world, some of us cannot be helped. My burn is not your fault."

He tilted his head, seeming to consider her as one might an interesting but strange zoo animal. In the dim evening light, his eyes were the color of a deep mountain lake on a clear day. "Do I seem like I want to save the world?"

"Maybe it's just me you want to save?"

"You, Pepper Shaker, don't need saving. You're fierce." He returned to the island and arrived back at the table seconds later with a bottle of ketchup and his plate. When he sat, she set aside her ice pack, anxious to eat.

"Let's chow." Stone took a good-sized bite out of his burger. After chewing for a moment, he grinned. "That's darn good." He chuckled as he pierced a potato chunk with his fork. "For two people who don't cook, we did pretty well."

She smiled back at this giant man who attacked potatoes with as much gusto as he did the rest of life.

"Although I happen to like everything spicy. As a matter of fact, I need a little pepper sauce for my burger."

In two long strides, he was at the refrigerator and leaning into it, displaying his fine rear. He might not be the designer-jean type of man, but the ones he wore hugged his muscular butt just fine. "Score. He has my favorite." He held it up for her to see. Pepper sauce. Dack loved the exact same one.

"You're not really going to put that on your burger?" she asked.

He sat back at the table. "No, but it's going on my taters ASAP."

Pepper ate another few bites of her burger while watching him enthusiastically sprinkle pepper sauce on his potatoes. She might add spice to his life, but he added fun to hers.

The lights went out, and they were plunged into a darkness so thick that everything, including Stone, disappeared and it was nothing but the black, quiet night and the thumping of her heart between her ears.

"Stone." She blinked furiously, as if that would magically return her sight.

"Don't worry, sweetheart. I know where my phone is. We can use the flashlight to find some candles. Stay put."

As if she was going anywhere. She shivered. "Hurry."

She heard his footsteps and a second later, a thud. "Ouch."

"Are you all right? Stone?"

"Yeah, I'm fine. Miscalculated where the island is, that's all." His voice sounded far away.

"Is it there? The phone?" She swallowed against the panic.

"Not yet. It's here somewhere. I'm just feeling around for it." A second later, he uttered a triumphant exclamation. "Got it." The glow of the phone immediately illuminated his face in ghoulish contours. He fiddled with it for a moment before the flashlight feature lit up the room.

He crossed around the island to where she sat at the table, trembling.

She stood and threw herself into his arms with such force that he staggered backward a few steps before tightening his arms around her waist.

"It's all right. I'm here," he said.

Her arms clamped around his neck. "Don't leave me. I'm terrified of the dark."

He kissed the top of her head. "Don't worry, Pepper Shaker. I've got you."

"Will you stay close to me?" she whispered.

"Every minute until the lights come back on."

15

Stone

WHEN STONE WAS A KID, the power went out in their trailer on a regular basis. Not because of an act of nature, but because paying the electric bill wasn't always the priority it should have been. His father's management of the household funds was not as strong as the whiskey in his glass. When the power went out in Mr. Lake's house, he didn't even flinch. Nothing a few candles and a roaring fire couldn't solve.

However, his current companion did not appear to share his assessment of the situation. He could feel her quickened pulse beat at her neck as he held her. She was shaking, and her voice sounded like the beginning stages of hysteria. He didn't want to think too hard about the reasons why. For now, he would focus on reassuring her and keeping her physically close.

Her grip on his hand as they slowly crossed the room endeared her to him in a whole new way. As much as it pained him to witness her palpable fear, it made her even more precious to him. Although he suspected this quality made him a Neanderthal, he liked being her hero.

She was a beautiful bandit stealing his heart in unforeseen and immeasurable increments. He had no doubt they would survive the snowstorm. With or without power, they were safe from nature's harsh elements here in the house. It was his heart that would suffer from exposure. He would never be the same after a few more days alone with the complex woman next to him.

"Should we find some candles?" he asked. The flashlight was surprisingly bright. He loosened his grip to get a better look at her.

She stared up at him and blinked. "Yes. A lot of them. We need tons of candles."

"But first, let's take Mr. Lake some dinner and make sure he's all set for the night."

"Yes. He might be scared all alone in there," she said.

He doubted Mr. Lake was afraid, but he kept that to himself. "Hold the phone up for me so I can see what I'm doing."

She pointed the light over the cooktop while he put together a dinner plate for Mr. Lake. When he finished, he smiled in what he hoped was a reassuring way in Pepper's direction. She sent one back to him, but he could tell her heart wasn't in it.

"Keep hold of my hand. I'll lead the way."

She placed her icy fingers in his. With the aid of the flashlight, they easily made their way out of the kitchen and into the living room. He stopped them at the fireplace. Flames had died down, and the logs burned bright orange. He suggested they put another few pieces on in order to light and heat the room. She let go of his hand long enough to toss several more on top of the others but was right back with her iron grip the moment the task was done.

Pepper remembered her phone was in her purse by the door. They grabbed it for the extra light and headed down the hall to their patient.

Mr. Lake was awake and sitting up in bed reading from an e-reader. Dim light from the screen cast shadows across his face when he looked up at them. "Howdy there, lovebirds. Is that dinner I smell?"

"We thought you were asleep, or we would've brought you dinner earlier," Stone said.

"Strangely enough, the power going out woke me up." Mr. Lake set aside his Kindle and held out his arms for the plate. "A burger sounds mighty fine. Thank you very much."

When Pepper asked in a worried voice about candles, he assured them there were ample battery-operated lanterns in the hall closet and to take as many as they needed. In addition, they learned there were three bedrooms on the first floor and another three upstairs, as well as a third-floor loft with an additional four beds. Mr. Lake said there were extra toothbrushes and toothpaste in the same closet with the lanterns, along with towels and soaps, and to take what they needed. Stone asked if he wanted another pain pill. Mr. Lake said another after dinner might do the trick, but would Stone help him get over to the bathroom first?

It took a few minutes, but Stone successfully escorted him over to the bathroom to do his business. They gave him another pill and filled his water glass. When he was comfortably back in bed, Pepper kept Mr. Lake company while he ate. Stone left them to grab the lanterns from the hall closet.

They were essentially camping lanterns and would be quite useful for their needs. He set one next to Mr. Lake's bed and turned it on with an easy flip of a switch. Although dim, it was adequate to light the room.

Stone could already feel how the house had cooled. Mr. Lake verified his suspicion that the heat was powered by electricity.

"Would you like extra blankets?" Pepper asked when Mr. Lake was done with his dinner.

He patted the top of his down quilt. "Not necessary. These down comforters hold heat. You'll be warm and toasty all night. Other than your head." His weathered face crinkled as he smiled. "Nights like this have me wishing for a nightcap like the olden times."

Pepper took the blankets from Stone and placed them on the end of the bed. "Well, just in case, we'll leave these here."

"Is there anything else you need?"

"Not a thing," Mr. Lake said. "I'm going to read and then get some sleep. You two enjoy the rest of the night. I won't hear a thing."

Won't hear a thing? Was he referring to the sounds of sex? He glanced at Pepper, feeling awkward. If she was blushing, it wasn't visible in the dim light.

Stone turned on two of the lanterns and set one on each table on either side of the couch. With these additions and the roaring fire, the room seemed like any winter's night. A romantic one, at that.

She wrapped a throw blanket around her shoulders and sank into the couch, looking small and frightened. His heart twisted in his chest.

He sat next to her and stroked her hair. "You okay?"

She nodded and reached through the folds of blanket to cup his face. "It's a silly thing. I'm fine. Just stay close." Her eyes darted around the room, as if she expected a monster to jump out of the shadows.

"You want a drink?"

"Is there any scotch?"

"Scotch?" He wouldn't have guessed Pepper for a scotch drinker. Then again, the woman was an exercise in juxtaposition.

"Neat. And make it a generous pour." Her voice still sounded shaky, despite the lanterns' light and her reassurance that she was now fine.

He kissed her cheek before hustling over to the liquor cabinet. There was a decent selection of booze, including scotch. Not one to disobey a woman's request, he poured a three-finger portion for her and for himself.

She thanked him for the drink, then took a deep sniff and made a throaty groan of appreciation before taking a sip.

He sat next to her and tried not to wonder, what besides scotch could make her moan with pleasure?

"I must seem ridiculous to you," she said as she swirled the amber liquid in her glass.

"Not at all. I think it's sweet. And, not that I'm proud of it, but I like being your hero."

She smiled a little wickedly at him. "You like being my hero?"

He brushed her mouth with his finger. "It's the role of a lifetime."

"You're very good—very authentic."

"I have a very special and talented costar," he said.

He had no intention of telling her how much he was enjoying himself. With or without power, there wasn't much better in life than being here with her. Sure, the power outage wasn't ideal, especially because it scared Pepper. However, having her all to himself without interruption? That was a dream come true. They'd get out of here tomorrow, most likely, and get Mr. Lake to a hospital. For now, he had every intention of soaking in as much Pepper as he could.

"Stone?" she asked with her gaze still dipped toward her drink.

"Yeah?"

"I can't sleep alone. Not in a strange house in the dark. You'll have to stay with me."

"Stay with you?" Surely he'd misheard her.

"I'm serious. I'll freak out if I'm alone with nothing but that lantern." Her usually centered voice had dissolved into the pitch of a frightened child. "I need you to stay with me, but I'm not ready to take this to the next level."

"Sweetheart, I'll be wherever you need me to be. Of course I will. And I promise to be the perfect gentleman."

"We could stay in the loft."

"The loft." He put space between the two words. "Not one of the bedrooms?"

"There's probably bunk beds and stuff in there."

Oh, right. He understood now. The loft would feel safer to her. "I always wanted to go to summer camp." He used his teasing, goofy voice, understanding how hard this was for her—how vulnerable and exposed it must feel to be trapped on a mountain with a man she knew wanted her. "But no ghost stories."

"Ghosts are not as scary as some people," she said softly.

This woman broke his heart. "I know, baby."

She looked up at him, the red glow of the fireplace reflected from her smoky eyes. "Not you. You're not scary to me. But I...I need time."

"I'll be here when and if you're ready." He stroked her hair once more, marveling at the softness of her curls. She tucked her chin into her neck and closed her eyes. Her eyelashes were long and thick. The lashes of an innocent. A sigh escaped as she pressed her cheek against his hand.

"A woman like you is worth waiting for."

"Do you mean that?"

"I'm not perfect, but I'll never lie. Especially when it comes to how I feel about you. I've been waiting a long time to meet someone like you."

She sipped from her glass without looking at him. "I've had boyfriends in the past."

"As much as I'd like to pretend that wasn't true, I assumed so. I've had relationships too. It's not like we're teenagers."

"Right, true. But there's something I need to tell you—about sex. About sex and me." She halted, clearly unsure of what to say next. "Sex has been only physical, like a sport or game. Emotion or love doesn't factor into the equation. It's the only way I could think of it after what happened."

"Pepper, what happened, exactly? What did they do to you?" His heart ached at the way her shoulders slumped forward. She hung her head, and once again her curls robbed his view of her face.

"Hey, it's all right. We can talk about anything else. The weather, for example." He tucked her hair behind her ear. His chest tightened as tears swam in her eyes. Damn, the woman was stubborn. She took in a deep breath and clenched her teeth. He could almost hear her pushing the sadness away with the strength of her will. Did she ever allow herself to cry, or did she swallow tears and shove aside deep pain? Was that why she moved through life like a spinning top?

When her tears had disappeared under the command of her grit, she twitched her lips upward in a dim smile and shook her black curls. "We have to talk about it. At least this once. I need you to know what happened. Otherwise, you won't know who I truly am." She continued to stare into her lap but placed one of her hands over his. Her voice quieted. "It was on the subway. Late, past midnight. It was the night I went to see my father. The night he told he wouldn't come to my showcase. I was devastated, which, considering what came next, is ironic." She stopped and took in a deep breath. "I was upset and felt reckless. I stopped into a tavern where I'd worked the summer before. The bartenders would slip me a few drinks even though I was underage. I was tipsy by the time I headed to the subway. I had my headphones in, listening to music and not paying attention. Suddenly, they were just there, trapping me in a corner. Four of them. All dressed in navy whites. One of them raped me. Before the others could, the police came. A witness called 911."

He realized he'd been holding his breath and let it out slowly. His stomach clenched as the truth rocked through him. Rage like he hadn't felt since Autumn's accident surged through him. He would kill them if he could. Make them suffer first. What did he say? How could he let her know how sorry he was, how he wished he could take it all away? There was nothing to say or do, no way to save her from violence that had already happened. "God, Pepper, I'm so sorry."

"It was hard. And it made me hard." Tears, at last, fell down her cheeks.

"I know, baby." He wiped her face with the cuff of his shirt, wishing that the exercise of drying her tears would make her pain subside. His was a futile desire. Nothing could change the past. Even love couldn't erase what those men had done to her.

"Do you know what I've learned in therapy?" She sniffed and wiped her eyes. "The one thing? That no matter how deeply and well my mother and Dack loved me, everything good they did was wiped away in one night." Her voice had dipped to a smidge above a whisper.

The ways in which she'd unfolded her layers tonight overwhelmed him. He'd liked her clever and sassy persona, but this vulnerable woman in front of him was complicated and precious and so very lovable, none of which he'd been prepared for. With every minute that passed, his heart increased piece by piece, and Pepper filled every one of them. By this time tomorrow, she would be the only thing he knew, the only thing he wanted.

"I'm telling you this so you understand why I want to wait," Pepper said. "With you, everything's different. I want it to be different. I feel things for you I haven't felt before. Things I can't explain. A connection, I guess." She raised her eyes to him. "Do you feel it too?" She laughed and sobbed at the same time. "Maybe I should've asked that first."

"Yes, yes. I feel it too. Isn't it obvious?" His chest hurt with the surge of love that opened him, changed him, made him feel heroic. *He* was special to her. *Him.* Stone Hickman. How could this be? Only moments ago, the possibility of his affection being returned had seemed improbable. He'd hoped, of course. Oh, how he'd hoped. He had vowed many times over the last few days that he would do his best to win her heart. But he was an ordinary man. Not rich or slick or even handsome with his rugged face and calloused hands. Yet now, as Pepper's exquisite gray eyes softened into a hazy blue, he understood that she believed in them, too. Something extraordinary was developing between them. A love worth fighting for? Believing in? "I learned a long time ago that the best things in life are worth waiting for. I'll wait as long as you need me to."

"It won't be forever."

"I'll never pressure you. I promise." He smiled. "But know this—I'm crazy about you. Nothing will change that."

She touched his face with her fingertips. "You're not like any man I've ever met."

He kissed her, gently. "You're one of a kind too, Pepper Shaker."

They were quiet for a moment, looking at the fire.

"What about your dad?" he asked. "Did you see him again after that?"

"No. His rejection was all mixed together with the other thing. I vowed never to see him again, and I haven't."

"Do you miss him?" Stone had an image of Kyle in the months after their mother left standing at the window, watching and waiting for their mother's return. Even years later, when they were teenagers, he caught Kyle standing there. Still waiting. When had he stopped looking and hoping?

Her mouth twisted. "No, not anymore." She jutted out her chin in that way he'd once interpreted as haughty but that he now knew was a defense mechanism, like a signal to her brain to remain tough and unmoved. "Obviously, I was a slow learner, but I'm a stubborn, hard thing when I decide something. That was it. He called a few more years after that to arrange my birthday lunch. Or, rather, his secretary called. I didn't return the call. After a few years, he stopped calling."

The logs flickered and sputtered as the flames died down, as if telling them if it was time to retire. The room had cooled as well. "Let's go upstairs and get ready for bed," he said. "It's getting cold."

She agreed. "We'll have to do the dishes tomorrow when it's light."

He laughed. "I'd forgotten about the dishes."

"And I'm the messy one?"

"I *did* see the contents of your suitcase," he said as he helped her to disentangle from the blanket.

"Lisa and Maggie torture me about my messiness. I think people should accept me for how I am."

He rose to his feet and offered his hand. "I accept you as you are."

She kissed his cheek. "You're a true gentleman."

Pepper carried both lanterns so he could take the borrowed toiletries and towels. They climbed the first set of stairs and then another to the loft.

He couldn't help but smile when they entered the loft space. It was a kid's paradise. Four nooks with double beds were built into the slanted ceiling space at one end of the room. A pool table took up a large portion of the other end, along with a dartboard and shuffleboard. A plump L-shaped couch was arranged around a large-screen television. There was also a bar area with a bistro table and barstools.

"Is this heaven?" Stone asked as he set his pile of toiletries on the table.

Pepper handed him a lantern and turned in a full circle. "I'm just happy there's a bathroom. I won't have to go downstairs in the dark."

"Can you imagine how much fun it would have been to stay here as a kid?"

Pepper's eyes sparkled in the lantern light. "I'm imagining how fun it's going to be right now."

"Right?" He noticed the beds were doubles built into nooks, giving whoever slept in them a sense of privacy. Perfect for a bunch of cousins. Or for a couple who wanted to take their physical relationship slowly. "You were right. This loft is perfect for us."

He wandered over to the window positioned under the slanted ceiling on the other end of the room and held the lantern against the glass. At least two feet of snow covered the roof. Would they ever get out of here? Did he even want to?

"Did you know I'm a pool shark?" Pepper asked from behind him.

He turned from the window. "Is that right?"

She'd placed her lantern on the pool table and was over at the bar area pouring them both another drink. "You want to play? It'll be a little challenging without much light."

"I'm in."

Stone figured out how to hang the lanterns from the funky wood chandelier over the pool table. Pepper had been right that the lighting situation made the game more challenging. The shadows played tricks on his eyes. Not that better lighting would have helped his game. Turned out, Pepper had not lied about her pool-playing abilities. She killed him in back-to-back eight-ball matches. He suggested they play nine-ball, hoping to redeem himself. Redemption did not happen. She ran the table.

He leaned against his pool stick and shook his head. "You didn't even give me a chance to sink one ball."

"I didn't make the rules." She shook her dark curls in that way that made his blood run hot.

"You've damaged my fragile male ego."

She rolled her eyes as she lifted her glass in a mock toast. "Your ego seems unflappable."

He poured himself another drink, feeling loose. Hanging out with Pepper was way too much fun. He was in trouble. So much trouble.

"Seriously, how did you learn to play like this?"

"Dack," she said as she flopped onto the couch. "That's how we bonded when we first moved in with him. The poor man. He was almost thirty-five when he met my mom. He'd never been married before and had no children, not even a niece or nephew. And then, enter Pepper from stage right."

"He was lucky to have you."

She brushed her hair away from her forehead and rose to her feet with one hand planted into the arm of the sofa, as if she felt a little unsteady. "It seems like a week ago I last brushed my teeth."

He laughed. "Me too."

She picked up one of the lanterns and grabbed a towel, toothbrush, and toothpaste from the pile. "I'll just be a minute."

While she was in the bathroom, she sang softly under her breath. Smiling at the lovely tone of her voice, he stripped down to his boxers and undershirt. After that, he opened a few cupboards until he found extra blankets. He put one on each of their beds, then took the lantern with him to the window and peered out at the falling snow. Still coming down in droves.

Would it ever stop?

16

Pepper

PEPPER CAME out of the bathroom with a scrubbed face and clean teeth. She was still dressed in her jeans and sweater and figured she'd sleep in them. She wished she had her flannel pajamas with the candy cane pattern, sent to her last Christmas by her mother. Since she was a little girl, Pepper's mother had bought matching pajamas for them and Dack. Last year had been no exception. She was certain to send them this year as well. An image of Stone with her family at Christmas, wearing a pair of matching pajamas, flashed through her mind. She smiled at the thought. With his easygoing attitude and good sense of humor, even if they were in a pattern of cheesy Santas, he would gladly wear them. He might even propose a photograph in front of the fireplace, reveling in the idea of family traditions because he'd grown up without them. Sentimental. Family oriented. Sweet. Like her stepfather. She put that thought aside for now.

Stone stood by the window, inches from the glass. In profile, his face with its long, pointed nose and stern jaw appeared almost regal, like a playful yet brave son of a king, not yet forced to take command of a country, but ready when called. A worried sigh bunched his shoulders. How the heck did a man in a pair of boxers and a T-shirt look that sexy?

He turned to face her. "Hey."

"Hi." Pepper patted the arms of her sweater. "I can't tell you how much I wish I had my Christmas pajamas with me." She told him about the tradition of the Christmas pajamas. "We open them Christmas Eve, and my mom always acts like it's a surprise when we all know what's in the box. Then she makes us put them on and we all watch Christmas movies until midnight."

His expression grew wistful. "That's a nice tradition."

"As long as you don't mind cheesy patterns."

"I'd wear them and get a photograph," he said.

She'd predicted that one.

"If you're all done, I'll use the bathroom before we turn out the lights." He moved away from the window. His bottoms hung low on his hips. The thin T-shirt clung to his lean, muscular stomach. This was what Stone looked like before bed? She averted her eyes, shy. They would be sleeping just feet from each other. Was this a good idea? She shivered, imagining herself downstairs alone in one of the bedrooms. She'd be shaking like a leaf and fully expecting a monster to jump out of the closet.

Her concerns must have shown on her face, because he crossed over to her and planted a kiss on her head. "Remember, no pressure. I'm a gentleman for as long as you need me to be."

She dropped her forehead onto his thick chest. "I know."

"I'm sure it feels weird to be sleeping in the same room."

"A little, yes," she said into the fabric of his shirt.

"And you're just a little shy. Which I find very sweet." He kissed her head again and let her go.

The moment he was inside the bathroom, the cold crept in under her clothes.

She carried the lantern into bed with her and set it in the alcove that served as a bedside table. Leaving the light on, she snuggled under the down comforter. The sheets were cold against her hands as she pulled the covers up to her neck. Her feet, however, were toasty, encased in thick socks. This bed was like a cocoon, small and enclosed. The way a sleeping space should be. She yawned and nestled further into the soft mattress, like a happy cat in a box.

She listened to Stone's heavy steps and the occasional creak of the floor, then the whir sound of him brushing his teeth and finally the clink of the toilet's seat cover. Stone, her very own hero. His performance as leading man in what could have been a tragic day had been stellar. There wasn't even a hint of hesitancy or fear during any of the myriad crises they'd encountered. He didn't flinch when she did her crybaby move when the lights went out and begged him to sleep with her.

The dark. She'd never been afraid until the night on the subway. Since then, she was afraid of what she couldn't see. Would there be someone lurking around a corner or under a bed? No place was safe in the dark.

The door to the bathroom opened. Stone crossed over to the beds with the lantern in his hand. "You look snug."

"I am," she said.

He threw her a kiss. "Good night, Pepper Shaker."

"Night."

The lantern threw shadows across his face as he left her. On the other side of the wall, the wood creaked from his weight. She heard him moving around before letting out a big sigh. "This bed feels better than it should." His voice came through slightly muffled.

"We had a long day."

"Will you be warm enough?" he asked.

"My nose is cold but the rest of me is fine."

"Duck your head under the covers. That's what we did when we were kids," he said.

When they were kids. Without heat. Or enough food. She ached for that little boy.

"Do you have any photographs of when you were little?" she asked.

"Autumn may have one or two. We weren't a picture-taking family."

"Do you snore?" she asked.

"No way."

"We'll see about that," she said, chuckling.

"Do *you* snore?"

"I'm much too ladylike."

His laugh penetrated the wall between them and nudged into her heart. It was a low, deep rumble that seemed to originate from his belly and made her feel as warm and cuddly as the comforter she was currently burrowed under.

Scratch, scratch, scratch. She sat upright. What was that? It was coming from the wall next to her bed. She tensed, listening for it again. *Please don't come again.*

It did.

Was it the sound of tiny feet scurrying up and down the wall? *Rats. Oh God, rats.*

"Do you hear that?" Her voice sounded high and tinny between her ears.

"Um, yeah."

She clutched the comforter to her chest. Why had she turned off her lamp?

Silence and then the sound of the tiny, disgusting feet came again.

"It's rats. There are rats in the wall right next to me," she said.

"They can't get to you. They're in the wall."

Did he sound amused?

"How do you know? What if there's a hole?" She shuddered and reached for her lamp. With her fingertips she felt for the switch and turned it on. She blinked as her eyes adjusted to the light. "Stone?"

"Yeah?"

"I'm coming over to your bed."

Dead silence, except for the scurry of little feet. Oh my God, she hated rats. Rats in the dark were even worse. She wouldn't be able to see them if they decided to crawl out of the hole and eat her face.

"Stone, did you hear me?"

"Yes, I heard you. Come on over."

She crawled out of the bed and crossed over to his nook. By the time she reached him, he was sitting up. And yes, he looked quite amused.

"It's not funny." She handed him the lamp and crawled on top of the comforter until she reached the pillows. He'd scooted to the far side of the bed, but was so large he took up at least three-quarters of the mattress. She slipped in beside him and rubbed her fingertips down the wide-planked wall. Would the rats come over here or stay on the other side of the stairwell?

"Why in God's name do they make empty walls?" she asked.

The lantern shook when he laughed, and made a pattern on the ceiling. "They may have eaten through the insulation. That happens sometimes."

She shuddered again, then turned on her side to watch him. "Which means they could totally eat my face."

"I'll protect your face at all costs." He held the lamp up. "Are you ready for me to turn this off now?"

"You have to stay close to me."

"It's impossible not to. This is a small bed for a guy like me, even without a girl in it." He set the lamp on the shelf next to the bed and turned it off. "Not that I'm complaining. I love having you here." His husky voice might be the end of her resolve.

She blinked into the darkness. Nothing. She couldn't see a thing. Her nose worked just fine, however, and it smelled the spicy, clean scent of Stone. Additionally, her sense of touch seemed to be fully functioning. She felt the weight of Stone as he settled next to her. The heat from his skin warmed her own, even without touching, distracting her from the killer rats not feet away.

From what she could tell, he was on his back. She remained on her side, hoping to catch a glimpse of his profile in the dark. Still nothing. How could it be that even without sight, she was so keenly aware of him?

Would her sense of taste be as tuned in as her other senses?

God, her mind was in the gutter.

"Pepper?"

She jumped at the sound of her name. "Yes?"

"Do you understand you're torturing me?"

"What do you mean?"

"We're in a very small bed and you're the sexiest woman in the history of the world. Do I need to say more?"

She sighed with pleasure at the compliment. What had happened to her resolve to remain strong? "I'm sorry, but I can't sleep over there by the rats."

The bed moved as he let out a sigh, and he must have rolled to his side because she felt his breath on her neck. "It's so dark." He shifted slightly and his arm brushed her left breast. "Sorry. I can't tell exactly where you are."

Desire flooded through her. Was it the whiskey or the dark or just this man and his inconsiderately fantastic-smelling neck?

"Are you okay?" he asked. "Is this freaking you out?"

"No. I'm not freaked out. I'm...a...I'm feeling things I probably shouldn't."

"About me?" he asked.

She could feel his smile even if she couldn't see it.

"You smell really good," she said. "And you're warm and big."

"You're soft and little." He chuckled, and her heart ached in the most exquisite of ways. "And *you* smell like the best thing God ever made."

She scooted next to him and found his mouth with hers. They kissed as he rolled onto his back, taking her with him. "I wish I could see you." She propped herself up with her hands on his shoulders and straddled him.

"Pepper." His voice was quiet, a warning.

She kissed him again, then trailed her mouth down his neck. Her hands found their way under his shirt.

"Is this what you want?" His hands wrapped around her legs. "Are you sure?"

"I'm sure." They kissed again. He rolled her over so his tall, hard body covered her. His fingers worked their way up her waist to brush her breasts. She arched against him.

"Your skin…it's so soft." His lips were on her neck, spreading fire. He unzipped her jeans and tugged them off her legs.

She laughed as she wrapped her bare legs around his waist. "I'm sorry there's no lace or sexy underwear."

"I wouldn't be able to see them anyway."

"Help me out of my sweater." She lifted slightly.

With one fluid tug he had her out of her top. By the time she'd lain back against the mattress, he'd done the same with his clothes.

She moaned. "Make me forget all about those rats."

And he did.

17

Pepper

Pepper opened her eyes to the sight of white wainscoting. The room was quiet, unnaturally quiet. She was naked under a thick down comforter. The spot between her legs throbbed, and her limbs ached. Stone. Her and Stone. Glorious, mind-blowing Stone. Stone and sex. Lots of sex. No, that wasn't right. It was not just fun, satisfying sex. They'd gone to another level of intimacy, one that included her mind and heart and body. He'd done it. Broken through to a part of her she feared had been killed on that night when her innocence had been robbed.

She smiled and stretched under the covers. What was this feeling? She was full, as if she'd eaten a good meal. Her body hummed the way it did after a great dance workout. And her mind was as quiet as the snowy world outside the house. She was happy. This was what it felt like to feel completely content. In love. She was in love.

She looked over to the windows. Sunshine streamed through

the glass. She caught a glimpse of blue sky through snow-covered trees. The storm had passed. She rolled over and there was Stone, just visible in the early-morning light. Stone. He slept on his side with his arms in front of him. The lines around his eyes smoothed in sleep and made him seem vulnerable and young. His dark hair sprang up from all directions. A scratch on his neck from her fingernail hinted at their antics from the night before. Morning stubble covered his chin, making him look rugged and tough, although his peaceful breathing told another story.

She wanted to touch him but kept her hands to herself and watched him breathe instead, remembering the conversation in the darkened room.

They'd made love for the first time, a feast of limbs and bodies and whispers of devotion and admiration and this utter honesty. She'd been cracked wide open and filled by him.

Afterward, she lay half sprawled on top of him with her head on his chest and his arm tucked firmly around her shoulders.

"You've told me about that night—the thing you didn't want to talk about. I'm humbled and grateful you trust me with it."

"Me too," she whispered.

"Now it's my turn. If you're to truly know me, I must tell you the story of my family," he said.

"I'm listening."

He told her more about his mother's departure and his father's breakdown and the ways in which the Hickman children had suffered from poverty and bullying. "One day, I took care of the Miller boys by beating the crap out of them. But we paid for it. We paid dearly."

She listened in horror as the story unfolded of the Miller brothers and their revenge. He shared the details of Autumn's accident. In a halting voice, he told of how the horrible brothers had chased them on a rainy afternoon and nearly killed Autumn.

"Kyle felt it was his fault. He disappeared. Changed his name. The only way we knew he was alive is that he sent money. Twelve years went by, and it was like our mother's abandonment all over. Like no one we loved would ever stay. A few years ago, Autumn found Kyle. We went to see him and worked through it all. Even though we didn't understand how he could blame himself and disappear, we forgave him. We decided to move to Cliffside Bay and be a family—to make up for lost time. Autumn finally was able to move into her new house and start her job. We've all been so happy together. Kyle's wife and family have become our family. The children are a second chance to live the childhood we would've wanted."

"A happy ending." She kissed his hand. "You guys made it through."

"I thought so, but something's happened." He told her about the deaths of the Miller brothers in a house fire. It had been determined an accident, but he'd always worried it had been set by his father. "But it wasn't him. It was her."

"Her?"

"My mother. Do you remember the day you saved me?"

"Yes."

"She had just approached me on the street. I hadn't seen her since I was six years old, and there she was. When we sat down with her, she told us what really happened to the Miller brothers. It was her. She did it, not him."

Pepper's body tingled with horror.

"This is my family. My mother's a murderer. And now she's back, and we're trying to help her."

She held him as tightly as her limbs would allow. "Why didn't you tell me before now? I've been spilling my ugly secrets."

"It's the dark. It gave me the courage to tell you. I didn't want to see your face when I told you the truth about my family. Because if you'd looked at me in disgust, it would have killed me."

"I would never look at you in disgust." She pressed against

him. "I understand about shame. I do. But you don't ever have to feel shamed with me."

"This is my family, Pepper. This is who I am."

"No, no. You're Stone. One of the good ones. The best one." She spoke urgently, determined that he understand. "You're the man I love."

His body went completely still. "You love me?"

"I do. I was wrong about everything. I understand now how it happened with Rafael and Lisa. You and me—we're supposed to be together. We're supposed to love the shame away."

"Yes, maybe."

She smiled in the dark and played with the hair on his chest. "Now it's your turn. You're supposed to tell me how you feel."

"I've always been better with my hands and body. How about if I show you how much I love you, adore you? How about if I leave absolutely no doubt that I've waited for you all my life and all I want to do is make you happy?"

"Those words did the trick, but if you feel the need to punctuate your meaning with another round, don't let me stop you."

He rolled her over and kissed her and then did exactly what he'd promised.

Now he stirred and opened his eyes. A split second of confusion, then shock crossed his face before joy spread over his face. "Pepper. You weren't a dream."

"No, baby. I'm not a dream. I'm real."

"Did it stop snowing yet?" He yawned as his eyes flitted to the windows. "Is that sunshine?"

"Yes. Sadly, we might have to go home."

He reached for her under the covers, his eyes somber. "No regrets?"

"Not one. You?"

"Not one." He smiled as he pulled her closer. "You're beautiful in the morning."

"So are you."

For the next hour, they made love in the light of day with the sun splashing yellow, and Pepper no longer remembered the darkness that had brought them together.

Around nine that morning, the electricity came on. By that time, Stone had already checked on Mr. Lake and helped him to the bathroom. Pepper showered and dried her hair, then made coffee and prepared scrambled eggs and toast. Stone had gone outside to investigate and get some wood for the fire. When she had everything ready, she took a tray to Mr. Lake's bedroom. She knocked softly on the door. He called for her to come in.

Sitting up in bed, he had the television remote in his hand. A news program played on the screen. "I thought I smelled breakfast."

She set the tray over his lap and then helped adjust the pillows to make it easier for him to sit up straight. "Are you hungry?"

"Famished." He grinned as he spread a teaspoon of blackberry jam on a piece of the sourdough toast. "The news said the whole area was hit but that this particular area got the brunt of the storm."

"We had no idea it would get bad so fast," she said with a shiver.

As Mr. Lake ate his breakfast, they chatted about the unlikely blizzard and the feasibility of renting the house for a December wedding.

"It's a bit of a crapshoot," Mr. Lake said. "Now if they wanted to wait until the summer, we'd be a sure bet. I'll tell you, though, in all honesty, the weather yesterday was a real fluke. Normally we see it coming."

See it coming? What good would that do if it ruined Lisa's wedding? If everyone was stuck in the house on the day of the wedding and unable to get to the church, it would be a disaster. Lisa's dream of having it here was becoming less and less appealing. She would go home and advise Lisa and Rafael to stick with plan A. The small church wedding and reception at Dog's Brewery might be exactly the thing to do. She walked over to look out the window. Sun sparkled off the snow and the frozen pond. Tree branches bowed like graceful ballerinas. "It's so pretty."

"Yes, it is. Tell me about your friends and what kind of wedding they want."

While he ate his breakfast and took sips of coffee, Pepper told him of Lisa's discovery of the town and church all those years ago.

"I felt compelled to come check it out for her. But then we found out there's no way the lodge could accommodate them. And then we ran into the storm here. So now I'm not sure this is the greatest idea."

"I can understand why. But if she decides she wants to rent out the house, just let me know. I'll give you guys a deal since you and your burly fellow saved my life."

"I love this house."

"People have been known to fall in love here."

"So I've heard." She blushed. *I'm one of them.* "Why do you want to sell?"

"Since my wife died, it just feels right to sell it. This was her dream house. We had a lot of good times together here, but it's painful to be here without her. I miss her every second of every day."

"I can understand, but it's such a wonderful place. Aren't your children interested in keeping it?"

"We only have one son. Philip. He never cared for it here. More of a city kid, that one. He works in high tech. Silicon Valley. Never takes a vacation."

"What did you do, Mr. Lake?"

"You ever hear of Murphy's Burgers?"

"Sure. They're all over the Midwest, right?"

"That's correct. I opened the first one back in 1960. I was

twenty-two years old and didn't know I could fail miserably. I didn't, though. This may surprise you, but there's money in burgers."

"Stone's going to die when I tell him he made a hamburger for the owner of Murphy's."

"Tell him I approved wholeheartedly." His eyes narrowed as he regarded her from his bed. "You look a sight better than you did last night."

"The sun and power returned, improving my mood considerably." She took the tray from his lap and set it on the table by the door.

Stone arrived, pink-cheeked and rubbing his hands together. "I have good news and bad news."

"Tell us the bad news first," Mr. Lake said.

"There's no way we're getting out of the driveway anytime soon. There's about four feet of snow trapping the car."

"And the good news?"

"The phone's working. I called the local hospital and they're arranging for a helicopter to lift us out of here."

"I have always wanted to ride on a helicopter," Mr. Lake said.

"What about the rental car?" Pepper asked.

"I called the rental company and explained our situation. They'll send someone to get it once the roads clear."

"What about the money? That'll cost a fortune," Pepper said.

"No, they said they'd eat it, given what happened," Stone said. "We will need to figure out how to get back to Denver, though."

"I know just what to do," Mr. Lake said. "Leave it to me."

18

Stone

The medical helicopter arrived around noon with a great flurry of snow and the deafening sound of its engine and rotors. When Stone had spoken to the medical team earlier, they'd debated the best place to land the helicopter and had decided on the flat patch of land between the pond and house. Stone had shoveled most of the snow from the back patio and stairs. He'd also shoveled a walking path from the bottom of the steps to the middle of the yard and marked it with red hand towels from the kitchen. The pilot descended perfectly between the four red flags. Stone watched as the helicopter hovered inches above the snow, then landed on what looked like enormous skis. The door opened, and two men dressed in orange ski gear and snowshoes exited. One of them reached back into the vessel and came out with a stretcher loaded with a pile of blankets. With each man holding an end of the stretcher, they made their way toward him.

When they reached the bottom of the steps, they introduced

themselves as Nelson and Brooks. "Nice path," Brooks said. "Mr. Lake was lucky to have a former marine, huh?"

"I guess so," Stone said with a laugh. "Come on inside."

Pepper had Mr. Lake sitting in a chair with his splinted leg propped up on a stool just inside the patio doors. Nelson and Brooks quickly got him onto the stretcher and tucked blankets around him.

Pepper leaned over him and gave him a peck on the forehead. "We'll see you at the hospital."

"Will do." Mr. Lake smiled at her and then Stone. "Thanks for everything, kids."

"The pilot will be back for you two within the hour," said Brooks.

"We'll be ready," Stone said.

Mr. Lake's son was on his way from California and would arrive sometime that evening.

Stone and Pepper held hands and watched from the window as they loaded Mr. Lake into the helicopter. Minutes later, they were gone in a spray of snow and roar of the engine. They waited by the window until the sound of the rotors finally faded, leaving them in the silence once more.

"This has been an adventure. I'll say that," Pepper said. "But I'm pretty excited to go home."

"Can't say I disagree. Although if I had to choose someone to be snowed in with, it would always be you."

Pepper laughed and threw her arms around his neck. "You sure know how to show a girl a good time."

SEVERAL HOURS LATER, after making sure Mr. Lake was comfortably settled at the hospital, they returned to the lodge.

The doctors had advised Mr. Lake to stay overnight. He was elderly, and they wanted to keep a close eye on him. Tomorrow, if the roads were cleared, his son would take him home to Denver.

One of his nurses mentioned what a splendid job Stone had done on the splint. "You saved him from a whole lot of trouble there."

Pepper had beamed up at him, and he felt like a rock star.

She'd called the lodge earlier to let them know what had happened and asked if they might be able to help them get a new car rental. They'd assured her it was no problem and were glad they were safe.

The moment they walked into the lodge, Mindy flew across the lobby and hugged them as if they were her long-lost friends. "I was worried sick. When you didn't return yesterday afternoon, I knew something was wrong. I was picturing you stuck somewhere in the middle of that blizzard and freezing to death. Then the news reported about the power outage on the mountain. When you called this morning, I felt like I could breathe again."

"We arrived before it got too bad, and it's a good thing we did," Stone said.

Mindy's eyes widened with horror when Stone told her what they'd found when they arrived.

"Poor Mr. Lake," Mindy said.

"He's fine now," Stone said. "His son will be here this evening."

Mindy looked from one of them to the other with an excited gleam in her eyes. "Strangely enough, I have other news. The couple booked for December called this morning and canceled their wedding here. The storm scared the bride's mother." Mindy smiled. "So that block of rooms and the reception space is now available for your friend if you want it."

"Thank God," Pepper said. "Because there was no way I could recommend Mr. Lake's house. Not after what we experienced."

"I guess the storm was a blessing in disguise?" Stone asked.

"As my mother used to say, 'All's well that ends well,'" Mindy said. "Come on back. We can get it all booked."

THEY WERE JUST WRAPPING up with Mindy when she got a phone call from Mr. Lake. "He wants to treat you to a week here at the lodge, plus meals. Can you stay?"

Stone looked over at Pepper. "I can. How about you?"

"Unless my agent calls with an audition, I'm all yours."

Mindy watched them for a moment. "Mr. Lake's house did its magic, didn't it?"

Pepper flushed. Stone laughed.

"Should we get your wedding booked while you're here?" Mindy asked.

"No offense, but I think we might prefer somewhere warm," Stone said.

For the next seven days, they spent a large portion of time in bed enjoying each other. They slept late and ordered room service for breakfast. The afternoons were spent exploring town or going on hikes in rented snowshoes. One night, they went to a movie in town and ate popcorn and laughed over slapstick comedy. They dined out at Simon's two out of the seven nights, but branched out to several others as well, coming to the conclusion that Emerson Pass had a lot of good restaurants.

And they talked and talked and talked. Stone learned about Pepper's dreams. She wanted a theater of her own where she could produce plays about women, and a juicy role in a movie or television show she could sink her teeth into. He read this Hedda Gabler play she was so crazy about, which he only vaguely understood. She laughed at him when he said he would have liked it a lot better had it not ended in a suicide. In reparation, he made her listen to country music. One day, he caught her singing one they'd listened to earlier in the shower. It was uncanny how quickly she could pick up on a song.

He told her how he wanted a big family and a happy home like Kyle. They dissected the situation with his mother and concluded that Kyle was right. There was no way they could abandon her when she needed them.

He learned more about Pepper's biological father and what a giant jerk he was. He also heard many stories about her mother and Dack, and almost danced a jig when she asked if he'd like to meet them soon.

He was in love. Plain and simple.

Pepper Griffin was his unicorn and his rainbow and every single good thing in this world. There was no one he'd rather have next to him when the sky rained canned peas.

19

Pepper

AFTER A WEEK and several days away, Pepper let out a sigh of relief when their plane landed in San Francisco. They'd left that morning from Emerson Pass and driven to Denver on clear roads. The flight had been without incident, other than being crammed in a row of three with Stone and an even larger man with a pregnant-sized beer belly. She'd been stuck in the middle with nowhere to put her arms, other than in Stone's lap. Which was just fine with her.

As they taxied to the gate, drizzle fell from a gray sky. When they reached the gate and waited to exit, Pepper turned on her phone. Immediately, the screen flooded with notifications. There were half a dozen voice mail messages, one from a number in New York, one from Lisa, another from Pepper's mother, and one from her agent. They'd only been on the plane for three hours. She sighed and held up her phone to show Stone. "Back to reality."

Stone frowned as he reached into his pocket and pulled out his phone. "Mine's buzzing like crazy too."

She squeezed his hand. "We can turn them off when we get home—pretend we're back in Colorado."

He flashed her a wolfish grin. "We can call it 'Colorado time' from here on out."

"It'll be our code word at parties for when we want to go home." She leaned closer and whispered in his ear. "And ravish each other."

His eyes sparked. "Great idea."

She turned back to her phone. Curious about the call from New York, Pepper listened to that one first.

"Hello, Pepper, this is Arthur Freidman." It was a deep, resonant voice. His precise speech indicated breeding and wealth and someone important and self-confident. "I'm not sure your father ever mentioned me to you, but I'm his attorney. I'm terribly sorry for your loss."

Her stomach fell to the floor. Loss? Who had she lost?

"Although I worked for your father for thirty years, he was somewhat elusive about his personal life. I had no idea he was ill until I got the call from his assistant this morning. The last time I met with him was a little over six months ago when he came in to talk to me about the details of his will. It was then that I learned of your existence. He gave precise instructions about his wishes, some of which concern you. It's my understanding you're in California now, and I apologize for the inconvenience, but I'll need you to come to New York so that I can discuss the details of your inheritance."

Inheritance? The bastard had left her money? No, it wasn't possible. Maybe a pittance? Or a cruel reminder that he found her untalented and uninteresting?

The voice mail from Arthur continued. "If it is at all possible, I'd like to meet with you at your earliest convenience. Please give my offices a call so we can arrange a time." There was a slight pause before he spoke again. "I'm aware of the nature of your relationship with your father and that perhaps your first instinct would be to forget this call. However, without saying too much over the phone, it will be worth your efforts to make the trip. I'll look forward to hearing from you."

She hung up and stared at the screen, numb and confused. Her father was dead and had left her something in his will. How were either of those things possible? She tried to remember how old he was but drew a blank. He'd been at least twenty years older than her mother, who was only fifty, which would make him early seventies. Not young, but not old enough to die.

"What is it?" Stone asked.

She looked over at him. "My father died. That was a voice mail from his attorney. He left me something."

His eyebrows raised. "Your father? How?"

"I don't know. He didn't say." She remembered her mother's voice mail. "Hang on. I need to listen to my mom's message."

As she'd suspected, her mom's message was about her father's death. She didn't come right out and say it, but it was obvious. "Pepper, honey, call me when you land. I have something important to tell you."

"My mom," she said to Stone. "I'll need to call her right away."

By now it was time to leave the plane. She would have to wait. On shaking legs, she stumbled into the aisle with her bag pressed against her stomach. Her heart thumped hard in her chest as she followed the person in front of her off the plane and into the gate. Stone guided her with his hand on her elbow away from the existing crowd. When they were in a quieter area, she collapsed into a chair. Stone sat next to her as she called her mother.

"Hi, sweetie," Mom said. "Did you get my message?"

"Yes. I already know. His attorney called. He left me something in his will. I have to go to New York to meet with him."

"He left you something?" Her mother's voice sounded unnaturally high, like she was trying to hold it together.

"Apparently."

"I'm amazed," Mom said. "I saw it on the news this morning. That's how I found out. He died of congestive heart failure."

"Heart failure." How ironic. His heart had failed a long time ago. She glanced at Stone. He was bent at the waist with his elbows resting on his knees. She let her head fall onto his shoulder as she wrapped up the phone call. "I'll call you when I know more," Pepper said.

"I love you," Mom said.

"Love you more."

"Do you want to call the attorney now?" Stone asked in his gentle, thoughtful way.

She nodded and pushed the call-back button. An administrative assistant answered.

"Hi, yes. This is Pepper Griffin for Mr. Freidman."

"One moment, please."

Seconds later, Mr. Freidman's voice came through. "Pepper, thanks for calling."

"Sure. Your call came as a shock. I had no idea he'd died."

He responded with a second of silence before he recovered. "I'm very sorry. As his only child, I assumed you would know already."

"My mother saw it on the news, but I was traveling this morning so my phone was off."

"You weren't in contact with him personally then?" he asked.

"I haven't talked to him in over a decade."

Another few seconds of silence passed before he answered. "I thought that might be the case."

"Are you sure I'm his only child?" she asked with a wry smile at Stone. "The man had a habit of bedding young actresses." Maybe that's what did in his cold heart.

"You're the only one he mentioned in his will. Other than that, I can't say I'd know either way. As I indicated in my message, I didn't know him well personally."

"Is there a reason you can't just tell me what he left for me over the phone?"

"He was very specific. We are to meet in person."

"All right. I'll try to get a flight out in the next few days. When I have something arranged, I'll call you."

"Thank you. I'll look forward to meeting you in person."

She hung up and looked over at Stone. "I have no idea what to do here. What to think."

He straightened and met her gaze. "Do you want to fly out now? You could buy a ticket on the next flight to New York."

"Get it over with, you mean?"

"The longer it's hanging over your head, the worse it will be."

"True."

"I'll go with you. If you want."

She stared down at her hands, trying to focus on his question. Her mind whirled and buzzed in confusion and shock. Her father was dead. He'd left her something. She tried to picture herself going alone to the attorney's office. New York was her town. She could do it by herself, but having Stone with her made the whole idea bearable.

"What about work?" she asked.

"I can take a few more days." He took her hand into his lap. "That's the beauty of being self-employed."

"I'm embarrassed to admit it, but I don't know if I can go without you."

"Don't be embarrassed. This is how it works. When you're weak, I'm strong."

His steady sweetness penetrated through her shock and cleared her mind. "As long as you're sure you can leave again, then yes, please come with me."

He leaned close and gave her a quick kiss. "Come on then. Let's get some tickets to New York."

"Shouldn't we get our bags first?"

"Good call."

PEPPER SAT NEXT to Stone in a New York taxi, headed to Mr. Freidman's office on the Upper East Side. The streets were busy with cars, all pushing and plodding with honking horns and gas fumes. Crowds of people inched their way up the sidewalks, most with phones in their hands even if they weren't looking at them. She glanced toward Central Park and wished she were here with Stone to have fun. She would show him all her favorite places and take him for a drink at the Irish pub that had been her hangout with Lisa and Maggie. They could go to the Theater District and look at all the marquees, and she could tell him which ones she'd performed in and which she wished she could.

"You okay?" Stone asked.

"Sure. Just nervous."

He picked up her hand and held it on his lap. "It'll be fine." He looked handsome in his new blue button-down shirt he'd insisted on buying for the meeting.

"The shirt looks good," she said. "Matches your eyes."

"Have I told you how beautiful you look?" he asked.

"I believe once or twice." She leaned against him. Her Stone.

She'd decided on her red wrap dress and black boots. They made her look polished and serious. For luck, she'd worn her charm bracelet. Not really understanding why, she'd done her makeup carefully and fussed over her hair until the moment they had to leave or risk being late. Impressing the attorney was stupid. Her dad was dead. The outcome of today's meeting was predestined. Still, she wanted him to see that she was a put-together young woman, not some money-hungry leech only interested in her father's money. The whole thing was funny, really. It wasn't as if she'd ever impressed her father when he was alive. Most likely, her presentation this morning would not have impressed him either.

She hated him just as much now as she did when he was alive.

She also loved him just as much.

She hadn't even fidgeted much on the way, although now, as they pulled up to the building, her feet twitched inside the leather boots. A voice in her head screamed—*run*.

She didn't. Instead, she took Stone's hand and let him help her out of the car. They walked together through the glass doors of the building and up the elevator to the eleventh floor.

The offices of Green and Freidman were posh with sleek furniture and polished marble floors. A few splashes of red were the only color in an array of gray. An attractive young man named Jason greeted them and offered them a beverage. She declined. Her nerves were too jumpy to hold a cup without spilling.

Jason escorted them back to Arthur Freidman's office.

Arthur stood when they entered the spacious office. With a view of the Manhattan skyline from picture windows and thick leather furniture and a mahogany desk, it didn't take much of a guess as to how much this man billed an hour.

The man himself was as sleek as his offices. Tall and slender, he wore a graceful dark blue suit. His face was unlined and cleanly shaven. Only his short, perfectly styled salt-and-pepper hair hinted that his thirty years of service to her father was possible.

"Great to meet you." He shook both their hands and motioned for them to follow him to a round table on the other side of the office. They did so. Pepper folded her damp hands together under the table. Her heart raced as she waited for him to begin.

"Thanks for making the trip out here." Arthur Freidman reached for a pile of folders from the middle of the table and fixed intelligent, restrained eyes on her.

With considerable effort, she held his gaze. "Mr. Freidman, you made it hard to say no."

"Please, call me Arthur."

She nodded in agreement.

Arthur opened one of the folders and pulled out an envelope, then slid it across the smooth surface of the table. "This is a letter he left for you."

She stared at the envelope for longer than socially acceptable, as if she might leave it and walk out the door. She slid her gaze to Stone. He gave her a reassuring smile and wrapped his hand over her knee.

"It's your choice whether to read it or not," Stone said. "We can go. You get to decide."

Under the table, she pressed the palm of her hand over his. It was as if they had a secret, touching under the table out of the view of Mr. Freidman. The warmth of Stone soaked into her. Strong, steady Stone. She could do this with him by her side. When it was over, they could walk out and get coffee or dinner and she would be fine again. Her father could not hurt her now.

Or could he? The contents of the letter had the power to hurt, to rip open the wounds she'd so long ago sewn together. She examined the front of the envelope. Her name was written squarely in the middle in her father's precise handwriting. All capital letters. No weak lowercase for her father.

She plucked it from the desk and held her breath, as if the paper itself smelled bad, then tore it open with a slice of her index finger. The paper was thick, expensive, posh. She unfolded the letter. Her father's initials were embossed at the top of the page.

Dear Pepper,

Despite my best efforts, I've become a cliché. Like so many men who face their imminent death, I've spent my last few months contemplating the content of my character. I'm sure we're in agreement about my parenting skills. I've not been a good father. There's nothing I can do about it now.

Knowing you're here only to hear the contents of my will, I'll be brief.

I'll start with this. I'm sorry. To say I wasn't cut out for fatherhood is terribly obvious. However, it's the truth. I didn't know how to relate to a child. Because of my behavior, I didn't have the opportunity to know you as an adult. I'd like to think I'd do things differently if given another chance, but the truth is—I probably wouldn't. We are what we are.

My father told me when I was a young man that money didn't solve problems between people, only created them. If that is true, then my grand gesture here in the third act will mean nothing to you. I have to offer it anyway. Arthur will explain the details but suffice it to say I'm leaving you the only thing in my life I ever did well. If I'd been able to love anything as much as I did my work, perhaps our story would be different. Sadly, my third act cannot bring a happy ending. In the end, my financial accomplishments are all I have to leave you. I hope you'll use the resources wisely and make something of yourself.

Sincerely,

Your father

Pepper handed the letter to Stone without a word. While he read, she focused on breathing. Her heart pounded. Sweat pooled between her breasts and dampened her palms. Leave it to her father to go out with a flourish and an extra bow.

"What does all this mean?" she asked Arthur. The letter was cold, matter-of-fact and confusing, like her father.

"I'll explain." Arthur reached back into the folder and came out with what appeared to be a legal document. She recognized the layout, because she'd once come upon the custody agreement between her parents. He cleared his throat and began to read. Pepper squeezed her hands together to squelch the nervous energy coursing through her body before it escaped in the form of a primal scream.

After some legal jargon, Arthur came to the crux of the matter. "'To my only daughter, Pepper Grace Griffin, I leave the entirety of my financial accounts and all assets.'"

Arthur set aside the document for a moment and looked up at her. "There are a lot of legal details, but the headline is pretty simple. It's not a stretch to say he was the most powerful man in the theater community here in New York."

"I was aware of that," she said drily.

Arthur's mouth lifted in a thin smile. "His production company helped finance several large productions a year, but that was by no means the entirety of his portfolio. Before he passed, he sold all his properties and investments so that it would be a clean transition for you." He reached for another piece of paper. "Your father's net worth was one hundred million dollars, give or take. That money is all yours. These are the details of the bank account we set up for you. As I said, he wanted to make it easy for you by liquidating everything into cash."

Pepper pressed her thumb into the pointy end of the surfboard charm on her bracelet. Her head felt unnaturally heavy, and her vision went blurry the way it used to back in math class in high school. "I don't understand," she whispered. Next to her, Stone had gone completely still.

"There's more," Arthur said. "He's made you his successor at his production company. He wanted you to run it."

"What? Me? No. I don't know how to run a company." She looked over at Stone. He stared back at her with a bewildered expression.

"This is a lot to process," Arthur said. "I'll be happy to continue on as your attorney to advise you about taxes and such. If not me, then I can make recommendations to you."

"We haven't spoken in over a decade," she said. "Why would he do this?"

"It was my understanding he had no other family," Arthur said. "It was his dying wish for you to have financial freedom."

"Freedom? Freedom from what?" She sputtered and sat forward in her chair with her finger pointed at the attorney as if it were his fault her father was a lunatic. "This isn't like a nice allowance so that I don't have to wait tables while I look for acting work, which, by the way, would have come in damn handy back when I *was* waiting tables and looking for acting work. Why would he do this now?"

"I'm sorry. I can't answer that," Arthur said.

She looked over at Stone, who was staring into his lap. His skin had drained of all color. "Stone?"

He raised his head toward her. His eyes were glassy and unfocused-looking, like a kid's in the principal's office. "Yes?"

She simply stared at him, shaking. "What am I supposed to do now?"

Stone seemed to snap out of his stupor. He sat up straighter and placed his hand on her shoulder. "Give it a moment to sink in. You can figure out what it all means later."

She shook her head. "No. This is wrong. I'm not supposed to have his money. Not now. Not ever. We had no relationship. I don't want it."

Arthur cleared his throat again. "I have to say, I've never had a relative react this way to learning they were now very, very wealthy."

The tears wanted to come, but she would not let them. Not here in front of Arthur. Later, she would let the angry tears flow, and Stone would hold her. Yes, anger. That's what he'd left her. How dare he leave her all this money when all she wanted was a relationship with him? Maybe an introduction to a few directors in town. Not this. Not money.

She rose to her feet and smoothed her dress over her hips. "I'll be in touch later. But I need a little time."

"Of course." Arthur stood and handed her a card. "This is the number to your private banker. They will explain to you how to access your account and advise you on how to structure your money." He shifted from side to side and grimaced in obvious discomfort. "Also, the board of your father's production company, or rather, your company, have asked that you meet with them tomorrow in your offices to discuss the transition plan. They indicated there were decisions to be made sooner rather than later."

She stared at Arthur, completely helpless as to what to do next.

Stone stood and took her hand. "Thank you, Arthur. Do you have the address? What time should she arrive?"

Arthur handed Stone a card. "Address is there. They asked that you come at two tomorrow."

"Thank you, Arthur. We have to go now," she said. *Get out of here.* That's all she wanted.

Stone placed his hand on the small of her back and guided her toward the door. They didn't speak as they crossed through the lobby and out to the elevators. She'd begun to shake in earnest by the time they exited onto the ground floor. "I need a drink," she whispered. "There's an Irish pub around the corner from here. I used to work there."

"Whatever you want." He tucked her arm into his, and they walked out to the sidewalk. A light, feathery mist wakened her senses. The sidewalks were crowded with people, shoulder to shoulder. Several times, someone bumped her, and Stone steadied her. Finally, they reached the pub. The Hound and Thistle. With any luck, Morris would be behind the bar. She needed to be somewhere familiar.

It was nearing four now, and the after-work crowd had not yet arrived. Dimly lit, with the dark walls and tall booths, the bar had an intimate, old-school atmosphere. A few people sat at the classic pub bar, another few at tables. The scent of beer and the detergent they used to wash the floor took her back to the time she'd spent here as a waitress. A modern Irish band played from the speakers.

Morris was indeed at the bar with a towel slung over his beefy shoulder and a blue T-shirt with the bar's emblem across the chest. He'd told her once he owned one for every day of the week. His wife kept them washed and ready for him.

"Let's sit at the bar," she said to Stone. "You can meet Morris."

They took seats on one end, a bowl of mixed nuts between them. Morris was busy pouring a beer for another customer and didn't see them right away. When he turned from his customer to greet them, his face lit up as he let out an excited yelp. "Pepper Griffin. About time you brought your skinny ass in here to see me. Where you been?"

"I've been out in California with Lisa and Maggie."

Morris set a couple of cocktail napkins in front of them. "Them two are everywhere lately. I saw Lisa's face on a bus the other day. I said to my Joanie—I know that girl. She used to work at the bar. Real proud of you girls." He placed his arms on top of his ample stomach and grinned at her. "What brings you to town? You got a role in something?"

"No. Some family business." She placed her hand on Stone's arm. "This is Stone Hickman. My boyfriend."

The men shook hands. "Nice to meet you." He turned back to Pepper. "I take it they grow them big out west?"

"Not all of them, but this one, yes." She smiled, suddenly feeling better. This was familiar. Cheap beer. Stale nuts. Morris. One hundred million dollars was not.

"What're you two drinking? On the house."

"I'll have a scotch, neat," she said.

Stone ordered an IPA. Morris hustled behind the bar, and soon they had their drinks. A group of young people dressed in suits swarmed the entrance and shuffled in together like one entity. Boisterous and loud, they plopped into seats at the end of the bar.

"Duty calls," Morris said as he took off to care for his other customers.

For the first time since they'd left the lawyer's office, she wondered how Stone was taking the news. She stole a glance at him. He was hunched over his drink. "Hey there, Stone Soup." She touched the side of his face with her fingertips. "You okay?"

He turned on the stool toward her. For the first time, she noticed that his hands shook. "I'm stunned, I guess."

She nodded before taking a generous sip of her drink. It didn't take the smartest person in the world to know that money like this changed the dynamics of every relationship. "I never thought it would be this."

"Yeah," he said, sounding miserable.

She clasped her hands around the tumbler. A dark dread hovered over her, like the clouds that had suddenly unleashed a snowstorm in Emerson Pass. "His money is a slap in the face. And the company? What the hell? Why would he do that when he thought I was so untalented?"

Stone's great shoulders moved up and down in a sigh. "I can understand why you feel that way. When my mom suddenly showed up, my first thought was—it's too late. Too much time has passed. Too much pain to work through or get past." He rested his cheek in one hand, looking into her eyes. "But this is a whole different thing. He left you a fortune. In an instant, everything changed for you."

"It means I have money now, yes. But what does it get me? None of the things I want." She halted as tears pricked her eyes. "All I ever wanted was for him to love me. I don't care how much money it is. It's not a replacement for all the years he missed everything." She thought about Zane's dad and what he'd done for Sophie. How he'd secretly attended all her events even though he couldn't raise her. "Sophie's dad kept a journal for her. He wrote entries to her the entire time she was growing up. That's what he left *her*. I can guarantee you it means more to her than money." Hot tears escaped and ran down her face. She used her cocktail napkin to wipe them away. "Do you know he never once told me he loved me? And now to do this—it's wrong."

Stone's face twisted in obvious sympathy. He stroked her arm. "I know it hurts, baby. I'm so sorry."

"I've been fine, you know. My career isn't where I wanted it to be, but at least I could say I'd done it on my own, with integrity. No favors. Without his money. It's like him to mess up my life just when it got good."

He lifted his head. "Maybe it's the path to everything you've wanted."

She leaned her face into his shoulder and let the tears flow. The money didn't matter. It was never what she wanted or needed from her father. "I don't understand why he never loved me."

"Sweetheart, it wasn't about you. It was him. Just like my mom. She left because she didn't know how else to be—how else to save herself." Stone stroked her arm. "That money's going to give you a lifestyle most people only dream about."

"I don't want it." She shook her head with such violence that her earrings smacked against her neck.

Stone tilted his head and scratched the back of his head. "You don't have to decide anything right now. Let it sink in. We'll sleep on it."

"I'll make it on my own. I promised myself the day I left his office that I would never ask for anything from him ever again."

"You didn't ask for this."

"I most certainly did not," she said.

"He never gave you anything in life. No encouragement. No money. And now he's finally done the right thing. This money is freedom. You can do anything you want. See the world. Buy a house. The possibilities are endless."

"Will you still love me if I'm rich?"

"I'll love you until the end of time," he said quietly. "Nothing will ever change that."

"Money changes people."

"Not if we don't let it. If *I* don't let it. My male ego will have to take a back seat." He smiled and brushed her cheek with his thumb. "Sweetheart, it's not the money that changes everything. It's the other thing—the company. Is running it what you want?"

"I don't know. This is all so strange." She hiccupped and swiped under her eyes. Damn her father. How could he do this? Just when she'd found Stone, suddenly this opportunity falls into her lap. An opportunity that would require her to stay in New York. "I'd have to live here."

A muscle flexed near his mouth. "I know."

"I want to be with you."

He turned to face her, placing his legs on either side of her stool, and picked up her hands. "What if I weren't in the picture? Would you want this?"

The idea of it, the possibilities, rose up like a crocus in the early spring. Her own company. She could run it the way she wanted. It could produce plays about women, for women. She could employ talented actresses who were still waiting for their break.

Who was she kidding? She couldn't even pack her suitcase without screwing up.

"I'm not sure I can do it," she said.

He brushed her hair back from her face. "You can. You're the smartest person I've ever met. You'll kill it."

"You make me feel like I could do anything."

"You can."

"I want to be with you," she said again. "More than anything."

"Listen to me carefully. This position could change your life, make your dreams come true. I would never stand in your way. You deserve everything, Pepper. I want everything for you."

She sucked in a breath, trying to stifle the sobs that ripped open her chest. "But my life is out west now. You. My best friends."

"We'll still be there." He covered her knees with his hands and bowed his head. She put her mouth in the thick pillow of his hair and breathed in his scent.

"What about you?" she asked. "What about what you want? A family? A home?"

He lifted his head and warmed her with his gentle smile. Her heart ached with love for him. "As much as I want those things with you, I want you to seize this opportunity. We have time.

We're young." His voice cracked. "That said, the thought of being without you makes me feel like I'm dying."

"Same." The unasked question loomed above them. If she asked, then she would know the answer for sure. She had to. She had to know. "You could stay with me."

His features twisted, as if he were in physical agony. "I would. In a minute, I would. But I can't bail on the guys. Not when we've got so much on the line. If I bowed out, we'd lose everything. We all put every last dime we had into the company. Our margins are too tight. If one of us bails, it means financial ruin for the rest of us. Regardless, I'm the linchpin. Without construction, there's nothing."

She wrapped her arms around his neck. "You're my linchpin."

He held her tightly against him. "We'll figure it out."

"I don't want to lose you."

"You'll never lose me. When and if you're ready to come home, I'll be there. Or if things start going well for my company, I'll live here part time. We'll figure it out."

One last reckless question. "What if I fund your company?"

He squeezed his eyes shut and shook his head. "Oh, baby, you know I can't let you do that. It's not in my DNA to be a kept man."

The tears came again. Even if he agreed to it, a man like Stone Hickman couldn't live in a concrete jungle. He belonged to the outdoors, to the sky and sea and stars. He worked with his hands to build things, not live in the middle of a city where the buildings already touched the sky. And he most certainly didn't sponge off the woman he loved.

"I don't even know if this is what I want," Pepper said. "What about acting?"

"You owe it to yourself to find out. Being away from you is going hurt like hell. It already hurts like hell. But holding you back from your calling would hurt more. I can't be that man.

You're special, Pepper. I've known it from the moment I met you. This company could be your destiny."

"I can come visit. You can come here."

"Yes. We'll make our time together special." His eyes had dulled to the color of blue jeans. "I don't want the feeling between us ruined by one of us trying to change or compromise, only to end up bitter and resentful."

"We'll make it work."

"Absolutely we will." He spoke firmly, decisively.

No amount of affirmative intonation could disguise his doubt. He wasn't that good an actor. The dull, defeated look in his eyes betrayed him. She could see it plainly on his face that he believed this city would suck her away from him, dazzle her with its romance and glamour. Stone thought of himself as the little boy from the wrong side of town. He believed her money and possible power would be the inevitable demise of them. Their two worlds would become further and further apart until they were strangers.

Did she believe it too? Everything in her told her he was wrong, but only time would tell. Damn time. Endless days without him next to her felt like a life sentence.

The distance threatened to slide between them—that dark, sneaky doubt and insecurity and memories of the past wanted desperately to tear them apart. It was just a sliver, but over time, it could become wider and wider until it wedged them apart forever. Unless they stopped it. But could they?

20

Stone

STONE HELD Pepper's hand as they walked the streets of the Upper West Side, pretending to take in the storefronts. But he was blind to them. All he could see was darkness. Days without Pepper were unimaginable, yet it would happen. He'd fly home tomorrow without her.

The moment he'd heard the lawyer's words, a sick feeling had washed over him. Just as he thought he knew his future, it evaporated in an instant. Everything changed.

As he'd said to her, it wasn't the money. It was the chance to prove herself, to do work that she loved and gave meaning to her life. They were alike that way. Their contribution to the world mattered to them. They both wanted to make it a more beautiful place. As of now, neither had accomplished what they wanted. He could never take that chance from her. She was a beautiful bird that deserved to fly. He could already picture her at the helm of a production company. Her quick mind and artistic aesthetic would bring a freshness and innovation to whatever she touched. She would shine and grow powerful and move through the world with a force.

The problem was, it no doubt would be without him. As much as he'd love to be here with her, this was not his destiny. A car honked just feet from them as if to illustrate his point. All these cars and people and buildings that stole the view of the sky would eat away at him until he was miserable. Over time, she would come to realize their worlds were incompatible.

What about Rafael and Lisa? They were making it work. Could they? Pepper would come visit. He would spend time here between projects. All kinds of couples had long-distance relationships. He would hold on to that splinter of hope. It was all he could do. The alternative was to admit defeat, and he wasn't yet ready to do so.

A nagging voice echoed between his ears.

It's not what you want. Admit it. You want the whole package, like what Kyle has. Family and a home and a wife who can live with you full time.

Shut up, brain. I'm in denial here. Leave me alone.

Pepper's voice interrupted the ones in his head. "Do you want to go back to the hotel or find a place to eat?"

"Let's go back. We can order room service and be alone. I don't want to share you with anyone on our last night together."

She didn't say anything, just lifted her New Yorker arm and hailed them a cab.

THE NEXT MORNING Stone woke early after a restless sleep. While Pepper slept, he showered. His eyes were scratchy, as if there were grains of sand under his lids. After they'd come home from the bar, Pepper ordered their dinner from room service. Neither of them ate more than a few bites. Apparently having your heart stomped was a real appetite killer. They'd crawled into bed together and made love as though it was their last-ever night together. Finally, physically exhausted, they'd fallen asleep wrapped together like bendable spoons.

When he came out of the bathroom from his shower, Pepper was sitting in the middle of the bed with the blanket pulled over her bare torso, looking sad and small. Puffy eyes stared at him woefully. He could barely look at her without breaking down himself.

"I have to leave soon for my flight." He tightened the towel tied around his waist.

She nodded as she pulled her knees up to her chest. "I know. I called a car for you. It'll be here in forty-five minutes."

He sat on the bed. "You'll come out in two weeks for the weekend. Time will fly. You'll be so busy. We'll text all the time and talk on the phone. It'll be fine."

"Sure, yeah," she said dully.

The sadness in her eyes was more than he could tolerate without losing it. He went to his suitcase and pulled out a pair of jeans and a shirt to wear. While he dressed, she slipped from the bed and went into the bathroom. After a moment, he heard the shower turn on.

No singing today.

Stone went to the window and drew back the curtain. The sight of gray and gritty Manhattan greeted him. Even from the twentieth floor, the sounds of horns and traffic called out to him. People crowded the sidewalks, shoving and pushing their way to work or shopping or school. Could he live here? Could he do it to be with Pepper?

Stay. Save yourself. Save her. You need each other.

But in the next second, he remembered the Wolves and his commitment to them. And Kyle and Autumn? They would understand if he chose love over them. They'd be fine. But what about him? Alone in a strange city with a woman who would probably be working most of the time. What would he do here? Get his contractor license? He could, he supposed. If he could afford to live here. Everything had fallen into place for him in Cliffside Bay. Walking away for a woman who would probably outgrow him was a disaster waiting to happen.

Pepper distracted him from the window and his thoughts when she returned from her shower. She'd fixed her hair and applied makeup, but none of it hid the dark circles under her eyes. It hurt him to see her this way.

"I want to go the airport with you, but I'm afraid it'll make me late for the meeting," she said.

He agreed, assuring her it was fine. "I hate goodbyes at the airport anyway."

"Not goodbye. See you soon."

He crossed over to her and pulled her into his arms. With his face buried in her curls, he breathed in her scent, wishing he could at least take that with him.

"I wish you didn't have to go." Her voice was flat and defeated. She didn't sound like his fiery Pepper.

"I'll see you soon." He pulled away to look into her eyes. His lips touched hers, and he lingered for a moment. "I love you."

"I love you," she whispered.

"I'll see you in two weeks."

"Two weeks."

He wrenched away and grabbed his suitcase, leaving without a backward glance. If he looked back at her, he might never leave. And that wasn't what either of them needed.

TWO HOURS LATER, after surviving security and crowds, he reached his gate, only to find out his flight was delayed by thirty minutes. He called Rafael. They hadn't spoken since he'd called him from San Francisco to let him know he was accompanying Pepper to New York and that they'd managed to fall in love in the middle of a snowstorm. Now he filled him in on the unsettling events of the last twenty-four hours. His friend didn't say much until he finished his sad tale. "I left her at the hotel, and now I'm flying home."

"Man, I'm sorry," Rafael said. "I don't know what to say."

"Tell me I'm doing the right thing."

"You are. Giving her space to see where it might lead is the only path to happiness for both of you. And you have commitments here. Bailing on them isn't in you. Everyone knows that, including Pepper, which is probably one of the reasons she loves you."

"I know you're right, but I feel pretty miserable right now."

"I know, man, but listen. You got the girl. She'll come back to you if your bond is as strong as you think it is. I promise you—it's going to be okay."

"I hope you're right." He hesitated for a moment. "How's it been for you—the whole money thing?"

"You mean because Lisa is rich and getting richer? I struggle every now and then. I'm not proud of it, but yeah, it still bugs me. That said, it gives me more incentive to make our business venture work."

"That's a good way to look at it."

"You'll get used to the idea after a time. It's still hard when you wish you could get her something and you realize she can get it for herself."

"These girls don't care about that stuff," Stone said. "You know what Pepper said when she found out her dad left her all that money? 'Why didn't he love me?'"

"That makes me want to murder the guy even though he's already dead."

"I know. They say money makes the world go around, but it's actually love."

"Amen, brother. Now, come home. We'll sew you back together until your girl comes back to you."

After he hung up the phone, Stone sat staring at his hands, crushed and broken. What had he been thinking? He was a joke.

Had he really believed that Pepper was going to marry him and have his babies and live in his small apartment in Cliffside Bay while he built his business? This woman was a star who belonged on the stage and screen with millions of adoring fans clamoring for her every word. He knew it was right to let her go fulfill her destiny, even as his guts were being twisted by invisible monster hands.

It was nearing six in the evening when he arrived home to Cliffside Bay. As soon as he stepped inside his apartment, the scent of his sister's spaghetti sauce filled the air. Voices and laughter came from the kitchen. He left his bag by the front door and followed the noise of what sounded like happy people. Autumn, wearing an apron over jeans and a pink sweater, stood at the stove with a wooden spoon in her hand. Trey was at the counter making a salad.

"Big brother, you're home." Autumn moved across the room with the slight hitch in her step to hug him. "I missed you so much."

Trey stood, and they exchanged a quick brotherly embrace.

"How you doing, man?" Trey asked. "Good to see your ugly mug."

"You too," Stone said. Despite his heartbreak, the sight of these two people cheered him. "It smells fantastic in here."

"I made my special sauce," Autumn said. "Thought you might need a little comfort food."

"You know me too well." Stone smiled at his sister. Flushed from the heat of the stove, she looked even lovelier than usual. He wished for the thousandth time that she and Trey were attracted to each other. They had so much in common and already had the foundation of friendship. But without the attraction factor, it didn't matter how compatible they were. The irony was not lost on him. He and Pepper were in love but couldn't live together. These two practically lived together but could never be in love.

Trey opened the refrigerator and pulled out two beers, then poured a glass of wine for Autumn. "Take a load off," Trey said to Stone. "Tell us all about it."

"Rafael called earlier and told us what happened," Autumn said.

"Ah, the spaghetti sauce is making more sense," Stone said. He wasn't surprised Rafael had shared his news. These guys were starting to feel like family. As much as every cell missed Pepper, being home was a comfort.

"There's not much to tell that you don't know, then. Pepper and I spent the last ten days wrapped up in each other, and I'm madly in love with her. We were headed home to work on making our dreams come true, together. Then her bastard father left her his theater company and loads of cash, which means she can live her dream. Without me." Stone lifted his beer and took a long drink. Autumn and Trey exchanged glances, as if they knew something he didn't. "What?"

"Nothing really," Autumn said.

"Go ahead," Stone said. "I know you have an opinion."

"I've never been prouder of you. Encouraging her to spread her wings is so very cool," Autumn said.

"Once we get things running like we want, there's no reason you can't live in New York part of the year, and she could live here part of the year," Trey said. "Or do what Rafael and Lisa are doing."

"Sure. That's the plan," Stone said, not entirely believing it even as it came out of his mouth.

"Or maybe she could hire someone to run the theater?" Autumn asked. "Like an artistic director or something."

"She could," Stone said. "But she needs time to figure out how it's going to work."

"Why do you sound so pessimistic?" Autumn turned to stir her sauce and spoke with her back to him. "It's not like you."

"I'm just not sure I'm going to hold up against the allure of the rich people she's going to be around now," Stone said. "And I miss her like hell. Like I lost a limb. Or two."

Autumn set aside her spoon and turned around to face him, her eyes full of sympathy. "She'll be back."

"I hope you're right, but the odds are stacked against us," Stone said. "Think about it. She's mega rich. She's going to run one of the most successful theater companies in New York and probably get to star in several productions a year. She'll be surrounded by the elite society of New York. Take a guess how long it takes before she's moved on to bigger and better." Saying it out loud was a relief. "I'm just plain old me. I had to buy a shirt just to visit the attorney's office."

Trey grimaced. "The logic pans out. I hate to admit it, but I think you're right. You know how it is with women."

Autumn crossed her arms over her chest and glared at them. "Really now? And how is it with women?"

"You know, they're attracted to men with money," Trey said. "It's no secret."

Autumn rolled her eyes. "You have no idea what you're talking about."

"Look at my ex-wife if you need proof," Trey said. "The guy she cheated on me with and subsequently married is richer than God."

"No one's richer than God," Autumn said with a pious knitting of her eyebrows.

"You know what I mean." Trey gave her a sheepish grin.

"You two have major chips on your shoulders," Autumn said. "It's sad. If she loves you like she says she does, she'll make an effort."

"I don't know." Stone sat at the table, suddenly weary. "We're so different. She's the city and I'm the country. If I move there, I'm miserable. If she comes home with me, she gives up the opportunity of a lifetime. The thought of losing her makes me want to throw up."

Autumn sighed. "You poor thing."

"Yeah, well, sometimes love ain't enough," Stone said. "Enough about me, what have you two kids been up to?"

Autumn gave him one more of her sisterly glares that told him this discussion would be revisited whether he liked it or not. "We actually have big news."

"News that will cheer you up," Trey said.

He doubted anything could cheer him. "What is it?"

"The permits were approved for Sara's house," Autumn said.

"We can start next week. This house is going to be huge for us," Trey said.

"Great news." He tried to sound enthusiastic but succeeded in conveying extreme weariness instead.

"Oh, Stone, you're in bad shape," Autumn said. "A month ago, this would have made you do cartwheels."

He pushed into his eyes with the heels of his hands. "Leaving her was the hardest thing I've ever done. Imagining my life without her is impossible."

When he removed his hands, he looked up to see Trey and Autumn staring at him with expressions of helplessness.

"You guys will find a way," Autumn said. "If you love each other, nothing's impossible."

"Sure. One hundred percent," Trey said without meeting Stone's gaze.

Stone almost laughed at Trey's insincerity. His friend was a skeptic when it came to romantic relationships. Not that he could blame him. Trey's ex-wife had cheated on him and then taken the business he'd spent ten years building.

"I'll be fine. Don't worry. Let's eat," Stone said. "That sauce is making my mouth water." One foot in front of the other. Concentrate on his life here. The business. His friends. His family. This was his life. With or without Pepper, he had to keep moving forward. That's what the marines had taught him. Even if he felt as if he were dying, life must go on.

21

Pepper

AFTER MEETING with several attorneys and the board members of the theater, Pepper went home to the hotel and stripped off her uncomfortable clothes and shoes and slipped into the bathrobe. The day had exhausted her, and not only because she'd barely slept the night before. Her tearful goodbye to Stone seemed like a lifetime ago. Somehow, she'd gotten through the day without breaking down. In fact, her traitorous brain almost tricked her into believing it had all been a bad dream. She almost expected Stone to be waiting at the hotel. He wasn't. An empty can of shaving cream next to her toothbrush was the only proof that he'd been there at all.

She ordered some dinner up but didn't have the heart or appetite to eat. All day her phone had been blowing up with messages from Lisa, Maggie, and her mom. Everyone but Stone. She needed to return the phone calls and share the remarkable turn of events. She dreaded telling the same story three times and wished she could send a simple text instead.

Dad left me his theater company and gobs of money. Stone had to go home to Cliffside Bay instead of staying with me. I chose to stay here and pursue the dream I thought I wanted but all I can think about is the man who hates crowds and cities and noise.

She pushed aside her dinner and picked up the phone. She punched in Lisa's and Maggie's numbers for a three-way call. Amazingly, given their schedules, they both picked up. Five minutes later, they knew the whole story. For the second time in the history of their friendships, they were stunned into silence. The only other time that had ever happened was when Maggie called to tell Lisa and Pepper that everyone in Cliffside Bay had believed she died at eighteen in a car crash.

Maggie was the first to break the silence. "After like twelve years of no contact, he decides to leave you his theater and all his money?"

"I know it's unbelievable," Pepper said. "My dad always knew how to mess with my head."

"Are you all right?" Lisa asked.

The sympathy in her voice was too much. Her resolve to stay numb and strong disintegrated. "No. I'm all messed up. I don't know what to do or think. And I miss Stone so much it feels like I'm dying a slow and painful death."

"Do you need me to come out there?" Maggie asked.

"No, no. You have the baby, and you're finally home," Pepper said.

"Is the theater what you want?" Maggie asked. "Because you're not sounding so sure."

"I'm not," Pepper said. "A month ago, if you'd told me I would rather go back with Stone and live a simple life in Cliffside Bay, I would have said you were delusional. Did you guys ever notice how loud it is here? I mean, last night when I was trying to sleep all I could hear were horns and engines and people screaming. Maybe it didn't seem so loud when you guys were here to keep me company. I feel alone without you. This whole thing feels wrong. Do I sound crazy?"

"You sound like you're in love," Lisa said. "And love changes us. Our work isn't everything, despite what we believed all these years."

"It's just one part of us," Maggie said. "Art's fed by love."

"Stone's so generous," Pepper said. "The moment we learned the details of the will, he told me how much he wants this for me. But what if he's wrong? What if the huge opportunity is him?" Pepper tightened the belt of the robe around her waist. "You can't imagine the meeting I just had with the board. It turns out I'm not even in charge. They are. They're all a bunch of scary old people who told me my main responsibility is making sure we're on budget and hiring the right people. All the artistic choices will be made by directors and designers. I'll be a businessperson. Like in an office all day long looking at numbers. It's my worst nightmare. I had no idea what my dad actually did."

"That sounds awful," Lisa said.

"I know. And get this—our annual numbers are low because of my dad's illness. They want me to get started right away." She sighed, remembering the edict from the board.

"Do you want to be a businessperson?" Maggie asked. "Or an actress?"

"You know the answer to that," Pepper said. "But am I wimping out? Am I letting my dad down?"

"Screw him," Lisa said, uncharacteristically crass. "He never did one thing for you. Get out of there. Take the money, don't get me wrong, but resign from the company. Seriously, honey, you would be miserable."

"I agree," Maggie said. "Run as fast as you can."

"Not to throw even more complications at you, but I talked to Gennie today," Lisa said.

Gennie, otherwise known as Genevieve Banks, the most famous movie star in the world. Since Lisa's rise to fame, they had become friends. Recently, Gennie had started her own production company, making films about women. She'd offered Lisa a role in her next project. Pepper burned with shame remembering how jealous she'd been.

Sounding nervous, Lisa continued. "Pepper, she has a role for you in the film. It's a good one, too. Juicy and complex. She watched your scenes in the horror film and thinks you're perfect for the role of the salty bartender."

"What are you talking about?" She blinked. Her limbs tingled with what felt like electric currents. Had she heard her correctly?

"I didn't want to say anything until I was sure," Lisa said. "Almost all of your scenes would be with me. They're good ones, Pepper. Really good."

"I don't know what to say." Other than I'm a terrible, jealous, awful person and now you've done this wonderful thing for me.

"We always said if one of us got a break, we'd help the others," Lisa said. "But it would require you to come out here to film."

"I'd be an actress." And maybe a wife. She could live in Cliffside Bay with Maggie and Lisa when she wasn't filming. If she had children, they could raise them together.

"You guys, am I crazy to pass this up?" Pepper asked.

"No one can tell you what to do," Lisa said. "But we've always gone with our guts. What's it telling you to do?"

Go home to Stone.

"It's telling me that feeding my heart is the only way to live," Pepper said.

"Come home," Lisa said.

Come home.

"I will. I'll come home," Pepper said.

22

Stone

STONE LAY in bed and stared at the wall, listening to the soft footsteps of Trey in the bedroom next door. They were familiar sounds. The sound of the water going on and off as Trey brushed his teeth, then the flushing of the toilet. Trey was a good roommate, neat and courteous. They'd had fun together these last few months. Two bachelors partying and hosting parties, surfing and lounging on the beach. Two weeks ago, he'd been content. But now? All he wanted was to hear Pepper preparing for bed and then slipping between the sheets and wrapping her arms around him. How was he going to live without her?

He fell asleep finally and woke late the next morning to the sound of his cell phone ringing. Hoping it was Pepper, he sat up quickly and grabbed it from the table.

Kyle.

It was not Pepper, but his brother.

"Hey. What's up?"

"Not a lot. I was just calling to check in with you. I'm headed into town and wondered if you wanted to get some coffee or breakfast."

Word traveled fast in Cliffside Bay. His friends and family were worried about him. Touched, he asked if Kyle wanted to come up for coffee instead of meeting somewhere.

A few minutes later, his brother was in the kitchen, which smelled of freshly brewed coffee. Outside, fog hovered low, encasing the town in a blanket of white. Normally, Stone would have loved the cozy moment in his warm kitchen with his brother. Today, however, his heart hurt worse than the day before. This time yesterday, he was saying goodbye to Pepper. Would it continue to hurt more each day he was away from her?

He poured them both a cup of coffee and joined his brother at the table. Kyle added a teaspoon of sugar and some milk, then stirred it slowly, as if contemplating the cure for cancer.

"How are the kids?" Stone asked.

"Like wild animals." Kyle grinned. "They're not helping me convince Violet that we should try for another."

"You really have lost your mind. You're already way outnumbered."

"That's the kind of negative talk I hear from my wife."

They laughed together in the way brothers do, the culmination of their shared experiences echoing in the low rumble from their chests.

Kyle regarded him from across the table. "Trey told me the permits went through on Sara's house. Great news."

"Sure is."

"Listen, I've been thinking. If you want to take a breather and go out to be with Pepper, I have a few contractors I could recommend. They could fill in for you. Just temporarily."

He peered at his brother. "You know I can't do that. I made a promise to my partners. Not to mention that I need the money."

"I could help you out." Kyle picked up the discarded spoon and stirred his coffee again. Super casual. No eye contact.

"Absolutely not. You've done enough for me. This company is mine to make work."

"I respect that. I do. But hey, you know, love doesn't come along just anytime. When you find the one, you have to fight for her."

"I have to let her be herself. As much as it kills me to let her go."

"You guys will find a way." His brother folded his arms over his chest. "You know I'm super proud of you."

"Don't get all mushy on me now."

"Me? No way." Kyle took a sip from his cup. "This is the worst coffee I've ever tasted."

"What're you talking about? I make great coffee."

"It tastes like the day-old from the diner back home," Kyle said.

"That's hurtful, man."

"The truth hurts."

"Are you still trying to grow hair on your chest?" Stone asked. "Because I have enough."

"Seriously, this is really bad." Kyle grimaced as he set aside his cup.

There was a knock on the door, then Autumn's voice called out to them. "Stone?"

He sprinted to the doorway of the kitchen. "We're in here."

Autumn shrugged out of her coat and tossed it on the back of the couch. "I got a text from Kyle asking to meet you guys here. Everything okay?"

"Sure. We're having coffee. Want some?" Stone asked.

"A half cup, please." Autumn didn't have her cane with her today. She must have been feeling strong.

Kyle stood as they came back into the kitchen. "Hey. Thanks for coming." He gave his sister a quick hug.

Stone poured her a cup and placed it on the table as she settled into one of the chairs.

"I need to talk to you about Mom." Kyle shook his head.

"Still weird to say that word, other than in reference to my amazing wife."

Stone took in a deep breath, preparing himself for the discussion he really didn't want to have. "Sure is."

"Stone, while you were away, I took Mom to an attorney. He walked us through the steps of what an insanity trial would look like. It'll be brutal, and he doesn't think we can win. He thinks she's better off confessing to her guilt and sharing her motive. He said Autumn's injuries would be compelling."

Autumn stared at the surface of the table—her expression unreadable. "I kind of wish she'd just stayed away."

"I agree," Stone said. "I don't know if I can deal with all this right now."

Kyle nodded. "She agrees too. After we met with the attorney, she told me she feels terrible about disrupting our lives. She wants to turn herself in. No insanity plea. No major money spent on attorneys' fees."

Stone unfolded from his chair and walked over to the sink. His windows faced east, toward the hill. The view was as gray as his mood. An outright confession. His mind reeled with this new information. Maybe she hadn't come just for Kyle's money.

"There will still be a trial, but it'll be short and relatively straightforward," Kyle said. "Strangely enough, there are a lot of people who confess to crimes they didn't commit."

"Weird," Stone said.

"The attorney thinks she'll be sent to prison with the possibility for parole." Kyle shifted in his chair. "But her health's fragile. I don't think she'll last long."

"She shouldn't have to go to jail," Stone said. "Not after what they did to you—to Autumn."

Kyle looked at him for a long moment before answering. "I understand your perspective, but the truth is, she murdered two people. Not innocent men. But men just the same. She wants to pay for her crime and let us live in peace."

Stone turned to look at Kyle, who met his gaze. "I wanted to put that part of our life away. I thought we had. We'd moved on. We have one another and Violet and the kids and this great life and now she's here—causing grief and trouble."

Kyle nodded. "I know. But she's our mother. We can't turn her away. Not now." He paused. "I asked her over to the house tonight. She wants to meet the kids."

"You're letting her?" Stone asked.

"Violet's making me." Kyle's mouth lifted in a sad attempt at a smile. "Not really. Mom's probably going to jail. I wanted her to see my kids before they send her away."

"So, you've just forgiven her?" Autumn asked. "Just like that?"

"She's an old lady who knows she made a terrible mistake when she was young and messed up," Kyle said.

No one spoke for a good minute. Stone's thoughts crashed around inside his head. His instinct was to throw up his hands and tell Kyle he wasn't up for it. "What time tonight?"

"Six. Violet's making tacos."

"Taco night," Autumn said. "Like everything's normal when it's not."

"Isn't that the Hickman way?" Kyle asked.

THAT NIGHT, Stone drove Autumn to Kyle's. The beat-up Honda was already in the driveway when they arrived. He shut off the engine and turned to his sister. She had her arms clasped around a pale green purse.

"You ready for this?" he asked.

"Not really."

Dakota appeared in the doorway and then ran down the steps to Stone's truck. "We're being summoned," he said to Autumn.

Autumn smiled as Dakota appeared on her side and opened her door. No taller than the truck door's armrest, he beamed up at them. Kyle must have taught him to open a lady's door.

"Aunt Autumn, you look lovely tonight," Dakota said. "Your hair looks like a shiny ball."

"Why thank you." Autumn touched her fingertips to the knot at the back of her head. Her smooth auburn hair shone under the interior lights of the car. "It's called a French twist."

"Very nice." Dakota offered his hand and helped her from the car.

Stone untangled his long legs and jumped from the truck. He followed closely behind Autumn and Dakota across the driveway. At the bottom step leading to the front door, Dakota stopped and turned to look up at them. "Things are a little weird inside. Mom's dropped like four things. Dad cut himself shaving and now has one of Mollie's Barbie bandages on his chin." He looked at his feet and spoke in a quiet voice. "Did you know I have another grandmother?"

Stone knelt on the grass to get a better look at his nephew. "I did. You all right about that?"

"I guess." Dakota shrugged. "She's inside right now. Mom told me to be on my best behavior and not to brag too much about myself. You know, the usual." His nose wrinkled. "But I'm worried about Dad. When I went downstairs this morning, he was in his office all slumped over like he was sad."

"Oh, well, that's nothing to worry about," Autumn said. "It's just that we didn't see our mother for a very long time, and it's made us sad and a little confused."

"Why didn't you see her for a very long time?" Dakota asked.

Stone placed his hand on the top of Dakota's head. "It's complicated."

"Complicated is what people say when they don't want to explain something to a kid," Dakota said.

Stone exchanged an amused look with his sister. "Maybe Aunt Autumn could explain it to you."

"She didn't want to be a mom." Autumn spoke slowly, obviously choosing her words carefully. "So she went away."

Dakota tugged on his ear and knit his brows. "My mom doesn't see her dad either. Did you know that?"

Stone nodded. Violet's father was verbally abusive and a bunch of other nasty words. She'd cut him out of her life when Mollie was a tiny baby. From what he understood, Violet's mother visited occasionally, but without her husband and always in secret. "He's not a very nice man, and he made your mom feel terrible all the time, so now she doesn't see him."

"My mom won't leave me and the babies, will she?" Dakota asked so quietly Stone almost missed what he said.

"Absolutely not," Stone said. Poor little dude. He'd been worrying about that? Great. Another way in which Valerie Hickman could mess up their family.

Autumn rushed in next. "She loves you all very much. And she's the best mom in the whole world. Our mom wasn't like yours."

Dakota lips trembled as he blew out a long breath. "That's what I thought, but a guy worries sometimes."

"Sure we do. I worry," Stone said.

With earnest blue eyes, Dakota looked at each of them in turn. "I never knew a mom could leave."

"Most don't," Autumn said. "Yours most certainly will not."

"Got it?" Stone asked.

"Got it." Dakota smiled. "If my new grandmother isn't nice, I'm not going to be her friend."

"Good plan." Stone lifted his hand and they did a fist bump.

"Hey, give me some of that too," Autumn said.

Dakota lifted his little-boy hand to her smooth white one. "You guys aren't ever leaving either, right?"

"Are you kidding? We'd never be able to stay away from you," Stone said.

"We're so glad we live close to you now," Autumn said. "As

a matter of fact, you and the babies were one of the reasons we wanted to move to Cliffside Bay."

"Really?" Dakota asked with a pleased grin.

"One hundred percent." Autumn shot Stone a look that told him exactly what she was thinking. *This kid has my heart.*

Mine too.

A yearning for Pepper crashed into him as he followed his sister and nephew up the stairs and through the front door. He wanted her to know his family, to become friends with his sister and sister-in-law, and to show off his adorable nephews and nieces. She should be by his side, especially tonight when her presence would calm his nerves and give him the perspective he needed. But she was living her dream three thousand miles away. He had to face the truth. She might never return to him. He had to figure out a way to live without her.

The scent of chili peppers and onions came from the kitchen. In a slow jog that increased in speed as they passed into the hallway, Dakota led them toward the kitchen. When they arrived, the little boy announced them, as if they were English royalty.

"Mama, Uncle Stone and Aunt Autumn are here."

Violet was at the stove, heating tortillas. She looked up and greeted them with a smile. "Hey there."

Three empty high chairs were tucked against the empty wall.

"Our nanny's working late today," Violet said. "She's putting the babies to bed."

"I get to stay up." Dakota climbed onto a stool at the island and swiped a slice of tomato from the lazy Susan.

"I saw that, young man," Violet said. "No one wants your grimy hands in the food."

"Sorry, Mama," Dakota said.

Violet pointed toward the living room. "They're in there. Kyle asked you to join them when you arrived."

"Do you need help?" Autumn asked.

"No, it's just tacos," Violet said as she waved the spatula. "Go talk. That's more important." She looked at her son. "I have my helper right here."

Dakota straightened and squared his shoulders. "I'm a great helper."

Stone looked at his sister. "Let's get this over with."

She nodded. "Lead the way."

Kyle and their mother were sitting across from each other in the living room. The gas fireplace and several lamps lit the room in a soft shade of yellow. Outside, night had almost closed in, with just a fraction of daylight fighting for existence. The living room had high ceilings and large picture windows that looked out to a stone patio and swimming pool. Decorated in blues and whites by Trey, the vibe was genteel and timeless, yet practical. Like Violet.

Their mother set aside the can of diet soda in her hand and stood when they approached, as if she wanted an embrace. Stone hung back, but Autumn gave her an obligatory hug before lowering herself onto the couch.

"Autumn, you look so pretty with your hair like that," Valerie said.

"Thank you. Dakota thought so too."

"Hi, Stone." Valerie wore faded jeans and a pink sweatshirt. Her hair was pulled back in a ponytail.

"Hey. Good to see you." Why had he said that, as if they were merely casual acquaintances? Maybe they were, when it all was said and done. He didn't know her, not really.

"It's good to see you," Valerie said.

Kyle gestured toward the bar. "Help yourselves to a drink."

"I'll get it," Stone said to Autumn, only too happy to have an activity with which to busy himself.

There was an open bottle of white wine, so he poured a glass for his sister and grabbed a beer for himself. While he busied himself with this, the others made awkward conversation about the weather.

He returned to the main sitting area and gave the glass of

wine to his sister. When he sat next to Autumn on the couch, Kyle seemed to take that as a cue to start the real discussion.

"Mom, I filled the others in on our meeting with the attorney." He turned his attention in Stone and Autumn's direction. "She's just told me the extortionist contacted her this morning and said she wants the money the day after tomorrow. Which means she needs to go to the police tomorrow with her confession as well as proof of this woman's threat."

"As Kyle shared with you, I don't want to fight." Valerie twisted a cocktail napkin between her fingers. "I'm going to confess my guilt and take whatever the judge gives me. I've caused you all enough trouble. I don't want Kyle spending his money on attorney fees."

Kyle raised his designer-shoe-clad foot over his knee. "I think I have a better idea. Stone, you know how you always say that any of life's questions can be answered in the lyrics of a country song?"

"It's true," Stone said with a smile.

"It came to me today when I was driving Dakota to school and a Dixie Chicks song came on the radio. You remember the one about the abusive husband?"

"Earl?" Stone asked.

"The two girls poison him," Autumn said.

"Mary Anne and Wanda," Stone said. "They stuffed him in the trunk."

"Right. The cops filed a missing persons report and that was it. The guy was so awful that most people were glad he was gone. So, this got me thinking." Kyle's eyes glittered as he continued. "When the Miller brothers died in the fire, the cops barely investigated. A little more digging and they might have found their way to you, Mom. Instead, they talked to Dad and that was it. Because no one cared they were dead. They'd terrorized more than just us in that town, right?"

"No question," Stone said.

"That led me to my idea. What if we call this woman's bluff?"

Kyle asked. "Mom, you could tell her to go ahead with her plan because you're perfectly ready to go to jail. But if she decides to go to the police, we'll nail her ass for extortion."

"Which will make her keep her mouth shut. Kind of a reverse blackmail," Autumn said.

"Exactly," Kyle said.

Stone stared at his brother and then his sister. Their minds were so devious.

"And if she goes to the police, then fine. They'll dig around to see if they can make a case against you. Or maybe they won't. If, and this is a big if, you're indicted, then we can talk about a confession. Until then, I say you just lie low. Continue to live your life, and if they come for you, then fine. My guess, they won't. No one missed these guys. No one cared they were dead except for their equally disliked father. Who is also dead, by the way. I did a little research and he was killed in a bar fight five years ago. The Miller brothers were the last of the clan. There's no one else who cares enough to look into this with any interest."

Stone looked at Valerie to gauge her reaction. She'd twisted the napkin into a ball by then but nodded in what appeared to be agreement.

"What do you think?" Kyle asked.

"It makes sense to me," Autumn said. "I'm not sure why we didn't think of it before. Fear clouds logic, I guess."

"Well, thank you," Valerie said. "I guess this means you're rid of me."

Kyle studied her. "Is that what you want?"

"I know I don't have any right to be here or part of your lives, but it would be nice if I could be. Not a lot. Maybe just a visit every now and then so I could see the children. I don't deserve it, but I'd be so grateful for a second chance." Her eyes filled. She pulled a tissue from the pocket of her ratty jeans and wiped her face. "But you kids will have to decide what you want."

They were quiet. Stone watched a moth fluttering around an outside patio light. How long was he supposed to hold on to this anger? What purpose did it serve? He thought of Pepper then, about her father's letter. At the end, he'd been sorry he hadn't been the kind of father that Pepper needed. Still, he'd been unable to change. Perhaps Valerie Hickman was the same. She'd left because it was all she was capable of at the time. Was that circumstance or her psychological makeup? Who knew? However, unlike Pepper's father, she was here now. She wanted to be part of their lives.

He looked over at the old woman and took in her thin skin and weathered hands. She'd paid for her mistakes. That was plain to see. The anger drained from him. His heart opened. "Kyle's kids are the coolest. I know they'd like to have a grandparent around."

"They would," Kyle said.

Valerie brightened just slightly. A hopeful pink tinge colored her cheeks. "I'd like to be their grandmother. I'd love it, I mean. The chance to see them grow up would give me something to look forward to. I don't have much else."

"We can take it slowly," Autumn said. "Get used to the idea that you're back in our lives."

"Nah. That's not how the Hickman siblings roll," Kyle said. "Let's get you a little place in town. You can retire. Put your feet up. Join one of those old lady book clubs. Go to the beach with the kids."

"Get to know us," Stone said.

Valerie fidgeted, smoothing her sweater. "That's very sweet, but I don't have any retirement money saved. It was all spent on my husband's bills. I can't afford to leave my job. And this town is much too expensive for me."

"Mom, I'm super rich," Kyle said.

Stone chuckled. "He's rich and he's generous. Too generous, in my opinion."

"Nah. God doesn't love a stingy man," Kyle said. "Mom,

don't worry about it. I got you covered."

"I can always help you fix it up," Stone said. "I'm not rich but I've got these." He lifted his hands.

"Autumn?" Valerie asked through tears. "Is this what you want?"

"I don't know." Autumn had her arms wrapped around her middle. Her gaze was fixed on the tray in the middle of the square coffee table.

"Autumn, you and Stone forgave me for leaving," Kyle said. "And I didn't deserve you to."

Autumn's bottom lip quivered as she nodded. "It was more complex than that."

"So is this," Kyle said.

That was just it. If you delved into any situation and examined it from every angle and point of view, one arrived at complex. *It's complicated.* That was the truth. Every person on the planet had been given certain strengths and weakness but without nurturing support, it was hard to succeed.

After a horrendous childhood and marriage, their mother had done the only thing she could do at the time to survive. She'd left. Just as Kyle had.

But now they could do better than that. This was not a matter of survival. Among them, they had the means and the love to give their mother a taste of milk and honey during these last years of her life. They had it within their power to make her life easier. Because it wasn't really a matter of what a person deserved or not. She hadn't deserved a terrible childhood any more than she deserved forgiveness now. Her circumstances had been out of her control. She'd done the best she could.

What could they control? Right now. This moment. And their reaction to it. Their conscious choice to forgive, to love. He couldn't be sure, of course, but he had a strong suspicion that all roads to good were laid with bricks made of love. One could always choose love.

"Do you like to play cards?" Stone asked his mother.

Valerie had been silently weeping, but she dried her eyes and looked over at him. "Yes, I do."

"I have a few ladies I'd like to introduce you to," Stone said.

"Autumn, I'll only stay if you want me to," Valerie said.

Autumn raised her face. The stony expression had softened a smidge. "I'm not making any promises that we'll be baking cookies together by Christmas, but I'm open to getting to know you."

"Thank you," Valerie whispered.

"In the meantime, let's have some tacos," Kyle said. "My perfect wife and precocious son are waiting for us in the kitchen."

THE NEXT MORNING, Stone announced that dinner for the building was on at his place. He and Trey were making chili. They'd soaked the beans the night before and put them in the slow cooker with onions and spices. As the smell of chili pepper and onions filled the house, they spent most of the day watching football together on the couch like an old married couple. As much as he wanted to, Stone couldn't shake his sadness. Missing Pepper was an all-consuming, full-time ache that started the moment he woke in the morning and plagued his sleep with nightmares.

He'd been home for three days. They'd talked on the phone a few times and exchanged a few texts, but he hadn't heard from her all day. She'd been elusive about her meeting with the board, saying only that it wasn't what she expected, and she'd tell him about it soon.

Soon? What did that mean?

She was already drifting away from him. He could feel it with every text that went unanswered today. She was probably meeting with important people and planning trips to the South of France on some rapper's yacht.

But he couldn't wallow around the rest of his life. He needed to carry on. Thus, he'd put out a text to the rest of the tenants. Group Dinner was on.

Rafael and Lisa had returned home from her filming. He'd heard them come home late last night as he lay in bed trying to fall asleep. They'd agreed to come for dinner, as had everyone else.

It was the fourth quarter of the heated San Francisco-versus-Los Angeles game when a knock on the door interrupted their clenched-jaw watching.

"I got it." Stone ambled around the couch to open the front door.

The sight before him weakened his knees.

It was Pepper. Gorgeous, sexy Pepper Griffin in a long red coat and black boots. Her hair was its usual mass of curls that cascaded around her small face.

"Surprise." Her mouth widened into a smile.

He clutched his heart and pretended to stagger. "What are you doing here?"

"Should I have called? You're not having a heart attack, are you?"

"Is it really you?"

"The one and only." She appeared breathless, as if she'd run up the stairs at full speed.

He continued to stare at her, sure she was a hallucination. She moved closer and threw herself into his arms. "Aren't you going to kiss a girl after she paid outrageously for a last-minute flight?"

"Yes. Yes, I'm just so stunned." He pulled her closer. "Why did you come?" he asked softly with his mouth pressed close to her ear.

"I missed you," she whispered.

He set her on her feet and kissed her. "I missed you too." The scent of her perfume both intoxicated and soothed him.

Trey was on his feet by then. He stood on the other side of the couch, obviously surprised, but grinning from ear to ear. "Pepper, welcome back."

She thanked him as she plunged her hands into the pockets of the red coat and flushed scarlet. "Good to be here. Sorry to barge in on you like this."

"Not at all. I was just on my way out," Trey said. "To Rafael's. For the game." He stopped to give her a quick hug before making a hasty exit.

She unbuttoned her coat. Remembering his manners, Stone scooted close to help ease it from her shoulders. He held it against his chest, feeling the warmth of her body trapped in the wool before hanging it in the closet. When he turned back to her, she was sitting on the couch with her hands clasped over her knees.

She patted the couch. "Come sit with me?"

He strode across the room, anxious to be near her, and sat close to her. When he reached for her, she put a hand gently on his chest.

"Wait. Before we get carried away, I have something to discuss with you. I'm afraid it's going to disappoint you. I'm afraid *I* might be a disappointment to you. You had such high hopes for me—so willing to sacrifice for me to pursue my dreams, but I don't want it, Stone."

"Don't want what?"

"The company. My dad's company. The whole thing scared me to death. All the board members are stuffy, old-money New Yorkers. At the meeting, it was so obvious they thought I was a twit and not worthy of the job. They're right, Stone. I don't know the first thing about running a production company. They hurled all these questions at me one after the other. I didn't know the answer to any of them. They were talking about math stuff and projecting spreadsheets on the wall and business doctrine and how I needed to jump in right away because my father had let things go when he was sick. I would have to sit at a desk and be all serious and never have any fun because all I'd do is work. I'm sorry, but I don't want to be that person. I'm so sorry I've let you down." She burst into tears.

"Oh, baby. Don't cry. I would never want you to do something you didn't want."

"I'm not letting you down?" She sniffed as she met his gaze.

"How could you let me down? I want you to be happy. I'm not like your dad, Pepper."

She stared at him, unblinking. "You don't think I'm wimping out?"

"God no. This is your life. You get to choose. I'm proud of you no matter what."

"The entire meeting felt like a nightmare. And then I went to meet with my private banker, and Stone, it's so much money. It's more money than we could ever spend in a lifetime, but it's not mine. Not really. It feels so weird to look at all that money and think I'll never have to worry again and I could give you and our kids anything you wanted. But then the next thing I think is how undeserving I am. I didn't do one thing to earn it. Yes, my dad was a jerk, but still. This guy, this banker guy was all starched and lacquered and he talked like that character in *Rain Man*. You know the one?"

"With Dustin Hoffman?"

"Yes, he talked like that guy, and I couldn't follow a thing he said. I called Dack in tears and made him promise to come with me next time. Stone, this life my dad left me is all wrong."

He flooded with warmth and hope. There was a catch. There had to be a catch. "But what about the theater? What about acting? You have to be in New York for that, don't you? What about Hedda?"

"Dreams change. People change. You changed me." She rested one of her white hands on his knee. "As soon as you left, I knew my life was meaningless without you in it. If I stayed in New York and took over my dad's company, I would become him. I'd be alone. And no matter how much I love the theater, it's nothing compared to how I feel about you. I want to be here.

With you. More precisely, wherever you are is where I want to be. For the rest of my life."

He couldn't speak, and even if he'd been able to open his mouth and form words, what would he say? Nothing could describe the intense joy that flooded him.

"All that to say—I've come home to throw myself at your feet." She flashed him the same nervous smile from earlier and watched him intently, as if the code to the meaning of life was written on his forehead.

"No throwing necessary." His words came out strangled from the force of his effort to not cry like a baby in front of the woman he loved more than his own life. "You know I love you. Every second without you has been physically painful."

She dropped to the floor onto her knees and took both his hands in hers. "Stone Hickman, you're everything in a man I've ever wanted and more. When I'm with you it's like I'm the confident and calm woman I'm supposed to be. Seeing myself through your eyes makes me feel like the person I always wanted to be. I want to be your wife and make a home and a family with you."

"You do?"

She laughed as she brought his large calloused hand to her soft mouth. "The meaning of my life is right here." She tapped the rough skin on the palm of his hand with her finger. "Everything I want and need is in these hands that build things and caress my anxiousness away and will someday hold our newborn baby. I've been looking for purpose from my work when all along it's been right in front of me—my parents and Lisa and Maggie. And now you. My calling and purpose are to love you. Lisa and Maggie reminded me of something. The kind of work we do—art—can only be fed through our human connections. Through love. When I thought of it that way, I knew exactly what I had to do. I had to come home and be with you. The rest of it means nothing without you."

Her face blurred in front of him from the tears that swam in his eyes. What a sight he must be. A giant crying in front of a princess.

Pepper reached into the pocket of her dress and held up a thick silver band. "Stone Hickman, will you marry me and build a life and a family with me?"

His mouth fell open before he started to laugh. "You're proposing to me?"

"Yes, I am. Do you have a problem with that?"

"No ma'am, I do not. Nope. Not me. I'm an enlightened man at the mercy of a badass woman."

She grinned up at him. "This doesn't mean I don't want something sparkly on my own finger, but as you're aware, I have particular taste and would appreciate being able to pick it out myself."

He laughed again. "I wouldn't have it any other way."

"So, what's your answer? Will you marry me?"

"Yes, Pepper Griffin, I will marry you." He tugged her off the floor and onto his lap. She wrapped her arms around his neck and peered down at him with eyes that sparkled brighter than any diamond ever could. "However, I will have to put my foot down on a winter wonderland type of wedding. I think I've had enough of snow for quite some time."

"No arguments there." She leaned closer and kissed him, and his heart pumped hard and fast. This incredible woman wanted to be his wife. She loved him enough to make him the center of her universe.

"Are you sure you can give all of it up for me?" he asked.

"I'm not giving up anything. I didn't want to be a fund-raiser or answer to a board of stuffy directors. One day in my father's world and it was clear to me why he was such a nasty person. It was the only way to survive. It's not me, Stone. If my father had known me at all, he would have known that."

"What will happen to the company?"

"Several of the board members are buying me out. I'll have

another tidy sum to add to what my father left me. I'm so rich now." She grinned. "Am I more attractive because of it?"

"You're as stunning as you've always been."

"You loved me when I was broke, so I know I can trust you." She fluffed his hair and kissed his forehead. "God, I love you."

"Still, I'm a man, you know. Fragile ego and all."

"You're the opposite of that kind of man. A man like that would not have insisted I pursue my dreams. Anyway, when we get married, my money will be your money."

Perhaps this was true. Still, he didn't want to be a mooch, and he said as much to Pepper.

"You could never be a mooch," she said. "Plus, you made a commitment to the guys. You have to keep working."

"True enough." Having Pepper by his side would give him even more motivation to make Wolf Enterprises successful.

"All that said, I can't live here with you and Trey. We're going to have to get started on a house of our own. I can fund it now. I have tons of ideas of what I want, too, and David's just the man to design it for us."

He laughed. "Whatever you want, I want. As long as I get a man cave to escape to when Lisa and Maggie are over."

"A man cave in exchange for a pole in our bedroom sounds fair."

"Don't tease me when you have no intention of putting a pole in our bedroom," he said.

"Can you imagine it, though? My mother would probably faint at the sight of it."

"Not to mention Lisa," Stone said.

"That makes me want to do it even more." She bounced on his lap. "Anyway, I have other news. You're looking at an actress in the next Gennie Banks movie."

"No way."

"Yes. Lisa didn't want to get my hopes up if it didn't work out, so she had to keep it from me until they were sure. But it's a good role. A role that could lead to others."

He let out a whoop. "I knew it, baby. It's all going to happen for you."

"We just never know what's going to come next, do we?"

"True. Which is why we must remain optimistic, even when things seem bad."

"Things seem pretty good right now." She grinned before nipping his ear with her teeth, then trailed kisses down his neck.

"As long as you're with me, I'm good. Nothing else needed."

She answered him with a long, sweet kiss.

23

Pepper

PEPPER SQUEALED when she heard the knock at Stone's front door. "They're here," she called out to Stone, who was at the coffee table arranging a plate of pastries.

It was Thanksgiving Day, and her parents had flown into San Francisco the day before to take in the sights before driving out to Cliffside Bay this morning. They had a room booked at the lodge for five nights. Later today, they would all head to Violet and Kyle's for Thanksgiving dinner.

She slid her engagement ring off her finger and stuck it in her pocket, then sprinted across the room and flung open the door. Her parents stood there, beaming at her. She threw herself at her mother. "I'm so happy you made it." She hugged Dack before dragging them inside where Stone waited.

"This is my Stone." My rock, tree, stone—everything strong and steady and good. "Stone, this is Mom and Dack."

Stone smiled and held out his hand to her stepdad. "I'm pleased to meet you, Dr. Mack. Mrs. Mack."

"Nice to meet you, son," Dack said. The men shook hands. Slim and just under six feet, Dack looked small compared with Stone. His once-blond hair was now silver but if anything, it made him even better-looking. "No need for formality. You may call me Dack."

"Thank you." Stone turned to her mother next, but she was having none of that. Only a hug would do for Lila Mack. She embraced him, then pulled back to get a good look. "You're just as handsome as your photo but so much taller than I thought you'd be. And bigger."

"I've heard that before, ma'am," Stone said. "Mrs. Mack, you and Pepper look so much alike, only like sisters, not mother and daughter."

Mom slapped Stone playfully on the arm. "Well, aren't you sweet? And please, call me Lila. Mrs. Mack makes me feel like an old lady."

Her mother looked lovely, as always. She wore her wavy dark hair in a similar cut to Pepper's, only slightly shorter. If there were any grays in that glossy head, her colorist made sure they were well hidden under expensive color treatments. When Pepper was a child, her mother had always seemed younger and prettier than all the others. To Pepper, then and now, she was the most beautiful woman in the world. "Mom, you're gorgeous and way too young to ever be called old."

"I was just telling her that when she was fussing in the mirror this morning," Dack said as he handed his coat to Stone.

"I'm fifty. Things are starting to slip. Mostly downward." Mom shrugged out of her long coat and set it in Stone's outstretched hand. "It's horrifying."

"As you can tell, Pepper gets her beauty and her vanity from her mother," Dack said with a twinkle in his brown eyes.

Pepper shared a smile with her mother as she reached for the coats. "Dack, stop teasing us in front of Stone." She hung the coats in the closet. When she turned around, both her parents were staring at her.

"Pepper Griffin hanging up coats instead of tossing them onto the couch?" her mom asked. "What's happened to my daughter?"

"Stone's trying to reform me," Pepper said. "Apparently, I'm messy."

Both her parents laughed a little too loudly. "Good luck, Stone," Dack said. "We've been working on her a long time."

"She came out of the womb that way," Mom said.

"Stone loves me anyway, even though I'm a tad untidy." Pepper tossed her curls and flashed Stone a smile. He gave her a slight one in return. His hands fidgeted at his sides in a very non-Stone way. He was nervous. How sweet. She'd never seen him nervous about anything, including navigating through a snowstorm with near-zero visibility.

"Please sit. Would you like coffee?" Stone pointed at the table in front of the fireplace, set with pastries and a canister of coffee.

"We had a big breakfast at the lodge," Mom said. "But coffee sounds good." She shivered. "The fog has me chilled."

Her parents sat together on the couch. Pepper poured them each a cup of coffee before sitting in the chair opposite Stone's. When everyone had fixed their coffee how they wanted, Pepper caught Stone's eye. He gave a slight nod. Having saved their big news until they could tell her parents in person, they'd planned on telling them about the engagement this morning. Keeping it from them the last few weeks had been nearly impossible. However, she wanted to see their faces when she told them. A girl only got engaged once.

Across from her, Stone swallowed and set his coffee cup on the table, clearly too nervous to hold it without spilling.

"Mom, Dack, we have exciting news. We're getting married." *Remember this moment.*

Her mother's eyes widened, then turned upward as her face transformed from shock to joy. "You're getting married?"

"And before you say anything, we fell in love before we knew about Frederick's money. Stone loved me way before that."

"I did. I've loved her since the first moment I ever set eyes on her," Stone said. "I even loved her when she hated me."

"It's true." Pepper laughed. "I was awful to him, and he still loved me. He saw from the beginning how we belong together." She fetched her ring out of her pocket and slipped it on before holding out her hand for them to see the princess-cut diamond surrounded by a dozen small ones arranged in a circle. "We even have a ring."

"It's beautiful," Mom said before turning to Stone. "And for the record, it would never have entered my mind that you'd marry my daughter for her money."

"Why?" Stone asked.

"Because my wife's the least suspicious person in the world." Dack rose to his feet, which prompted the rest of them to do the same.

"Me? What about you? He's a complete romantic," Mom said. "Do you know he said he fell in love with me at first sight?"

"How could I not?" Dack asked. "I mean, look at her." He took Pepper's hand. "Let me see that ring."

"I picked it out, because you know, it's me and I had to have my way," Pepper said.

"Your mother picked hers out, too." Dack looked over at Stone. "It's best to know your place when it comes to these two."

"Yes, sir." Stone's tense expression had dissipated some, but a muscle in his cheek still flexed.

Dack shook Stone's hand again before grabbing him into a half hug. "Congratulations. We're very happy."

Mom drew her close and stroked her hair. "My little feisty Pepper's finally been tamed."

"I love him so much, Mom," she whispered.

Mom let her go and turned to Stone. She lifted her hands to

his face. "You'll be good to my baby. I know you will. You've got an earnest face and honest eyes."

"I'll do everything in my power to keep her safe."

Dack turned to Pepper and pulled her close. "You've always been full of surprises, Pepper girl."

Pepper felt the tears coming and didn't even try to keep them back. "I know, Dack, but you've loved me anyway."

"More than you'll ever know." Dack's eyes grew shiny. "You and your mother are my whole life. I'm so proud of you."

"I guess this means you're staying in California?" Mom asked as she wiped her eyes.

"Yes, but we'll be out to visit tons," Pepper said. "Or you guys can come here."

"We're going to build a house on the property next to my brother," Stone said. "When we go out later, we'll take you by to see it."

"A big one so we can have a million children," Pepper said.

Mom's mouth dropped open, and her hand flew to her heart. "Children? Again, Stone, what have you done with my daughter?"

"Mom, as it turns out, once I found the right man, everything changed."

Mom looked over at Dack. "Shall we tell them our news?"

"Seems like an appropriate time," Dack said.

"Your father's retiring at the end of the year. Which means we'll have a lot more time to visit," Mom said. "Or maybe have a second home."

"Really?" Pepper bounced on her toes.

"I'll be able to help you with all those children you're having," Mom said. "Whenever that is. It's not imminent, is it?"

"Mom, no." Pepper flushed. "I have a movie to film in the spring. I need a few more years to get my career going."

"Don't wait too long," Mom said. "I'm not getting any younger."

Dack gave an indulgent shake of his head. "Maybe we should look for real estate this weekend."

"Dad, really?" Pepper asked.

"We want to be where you are," Dack said. "And now I'll have a son to add to my good fortune."

Pepper looked over at Stone, knowing that Dack's words would mean a lot to him, but even she was surprised when his eyes filled. He needed and wanted a father figure in his life. And Dack was just the man for the job.

She might explode with happiness.

24

Stone

STONE USHERED his soon-to-be father-in-law onto a stool at The Oar. They'd left the ladies at the apartment to prepare a sweet potato dish to take to Kyle and Violet's later. He'd asked Dack to come out for a beer for an important reason, one that had been eating at him for weeks. He had to apologize for not asking for his permission to marry his daughter.

Sophie was behind the bar, looking like sunshine with her blond hair and big smile. The gloomy and foggy weather was no match for her. Stone introduced Dack to her. They shook hands across the bar.

"Pepper's dad. I'm so glad to meet you," Sophie said. "She talks about you all the time."

Dack smiled as he settled onto the stool. "It's great to be here. We've heard so much about all of you and Cliffside Bay that we feel like we know you already."

"What're you boys drinking?" she asked.

They both ordered one of Zane's local IPAs. In seconds, with swift and efficient movements, Sophie had them poured and in front of them. "Enjoy." She left to take care of another customer.

"Sir, I brought you here to apologize," Stone said.

Dack's eyebrows raised. He wiped a spot of foam from the side of his mouth with a cocktail napkin. "Apologize?"

"Yes. I'm sorry I didn't ask you for permission to marry Pepper."

Dack barked out a laugh. "I'm not sure if you've noticed, but she's not one to answer to anyone. She's not named Pepper for nothing. Seems to me she's pretty clear about who she wants. My permission isn't necessary."

"I need you to know the truth, sir. I'm not from your world. I grew up in a trailer on the edge of a pig farm. My company's just starting out, so I'm basically cash poor. The property where I'm going to build our house is owned by my brother. All that aside, I love your daughter with everything I am. I'd do anything for her. I'll support her dreams and take care of her heart. But I wanted you to understand who and what I am."

Dack put his hand on Stone's shoulder. "I don't know how much Pepper told you about me, but I didn't come from the world I live in now, either. Single mom. Trailer park. Earned a scholarship to college and fought my way into medical school. I don't care where you came from, only where you're going."

"Yes, sir."

"Well then, let's have a beer and get to know each other."

Stone found himself telling Dack about his childhood and his mother's return. He left out the murder, figuring his future father-in-law didn't need the burden of that knowledge. Dack was a good listener, asking a question now and then, but mostly listening.

"So, my brother's going to help her get on her feet. Possibly move her here. The whole thing's been hard, but she's family.

We're a strange family, but family just the same." He kept the gritty details of the extortionist to himself. All had worked out in the end. Kyle had been right. She'd backed down the minute they said they were going to the police. They'd all breathed a sigh of relief.

"Most of the time our families don't come in neat little packages you can put on a Christmas card. I commend you and your siblings for giving her a second chance. She's paid for her mistakes. There's no reason to make her suffer more by keeping those grandkids away from her."

"I agree, sir. Thank you." Was this what it was like to have a father figure? If so, he was all in.

They finished their beers as Stone gave Dack the rundown on the crew he'd meet tonight at Violet and Kyle's. "You know Maggie and Lisa, obviously. But you'll meet Jackson and Rafael's mother and their friend, Ria. My sister, Autumn, will be there. And my brother and his wife, Violet, and their four children."

"Four?"

"All under six years old."

"She's a busy lady," Dack said.

"An amazing lady. The rest of the Wolves will be there too."

"Wolves?"

"My business partners. That's what we call ourselves. Long story."

"I can't wait to hear it."

"And my mom." He took in a deep breath and let it out slowly. "My mom, who hasn't been at a Thanksgiving dinner since I was six years old."

"It'll be just fine, son. We'll be right there with you the whole time."

Son. Stone sighed with contentment. Life was coming up rainbows and unicorns.

As THE SKY darkened into evening, Stone, Pepper, and her parents arrived at Kyle and Violet's. He rang the doorbell while balancing the dish of sweet potato casserole in one arm. Violet greeted them with smiles and hugged Lila and Dack as if she'd known them all her life. She ushered them inside and helped them with coats, which she tossed onto the already-steep pile on the foyer bench. The sounds of laughter, children's footsteps, and various voices in conversation mingled with country music. Thanksgiving was such a good day. Especially this one, because Pepper and her parents were by his side.

Violet flashed her wide, gentle smile as she wrapped her arm around Pepper's waist. "My soon-to-be sister-in-law. I love the way that rolls off my tongue."

"Me too." Under the soft lights, Pepper's eyes were closer to a smoky blue than gray today and matched her dress. She had never looked prettier to him than right now.

To Dack and Lila, Violet said, "Your daughter makes everything a little more interesting."

"That she does," Dack said with a loving glance at Pepper.

Violet winked at Stone. "My husband's also one who livens and brightens the world. You and I will have to be happy as the quiet, steady ones."

"Someone has to do it," Stone said.

Violet linked her arm through Pepper's. "Come on in. You're almost the last to arrive. We've already started in on the wine."

Stone wanted to skip with joy as he followed behind the ladies and Dack and Lila down the hall toward the kitchen. Every person he loved in the world waited at the end of this hallway. His life might be simple, but it was exactly the one he'd wished for all the years of his childhood and then his time in the service. Soon, he and Pepper would be married and have a home like this one. They might host Thanksgiving next year in their new house. The thought of it made him dizzy with glee.

When they reached the door to the kitchen, Stone detected

the scent of sage and sausage. Violet had made her famous stuffing. He couldn't smell turkey, however. "I don't smell a turkey. We haven't gone vegetarian, have we?" His brother's wife was always trying to get them to eat healthier. "Please tell me you didn't make good on your threat to make a tofu turkey."

Violet laughed as they entered the kitchen. "No, it's the exact opposite. Kyle got a wild hair and decided he needed to deep-fry the turkey. Which, for the record, I highly disapprove of. He's out on the patio with Jackson and David—supervising the fryer and drinking scotch. The three of them will be half-lit before dinner." Despite her words, Violet didn't seem in the least bothered by her husband's antics. She loved him, wild hairs and all.

The kitchen was a bustle of activity. Lisa and Maggie were at the counter cutting vegetables. The twins and Maggie's baby, Lily, were in highchairs in one corner of the kitchen, having their dinner. Steam fogged up the windows. Various casseroles occupied both ovens. The counters were full of all the usual side dishes: cranberries, mashed potatoes, stuffing, a salad. God bless this holiday. It was the best day of the year.

He added their sweet potato casserole to the mix as Maggie and Lisa swarmed Dack and Lila.

After hugs and exclamations of delight and declarations of how good everyone looked, and it had been too long, and it's so good to see you, Maggie and Lisa returned to their task. Violet poured Lila and Pepper glasses of wine; if the two empty bottles were any indication, the other ladies had a good start on them. Stone grabbed beers out of the beverage cooler for Dack and himself.

"These are my niece and nephew," Stone said to Lila and Dack. "Hope and Chance."

"I love their names," Lila said.

"They were quite the surprise," Violet said. "Thus, the names. We already had two when I found out I was pregnant. I can't remember a thing since."

"They're adorable," Dack said. "And in my professional opinion, look very healthy."

Stone plopped a kiss on each of the babies' heads. Hope reached out to him with fingers smeared with mashed potatoes and let out a screech of delight.

"And this beautiful girl belongs to Maggie." Pepper twirled a red curl around her index fingers as Lily grinned up at her. "Pep-pa," Lily said.

"Oh, Maggie, I would have known her anywhere," Lila said. "She looks just like you."

"She has my husband's eyes," Maggie said. "But yes. Her coloring is all mine."

Stone turned to Dack. "We better get out of here before they put us to work. Come on, let's go see what my brother's done to this poor turkey."

"Wait? I'm supposed to help in the kitchen?" Pepper asked. "That doesn't seem like me."

Lisa smacked her on the behind with a towel. "You can just sit there and look pretty."

"Oh, good. I was worried for a moment." Pepper plopped onto a barstool at the island and took a deep sip from her wine.

Before they left the women, he asked Violet if his mother had shown up yet. He hadn't seen her car in the driveway.

"Not yet. She said she was coming," Violet said.

But maybe she'd bail at the last moment. Whatever. He wasn't letting her ruin his evening. He gave Pepper a quick kiss on the cheek and left with Dack to find the men.

He spotted Kyle, Jackson, and David outside on the patio with drinks, keeping a close eye on the flightless bird. Trey, Nico, and Autumn were on the couch huddled over a laptop computer. Laine and Mollie played with dolls in the corner of the living room.

Stone greeted them. "Hey, gang. Meet my future father-in-law."

Nico set the laptop on the coffee table when they all three stood to shake hands with Dack.

"Welcome to town," Autumn said. "We're so pleased about the engagement. We love her very much."

"Everyone loves Pepper," Trey said. "It's impossible not to."

"Thank you," Dack said.

The three settled back on the couch while Stone and Dack each sat in one of the chairs.

"Where are Dakota and Oliver?" Stone asked.

"Upstairs, playing trains," Autumn said. "They're thick as thieves up there."

"You guys aren't working, are you?" Stone asked, gesturing toward the laptop.

"Not work, exactly." Nico glanced slyly at Trey.

Autumn giggled. "It's a chore, but not work."

"We're finding a man for Autumn." Nico grabbed the laptop from the table and sat back down on the couch.

"We're perusing three dating sites," Trey said. "It's proving difficult to find a man worthy of Autumn."

"Nico came up with a rating system," Autumn said. "Based on appearance, education, employment, and similar interests."

"We haven't found the right combination yet," Nico said. "But he's out there."

Stone would have liked to suggest that perhaps one of the two of them might date his sister. However, he kept his mouth shut. His sister would kill him if he dared say anything even remotely close. They were her *friends*, she'd told him when he'd suggested it before. And, she'd added, friends were more important than guys who would eventually break her heart when they saw what she looked like without clothes. He'd flinched when she'd said that, sick to his stomach. He imagined his fighting days were past him until he thought of someone hurting his sister. Nothing made his fists clench faster.

"What happens if you find one with potential?" Stone asked.

"*I'm* going to help Autumn write to them," Trey said. "We decided a guy would know more what a guy wants to hear."

"It's kind of a twisted Cyrano type of thing," Nico said. "Only Autumn doesn't have a big nose."

"She has a particularly adorable nose," Trey said. "Sprinkled in freckles, which are the best kind."

Stone studied Trey, but there didn't appear to be anything at play, other than a good buddy trying to build up his friend.

"I'm fine in the nose department, but what about my leg?" Autumn asked.

The guys were quiet. No one, other than Stone, had ever seen her bare legs. Tonight, she wore blousy slacks and a green cotton sweater that matched her eyes.

"They don't think I should mention my lame leg in the profile," Autumn said. "But that seems like false advertising."

"Any guy worth his salt isn't going to care about your leg," Nico said. "Anyway, you're beautiful, smart, kind, and funny."

Again, if she was so great, why wasn't one of them snatching her up? *Were* they deterred by her leg?

Stone looked over at Dack, who appeared to be listening with interest and compassion.

They were interrupted when Dr. Jackson Waller came in from the patio. More introductions ensued, ending with Jackson and Dack breaking apart from the group to talk about practicing medicine in small towns. The other three went back to looking at male profiles. Stone decided it was time to say hello to his brother and David. He grabbed another beer and joined them.

They were sitting on the outdoor lounge chairs, drinking scotch and talking about…not sports or politics or business but about their kids. Stone hoped someday he might be able to join in the discussion. The fryer was silver and on legs, looking remarkably like a larger version of Dakota's toy spaceship upstairs in the playroom.

"Hey, little brother," Kyle said. "Have a seat. Tell us about the in-laws."

Stone grabbed a chair and joined them. David looked relaxed for once. The fatigue around his eyes had smoothed, and his jaw appeared less tight. Being out here with Kyle was doing him good.

He told them about his day with Dack and Lila, how gracious they were and welcoming, as well as his apology about his lack of decorum regarding the proposal.

"How're you doing?" Stone asked David. This was his first Thanksgiving without his wife.

David lifted his shoulders in a shrug. "I'm good. Better than I thought I'd be. My sister was right to suggest I move out here. To tell you the truth, I wasn't sure. Except for college, I'd never lived anywhere other than the town I grew up in. It's been good for me to be someplace new, and I couldn't ask to have met a better group of people. You guys and Lisa's friends—I feel supported and damn grateful. Being close to Lisa is great for the kids, too. She's so good with them, and they adore her. Honestly, I never realized how lacking my wife was as a mother until I saw Lisa with them. Violet's been a lifesaver, too. She hooked me up with a part-time nanny and is always inviting the kids over to play. So, all in all, I'm pretty good."

That was the most Stone had ever heard David say at one time.

"And your brother's been plying me with good scotch for the last hour, so I'm feeling no pain."

Kyle laughed. "I'm happy to have the company."

"Still, can't help but dread December, man." David clicked his tongue against the roof of his mouth. "Christmas and my sister's wedding mean time with my mother. She's still super ticked at me for moving out here and taking the kids from her."

They talked for a few minutes about the wedding and David and Lisa's family. Although his parents were together, it sounded as if they weren't exactly the perfect family. Welcome to the club.

After that, the conversation drifted to work when Kyle asked about the status of Sara's house. Since they'd broken ground at the beginning of the month, they'd made great strides. If all continued to go well, she'd be able to move in at the beginning of the summer. To Stone's surprise, she'd been an easy client. Not that she'd ever been anything other than sweet to him, but he wasn't oblivious to the fact that she was rich and therefore might have been used to being demanding.

"I may have your next few jobs," Kyle said. "Jackson just told me he's moving his medical practice from their current building."

"Why's that?" Stone asked.

"They need more space. Something about the number of babies upping the population. With Kara scaling back her hours, he's going to hire another nurse practitioner and expand the practice. He can't keep up with the volume, especially since his dad wants to golf and spend time with his wife, not get called into work every other day. Anyway, he and Maggie bought the building in back of the post office for his new practice. They're gutting it and basically starting from scratch. Doc wants to sell the old building for the cash. Coincidentally, the dance studio next door is also in flux. Miss Rita's tried to retire, but the woman who wanted to buy her out couldn't make it work. She can't find anyone who wants to take over the studio or buy the building. She came to me the other day to ask if I was interested. So, long story short, I'm buying them both. Since they're next door to each other, it gives me the option to tear them both down and build something bigger."

"Do you know what you want to do?" David asked.

"Nothing concrete. All I know is that it's prime real estate for a business that appeals to tourists." Kyle sipped from his scotch. "The problem is my wife. She wants it to be used for something that benefits the town culturally or artistically. And she's totally against tearing the existing structures down unless we build something pretty. The architecture has to enhance the beauty of the town, not take away from it. You know how she is."

Stone nodded, smiling. Violet had grown up in Cliffside Bay and was practically militant about preserving the quaint aesthetic as well as the history. She and Kyle had fallen in love as they went head-to-head over the building of the resort on the edge of town. Stone hadn't yet moved to town, but apparently Violet was a lone picketer in front of the construction site.

"What's she want? Like an art gallery?" David asked. "Because that would be cool."

Kyle groaned. "Yeah, because I love to invest in a business that bleeds cash. Unfortunately, that's exactly the kind of thing she has in mind. I'm totally screwed. I'm serious. I cannot cross her on this. I promised. But it goes against everything in me to invest in a venture that doesn't make money."

"That's a bummer about the dance studio closing," David said. "Every time we go by there, Laine points at the tutus on display and says, 'Me want.'"

"Mollie Blue's the same way. Violet says they always have to stop and watch the little dancers if the curtains are up when there's a class going on."

Stone had a sudden thought. An idea that might please everyone, including Violet, Pepper, and Kyle. This line of thinking was interrupted by the appearance of Valerie Hickman. She'd shown up after all. The men stood to greet her. Kyle hugged her, which surprised Stone. Remembering his vow of forgiveness, he did the same. Valerie trembled. His arms seemed big and oafish. She was no sturdier than a toothpick. A sharp sting pierced his chest. She was an old lady—fragile and vulnerable, probably scared to come to this enormous, perfectly polished house. Maybe she'd sat in her car, willing herself to go, but too afraid to start the engine. This house full of successful people, happy families, must feel foreign to her. She wasn't like Pepper's mother and father, at ease with rich people because they were too.

"I'm glad you came," Stone said quietly.

She looked at her feet. "I almost didn't. All these people I don't know. I didn't have anything nice to wear." She crossed her arms over her chest, as if to steady herself. "But I promised your brother, and I didn't want to let him down."

He took in her clothes then. She wore a pair of black pants and a thick sweater. The yarn had balled, and there was a small hole at the collar. Her black shoes were scuffed. "Our friends are really nice. And you know Pepper already."

Last time she'd come to visit, they'd all had lunch together at The Oar. Pepper had made it easier. She'd asked Valerie questions and gotten her talking about television shows she enjoyed. At the end of the meal, Kyle had asked her again if he could move her to an apartment or house closer to them. She'd refused. Again. "I can't let you do that. I'm fine. Really."

Kyle had told him later that he'd tried to slip her some money, but she'd declined that too. However, she was here tonight. Progress. He had a feeling if anything changed her mind about taking Kyle's offer, it would be the grandchildren.

Now, Kyle leaned over the fryer and let out a shout. "Our bird's done. Boom. I'm the king of the turkeys."

Valerie laughed, high-pitched and quick, as if she were out of practice. He'd never heard her laugh before. Not since her return, anyway. A sudden memory exploded in his mind. They'd been outside on a warm day. Her hair had glistened in the sun and looked almost red. Like Autumn's hair now. She'd knelt over to pick Autumn up from the grass and when she rose, his sister had taken a chunk of the silky strands in her pudgy toddler fist and said, "Mama pretty."

His mother had hugged Autumn close and laughed, faint and sad. "I used to be, little girl. Until this world used me all up."

Had she ever had much to laugh about? Stone's throat ached at the thought of her hard life. Darned if he was going to cry in front of his brother and David, but sadness rocked him like waves against a doomed ship in a storm.

Kyle and David lifted the turkey out of the pot and onto a

waiting platter using heat-resistant gloves. The scent of oil and crispy skin filled the air.

He turned back to look at Valerie. She was watching Kyle's every move. Although her mouth was set in a smile, her eyes glistened with unshed tears. Her hand was at her throat, playing with the cross that hung in the hollow of her neck.

"You all right?" Stone asked her.

She jumped, as if she'd forgotten he was there. "Yes, I'm fine."

"You sure?"

She spoke quietly in her dry voice. "Yes. So many Thanksgivings went by. One after the other until there were no more. I always thought, maybe next year. Next year, I'll go get them. But I was too afraid, too passive, too guilty. Then, finally, it was too late."

"You're here. It's not too late. We have another chance."

"How is it you boys can forgive me?" Tears spilled down her wrinkled cheeks. "I never forgave my parents. Not after all the ways they hurt me. You boys should hate me."

Kyle had turned to them by now. He approached, still wearing his gloves. David discreetly took the platter with the turkey inside the house.

"We can't hate you," Kyle said. "You're our mother. What would be the point of holding on to anger when we have this second chance? In the history of man, no good has ever come from clinging to a grudge or refusing to let go of the past. We're here. Our babies are the present and future, a chance for redemption—the ultimate second chance." Kyle looked up at the sky for a moment before returning his gaze to Valerie. "Stone and Pepper are getting married. Think of the wedding. Stone all dressed up waiting for his stunning bride to walk down the aisle. Think of the children's school concerts and the births of Pepper's and Autumn's babies, graduations and Thanksgiving dinners. Oh heck, think of Christmas morning. And all the beautiful days in our future. You don't have to miss anything else. We made it through the hard times to all of this." He waved a gloved hand toward the house. "Right now, that kitchen is filled with people who love us. We made it to the other side, and we want you here for the rest of the ride."

At this point, Stone realized he was crying. Just then, Dakota came running out to them. He stopped dead in his tracks at the sight of all of them crying. It was only a second's hesitation, though. He recovered his wits and hurled himself at their legs. "Don't cry, guys. It's a happy day."

Kyle yanked his gloves from his hands and tossed them onto the table. He lifted Dakota in his arms, holding him tightly around his legs. "You're right, my little man. *You* make it a happy day." Dakota wrapped his arms around his father's neck as Kyle held him close to his chest with one strong arm. "I love you, Daddy."

"I love you too," Kyle said, smiling over the top of his head. "This is the future, right here."

Dakota lifted his head. "I love you, Uncle Stone."

Stone wiped his eyes with the back of his hand. "Oh, buddy, I love you too. So much."

Dakota turned to his grandmother. "I love you too, Granny."

A sob rose out of her. A cry of pain and joy and gratefulness. "You do?"

"You're my granny. Mama says a heart has room to love gobs and gobs of people. Did you know that, Granny?"

"I did, actually."

Dakota slid down his father's tall body. "Mama says it's time to carve the turkey. May I help?"

"You may," Kyle said.

"Mama makes us say 'may,' Granny. Sometimes we forget, right, Dad?"

"Sometimes. But we're slowly getting there. One day at a time." Kyle smiled at his mother. "Come on, Mom. Let's go stuff ourselves."

Dakota placed his hand in his grandmother's. "May I escort you to dinner, Granny?"

"You may," she said.

And she laughed, a little less out of practice than the last time. If anyone could teach a person how to laugh, it was Dakota.

25

Pepper

A LIGHT MIST fell from the sky as Pepper walked her parents to the entrance of the lodge. Stone had waited in the truck while she said good night to them.

Before they reached the doors to the lobby, Pepper clasped her mother's hands in hers. "Thank you for spending time with my friends. I love having you here." Behind them, the valets ushered guests in and out of the lobby.

"It was a great way to spend Thanksgiving," Mom said. "Seeing all you girls happy is something to be thankful for." Her mother's voice cracked with emotion. "Stone's family, your friends, this beautiful town—well, we couldn't ask for anything better for our little girl. We're so proud and happy."

"And you like my Stone, right? You approve?" Pepper asked.

"Of Stone?" Dack asked. "How could we not?"

"He's a wonderful young man who obviously adores you," Mom said. "We approve."

"Can you believe I finally found someone?" Pepper asked.

Her mother captured Pepper's face in her hands. "I never doubted for a moment that you'd find the right man." She glanced at Dack. "Sometimes it takes a time or two before you find the exact right match."

"I never thought I'd think anyone was good enough for you," Dack said to Pepper. "I was prepared to spend the next few months worried and unable to sleep because I'd be sure you were making the wrong decision. But the minute I met him and saw his earnestness and how he looked at you, I knew. This man is good enough for my Pepper girl. Frankly, I didn't know there were young men like him or Kyle, or their friends. I thought men of integrity and grit and manners were a dying breed. Three years ago, when you and Maggie and Lisa came up to visit, I thought after you all left—what is wrong with the men of New York? How could they let any of you go? I told your mom, we may as well give up on grandchildren from any of you girls. Thank God Maggie found her way back to Cliffside Bay."

"Dack, I had no idea you were so worried about us." Pepper laughed through her tears. She threw her arms around his neck before backing away slightly to look at him. "Thank you for being my dad. For all three of us, you were the only man we knew who taught us what we should expect, what we deserved."

"You three girls deserve the world," Dack said. "Don't forget that."

They said good night and she watched as they disappeared into the lobby. She ran through the damp air to Stone's truck and slipped in beside him.

"Well? Did I pass the test?" he asked.

"I'd say so, yes. They love you. I knew they would."

He let out a long breath. "Thank God."

She kissed his cheek. "This is such a good day. Not a canned pea in sight."

"It's all rainbows and unicorns with you, baby." He brought

her hand to his mouth and kissed her palm. "You came back to me, Pepper Shaker. I'll never take that for granted. I'm a blessed man."

"Have I told you today how much I love you?"

He grinned as he put the truck in drive and inched out of the driveway. "I think you may have shown me this morning."

She slapped his arm and laughed. "There's more where that came from."

"You're going to love me even more in a moment," he said. "I have an idea."

"An idea?"

"You'll see."

They headed down Main Street toward the Victorian, but instead of turning into their driveway, Stone drove another block and parked in front of the dance studio. He shut off the engine and turned to her.

"What are we doing?" she asked.

"My idea's a little crazy but hear me out."

"Sure."

He gestured toward the dance studio and clinic. "Kyle wants to buy the buildings and start a business that would appeal to tourists but that also passes the Violet test. She wants something that enhances the lives of the residents, as in art or culture. Depending on what he comes up with, he might tear the current buildings down and make one structure."

She thought about the size of the current buildings. "That would be a huge space. Like Target-sized."

"Violet made sure the city council agreed to keep big businesses like that out."

"I'm with her. Why would anyone want to ruin the vibe of Cliffside Bay? Plus, it would drive all the little guys out."

"Agreed. With that in mind, what if it was an enterprise that brought tourists and enhanced the community?"

"Like?"

"Like a theater," Stone said. "A small company that does

professional productions during the summer and dance and theater classes for kids during school months. This solves the problem of losing the dance studio and provides yet another reason to come to Cliffside Bay and spend lots of money."

She closed her eyes for a moment as images flooded her mind. A two-hundred-seat theater space. Below would be studios for dance and acting classes. When she opened her eyes, Stone was staring at her with a definite gleam in his eye. "I think it would be wonderful."

"And who better than you, Lisa, and Maggie to head up the idea?"

"Us? You mean, run the theater?"

"Be the idea and money behind it and hire staff to do the day-to-day. Think about the draw the three of you would have for audiences. Lisa's fame alone would bring people in droves. You could employ worthy actors and directors. Who wouldn't want to spend the summer in Cliffside Bay working in a theater? The three of you can form a nonprofit to take advantage of tax breaks."

She turned to face him. "You've really thought this through."

"I talked it over with Kyle after dinner. He's all for it."

Her mind whirled with ideas. "We could start with a summer production, and if it goes well, add a spring one."

He slapped the steering wheel. "Love it."

"We could exhibit art in the lobby and feature the Dog's Brewery beer at the concession stand." Her head almost exploded with the next thought. "My mom could run the children's programs."

"She could."

"It's the ultimate revenge, using Frederick's money to fund a theater run by me and Mom." She drummed her fingers against the dashboard. "But we should buy the buildings. You and me. It can be another investment for us, and the company wouldn't have to pay rent. Do you think Kyle would be open to it?"

"I can talk to him." He suspected Kyle wouldn't care. It

wasn't as if he needed the money. "You ladies can work with David on the design."

"Yes, something innovative yet classic."

"Given the codes, we'll have to keep the height the same as the other buildings, but we can dig into the ground." His eyes flashed with mischief. "Between building our house and this theatre, the Wolves are going to be busy."

They sat there grinning at each other like a couple of love-struck fools. Which they were.

"Do you know something, Stone Hickman? I no longer feel broken." She placed her hand over his. "I think you've healed me."

He looked at her for a long moment, his expression serious. "I'll spend the rest of my life grateful you chose me. Being loved by you is the deepest honor of my life."

"It's the other way around. Without you I was adrift, lost. You've grounded me in the best way. You're my real-life hero."

He smiled. "I *do* love to hear that, even if it makes me seem old-fashioned."

"You're just the right combination of old-fashioned meets modern man. My man."

"That I am." He leaned over and placed the softest of kisses on her mouth.

The rain intensified and beat against the roof of the truck like the bass of a country song. In an unspoken agreement to stay for a while, she snuggled under his arm. He held her close as they watched rivulets of water slide down the windshield. Outside, white holiday lights twinkled from the bare branches of the trees that lined the street. Through the wet window, they blurred into diffused yellow light and looked like a painting.

She sighed with contentment and nestled closer to Stone. So much of her adult life she'd spent running and spinning in a desperate attempt to escape from the darkness that had broken her. Yet, here in this innocuous moment, serenity had replaced her restlessness. Who knew she'd find magic in the bed of a truck with a guy from Oregon? Not her.

Finding joy in life was not complex. She knew that now. It was not found through the pounding of footsteps on hard pavement, or this never-ending cycle of activity. Or, wonder of all wonders, not even in accomplishments.

This quiet moment whispered the truth. To find joy, listen to the rhythm of raindrops on a metal roof. Watch as lights through a wet window become a watercolor. Move closer to the one you love. Be thankful.

Be still.

For in the stillness, love appeared.

THE END

MORE CLIFFSIDE BAY

I hope you enjoyed the first installment of Part II of Cliffside Bay as much as I loved writing them. The tales of the Wolves continues with Scarred: Trey and Autumn. Will these two best friends become more?

Before you find out, be sure to download so you don't miss any of the Cliffside Bay fun. Chateau Wedding (Cliffside Bay Novella to be read after Healed)
And then: Scarred: Trey and Autumn

To read the first chapter of Scarred, simply turn the page.

Much love, Tess

P.S. I love to hear from you. Don't hesitate to reach out if you're enjoying my books at tess@tthompsonwrites.com

SCARRED: TREY AND AUTUMN

Trey

The first evening of summer smelled of the sea and honeysuckle. A warm breeze kissed Trey Wattson's skin with a promise of the long, languid days to come. All memories of the sulky grey days of the northern California winter seemed only a dream under the clear night sky. Stars twinkled down at them, competing for attention with the white lights strung between the pool house and outdoor kitchen of the Mullens' stone patio. A half-dozen couples danced, silhouettes on the other end of the pool deck. Others mingled near the pizza oven and bar area, drinking beer from etched pint glasses or champagne from skinny flutes. Their laughter combined with a country ballad that streamed through unseen speakers. Beyond the patio, a stretch of freshly mowed grass ended at the edge of a steep cliff, with the sea below. A steel fence kept intruders out and little children in while maintaining the integrity of the view.

Trey sat in a lounge chair just outside the open doors of the newly decorated pool house with his legs stretched out, watching as the party went on around him. Unlike the rest of the men, who were dressed in cargo shorts and T-shirts, he wore pressed khaki pants and a cotton shirt the color of the cobalt-tiled pool. His wavy brown hair, almost tamed by products and a meticulously styled cut, disobeyed by flopping over his forehead. These days, he spent too long deciding what to wear and how to comb his hair. Falling in love with a woman did that to a man.

Next to him, the object of his tortured heart, Autumn Hickman, shared an oversize lounge chair with her friend Sara. Their heads were together, chatting as women do about things men were not privy to and probably didn't want to be. If he'd strained, he might have heard what they whispered to each other, but it was of no interest to him. He was content to sit next to Autumn and occasionally catch a whiff of her perfume.

Kara and Brody Mullen's property was an oasis from noise, traffic, and tourists who would flood the stores and beach all summer. Here, it was as if the rest of the world didn't exist. Thick woods to the south and north hid a cottage and Brody's brother's house. Although not visible from here, the town of Cliffside Bay was five miles down the road, in the valley between two competing slopes.

His gaze fixed on the host and hostess. Kara and Brody, separated by her very pregnant belly, swayed to the music at arm's length like two kids at a Catholic school dance.

Tonight's party was to celebrate the redecoration of their pool house. Trey had spent the last few weeks transforming it from bland to bright and cheery. Kara had asked for citrus colors to brighten up the dried-grass and eggshell interiors of the pool house. He'd combined lemon-yellow walls with lime and orange accents but kept the eggshell cabinets and colors subtle. No one wanted a room that looked like a carton of Popsicles. The outside patio furniture mirrored the inside, including striped lime-and-orange umbrellas, which he'd had specially made.

To thank him for his work, Kara had invited him to the party. He didn't usually run in the same circle as the former professional quarterback turned color commentator and his stunning wife. The Mullens were good people, without a hint of pretension, but they were rich and like finely bred racehorses, stronger and smarter than the rest of the world. Brody was tall with a muscular body made for football and a chiseled face perfect for television. Kara was dark-haired and athletic. A nurse practitioner, she was as smart as she was compassionate. They hung with a group of four other couples, all rich and shiny and as close as family. They called themselves the Dogs and the Wags. Trey was simply their decorator. Not that he was complaining. He and the other four partners of their construction company, Wolf Enterprises, were grateful for their business.

On the poolside dance floor, Brody placed his hand on Kara's stomach. Darned if Trey's eyes didn't sting at the sight of them. What had happened to him over the last few months? As if he didn't know. Right. He knew. He knew exactly.

Autumn had happened. Like a strong riptide, she'd pulled him under and out to sea. Autumn and her ridiculously charming cottage. She'd hired him to remodel the 1940s beach bungalow. What should have been a simple job had turned into much more than that. The job and the woman had changed him. Before any of the walls had succumbed to his jackhammer, he'd fallen into Autumn's current, never to return to his bitter, disillusioned, cuckold self. Or was it former cuckold? Was that a temporary title, expunged after a divorce?

Autumn's presence in his life had turned back time to the man he was before his heart had been shattered. He'd once been a romantic, a dreamer. A man who believed in marriage and loyalty and building a life with the woman he loved. His ex-wife had killed that man. Like the dish running away with the spoon, she'd run off with their intern. That had been that. He'd fallen from the moon, done with love. Ruined. Shattered. Scarred. His heart transformed into a bitter mass of humiliation and rage. He was no longer a romantic-comedy-loving fool. No, he was a cold, hard lone wolf who watched action films and drank scotch and felt nothing but disdain for his former self.

That had been his intent, anyway. He'd been determined to be a lone wolf, except for hanging out with the other mangy Wolves of Cliffside Bay. His friends were one thing. Sure, he could love the other Wolves and his mother and sister. His heart wasn't totally dead. Just dead to the idea of romance.

Or it *had* been. Past tense. He'd tried to retain the promise he'd made to himself. For months, he'd kept his lovesick feelings hidden first from himself, then from her and everyone else in their lives. He'd pushed his feckless thoughts aside time and again. Yet there they were. Like the honeysuckle's blooms and long summer days, love had come around again.

He loved Autumn Hickman. He wanted her to be his forever.

"Trey," Autumn said, startling him from his meandering thoughts. "You're quieter than usual. All good?"

He turned to look at her. "Yes, just watching."

"Nothing odd there." Her mouth curved into her gentle smile and his stomach fluttered. He'd not known a smile could do that to a person.

"How about you?" he asked. "You okay?"

"Yes, more than okay." Autumn's hair, a color somewhere between brown and red, shone under the lights. She smiled again, looking younger than her thirty years with her fair skin caressed into a pink blush by a few glasses of wine. "Thanks for bringing us tonight."

"Seriously," Sara said, poking her head around Autumn to look at him. "I haven't had a night out in ages." She sighed, seeming slightly tipsy. "If only I had what those two have." She pointed to the Mullens. "I most certainly do not have that, do I now?" Sara was raising her baby daughter alone, with the help of an au pair, after her husband's death.

"You will," Autumn said. "It's only been a year."

"Isn't one year supposed to be the magic number?" Sara asked. "The time I'm supposed to feel better?"

Autumn tilted her head to rest on Sara's shoulder and patted her friend's hand. "Give it a little more time."

"I've had too much wine and now I'm feeling sorry for myself." She said this with a lighthearted lilt to her voice, but Trey suspected the words were very true. There was no timeline for grief. He wished there were.

Sara glanced at her watch. "I should call my nanny and check on Harper. Mimi's old-school. She won't go to bed until I call and tell her I'm fine and what time I'll be home. It's like living with my mother." She rolled out of the chaise with a husky giggle. "This chair's way taller than it was a minute ago." She straightened her dress and patted the back of her auburn tresses. "I'll call her from the house. Too noisy out here."

As Sara walked toward the house, the first notes of an eighties rock ballad came from the speakers. A Journey song—one of Autumn's favorites.

"Would you like to dance?" he asked.

She hesitated, almost like a silent hiccup. Autumn had to ration her dances. Her damaged legs grew weak after a long day. After dinner he'd sensed she was fatigued and had suggested they sit by the pool instead of joining the dancing couples. Autumn had been in a car accident when she was fourteen, both her legs broken in multiple places. Her left leg had been so mangled they'd considered amputation. In the end, they did what they could, including taking skin from her hip to replace what had been torn from her legs. For the most part, through physical therapy and several surgeries, doctors had been able to restore the functionality of her legs. Still, she tired easily and she never, ever showed her bare legs to anyone.

"Do you feel up to dancing?" he asked.

She rested her fingertips on his wrist, smiling over at him. "Do you know you're the only one who's ever asked me to dance?"

"Really?"

"It's true. You, Trey Wattson, are the first man ever to ask me to dance. Men are too afraid I'll stumble and embarrass them or myself."

"I'd never let you stumble. It's my job to make sure you're safe." He would hold her tightly, make sure she didn't fall or trip.

She smacked his shoulder. "What're you talking about? I'm not your responsibility."

I want you to be. Out loud, he said, "Last time I checked, you were busy looking after me."

"How so?" Her finely shaped brows knit together.

"Sara told me what you did the other day. In the city." While shopping for furniture in San Francisco, the ladies had stumbled into the showroom of Wattson and Smith Design before realizing it was the former showroom he shared with his ex-wife. The name had once been Wattson and Wattson Design. Smith was the name of the intern. *River* Smith. A boy with hippie parents. He didn't actually know River Smith's background, but that didn't stop him from making assumptions. The twerp had slept with Malia in Trey's house. Gloves were off, knives sharpened. After all, the little upstart had taken Trey's whole life.

"Oh, that? That was nothing. Any friend would do it." The lights from the pool threw shadows across Autumn's face. He couldn't be sure, but he thought he detected a hint of triumph in the set of her jaw.

After the divorce, he'd left San Francisco and moved to Cliffside Bay to start another business. A few years into his fledging interior design business, he'd met the other Wolves and agreed to join them in partnership. They were now gaining steady business, and Trey was finally starting to climb out of the financial hole he'd created when he let his ex-wife take everything he'd worked so hard to build.

He could have fought harder, spent more money on attorney fees, but his inner warrior was stuck in the trenches. The humiliation had been so intense, the betrayal so hurtful, that he'd walked away from the entire mess and entered survival mode. Even though he had to start again, it was the only thing he could do at the time.

He now found himself at the other end of his starting-over period. He was ready to live fully without the burden of his bitterness. The past was the past.

"What did you think of her?" he asked Autumn.

"Your ex-wife?" Autumn touched her fingertips to her temple and tilted her head, continuing to look out to the pool. "She's very beautiful."

"I used to think so."

She turned toward him. "You don't now?"

"No. Not when I know the inside doesn't match the outside."

She nodded, smiling as a slightly evil glint came to her eyes. "She was taken aback when we said we knew you. In fact, she went a little green."

He chuckled. "Is that when you told her off?"

"I didn't tell her off *exactly*. I simply told her we knew her former partner and pointed out how well you're doing in Cliffside Bay. I might have dropped Brody Mullen's name as an example of one of your new clients and said something about how you can't keep true talent down, even when someone without any steals his business." She laughed. "I don't know what came over me. When I saw her, I just wanted to make her hurt for what she'd done to you."

"I'm fine now." He lifted one shoulder in a shrug. "I don't care anymore. I'm glad it all happened. Now I have the Wolves and Cliffside Bay." *And you.* "But thanks for making her a little green."

With her face propped in her hand, she regarded him. "Careful now, Wattson, you're losing all your bitter edges."

"You didn't answer my question. Do you want to dance? I'll be there to catch you if you stumble."

She stared at him for a few seconds longer than she should have. Did she know his words covered more than just dancing? If so, she didn't let on. Instead, she held out her hand. "I'd love to dance. At least for a song or two."

He rose to his feet and helped her up with a gentle tug. Still holding her hand in his, he led her across the pool deck to the makeshift dance floor. When they reached where the other couples were dancing, she went easily into his embrace. Neither tall nor short, she came up to his shoulders. She almost never wore high heels; he supposed they were too unsteady. Tonight, she wore a white-and-yellow maxi dress that made him think of a fresh daisy.

He gazed down at her. The swoop of her long eyelashes reminded him of a cresting wave. She nestled against him, resting her cheek on his chest. Her hair smelled clean and sweet. He'd never known anyone to smell as good as Autumn. She shifted slightly in his arms, and a faint squeak came from her throat, as if she were settling against his body for a long nap. A feeling of bottomless tenderness washed through him. If it were possible to hold her with more care, he would. Yet she was as strong and tough as anyone he knew. The pain and rehabilitation from her accident would have taken most girls of fourteen down. Not Autumn. Under her delicate appearance lay level upon level of strength.

Next to them, Zane and Honor Shaw, in a rare night out without their two kids, danced with their bodies pressed so tightly against each other they might as well have been superglued. Lance and Mary Mullen, having confessed earlier that this was their first night out after their second baby, a little boy, had arrived the last week of April, were currently staring into each other's eyes as they moved around the pool deck. No one looked at his wife with more adoration than Lance. Although a savvy hedge fund manager type, Lance had opened a bookstore to make his librarian wife happy. If that wasn't love, he didn't know what was. He'd had such a great time planning the interiors for the Cliffside Bay Bookstore with Lance. Like him and Autumn, the Mullens had started out as friends before they fell in love. This gave him hope that someday Autumn would look at him as a man instead of just a friend.

Autumn's oldest brother, Kyle, danced with his wife, Violet, near the edge of the pool. They had their arms around each other, almost propping each other up, like those old photos from the 1930s of couples in a dance contest. Violet yawned and buried her face in her husband's neck. They'd be headed home soon. Trey figured four kids under the age of seven made for early bedtimes.

What was it like to go home to a houseful of children with the love of your life? Trey had thought he'd have that with Malia. The bitterness rose in his throat, but not as strong as it used to be. Really only a twinge now. He'd let it go, moved on. Because of Autumn.

He wasn't even sure when his feelings had changed from platonic to love. One day he woke up and knew. *I love Autumn Hickman.*

That truth had frozen him in place. He didn't know what to do with his feelings. Did he tell her and risk rejection? Was it possible she felt the same way? He doubted it, which kept him from saying the words out loud to her or anyone else. His tender heart, so recently hurt, seemed content to remain hidden.

One day she'd announced her desire to meet a man. *The* man. Then she joined an online dating site, and his nightmare began.

It was the frenzied pace of Autumn's coffee dates that woke him from his apathetic longings and made him want to take a sledgehammer to an abandoned building. The men were everywhere, raising their virtual hands from inside the online dating site. *Pick me, Autumn. Pick me.* This week alone, she'd met three different men for coffee. Men grew from trees on that godforsaken site. All a man had to do was see her pretty face and decide to click *yes, please match me,* as if that made them worthy of Autumn.

Trey wasn't a math guy, but he figured the odds of her meeting the wrong man disguised as the right man went up with every sip of iced latte. He had to do something. His passivity was getting him nowhere. He was disgusted with himself that he'd let his bitterness over his divorce keep him from making his move before she'd put him steadily in the friend category.

He was the one who knew exactly how Autumn liked her latte: two shots of espresso, nonfat milk, no foam, and one squirt of sugar-free caramel syrup. She asked for it over ice in the spring and summer and one hundred forty degrees in the fall and winter. Not that she would make a fuss if it wasn't exact. She wasn't like that. But he made sure, whenever they were together, that she got precisely what she wanted. *He* knew what she liked. Not some stranger. He ordered it for her every Saturday morning from the coffee shop in the Cliffside Bay Bookstore. Or he had, until she'd decided to explore online dating. Now her Saturday mornings were busy with other men. Unworthy men who drew her away from their comfortable Saturday morning stroll down to the coffee shop, where they'd spent hours reading together.

Comfortable. That was the very word that did him in. They were so darn comfortable together. He provided comfort instead of stirring her emotions. And he certainly hadn't awakened any feelings of desire. He was like a Labrador puppy, all soft and fuzzy and harmless. Women wanted a little danger, maybe some mystery, not good old comfortable Trey.

They saw movies together and shopped for antiques or had coffee at the bookstore. All activities that encouraged comfortable silences. These activities had contributed to his downfall. They kept the words stuck inside him.

She lifted her face to look into his eyes. "What is it? You stumbled."

"Did I?" The muscles in his left cheek twitched as they fought to keep his persona intact. He'd once been an amateur at hiding his feelings, but after his divorce, he'd become an expert at conveying a lighthearted stoicism. No one could know the depth of his wounds.

"You're supposed to hold me up," she said, smiling. "Wasn't that our agreement?"

"I'd like to. I want to." The words spilled out of him, pushing against their prison at the base of his throat to break free. "I mean, would you…would you ever consider me… Could I ever be one of the guys you'd let take you to coffee?"

She loosened her grip on his shoulder and punched him lightly on his upper arm. "We go to coffee all the time."

"A date type of coffee."

She went still in his arms and looked up at him with an amused expression in her eyes. Then she laughed. "Very funny. I know your stance on love and marriage. You've only been saying you're done with love and marriage every day since I met you. Anyway, even if you were serious, I would never risk what we have. Eventually, the whole thing would blow up, and I'd be without my best friend." She fluttered her eyelashes and spoke lightly, as if the next sentence was supposed to be funny. "Plus, you like pretty objects, not awful, damaged things like me."

He wanted to say a good many words in response, but now his throat had closed back up and they were trapped once more. If he'd been able to, he would have told her that whatever her scars and damage, it didn't matter. He didn't care what her legs looked like. He knew her heart. And it was as lovely as anything he'd ever seen.

She was right. He liked beautiful things, and she was one of them.

"Why would things blow up?" he asked.

"Because they do. You, of all people, know that."

"I suppose they do," he said as his throat constricted and his stomach lurched.

"And you and me—we're forever. Best friends never leave each other." The dancing couples swayed around them, but for him the world stopped. It was only Autumn's face that he saw. The fierce love in her eyes broke his heart and made it soar at the same time.

"Anyway, stop saying all these weird things," she said. "How much wine did you have?"

"Not much. I promise," he said, matching her teasing tone.

She laid her cheek on his chest. "I'm tired suddenly. Would you take us home now?"

"Sure. I'll get Sara and meet you at the car."

He dropped Autumn off at her cottage by the beach, then drove Sara out to her place. She lived up a country road not far from Jackson and Maggie's place. They passed by the gate with the sign that read The Wallers and then shortly thereafter, another that read "The Hickses." Kyle was Autumn and Stone Hickman's brother, but he'd changed his name when he went into the commercial real estate business. "Long story," Autumn had told Trey when he first asked about the name change. Later, she'd explained that he'd wanted to separate from everything from his childhood. She and Stone had been estranged from Kyle for over a decade. Just two years ago, they'd reunited, and Stone and Autumn had decided to join their older brother in Cliffside Bay.

Trey had decorated both the Wallers' and Hickses' homes. The Waller place had been a remodel of a crumbling house built in the style of a French château. He'd enjoyed working with Maggie Waller to honor the ornate architectural aspects of the interiors while bringing in a modern feel at the same time. The Hicks house had been the first project he and Stone Hickman had done together and had cemented their friendship and their decision to become partners. The other members of Wolf Enterprises had been added later: David Perry, architect; Rafael Soto, business manager; and Nico Bentley, landscape architect.

Before they formed Wolf Enterprises, they'd jokingly named themselves the mangy Wolves of Cliffside Bay. When Rafael, Stone, Trey, and later Nico and David had decided to partner up, they were broke and broken. In the last year, things had changed drastically for Rafael and Stone. Rafael had married Lisa, a beautiful blonde, currently the "it" girl of Hollywood. Stone was engaged to Lisa's best friend, Pepper, also a rising star of stage and screen.

Sara didn't say much as he rounded a corner and then took a right turn into her long driveway. When he pulled up to her house, with its newly landscaped yard, thanks to Nico, she turned to him. "Did something happen at the party?" The tone of her voice had lifted from its usual husky tone to a slightly teasing intonation that said loud and clear—whatever it was that upset Autumn most likely had to do with him. "Autumn was strangely quiet on the way home."

"She was, yeah." Autumn's silence on the way home, as opposed to her happy chatter on the way there, had been starkly noticeable. He'd thought she'd dismissed his awkward advances as a joke. Her quietness indicated something else. "Maybe she was just tired."

"No, that wasn't it. I've been her friend since freshman year of college," Sara said. "We know each other well. She knew, for example, that moving here was just what I needed...after everything."

He nodded, unsure what to say. *Everything*. What a loaded word that was. Sara's daughter had been only a few weeks old when her husband was killed. Autumn had convinced her to move to Cliffside Bay. Here she could start over and heal. Trey and Nico had done the same after their disastrous breakups. Sara had bought a piece of property and subsequently hired Wolf Enterprises to build her a home. Currently, Trey was helping her decorate the interiors. As an heir to a massive fortune, money was no object, yet Sara was particular, wanting an eclectic combination of unique pieces found at antiques stores and boutique furniture sellers. All of which made an interesting but complex design experience.

He sighed as he gripped the steering wheel. "I kind of hinted that I'd like more than friendship."

Her mouth dropped as her even features stretched long in both directions. "You did? You do?"

"She thought I was joking and then shut me down fast." He placed his forehead on the steering wheel between his hands. "I made a complete idiot out of myself. Worse, I think I freaked her out."

Sara cleared her throat. The leather seat groaned as she shifted toward him. "Why would she think it was a joke?"

He lifted his head to look over at her. "I've been telling anyone who would listen that I have no intention of ever getting seriously involved with anyone. I meant it until I met Autumn."

She scratched behind her ear and narrowed her eyes, staring out the front window. "You *have* been vocal about your feelings on romance. Not that I can blame you. Having been cheated on myself, I know how hard it is to get past the betrayal." Sara Ness had a way of speaking that reminded him of a history professor he had in college. Well-spoken but a bit aloof, as though she was preparing for an eventual seat on the Supreme Court.

"I should've asked her out right away. Maybe everything would be different now."

Sara pressed the palms of her hands against the faux wood strip that ran along the dash, as if working out what to say next. "When thinking about Autumn, you must keep in mind everything she's been through. There's a reason Autumn and I are so close. At school, we were odd ducks in a lake of swans. She sees herself as unworthy of a man like you, so she never lets herself go there in her mind."

"A man like me?"

"Physically perfect."

"I'm hardly perfect," he said, thinking of his height and slight build compared to most of his friends.

She unfastened her seat belt and turned to face him. "I'll deny saying this if she ever asks, but I believe she has feelings for you, too. That said, she's never going to admit to them."

"Why?"

"She's terrified she'd lose you the moment you saw what she looks like without clothes."

"I don't care about her scars."

Sara ducked her head. Her copper-tinted hair covered her face for a moment before she looked back up at him. "It's happened to her before. Twice now. Men she cared for deeply rejected her when they saw all of her, so to speak." Her fists clenched in her lap. "They crushed her. Do you know how brave you have to be to put yourself out there like that when you've been through what she's been through?"

Kind of. Only his wounds were internal.

Sara tossed her hair behind her shoulder. "Men, especially young ones, can be so cruel. Any girl who's ever been called a fatty knows that."

He opened his mouth to agree when he realized she must be talking about herself. *Odd ducks in a lake of swans.* Maybe they'd felt they were ugly ducks instead of just odd. Had Sara been overweight? She wasn't now. Not super thin, but just right, with curves and muscles. He remembered, suddenly, the magnet she had on her refrigerator. *Nothing tastes as good as thin feels.*

"I'm sorry," he said. "Guys can be such idiots." His heart ached for Sara and Autumn. He knew how college had been—guys evaluating girls, rating them on a numbered scale. Jerks. He and Nico had not participated in that kind of thing, but they were witness to it more times than he cared to admit.

"Both of us spent a lot of nights in, watching movies and eating ice cream. Until I stopped eating ice cream. But my body issues could be dieted away. Autumn's can't. With that comes a feeling of hopelessness and a basic distrust of most men."

"I can understand, but I'm not that way," he said. "I adore her. No scarring or misshapen legs can change that." He paused, swallowing against the ache at the back of his throat. "Actually, I love her. I have for a while now. She's my favorite person. I could never get enough of her. *All* of her. But I have no idea how to win her heart."

She gave him a good, hard look. "If you truly love her, then you're going to have to get creative. She will never let you in if she thinks there's a chance you would reject her. If you break her heart, she'll never recover. There will be no more trying. No more coffee dates with these guys she finds online, hoping that one of them will be decent enough to look past her physical imperfections. She'll curl up on her couch with her books and movies and comfortable pajamas and that'll be it." She didn't have to add *like me* for Trey to hear it loud and clear.

He returned her stare, hoping his sincerity showed in his eyes. "I'm not going to break her heart. I had mine broken, so I know."

"Well, then, Trey Wattson, what're you going to do?"

"I'm not sure." His friends might be able to help. The Wolves had promised to always have one another's backs, in both work and their personal lives. Maybe they would help him come up with a plan, as they did for their construction and remodel projects. This would require asking for help and speaking his secret out loud. Not easy for a man like him, but these were desperate times. He must reach deep inside for courage. "I'm not going down without a fight."

Sara smiled at him and patted his hand. "All you need is patience and persistence and total honesty about your feelings. She loves you, which is why she's so terrified to lose you." With that, she was out of the car and bounding up her stone walkway to the double front doors. He waited until she was safely inside before pulling out of the curved driveway and onto the road that would take him back to town and his quiet, lonely apartment.

The next day, Trey met the other Wolves at their favorite local haunt, The Oar. They sat around a table by the window, sharing a pitcher of the local IPA and eating burgers. Trey pushed his turkey burger around his plate, his appetite suppressed by his lovesick heart. While the others talked about baseball, he looked out the window. Tourist season had wakened their slumbering town. Families carrying beach umbrellas and baskets headed toward the strip of sand at the end of town. Teenagers hung out in clumps in front of the grocery store, playing hacky sack or gossiping and flirting. Young women in bikinis tops and shorts strolled by the business windows, showing off their tans. Surfers, wearing wetsuits with the torsos hanging from their waists, carried boards tucked under muscular arms. Cars inched along Main Street. Drivers craned necks as they looked for parking. They wouldn't find anything downtown. Not on a warm summer day.

And summer had come to Cliffside Bay with a sudden urgency, as if the dormant flowers and trees were anxious to please the sun. Bright-colored flowers decorated the baskets that hung from the awnings of businesses. Red-leaved cherry trees, oaks, and maples dotted the hillside above town. Rhododendrons burst with lush, fat clusters of red and fuchsia flowers. Birds sang their happy tunes from the newly budded oaks that lined Main Street.

Between the lunch and dinner crowd, The Oar was surprisingly slow. The Wolves planned it this way on Saturdays during the summer, often meeting around two for a leisurely lunch during which they talked business. Because they were busy during the week working on the projects themselves, they weren't often all together, as the houses were in various stages.

"Hey, earth to Trey." Nico Bentley's light brown hair caught the sunlight coming in through the window as he set aside the remnants of his veggie burger. After a diagnosis a few years back of high cholesterol, the guy had totally changed his diet. Unlike their college days together, which consisted of burgers, fries, and beer, now it was all red wine, poultry, and vegetables. Looking at the guy, you'd never think he had cholesterol issues. He was a lean and muscular surfer type, tanned to a golden caramel from all his time outside.

"You okay, man?" Stone Hickman slipped an errant slice of jalapeno back into his beef burger. He liked everything spicy, including his fiancée, Pepper Griffin. And no joke, Pepper was aptly named. Stone placed one muscular arm on the table. "You've been super quiet." Stone, as steady as his Pepper was feisty, was also one heck of a general contractor. One only had to look at their completed houses to know the kind of work he did and the integrity with which he approached each endeavor. God didn't make them better than Stone Hickman.

"Yeah, you look a little rough today." Rafael's dark brown eyes focused on Trey for a split second before returning his attention to a steak fry and pool of ketchup.

"I'm good," Trey said. Lying about his feelings came as naturally as breathing. He could thank his father for that attribute. Talking about emotions had been forbidden in the Wattson house growing up. The few times Trey had made the mistake of showing weakness or fear, it had been sufficiently snuffed out by his father's ridicule. "Just a little tired."

"Late night?" David Perry lifted the top bun off his chicken burger and slid the onions off with a swift flick of one long finger.

Rafael's wedding ring flashed gold as he lifted a fry to his mouth, then chewed appreciatively. "God, this is a good fry. I love my wife, but Lisa's trying to starve me with all the salads and bean sprouts."

David, who happened to be Lisa's twin brother, laughed. "The price you pay for living with a famous actress."

Stone shook his head ruefully. "Pepper isn't *trying* to starve me, but given her sudden desire to learn to cook, I just might."

Trey, despite his bad mood, chuckled before taking a bite of his turkey burger. Just yesterday, the fire alarm in their apartment kitchen had sounded off, loud and obnoxious, followed by Pepper's wail of dismay, like two discordant creatures calling out to each other. Other than her mishaps in the kitchen and her natural inclination toward messiness, he would miss Pepper when she and Stone moved into their own house. He'd grown accustomed to her lively ways and curious mind. She was always quick to suggest a party or a game, drawing Trey out of his shell. The sounds of Pepper's and Stone's voices in the mornings made him feel as if he shared a home with a family. A home completely different from the cold, quiet one he'd grown up in, but that was another story.

While Wolf Enterprises had built Pepper and Stone's home on his brother's property, they continued to share a two-bedroom apartment with him in the old Victorian Rafael had renovated into six apartments. When the house was complete, they would move, and Trey would be alone. They were days away from completion. He sighed, feeling sorry for himself.

"Hey, seriously, bro, you all right?" Nico asked. "You're like on another planet."

He met his friend's gaze. Although opposite in personality, Nico was his oldest friend. He was talkative and outgoing; Trey was quiet and reserved. They'd met in college in San Diego and had bonded over their controlling fathers and the expectations that they would follow them into the family business. In Nico's case, he was supposed to join the family law firm like his older brother, Zander. Trey's family had assumed he would follow his dad into the pharmaceutical business. His father was CEO of the company that made drugs for people with autoimmune diseases. As the major shareholder, his father had gotten very rich.

On a beach in San Diego, he and Nico had decided together to rebel against their fathers' wishes. Trey changed his major to design; Nico changed his to botany. Their families both withdrew their tuition money, and the boys were on their own. They'd graduated and both gone on to graduate school, funded by loans and more loans. At the end, though, they'd chosen what they each felt was their calling.

When Nico's fiancée had decided she preferred her bridesmaid, he'd been devastated. At loose ends, he'd gladly accepted Trey and the other Wolves' offer to join the firm as their landscape architect.

Sophie, The Oar's co-owner, approached with a bottle of

wine. "Hey, boys. Who wants to taste my latest find from my trip to Napa? Nico?" She held the bottle against her chest. Tall and tanned, with masses of blond hair, Sophie Woods was like a piece of lemon pie: sweet, zesty, and bright.

Nico smiled stiffly, then looked down at his plate. "Not today. Drinking beer with the guys."

Sophie's blue eyes flashed as she backed up a few inches from the table. "Is that how we're playing this?"

Everyone at the table seemed to freeze. Nico glanced up at her, his usual playful expression tense. "We talked about it. You know the deal."

Her eyes filled with tears. "You're an ass, you know that, Nico Bentley?"

"I'm trying not to be. That's the whole point," Nico said.

"Well, you're completely misguided." Sophie turned so quickly her tennis shoes squeaked against the wood floor. Seconds later, she stomped through the door to the back office.

"What just happened?" Stone asked.

"She was about to cry," Rafael said. "What did you do to her?"

"It's what I didn't do," Nico said before burying his face in his hands. He spoke through his fingers. "I had to put a stop to this thing. Before I did something we both regretted."

Everyone knew, including Nico, that Sophie had it bad for him. However, she was only twenty-two and a virgin. Nico was twelve years older and definitely *not* a virgin. Since his fiancée had left him for a woman, Nico seemed to be on a mission to prove that at least part of the female population of California found him attractive.

"What do you mean, put a stop to this thing?" Rafael asked. His dark eyes looked wary, as if afraid of what Nico was about to admit.

"Dude, I find her impossible to stay away from," Nico said. "It's like we're magnets or something. The attraction between us is off the charts. The other night I gave in and kissed her, even though we'd agreed to be just friends."

"She does *not* want to be just your friend," David said with his usual serious countenance. "That's been obvious for as long as I've been in town."

"I know, that's the problem," Nico said. "When she throws that luscious body at me, I'm powerless. Anyway, I told her after our kiss that I couldn't hang out with her anymore. It wasn't right, and she needs to find someone her own age. I mean, it's obscene."

"You're not *that* old," Stone said.

"It's not that I'm old; it's that she's so young," Nico said. "And innocent. It's not for me to take that from her. Plus, there's the problem of her brother."

"Zane?" Stone asked.

"Yeah. He pretty much told me he'd run me out of town if I so much as touched her." Nico took a long slug of beer from his pint and grimaced, as if he really wished he'd said yes to that glass of wine.

"Was he serious?" Rafael asked.

Nico nodded. "I think so. He's protective of her, as he should be."

Zane Shaw owned both The Oar and Dog's Brewery. Although they were half siblings and had discovered the other's existence only a few years ago, Zane had given Sophie part ownership in both businesses. As far as Trey could tell, the siblings were close. In fact, Sophie had been Zane and Honor's surrogate. You couldn't get closer than giving your brother a baby.

Nico ran a hand through his light brown hair. "Anyway, I guess she didn't take me seriously or she wouldn't have come over here all human-sunshine-like and offered me wine."

"You're right not to lead her on," Stone said. "But I don't see why the age difference should matter. Love is love."

"True. Look at Lisa and me," Rafael said. "Beauty and the beast."

"But you two are soul mates," Nico said. "Sophie's soul mate is out there probably working an entry-level job at some company and going clubbing at night. I'm home and in bed by ten after looking in on Mrs. Coventry. Just because there's a physical attraction between us doesn't mean we're right for each other. If she were older, she'd know that."

Before anyone could answer, Autumn walked into the restaurant and made a beeline toward them.

Trey sucked in his breath at the sight of her. She had her hair down and teased into waves around her shoulders and wore tight white jeans and a flowy, pale green blouse. She was without her cane. She must be feeling strong and rested. When she was fatigued, she sometimes used a cane for support, which she'd once confessed to him made her feel like a lonely old maid.

She flashed a smile around the table as she lowered herself carefully into the only empty chair. "Hey, guys."

"You look extra pretty," Stone said. "I don't know if I should let my little sister out of the house looking so good."

"I have a date," she said. "I'm meeting someone for a drink."

Trey's stomach clenched with a sudden rage. He blamed Nico for this. He was the one who had the bright idea about online dating. Then, in an attempt to squelch his jealousy, Trey had offered to help Autumn answer emails from these jerks. That hadn't lasted long. He'd had to recuse himself or risk giving himself away. What he'd really wanted to type as responses would not have been met with enthusiasm on the other end.

"Which one is this?" Nico asked.

"I haven't told you about him yet," Autumn said. "We exchanged an email just yesterday for the first time and he asked if I wanted to get a drink. He said he was trying to be more aggressive, rather than send a thousand emails back and forth."

"One email?" Trey asked. "Is that enough time to assess his character? He could be a total player."

"Player?" Autumn asked. "No. I didn't get that vibe. He seemed forthright."

She was so cute with her innocence and those wide-set green eyes and the way her brow furrowed in confusion when he said something stupid. "Well, goody for him," he muttered under his breath. "Just be careful. You're not letting him pick you up, are you?"

Her small mouth turned up in an indulgent smile. "No, of course not. I'm meeting him over at the Dog's Brewery."

"Is he local?" Stone asked.

"He lives up in Stowaway," Autumn said.

"That's almost an hour away," Trey said. "*Way* too far for him to be able to come see you much."

"It's only a drink." Rafael tilted his head, peering at him with a little too much curiosity. "Let's not get ahead of ourselves."

"Regardless, don't forget what I told you," Nico said. "No compromises. You find a guy willing to give up everything to be with you."

Autumn lowered her eyes. "He probably won't ask for a second date once I tell him how bad my scars are." She'd written into her profile a sentence about her legs being scarred and maimed from her accident. He and Nico had thought it best to leave it out, but she'd insisted. "It's a good way to weed out the guys who would care about something like that," she'd said at the time.

"Then he's not worthy of you," Nico said. "The right guy won't care."

Trey couldn't tear his eyes from her. The sage-green blouse really brought out her almond-shaped eyes. Her complexion reminded him of apple blossoms, white with a tinge of pink. The scattering of freckles over her nose made him want to count every one of them and give her the same number of kisses.

She touched the faint scar on her right cheekbone and looked up at Nico. "This might be a deterrent as well."

"You can't even see it," David said softly.

Trey turned to him, surprised. Other than to his sister, David rarely spoke to a woman unless spoken to directly. He had a shield a mile thick over his heart, which translated into a reserve that could be interpreted as aloofness. But Trey knew better. David was too fragile to put himself out there with most people, but especially women. Finding out your wife was dealing drugs from the back of her minivan with two little kids in the back seat could really mess with a man's mind. Betrayal ate away at you until your only desire was to hide behind whatever wall you could find.

"Maybe not in a dim room," Autumn said. "Which is why I suggested we meet at the brewery." In the right light, the scar on her right cheek *was* visible, even under her carefully applied makeup. He often saw her conceal the area with her fingers in what seemed like an unconscious habit. To him, her imperfections made her even more lovely. She was like a piece of artwork, imperfectly exquisite.

"Don't even think of it," David said. "Be yourself."

"He won't be able to stop himself from falling in love with you," Trey said. Had he said that out loud?

Other than Autumn, who looked back down at her lap, the entire table turned to him. Well, that answered his question. He *had* spoken out loud. Four pairs of eyes scrutinized him. He went hot, embarrassed. Why had he said it with such emotion, so emphatic? God, he was an idiot. They knew. The knowing glimmer in Rafael's and Stone's eyes told him everything he needed to understand. They could all see he was in love with her now.

"Well, I should go." Autumn stood so abruptly she knocked a knife off the table. "I should just get this over with. You guys have a good afternoon." She waggled her fingers, then headed across the restaurant and out the door. Trey watched through the window as she walked with a slight hitch to her gait toward her car.

When he shifted his gaze back to the table, all four of the guys were watching him. Watching *him* watching Autumn.

He grabbed his beer and guzzled from the glass.

"What is going on here?" Nico asked. "I've missed something, obviously."

Trey shrugged and took another drink from his glass.

"Trey, do you have feelings for Autumn?" Stone asked.

He looked back out the window just as Autumn's car passed by, headed east toward the end of town. She was hunched over with both hands wrapped around the steering wheel. Even from this distance he recognized the tension in her shoulders and the way she clenched her mouth when she was nervous or upset. His heart broke in two at the sight of her, so vulnerable, so brave for putting herself out there, for hoping that love might be waiting at the other end of the day. If she only knew that it was right here. Right here with him.

Stone nudged him with one of his giant shoulders. "Did you hear what I said?"

Suddenly it was too much. Keeping his feelings bottled up inside himself all these months was like holding on to the stern of a boat in a storm. Any loosening and he'd fall right into the ocean. Tears pricked his eyes. Horrified, he brought his beer back to his mouth, but he couldn't drink. He set aside the glass and swallowed.

"Dude, you're in love with her, aren't you?" Nico asked.

Across from him, Rafael shifted slightly and leaned over the table to pat his shoulder. "It's all right. We've got your back. You can talk to us."

"Are you?" Stone asked, with a tone as soft and compassionate as Trey had always wished his father to be.

Trey looked at his hands, helpless to think of any way to explain other than to come right out with the truth. "I'm in love with her and have been for a long time now."

"Why didn't you tell me?" Stone asked.

"Because I'm scared that she doesn't feel the same," Trey

said. "I've been humiliated enough by my ex-wife to last a lifetime. I don't think Autumn could ever feel the same way about me."

Stone muttered an expletive under his breath. "That's just her fear talking. It's about her legs." He cursed again. "I can't believe it. I hoped you felt this way, but I didn't think you did."

"I shouldn't," Trey said. "But I do."

"You were helping her with the online dating stuff." Nico was staring at him as if he'd never seen him before, despite their knowing each other for almost fifteen years. "Like a *buddy* does."

"I had to. I want her to be happy, even if it's not with me," Trey said. "Even though I feel like a truck is driving over my chest just thinking about her with anyone else."

"She's told me repeatedly that you guys are just friends," Stone said.

"I'm afraid that's all it will ever be between us," Trey said, feeling more miserable by the minute. "I wasn't ready when we first met. My feelings came slowly...and maybe I was in denial because I was afraid to get hurt again. But they're here now and not going away anytime soon."

"It's natural to feel reticent after having your heart broken," Nico said.

"And bitter," David said. "If only we could go back in time and make different choices, right?" He took a sorrowful drink from his beer glass.

"The ending of my marriage destroyed me," Trey said. "Autumn thinks she's the only one with scars."

David nodded. "It's like the person you used to be vanished with the betrayal, and now all you are is the pain and distrust."

"I keep thinking if I could just start over with Autumn, maybe I could be different, more open, less vocal about my vow to never marry again. That was so stupid. She took all that to heart."

"She doesn't want to get hurt," Rafael said. "That's clear as anything."

"And lose you as a friend *and* a boyfriend," Nico said. "It makes sense that she's kept a distance."

"A guy in Denver hurt her really bad," Stone said.

"I'd like to kill that guy," Trey said.

Stone raised his eyebrows, clearly surprised. Trey wasn't usually the type of man interested in violence. He spent his days figuring out how to arrange beautiful pieces into pleasing living spaces, not contemplating beating some guy's face in with his fists.

"Did she tell you about him?" Stone asked.

"She mentioned him just once," Trey said. "After a few glasses of wine one night." The story she'd told him had ripped a hole in his heart.

"What did he do to her?" Nico asked.

Trey winced, remembering how Autumn's voice had sounded when she told him the story. "She waited a long time to go to bed with him because of her scarring. When she finally did, he told her it was no problem, but he turned out the lights."

"Then bailed on her in the middle of the night," Stone said. "After...you know, with her first. I can't say that word in relation to my sister."

"What a total douche," David said.

No one spoke for a few seconds. Trey was vaguely aware of voices coming from the bar and the clatter of dishes and silverware, but they didn't penetrate the Wolves' vortex. Men rarely talked like this. Certainly not this group, anyway. It was as if they'd created a temporary space where they could put aside their male egos and talk, the way women did. They were so much smarter than men.

Stone bowed his head, then turned slowly to look at Trey. "I have an idea. It's probably a really bad one, but here goes. You said you wanted a chance to start over with her, right?"

"Yes, but that's impossible," Trey said.

"You guys ever see that chick flick, *You've Got Mail*?" Stone asked.

"Sure. Everyone's seen that one," Rafael said. "At least anyone raised by Mama."

"That's the one where they're writing to each other without realizing they know each other in real life, right?" David asked.

"That's right," Stone said. "What if we set up a fake profile on that dating site? You could start fresh. Show her you're ready for a relationship. Open up to her."

The conversation came to an abrupt halt, as if a time continuum glitch in the universe had skipped them forward without any idea of what just happened.

"A fake profile?" Rafael asked. "What good would that do? You'd just be lying to her and once she found out it was you—she'd be really mad."

"But what if they fell in love over letters like in the movie?" Stone asked. "I could totally see my sister doing that."

Nico was rocking back and forth the way he did when he was thinking through a problem. "But those two were both in the dark, weren't they? This isn't fair if Trey knows and she doesn't."

David picked up a knife and tapped the flat side against the palm of his hand. "Yes, but it's true what Stone says. It would be a great way to show her a different side. We all find it easier to express ourselves in almost any other way than verbally. I mean, we're all work-with-our-hands type of guys."

Rafael crossed his arms over his chest, a deep furrow between his brows. "Won't she guess it's him? I mean, if you're really going to get to know her and show her the true you, won't you have to tell her things about yourself? Things she probably already knows?"

Trey thought about the question for a moment before answering. "I'm kind of ashamed to say this, but as much time as we've spent together, I haven't told her much about my family or my childhood. She knows about what happened with Malia, but not how I felt about it. I could leave out the details of my job. I could just say I'm an artist."

"What about a photograph?" Rafael asked. "What will we do about a profile picture?"

That seemed to stump them. They were regular guys, after all, and not particularly smart when it came to deception.

David raised his eyes from where he'd been turning a cardboard coaster over and over between his fingers. "This might be a little out there…a lot out there."

"Go ahead," Stone said.

"She's afraid you can't love her because of her scars, right?" David asked. "What if you flip it around on her? What if you say you don't have a photo because your face is scarred?" He folded the coaster in half and set it on the table like a tent.

Nico's eyes blazed with excitement as he straightened in his chair. "As a way to get her to see how wrong she is—that physical imperfections don't make you unlovable. I like it."

Rafael tapped his fingers on the table. "No, I have a better idea. We're looking at this all wrong. She's a sensible girl. Very practical, right?"

"True," Trey said.

"We raised ourselves," Stone said. "There was no time or money for frills."

"Exactly my point," Rafael said. "I'm thinking you set up a correspondence with her as a friend. He…I mean, Trey, would tell her that her profile caught his attention because he too is scarred, only it's his face." He paused, obviously thinking through the rest. "He should live overseas, so there's no way they could meet. He'd propose an email correspondence to support each other in their romantic pursuits."

"Put him in Paris," Nico said. "It's romantic there."

Rafael shook his head, laughing. "What does that matter? It's not like she's there with him."

"It'll play in her mind," Nico said. "Girls love Paris." He snapped his fingers. "And he should have a woman he's in love with, but they're only friends. Like a parallel story that will open her mind to the possibility of Trey."

Rafael stroked his chin as he gazed up at the ceiling. "Yes, that's good. We want her to see that her thought process is all wrong. There's no better way to do that than see someone else making the same mistake you are."

"This is kind of twisted," Trey said as the anxiety slivered up from his gut to his throat. "I'm not a good liar."

Stone had been quiet during the last exchanges. Trey looked over at him. "Stone, what do you think? I'd be lying to your sister."

"It wouldn't be exactly lying," Stone said slowly. "You'd just be leaving out that Autumn's the woman you're in love with."

"And saying that you're scarred when you're not." Rafael grimaced as he picked up his beer. "That's a big lie."

"But I *am* scarred," Trey said. "They're just not visible."

Nods around the table told him they understood exactly what he meant.

"I painted an abstract self-portrait shortly after my marriage blew up," Trey said. "It's in the cubist style. I could use that for my profile picture."

"Cubist? Like Picasso?" Stone asked.

"Yes. My face is all fragmented to represent how shattered I was," Trey said.

"It's the perfect profile picture," David said. "And definitely not a lie."

"And something Autumn would respond to," Stone said.

Trey asked his friend once more, knowing how protective he was of his sister, "Are you sure you're okay with this? Autumn's your sister. You're the one person at this table who loves her as much as I do."

Stone was quiet for a moment as a myriad of emotions crossed his rugged features. When he spoke, his voice sounded hoarse. "Dude, you love her as much as I do? For real?"

"I'm hopelessly in love with her," Trey said. "She thinks her legs will repulse me, but she doesn't understand that I'm in love with who she is, not what she looks like. We fit together."

"*Everyone* can see that," Rafael said. "We've all been saying it for months."

"Except Autumn," Trey said.

"You love her." Stone slowly shook his head as a faint smile lifted his mouth. "And I believe in my heart she feels the same way about you. We have to do everything in our power to make her see what's right in front of her." He slapped the table. "If I could get Pepper to fall in love with me, then anything is possible."

"Same with Lisa and me," Rafael said.

"You have to go for it, even if the method's a little…what's the word?" Stone asked.

"Unorthodox," David said.

"All's fair in love and war," Nico said.

"Here's to Operation Autumn," Stone said as he raised his pint glass.

"We need a code word," Rafael said.

"Paris," Nico said. "Has to be Paris."

They raised their glasses.

"Polish up those writing skills," Nico said. "You're about to write one heck of a school essay."

"To Paris," Stone said.

"To Paris," they all repeated.

The Wolves gathered around Trey's desk in his bedroom at the apartment. He had his laptop open, with Rafael and Stone on one side of him and Nico and David on the other. The irony was not lost on him that five grown men were currently using their considerable creative and intellectual talents to come up with a profile they hoped would entice the site's algorithms to make a match of Trey Wattson and Autumn Hickman.

"Are you sure this is a good idea?" Trey asked for the twelfth time in as many minutes.

No one bothered to answer this time.

"How should I describe myself?" he asked.

Nico tapped him on the shoulder. "Move out of the way. I'll do it."

Trey let him have the chair and flopped onto his bed as Nico typed away. Rafael slid to the floor by the window. Dave sprawled over the armchair.

"Okay, read this." Nico handed the laptop to Trey.

Trey sat up and leaned against the pillows to read.

Nico had given him the handle Artyboy34 and written a short profile description.

"It's not bad," Trey said before reading out loud to the others. "'Artistic soul seeks same. The left side of my face was disfigured a few years ago. I'm looking for a woman who can see through my appearance to love me for who I am underneath the scars. I'm an artist living temporarily in Paris. Decent income by painting portraits of people with their dogs. It's a niche, but hey, who am I to judge?'"

Trey looked up from reading. "Pictures of people with their dogs? Isn't that a little weird?"

Nico shrugged. "It has to be believable. The truth is always stranger than fiction. Plus, I can totally see people paying for a portrait with their dogs."

"Or kids," Rafael said. "Maybe add that."

"No, it has to be dogs," Nico said. "It's quirky and kind of funny."

Trey scratched under his chin. "Is quirky what we're going for here?"

"You're quirky in real life," Stone said. "With all your cooking shows and antiquing."

"And glass ball collection," Rafael said.

"And obsession with textures," David said with a chuckle.

Trey shook his head, as if wounded. "You guys are hurtful, that's what you are. Anyway, here's the rest. 'I like art, music, sports, romantic comedies, cooking, and long walks on the beach.'" Trey laughed. "Long walks on the beach?"

Nico grinned. "I was just messing with you."

"You *do* like walks on the beach," Stone said.

"Yes, but it somehow sounds creepy in here," Trey said. "Like I'm the type who wants to lure unsuspecting young women onto the beach and then murder them." He deleted *long walks on the beach* and changed it to just *the beach* before reading the rest out loud. "The rest is good. 'I'm not perfect and I'm not looking for a perfect woman, but the woman perfect for me.'"

"I thought that was a nice touch," Nico said.

Trey took in a deep breath before loading a photograph of his painting for his profile picture.

Stone sat next to him on the bed. "There's no way she's thinking that's you." He pointed to a smudge of peach paint near the middle. "What's that?"

"My nose. Isn't it obvious?"

"Not really," Stone said. "But maybe you better stick with your dog paintings."

"My *pretend* dog paintings," Trey said.

"And their masters," Rafael said. "Don't forget that part."

"All right. Here goes," Trey said. He hit the Go Live button. "What if we don't get matched up?"

"You will. This thing matches you by ages and superficial interests," Nico said. "Trust me, there's no complicated algorithm that detects soul mates. I met my Allie on this thing, for example."

"It didn't detect that she liked girls?" Stone asked.

"Unfortunately, no," Nico said.

David uncurled from the chair. "Let's get Artyboy a drink and wait for the response."

"It's not coming anytime soon," Trey said. "She's on her date, remember?"

His stomach twisted at the thought.

ALSO BY TESS THOMPSON

CLIFFSIDE BAY

Traded: Brody and Kara

Deleted: Jackson and Maggie

Jaded: Zane and Honor

Marred: Kyle and Violet

Tainted: Lance and Mary

Cliffside Bay Christmas, The Season of Cats and Babies (Cliffside Bay Novella to be read after Tainted)

Missed: Rafael and Lisa

Cliffside Bay Christmas Wedding (Cliffside Bay Novella to be read after Missed)

Healed: Stone and Pepper

Chateau Wedding (Cliffside Bay Novella to be read after Healed)

Scarred: Trey and Autumn

Jilted: Nico and Sophie

Kissed (Cliffside Bay Novella to be read after Jilted)

Departed: David and Sara

Cliffside Bay Bundle, Books 1,2,3

BLUE MOUNTAIN SERIES

Blue Mountain Bundle, Books 1,2,3

Blue Midnight

Blue Moon

Blue Ink

Blue String

EMERSON PASS

The School Mistress of Emerson Pass

The Sugar Queen of Emerson Pass

RIVER VALLEY

Riversong

Riverbend

Riverstar

Riversnow

Riverstorm

Tommy's Wish

River Valley Bundle, Books 1-4

LEGLEY BAY

Caramel and Magnolias

Tea and Primroses

STANDALONES

The Santa Trial

Duet for Three Hands

Miller's Secret

ABOUT THE AUTHOR

Tess Thompson

HOMETOWNS and HEARTSTRINGS

USA Today Bestselling author Tess Thompson writes small-town romances and historical romance. She started her writing career in fourth grade when she wrote a story about an orphan who opened a pizza restaurant. Oddly enough, her first novel, "Riversong" is about an adult orphan who opens a restaurant. Clearly, she's been obsessed with food and words for a long time now.

With a degree from the University of Southern California in theatre, she's spent her adult life studying story, word craft, and character. Since 2011, she's published 25 novels and 6 novellas. Most days she spends at her desk chasing her daily word count or rewriting a terrible first draft.

She currently lives in a suburb of Seattle, Washington with her husband, the hero of her own love story, and their Brady Bunch clan of two sons, two daughters and five cats. Yes, that's four kids and five cats.

Tess loves to hear from you. Drop her a line at tess@tthompsonwrites.com or visit her website at https://tesswrites.com/

Made in the USA
Las Vegas, NV
26 August 2021

28948509R00193